PENGUIN BOOKS

SHADOW REAPER

Also by Lynette Noni

THE PRISON HEALER TRILOGY

The Prison Healer

The Gilded Cage

The Blood Traitor

SHADOW REAPER

LYNETTE NONI

PENGUIN BOOKS

PENGUIN BOOKS

UK | USA | Canada | Ireland | Australia
India | New Zealand | South Africa

Penguin Books is part of the Penguin Random House group of companies whose addresses can be found at global.penguinrandomhouse.com.

www.penguin.co.uk www.puffin.co.uk www.ladybird.co.uk

Penguin Random House UK

First published in the USA by Borzoi Books by Alfred A. Knopf, an imprint of Random House Children's Books, a division of Penguin Random House LLC, and in Great Britain by Penguin Books 2026

001

Printed and bound in Great Britain by Clays Ltd, Elcograf S.p.A.

The authorized representative in the EEA is Penguin Random House Ireland, Morrison Chambers, 32 Nassau Street, Dublin D02 YH68

A CIP catalogue record for this book is available from the British Library

ISBN: 978–0–241–74711–7

All correspondence to:
Penguin Books
Penguin Random House Children's
One Embassy Gardens, 8 Viaduct Gardens, London SW11 7BW

FSC
www.fsc.org
MIX
Paper | Supporting responsible forestry
FSC® C018179

Penguin Random House is committed to a sustainable future for our business, our readers and our planet. This book is made from Forest Stewardship Council® certified paper.

To Jen Azantian—

This book wouldn't exist without you
nurturing me back to life.
Thank you for being my agent, my friend, my miracle.

ELVERDINE ISLE
AMETRINE SEA
NEVARNOST TOWER
LAKE MIRTIS
WESTERN OBELISK
DOCKS
MISTWOOD
NECROPOLIS
N
E

Mount Mort
Mount Tembris
Mount Verta
River Mort
Northern Obelisk
Elders' Grove
Aravell
Eastern Obelisk
Uppercity
Farms
City of Aravell
The Summit
Scholars' Guild
Mount Verta
Entertainment Guild
Merchants' Guild & Market District
City Services Guild
Healers' Guild
Hunters' Guild & Nox Custodia Headquarters
Mount Tembris
Jonas's Apartment
Viri's Apartment
Mount Mort
Underlock
Undercity
Uppercity
Farms
Lake Mirtis

A Note on the Content

Please be aware that this is a dark YA fantasy book and therefore contains themes that may be triggering for some readers. For a detailed list, please visit my website.

Lynette

Glossary of Terms

Ellixen: another name for magic

Hallow Stream: three sources of pure magic fueling the world with ellixen

Blackmist: a deadly mist surrounding Elverdine Isle

Obelisks: four obsidian wardstones that suppress the power of the Hallow Stream and protect the city of Aravell from the blackmist

Wards: magical protective barriers

Impartation: a ceremony where children, on or before their fourteenth birthday, surrender their magic to fuel the obelisks warding the city

Burnout: the painful death or mindless existence that comes from a buildup of unstable ellixen

Reaper: a person who siphons ellixen from another. All reapers have enhanced senses, increased speed and strength, swift healing, and longer lifespans as a result of their stolen magic.

Hunter: a person who hunts reapers. All hunters have a magical mark inked into their palm—three interlocking circles representing their oath to protect, honor, and serve—that heats up when reapers are near.

Shallow: *(common)* a person with shallow levels of ellixen, most with too little to use for any magical acts

Mage: *(rare)* a person with strong levels of ellixen, enabling them to perform powerful magical acts. Most mages choose a specialty to train in, resulting in titles such as alchemist mage, celestial mage, healer mage, fabricator mage, enchanter mage, and more.

Ancient Mages: mages who lived in ancient times

Elder Mages: immortal mages considered deities. Also referred to as "the gods of old."

1

The slums of Aravell were eerily quiet at the midnight hour.

For most, it was risky to be out so late. The Nox Custodia imposed strict penalties upon anyone caught after curfew, and they were known to be creative with their punishments. But seventeen-year-old Viridia Solace wasn't worried about the Nox—one look at the insignia on her scarlet cloak and the city guards would keep their distance. She was more concerned by what lurked in the shadows. By *who* lurked in the shadows.

Her quarry.

The reason she was navigating the abandoned streets so late at night, when only the most desperate of citizens dared to peek around their sealed doors.

The most desperate of citizens—and the most dangerous of criminals.

Moving swiftly, Viri glanced down just in time for the moonlight to glint across a puddle on the cobblestones: vomit or urine or something equally unpleasant. Perhaps all three, judging by the foul odor. After years of hunting reapers deep into the slums, she still couldn't get used to the smells of unwashed flesh, decay, and overflowing sewage. Some days she feared she'd scrub her skin raw and yet never be clean again.

Shuddering at the phantom feel of ichor on her feet, Viri paused at a grungy intersection and considered which way to go: west, toward Lake Mirtis, or east, where the uppercity bled into the Tridus Mountains. She closed her eyes to focus her mind, and a moment later her hand began to warm, followed by a tugging sensation inside her, an instinct urging her west.

Setting off deeper into the darkness, she quickened her pace as the hunter's mark inked into her palm continued to heat up, guiding her to her prey. The mark—three interlocking circles representing her oath to protect, honor, and serve—was given to her the day she became a full-fledged reaper hunter. For most novices, training finished at eighteen, but Viri had earned her mark a year ago at just sixteen. A prodigy, her mentor had claimed. But really, she'd just had more motivation than most to see every single reaper get what they deserved.

Rowdy sounds reached Viri's ears from up ahead, the unexpected noise making her frown as she continued forward. She was closer to Lake Mirtis than she would have liked, and acutely aware of the dangers lurking beyond the Western Obelisk at the lake's edge. This far out in the slums, the obelisk's protective wards were significantly weakened, and that more than the Nox Custodia was why most sensible surface dwellers remained inside at night. Behind their carefully sealed doors, they were shielded from the drifting blackmist—and the agonizing death it afforded any who came in contact with it.

During the day, the four obelisks guarding the city forced the mist to withdraw to the outer reaches of Elverdine Isle. There it floated like a deadly cloud over the uninhabited forests and sea cliffs bordering the island, allowing the citizens of Aravell to go about their lives in relative safety. But come nightfall, when the ocean breeze picked up, not even the obelisks could keep the mist from wafting inland—which was why most Aravellians resided inside the mountains or beneath the surface in the undercity.

Viri, like any sane person, had a healthy fear of the blackmist, so she was eager to finish her hunt and return underground as soon as possible.

The mark on her hand suddenly seared, warning that she was nearing her target. A few steps later, she turned the corner of a dilapidated building to find the source of the rowdy noise: a run-down tavern on the verge of collapse.

For a moment, Viri just stood in the middle of the fetid street, wondering what careless patrons feared neither the mist nor the Nox. But then she shook her head and marched forward, ready to conclude her business. If things went to plan, she might even manage a few hours' sleep before dawn.

Approaching the tavern—named the Dripping Barrel, according to the broken sign above the entrance—Viri walked straight through the moldy, splintering doorway, marveling anew at the midnight revelry. It was common for nighttime socializing to occur in the undercity and inner-mountains, where there was no need for a safety curfew and residents could do as they pleased at all hours, but it was rare to witness the same here on the surface, where breathing the very air after dark could spell doom.

The patrons inside the Dripping Barrel seemed oblivious to the dangers of the outside world, their conversations loud and laughter unrestrained. The pungent scents of spilled ale and reeking bodies burned Viri's nose as she waded through the crowd, the mark on her hand still searing, telling her that not only was the reaper inside, but they were siphoning ellixen, right now.

Viri had always been more sensitive than most to the feeling of magic in the air—something that had aided her swift rise to becoming a hunter and protected her during many of her run-ins with the reapers—but not even she could pinpoint the exact location of her quarry. All she knew was that reapers never surrendered without a fight, and if this one had already begun siphoning, then their victim didn't have much time left.

Urgency thrummed through Viri as she approached the middle-aged man serving drinks behind the grimy bar and called for his attention.

"What'll it be?" he asked gruffly while pouring three ales in quick succession, foam spilling everywhere as he shoved them toward lively customers.

Viri gestured to the insignia on her scarlet cloak—the circular hunter's mark embroidered in silver over her heart—and said, "I'm looking for—"

"I don't want no trouble," the barman cut her off quickly. He eyed her up and down, taking in the black leather attire beneath her hunter's cloak, her braided red hair with its unusual silver streaks, and her startling lavender eyes. "Whatever you're looking for—*who*ever you're looking for—you won't find 'em here."

The burning of Viri's palm said otherwise, but when she scanned the tavern again, all she could see were cheerful patrons. There was no sign of magic—and no sign of death.

"Have you noticed anything out of the ordinary tonight?" she pressed. "Any new faces or—"

Once again, the man interrupted her, sliding a tankard down the bar with enough force to leave a trail of liquid along the scuffed wood. "I already told you, hunter—there's nothing for you here. Best take your business elsewhere."

As he spoke, Viri noted the bead of sweat that trickled from his temple down his weathered cheek; the way his gaze rested uneasily on her, then shifted away; the tremor in his hands as he continued pouring drinks. And then, finally, she saw the slightest lift of his chin as he motioned to a half-closed door in the back corner of the room.

Viri gave a subtle nod and moved that way, ignoring the stickiness gripping the soles of her boots as she carved a path between the noisy patrons—many of whom staggered away upon noting the color of her cloak—and approached the liquor-stained door.

Peeking through the narrow gap, all Viri could see was a rickety staircase dropping out of sight. She pursed her lips, knowing she would lose the element of surprise at the softest *creak* of the ancient wood. But a sudden, urgent blazing of her hand had her throwing caution aside and sprinting recklessly down into a musty cellar. Flameless everbeacons revealed a clutter of barrels and crates and glass flagons, but her gaze darted straight past them to the two small figures pressed against the back wall, to the hulking man stalking toward them—

And to the lifeless body he had just discarded.

A child, no older than twelve, his eyes closed, his chest unmoving.

Viri was too late to save him.

But she wasn't too late to save the two other children, a boy and a girl who were huddled together, the fear on their tear-stained faces indicating they knew exactly what kind of monster they faced.

They hadn't seen Viri yet. But the man—the reaper—stilled,

his neck swiveling her way, a sneer on his lips. With blond hair and blue eyes, he might have been handsome, if not for the fresh, undiluted magic emanating from him, the sacrifice of his young victim revealed in angry black streaks along the veins in his hands and up his bare forearms. Those streaks—visible only to hunters and reapers—would remain painted into his flesh until the power he'd stolen faded, offering irrefutable proof of his wicked crimes.

Crimes for which he was about to pay.

The reaper moved a step toward Viri, his sneer deepening, his eyes glazed as he adjusted to the surge of ellixen—of magic—flooding through him. The amount differed from child to child, but it was always enough to grant reapers increased speed and strength, enhanced senses, and swift healing. In some cases, it even added years to their lives.

Stolen years.

The price was too high, as was the guilt Viri felt for every person she failed to save. But there would be no more deaths tonight, no more victims for her to mourn. Only justice.

And one day, vengeance.

This soon after siphoning, the reaper would be stronger and faster than anything Viri could hope to match, so she couldn't let him make the first move and gain the upper hand. Quashing any hesitation, she lunged forward, uncoiling her gold fillium from around her wrist and flicking the whiplike cord through the air. The metallic weapon cleaved the space between them, her aim true if not for the man leaping away at the last second, his gray cloak flapping around him, glass shattering as he slammed into a shelf to avoid her attack. Viri immediately cast her fillium again, causing him to dodge once more—breaking even more glass—but he recovered faster this time and sprang toward her, his black-veined arms outstretched as if to strangle her with his bare hands.

Viri didn't give him the chance. She spun out of the way and lashed her fillium low, aiming for his ankles to impede his advance. In quick succession, she cast it twice more, but his enhanced speed kept him one step ahead of her attacks.

And then, suddenly, he was right in front of her, his fist flying toward her face. The move was so fast that his arm blurred, and only years of training had her twisting in time to avoid a shattered cheekbone. His knuckles still managed a glancing blow, and she hissed as the ring on his middle finger tore open her flesh. Blood instantly welled from the wound, but Viri ignored the pain and scurried behind a wooden barrel, trying to gain enough distance to cast her fillium again.

Her opponent was no fool—he knew what a single touch of her weapon would do to him, just as he knew its reach was limited at close range, so he rushed forward, not affording her any space, his fist coming at her once more. She ducked and whirled away again, but as she straightened, she heard the children cry out a warning as the man unsheathed a dagger and leapt toward her in a burst of speed, the blade glinting beneath the everbeacons.

Viri had been hunting long enough to have had experience with many kinds of reapers. Some were easy to capture, particularly those new to siphoning and unused to their ellixen-heightened abilities. The same was true for those addicted to the euphoric high that came with a fresh sacrifice, preferring to remain in their druglike state than resist arrest.

The man before Viri was neither a novice nor an addict—he clearly knew how to use his stolen magic, and he'd also had physical training. That made him dangerous.

But not as dangerous as Viri.

She'd noted his dagger the moment she had arrived in the cellar, she'd known he would pull it on her—and she'd been waiting.

The smirk on his lips and the triumph in his eyes as he stabbed his blade forward told her that he was just like every other reaper who was arrogant enough to underestimate her. They all assumed her fillium was the only weapon she carried, or at least the only one that could incapacitate them. Indeed, the man lunging at her was so focused on the threat of her metallic cord that he missed her pulling a vial from her cloak and using her thumb to unstopper it.

But he didn't miss her blowing the silver powder straight into his face.

The reaper's eyes rounded as the impedidust took effect, freezing him in place, the lethal strike of his dagger halted in the air between their bodies.

A quick glance down showed Viri how perilously close the blade was to gutting her, but she didn't waste time dreading what might have happened if the experimental—and highly illegal—powder hadn't worked, nor did she revel in the reaper's immobilized state. With so much ellixen coursing through his veins, the impedidust wouldn't hold him long, so she hastily slapped the dagger from his grip and used one end of her fillium to bind his wrists, nullifying his power. As long as the golden cord touched him, his enhanced abilities would be suppressed, his magic not only inaccessible but actively draining him of energy as it resisted the fillium's effects, rendering him weak and vulnerable—and completely at Viri's mercy.

She'd barely stepped back when the impedidust wore off and

the reaper staggered forward, not to continue his attack but to keep himself from falling over.

"What did you do to me?" he rasped, swaying drunkenly and struggling to remain upright.

Viri wasn't sure if he was asking about the fillium or the impedidust, but regardless, she simply declared, "On behalf of the Hunters' Guild, you're under arrest for the unlawful siphoning of ellixen and associated crimes against humanity."

"I'm innocent," he spat—or tried to. The words were slurred, his strength swiftly fleeing.

Raising an incredulous eyebrow, Viri glanced at the body of the boy lying mere feet away. But in doing so, she remembered the two other children, who watched with wide-eyed wonder, fear still on their faces but also tentative hope.

"Don't move," Viri told the reaper before starting toward the children.

"I don't take orders from you," he snarled, lunging after her—only to trip over one of the barrels they'd disturbed during their skirmish, leaving him groaning in a heap on the dusty, glass-strewn floor.

Normally Viri would have felt immense satisfaction in seeing him so weak—especially considering he'd tried to disembowel her just moments ago—but at the rate the fillium was draining him, it wouldn't be long before he lost consciousness. No matter how many times she witnessed her weapon in action, she would never get used to how debilitating its effects were. And while that was usually a boon, the last thing she wanted was to drag the reaper's heavy body all the way back to the Underlock, so they needed to get moving, *now*.

But first . . .

"Are either of you hurt?" Viri asked as she approached the children, wincing as broken glass crunched gratingly underfoot. She kept a tight grip on her fillium, with the other end still binding the reaper, who was cursing loudly as he tried to rise on wobbly legs, no longer a threat to any of them.

The children shook their heads and got shakily to their feet, clutching each other with trembling hands.

Seeing the evidence of their terror, knowing what might have befallen them, what *had* befallen their murdered companion, Viri had to breathe deeply to suppress her rage.

Justice, she reminded herself. The reaper would face justice for his crimes. By capturing him, she'd made sure of it—and she would continue to make sure of it for every other reaper she hunted on Elverdine Isle.

"You're bleeding," the little girl whispered, pointing at Viri's cheek.

Viri had forgotten all about the wound, though it throbbed now as she was reminded of the man's knuckles grazing her face. "I'm all right. It's just a scratch." She glanced toward the reaper, who had finally managed to get his legs under him, then turned back to the children. "Don't worry—he won't be able to hurt anyone else ever again."

Their eyes immediately skittered to the dead boy, making Viri swear inwardly at her careless words. Gently, she asked, "Did you know him?"

They shook their heads again, and she loosed a relieved breath. The loss of life was tragic, but at least these two wouldn't have to live with the trauma of witnessing a friend's death.

"Come on—let's get you out of here," she said, wanting to relocate them from the claustrophobic cellar as swiftly as possible.

Hustling them up the stairs and yanking on her fillium to force the stumbling reaper to keep up, Viri led the way back into the rowdy tavern, pushing through the crowd toward the bar. The man from earlier was still pouring drinks, though he paused when he saw Viri and her companions, his mouth opening and closing at the sight of the children. She understood his surprise—survivors were rare after a reaper attack. Too rare.

Raising her voice over the noise, she asked, "How far is the nearest wayportal?"

He shook off his shock. "There's one about a block away, just before you reach the lake."

Viri grimaced, not eager to approach the boundary of the obelisks' protection, but it was that or a long walk back through the uppercity dragging the quickly deteriorating reaper. She would have to take her chances.

Placing a gold coin on the bar, she said to the man, "For the mess downstairs." She then asked, "Do you have a kitchen here?" At his nod, she added three more coins before indicating the children. "These two could use something warm to eat. Keep them comfortable until the Nox arrive—they'll take their statements and see them home."

If the barman was displeased by the idea of Viri sending the city guards to his tavern, he said nothing, only pocketed the gold with a grunt of agreement. She didn't mention the third child, knowing the Nox Custodia would collect the body and notify his family.

Turning to the boy and girl, Viri smiled reassuringly and said,

"You'll be safe here until the Nox come. They won't be long." It went against her instincts to leave them after what they'd just been through—any time a hunt ended with survivors, part of her always wanted to stay and offer comfort. But she was a stranger to these kids, and they would be better off if she left now to notify the Nox.

"You're both very brave," she added softly, squeezing their trembling shoulders with her free hand. "In the coming days, when you can't help thinking about what happened tonight, don't forget that."

She watched them give hesitant nods, then helped settle them on stools at the quietest corner of the bar, where two bowls of fudge-covered ice cream were waiting. It wasn't the warm meal she'd requested, but when Viri looked at the barman in question, he shrugged and motioned to the kids, who were scarfing down the treat as if they hadn't just witnessed a murder and nearly met the same end.

Children could be incredibly resilient, Viri knew, though she also knew the horrors this pair had witnessed tonight would haunt them forever.

Just as the horrors she'd once witnessed would haunt *her* forever.

Blocking out her own memories, Viri left the children and dragged the reaper outside into the crisp midnight air. He continued to spit curses all the way along the grungy alley toward the lake, his steps more labored and his insults less creative as his energy faded. Viri paid him no mind, her focus on squinting through the darkness for any sign of the deadly blackmist.

Relief hit her when they passed a crumbling building and she finally spotted Lake Mirtis up ahead, the moonlight glimmering off its indigo surface, no mist in sight. Another few steps and she saw the wayportal—a ten-foot-high arch carved from silvery magestone—glowing against the darkness of the night.

They were a dozen feet from the portal when her captive stopped swearing long enough to say, "You won't get away with this, hunter." His voice dripped with menace. "The Reaper Priest will come for you. For *all* of you, but *you* especially."

Viri's feet halted without her permission, her eyes slicing to the man only to find a smug look on his face.

"You think I don't recognize you, Viridia Solace?" he continued, his lips twisting into a sneer. "That hair, those eyes—we all know who you are. You're marked, hunter. And one day, the Reaper Priest will—"

"He'll what?" Viri cut in. "Keep hiding, just as he's done for the last seven years?" Her voice was as sharp as steel to mask her sudden wave of emotion. "Every hunter on Elverdine Isle has been searching for him that whole time, including me. You say he's coming for us, for *me*? Then tell him to hurry the hell up." She cocked her head to the side and adopted her own smug look to cover the rageful racing of her heart. "Oh, wait. You won't be able to tell him anything, will you?" She yanked on the fillium, jerking him forward and eliciting another curse as he nearly fell. "You won't be able to tell *any*one *any*thing where you're going."

"He'll save me," the reaper snarled. "He'll reward me for—"

Viri scoffed. "He doesn't even know you exist. You're just one of his many murderous acolytes."

"I'm not. I'm—"

"Where is he, then?"

Silence met her question, just as she'd expected.

"If you weren't a worthless underling, you'd know the answer to that," she taunted. "But you have no idea, do you?"

Viri could *hear* the reaper gnashing his teeth. He wanted to lie—she could see it in his eyes. He wanted to claim some level of importance in the Priest's inner circle, something that might afford him leverage. But the fillium wouldn't allow it—another benefit of the golden cord, so long as it touched him. A magical truth teller.

"You've never even met him, have you?" Viri continued taunting.

More gnashing of his teeth, and she rolled her eyes, her tension fading. Any mention of the Reaper Priest—the current one, at least—was always enough to set her on edge, but despite this man's threats, he didn't know anything of use to her. He was nothing more than a follower, like all those Viri had hunted before him.

One day, she would find a way to his leader. It was the reason she'd become a hunter, the reason she'd earned her mark quicker than other novices, the reason she always pushed herself to be better, faster, stronger. Everything she'd put herself through for the last seven years had been with one single goal: to hunt down the Reaper Priest, the notorious monster of a man who had murdered untold numbers of innocents.

Including Viri's parents.

Unlike his underlings, the Reaper Priest wouldn't face justice. No, he would suffer.

Though not nearly as much as he deserved.

For a moment, Viri allowed herself to sink into her dark thoughts, her determination strengthening, as it always did when she thought of the Priest. But then she squared her shoulders and started forward again, tugging her captive toward the wayportal, ready to hand him over to the Nox and be done with this night.

She would find the Reaper Priest one day.

And when she did, she would finally have her revenge.

2

A few painfully short hours later, Viri was pulled from sleep by someone shaking her roughly, followed by a too-chirpy voice asking, "Did it work? *Did it?*"

Viri groaned and swatted at her best friend, Wynter Starling, before moving her pillow over her head. " 'S too early, Wyn. Go 'way."

"It's not early, and you're a little traitor." Wynter yanked the pillow away. "You promised to wake me when you got home."

"It was late." Viri opened her eyes into a squint-glare. "And unlike *some* people, I value my friends' sleep."

"I don't need sleep—I need answers. So spill."

When Viri tried to reclaim her pillow, Wynter tossed it across the room and returned Viri's glare with her own, causing Viri to grumble resignedly and sit up in bed. Wynter was right about the hour; a quick look out the sealed window of Viri's bedroom halfway up the side of Mount Tembris—the middle of three peaks in the Tridus Mountains—showed enough sunlight to indicate it was midmorning, at least.

"Meera's going to kill me," Viri muttered, having slept through her dawn training. Not even the calming view of Lake Mirtis glimmering in the sunshine could ease her dread at the thought of having to apologize to her mentor—who also happened to be the head of the Hunters' Guild.

Wynter tossed her glossy black hair over her shoulder, her sapphire eyes narrowing as she threatened, "She'll have to get in line if you don't hurry up and tell me what happened last night."

Viri knew her friend wasn't asking for an overview of the hunt, nor did Wynter care about the reaper who was now rotting in an Underlock cell deep beneath the mountain. There was only one thing Wynter wanted to know about Viri's night.

"Come *on*, V. I'm begging you. Did it *work*?"

Viri made her friend wait a beat longer—punishment for the rude awakening—but with a slow smile, she finally said, "It worked. You're a genius. But you already know that."

Wynter threw her hands up and let out a whoop of triumph. But then, just as quickly, she hushed herself, her eyes jumping anxiously toward the closed bedroom door.

"I take it your mom is home?" Viri guessed dryly.

Wynter chewed her lip and nodded, causing Viri to bite back a grin. Sarielle Starling—Wynter's mother and Viri's legal guardian—would *not* be pleased if she learned what her beloved daughter was doing in her free time. As it was, Sarielle claimed she had a heart attack every night Viri went out hunting, so if she knew her daughter was experimenting with the highly illegal practice of alchemy, she would be horrified. Not just because Sarielle was the Magistratus—the political leader of Elverdine Isle—but because alchemy was dangerous, in too many ways to count. And yet . . .

"You saved my life last night," Viri admitted, recalling the reaper's dagger just a breath away from impaling her. "Your impedidust kept me from being sliced in two."

Wynter's strikingly blue eyes widened. "Really?" she breathed. But then she tilted her head to the side, her gaze homing in on Viri's cheek. "Was that before or after you were sucker punched in the face?"

Viri touched her swollen, scabbed flesh, wincing as it throbbed beneath her fingers. "Does it look that bad?" When Wynter didn't answer, Viri pressed, "On a scale of one to ten, how much is your mom going to panic?"

"If she walked in here right now? Eleven, for sure." Wynter pulled a small glass jar from inside her gray trainee-physician robes and winked conspiratorially. "But if you put this on and wait a few minutes, that'll bring it down to a three. Maybe a two."

Viri took the familiar—and forbidden—healing salve from her friend and slathered it over her tender cheek. "Have I told you today how much I love you?"

"Not yet," Wynter said, reclaiming the jar and hiding it in her robes again, "but in your defense, you only just woke up." She settled more comfortably on Viri's bed. "Now tell me what happened with the impedidust. Don't leave anything out."

Viri did as ordered, sharing how she'd used the silver powder on the reaper and answering Wynter's numerous questions, all while ignoring the tingle in her cheek as the salve reknit her damaged skin.

"I forgot to factor in how strong they are after siphoning," Wynter murmured, her eyes glazed in thought. "I'll play around with the formula and see if I can make it last longer next time."

Viri shrugged. "It did what I needed. A few seconds is all it takes for me to get my fillium around them."

Wynter's glazed look vanished, her features turning stern. "You rely too much on that weapon of yours. It may be one of a kind, but if it ever stops working—"

"Then I'll have all your alchemy tricks up my sleeve," Viri interrupted, having heard this lecture before, "as well as my own hunter skills. Don't worry about me, Wyn. Fillium or not, I can take care of myself."

"I know you can." Wynter's expression softened. "But *of course* I worry. Just as you do about me."

"That's because you're sneaking around and breaking the law." Viri touched her cheek again, finding the swelling and pain mostly gone. "Though I have to admit, I'm certainly benefitting from it."

"Well, it's not like I can share my experiments with anyone else, is it?" Wynter said, pouting slightly. "They'd throw me in the Underlock with all those nasty reapers you capture."

"Maybe there's a valid reason why they'd throw you in there," Viri returned. "Like, oh, I don't know—to save your life? And everyone else's?"

Wynter waved a dismissive hand. "Alchemy's not dangerous if you know what you're doing."

"Which you *don't*. You're making things up as you go."

"That's what all the best alchemists do."

Viri huffed out a breath, half amused, half annoyed. "You have no way of knowing that, since you've never met one. Everything you know, you've taught yourself, thanks to some musty old books and that unnaturally big brain of yours."

"And now we circle back to how you're benefitting from it, and leave it there," Wynter said in her firmest end-of-discussion voice.

Sighing loudly, Viri gave in, but only because it was a conversation they'd had over and over, and no matter how hard she'd tried to sway her friend, Wynter was just too curious for her own good. From the moment they'd heard whispers about the ancient magical practice of creating and transforming matter into Elders-knew-what, Wynter had become obsessed with learning everything she could about it.

Fortunately, that was little, since the alchemist mages who had once inhabited Elverdine Isle had vanished long ago with all the other magical beings, taking most of their books and knowledge and leaving only traces of their power behind—the way-portals, the obelisks, the everbeacons, and a few rare, enchanted artifacts, all fiercely coveted. Viri's fillium was one such item, inherited from her hunter parents and carefully locked away until she'd earned her mark.

What Wynter was doing, though . . . The ancient mages had studied for *years* before they were allowed to practice alchemy unsupervised. In untrained hands, their experiments weren't just dangerous—they were deadly. And while no one on Elverdine Isle could perform magical acts like the mages of old, there was still the potions and powders side of the craft, where the wrong combination of ingredients could supposedly destroy an entire city. The risk was such that alchemy was the only truly forbidden form of magic on the island.

But that didn't stop Wynter, her obsession too strong to relinquish.

Sighing again, Viri shoved her friend none too gently off the bed, lacking the energy to argue. "I need to do some groveling with Meera, and *you* should be off studying how to heal people in legal, nonmagical ways." Arching a brow, she added, "Don't think I haven't noticed how many classes you've been skipping lately."

Wynter straightened her gray robes, frowning at the physician's emblem on her sleeve. "I hate it there."

"I know you do," Viri said, heading to her wardrobe for a fresh set of hunting leathers. "But I also know you love your mom too much to tell her that the sight of blood makes you queasy, lest you ruin her dreams of you becoming Aravell's top physician."

"Not just blood." Wynter shuddered comically. "People are disgusting."

Viri hid her smile by rifling through her hangers for a clean scarlet cloak. "You're a credit to the Healers' Guild, Wynter Starling. Let no one ever tell you otherwise."

"You said yourself that I helped save your life last night," Wynter shot back. "I'd be perfectly happy learning how to treat patients with magical means. But using mundane medicine? Witnessing illness, pain, death?" She shuddered again. "No, thank you."

"At the risk of repeating myself, your preferred method is *illegal*."

"It's only illegal if you get caught."

Viri snorted. "Try that line on your mom and see what she says."

Wynter blanched, then scowled, before pointedly changing the topic. "I'm surprised you're not in more of a rush."

Viri draped her outfit over her arm and reached for her boots as she replied, "Meera will be annoyed about this morning, but she'll see from the arrest logs that I didn't get in until late, so she'll understand." She would still kick Viri's ass during their next training session, but that would be the case regardless.

"I don't mean Meera," Wynter said. "I figured you'd run straight to Nox HQ the moment you woke up. I'm actually impressed by your willpower right now."

That made Viri pause. "What are you talking about?"

Hearing the bewilderment in her tone, Wynter's expression turned confused, then alarmed. "Wait—you don't know?"

"Know *what*?"

Wynter's alarm seemed to grow. "I overheard Mom talking with Captain Farrow this morning. Someone was captured last night. Someone important."

At the mention of Darik Farrow—the captain of the Nox Custodia—Viri relaxed. The city guards and hunters worked closely when it came to protecting the city, but they were still separate entities, with the Nox overseeing general law enforcement, and hunters specializing in reapers. The only news that might have caused Viri to sprint straight to Nox headquarters would have had to come from—

"Meera was too busy doing damage control to report in herself," Wynter went on, making Viri's thoughts stutter to a halt. "No need to let word spread and cause a panic—or so Darik told Mom."

Viri's blood turned to ice, then fire, as both dread and anticipation coursed through her. "Who was captured, Wyn?"

Wynter shook her head. "I didn't hear a name. All I know is that it's a high-ranking reaper. Someone in the Priest's inner circle."

The air left Viri in a *whoosh*.

Finally, after so many years of searching, this could be the break they needed in gaining access to the Reaper Priest.

“I need to go,” Viri said, rushing to her bedroom door, only for Wynter to grab her arm.

“Clothes, V.” Wynter indicated the bundle in Viri’s hands, spinning her toward her private bathroom. “As much as I love the image of you interrogating a deadly reaper in your pajamas, you should probably stick with your usual badass hunter vibe.”

Viri glanced down at her pastel-pink nightshirt and cursed before racing off and dressing in record time, finishing by coiling her fillium around her forearm.

“Go get ’em, hunter,” Wynter said as Viri hurried back into the bedroom. “I want a full debrief later.”

Viri was already sprinting out the door and down the long hallway of their apartment, Wynter’s words fading behind her. She could hear Sarielle in the kitchen—a rarity, given how busy her job kept her—and for a second, Viri considered heading in that direction. But her guardian kept a strict boundary between work and home, so she would be tight-lipped about anything Darik had shared. Better for Viri to go straight to the source.

Dashing out the front door, Viri bolted through the inner-mountain tunnels, inhaling the earthy, filtered air as she careened around corners at breakneck speed, her path lit by flameless everbeacons affixed to the black rock. Not for the first time, she was grateful that living with the Magistratus meant a prime cliffside location with few neighbors, limiting the foot traffic to the nearest wayportal. She was even more grateful that her late start kept her from colliding with the early-morning commuters she normally passed on her way to training. Instead, she was able to run straight for the shimmering magestone arch and leap through it without delay, mentally guiding it to the portal nearest to her destination.

The headquarters of the Nox Custodia were located deep within Mount Verta, the southernmost peak of the Tridus Mountains. While Mount Tembris had apartments like Viri's built all the way through it up to the summit, Mount Verta was mostly hollow in the middle, its thick rock walls carved by the ancient mages into upward-spiraling levels that housed the various guilds, city services, and market districts—giving citizens plenty of space inside the mountain to work, study, and socialize.

Since the Nox needed easy access to the Underlock, their headquarters sat at the base of the inner-mountain—a place Viri reached in mere seconds through the connected wayportal, exiting the shining arch straight into the white-marbled reception area of Nox HQ.

Two uniformed guards manned the public entrance, like always, and Viri gave them a quick nod as she marched past the front desk and into the elevator. As soon as the doors closed, she jammed her finger on the down button, rolling her neck against the skin-crawling feeling of magic as the ellixen-powered lift began its descent.

It was only a short ride down to the Nox's main administration level, where the city guards worked when they weren't on patrol. Usually, the cubicled space was quiet and calm. Today, however, Viri was met by chaos when she stepped out of the elevator, finding black-uniformed guards bustling about in apparent disarray and even a few red-cloaked hunters interspersed among them, clearly waiting for news. Viri knew she should join her colleagues, but she didn't have the patience, not when she needed answers *now*.

Striding between the workspaces and past open office doors, Viri headed straight to the farthest end of the floor, stopping when she reached a wooden door hewn into the mountainside, the golden plaque saying CAPTAIN DARIK FARROW. She was just about to knock when a voice halted her.

"It's about time you showed up. I was close to sending out a search party."

Viri whirled around to find her other best friend, Soren Archer, standing with his arms crossed over his Nox uniform, the silver buttons and buckles of his black trench coat all polished to perfection. With sandy-blond hair and warm brown eyes, he was the poster child of the Nox Custodia, not just because of his boyish good looks but also because he was a stickler for the rules, already rising through the leadership ranks. To Viri, however, he would always be the scrawny kid she'd met on her first day of training—her as a hunter, him as a city guard—the two of them paired in a joint sparring exercise to test their raw skills. They'd forged a bond in blood and bruises and been inseparable ever since.

Aside from Wynter, no one knew Viri as well as Soren, so it was unsurprising that he'd expected her to arrive as soon as she heard about the captured reaper. The teasing grin on his lips said as much, but that grin transformed into a frown when he took her in fully.

"What the hell happened to your face?"

"It's nothing." Viri waved off his concern. "Much better than earlier. I can barely feel it now."

Soren's features tightened as he realized what that meant. Like Viri, he didn't approve of Wynter's obsession with alchemy, but that was more because she was breaking the law and less because of how dangerous it was.

"Don't start," Viri said when his mouth opened. "Yell at Wyn later, not at me." She turned toward the door. "Right now, I need to see Darik and find out what's—"

"He's not here."

Viri whipped back around. "Where is he?"

"With Meera. They're talking to witnesses from last night."

"Witnesses?" Viri's brow furrowed. "What for?"

Soren ran a hand through his hair, mussing the pale strands, only for them to bounce straight back into a near-perfect coif. "The reaper—it's like he just . . . *appeared* here."

He.

The reaper was male.

Viri's skin tingled, her desperation to know more rising with every passing second.

"No one has claimed credit for his capture," Soren went on. "Captain Farrow thinks they're afraid of retribution from the Priest and keeping quiet to protect their family. But whatever their reason, we have a high-ranking reaper in custody and nothing but unanswered questions."

"Has he been interrogated?" Viri asked.

"Of course," Soren said. "But he's refusing to speak. Says there's only one person he'll talk to."

"Who?"

"The captain didn't say. He and Meera are staying quiet until they have more details."

Frustrated, Viri spun on her heel and began walking back toward the elevator.

"You better not be thinking what I think you're thinking," Soren warned, keeping in step with her.

"I want to see him," Viri said.

"Absolutely not."

She ignored the unyielding words. "I don't need your permission. I—"

"Actually, you do. He's in a high-security cell so deep in the Underlock that only Nox with valid clearance have access."

At the odd note in her friend's voice, Viri halted on the marble walkway between two empty cubicles and squinted at him. "What aren't you telling me?"

Soren seemed to debate within himself. "The reaper isn't just someone in the Priest's inner circle. He's . . . more than that."

Viri's heart stuttered, a strange premonition coming over her, sharp with dread. "Who is he, Soren?"

There was a long pause, as if he regretted saying anything, but then Soren met her gaze and declared, "It's Reeve Ashton—the Reaper Priest's most loyal servant and right-hand man."

Reeve.

Ashton.

For a moment, Viri heard nothing outside the ringing in her ears, her mind besieged with images of a young boy with tousled black hair and silver eyes that shone like stars. Other memories began to take form, but she shoved them away before she could see anything—or any*one*—else.

Swaying on her feet, Viri was vaguely aware of Soren going on to say something she already knew: that Reeve was infamous among Nox and hunters, considered a high-level target after whispers of his name and position had started circulating years earlier. The Priest was another matter—his identity was a carefully guarded secret, known only to those close to him.

Reeve Ashton was close to him. Perhaps closer than anyone.

Viri swayed again, prompting Soren to call her name worriedly. She snapped back to herself, her throat hoarse as she repeated, "I want to see him." Her features hardened with resolve. "You can help me, or you can report me. But either way, I'm going."

Seeing her determination, Soren swore under his breath, before saying, "He won't talk to you."

"Maybe not. But I still need to *try*." Her voice broke on the final word, the only evidence of the emotion she was struggling to hold back.

Soren's face softened. He'd met Viri mere months after her parents had died, so he was acutely aware of everything she was feeling right now, and how much this arrest meant to her. But at the same time, there were so many things he didn't know. Things he would never—*could never*—know.

Like the fact that she knew Reeve personally.

And just how much he had once meant to her.

"Viri . . ." Soren held her eyes, no doubt seeing the torment in them, then sighed loudly. "Fine, I'll take you to him. But if we get caught, you'd better call in all your favors with the Magistratus to keep us both from getting thrown in the Underlock beside Ashton. Agreed?"

Viri nodded quickly, which only made Soren sigh again and mumble about exasperating best friends as he nudged her in the direction of the elevator once more. The workspace around them was still buzzing with chaotic energy, but she barely noticed this time, focused only on summoning the courage she would need to face a ghost she'd thought long buried in her past.

It had been seven years since Viri had seen Reeve Ashton.

Seven years since her parents had been murdered by the Reaper Priest.

And seven years since Reeve had pledged loyalty to their killer, the two of them vanishing without a trace.

Until now.

3

The elevator descended swiftly beneath Mount Verta, whizzing past multiple levels of secured Underlock cells, every second adding to Viri's nerves.

"Just think of him like any other reaper," Soren said, watching her fidget and misreading her anxiety. "Don't let him intimidate you. There's nothing special about Ashton other than how close he is to the Priest."

Oh, if only that were true.

"I'm not intimidated," Viri said. "I'm just eager to hear what he says."

"Unless you've learned how to read minds, I wouldn't get your hopes up," Soren warned. But Viri wasn't worried about Reeve not talking—her presence should be enough to loosen his lips. It was the least he owed her after . . . everything.

"You never know," Viri said as they continued downward. "Maybe a few hours in the dark has made him rethink his silence."

The Reeve she remembered was stubborn to a fault, but she

needed Soren to see her confidence, especially with the favor she was about to beg of him.

Needing a distraction as the lift began to slow, she asked, "What's with the sparkles?"

At Soren's questioning look, she indicated his hands, which were covered in glittery dust.

He grimaced and tried unsuccessfully to wipe them on his clothes. "Jessy's newest craft project." In a grumble, he added, "Little sisters are the worst."

A smile touched Viri's lips as she thought of Jessalyn Archer, Soren's only sibling. At thirteen years old, she was a menace, yet still managed to be adorable enough to have everyone wrapped around her pinky finger—her big brother most of all.

Before Viri could ask how, exactly, the glitter had ended up on Soren, the elevator came to a halt, but the doors didn't open, something Viri had never experienced before.

"You so owe me for this," Soren muttered, pressing his palm to the command panel and waiting for the complicated magic—set in place by the ancient mages—to recognize him and his clearance level.

A moment later, it did, with the elevator doors opening to reveal a long, dark tunnel. It looked like every other level of the Underlock, the black rocky walls near suffocating, and the dimmest of everbeacons offering just enough light to keep Viri from being completely blind.

"Ashton is the only inmate down this far, but I'm not sure where they put him," Soren said as they stepped out of the lift into the moist underground air. The filtration wasn't as strong this deep beneath the mountain, the earthy aroma so thick and musty that Viri could almost taste it. "It might be a longish walk, depending on how isolated they want him to feel."

Likely very isolated, Viri figured. But that was good, since it meant there would be no witnesses to her reunion. There was only one problem to deal with first.

With a fortifying inhale, she halted Soren by grabbing his sleeve and made her request. "I need you to wait here."

He barked out an incredulous laugh. "You're joking, right?"

"I'm not." She planted her feet. "I want to talk to him alone. He might be more willing to share something if he doesn't see me as a threat."

"You're a hunter, V." Soren flicked her scarlet cloak. "You can't get much more threatening to someone like him."

Someone like him—because Reeve was a reaper.

Viri hadn't allowed herself to think about it, not once in the seven years since she'd last seen him. But of course that was what he'd become—a murderer, just like his master.

"I have a feeling about this," Viri said, knowing it was the only thing that might sway her friend. Her keen intuition was renowned among hunters and Nox alike, and Soren had seen for himself how many times her instincts had proven true.

"Feeling or not, I don't like the idea of you being alone with him," Soren said, his forehead creasing with indecision.

Viri felt a thread of hope and tugged on it. "He's locked in a cell. He can't do anything to me."

"He can say something to upset you," Soren argued. "Some words cut deeper than blades."

"At least that'll mean he's broken his no-speaking stance."

"I'm serious, Viri." Soren laid a hand on her shoulder, his brown gaze full of worry. "You're well known among reapers"—

he gestured to her unusual hair and eyes—"and Ashton hasn't evaded capture this long by being an idiot. He'll recognize you on sight."

That was true regardless of her reputation, but Soren didn't know that.

"He's also the Priest's closest confidant," he continued, "so you can be sure he knows what happened to your parents. He'll use that information to taunt you. To *hurt* you."

Viri swallowed, but said, "He can only hurt me if I give him the power to do so." She removed Soren's hand, squeezing reassuringly. He'd always been protective of her—overprotective, even, just as he was toward all his loved ones. But he couldn't protect her forever, nor did she want—or need—him to. "This isn't the first reaper I've gone head-to-head with, Sor. I've been taunted plenty of times, especially about my parents. I love you for caring, but I have a thick skin. Promise."

Everything she'd said was true, and yet . . . if Reeve dared mention what had happened that day seven years ago, then Soren was right to be concerned. But she couldn't allow herself to think about that, or she'd never make it to his cell.

"Please," Viri said quietly. "I need to do this."

Hearing her beg, Soren finally relented, though his grim expression showed it was against his better judgment.

"Be quick," he cautioned, heading back into the elevator. "Someone will have noticed me heading down here with you, and protocol means they'll flag it with Captain Farrow."

Viri nodded her understanding. She might not *technically* be doing anything wrong, but she was definitely bending some unspoken rules.

"I'll go run interference," Soren offered. He jerked his chin toward the command panel. "You won't need me with you to come back up—just hit the button like normal." His eyes turned hard as he finished, "I don't need to warn you that Ashton is dangerous. Don't give him any personal information; don't make him any promises. We don't bargain with killers. If he's willing to talk, glean what you can, then leave him to rot like he deserves."

"Don't worry, Sor," Viri said, her stomach churning despite her show of confidence. "I know what I'm doing."

She was lying through her teeth, but Soren gave an approving nod. "Come find me when you're done so I know you're all right."

Before she could reply, the elevator doors closed and he vanished from sight.

Taking a second to prepare herself, Viri glanced down the rocky tunnel, wondering if she could do this, while also knowing she *had* to. Even if Reeve refused to speak, she still needed to look into his eyes and see if there was any trace of the person she'd once known. Logically, she was aware that the eleven-year-old boy from her childhood was gone, replaced by an eighteen-year-old killer. But until she saw that for herself, she would never be able to fully believe it.

Mindful that every minute she delayed was another minute she risked discovery, Viri set off down the dimly lit path, building a mental wall brick by brick with every step. No matter what happened during this encounter, she wouldn't let Reeve get to her. She was a completely different person from the carefree ten-year-old girl he'd last known, and the same was true for him. They might as well be strangers. They *were* strangers, as far as she was concerned. He was a reaper, and she was a hunter. They were sworn enemies, now and forever. That was it.

Even so, her heart picked up speed as she continued along the tunnel, passing empty cells, each new corner making her pulse spike with anticipation. But no matter how far she traveled from the elevator, there was still no sign of life. So she kept walking, deeper and deeper beneath the mountain, her insides a riot of nerves.

Just as she was beginning to wonder if Soren was wrong about Reeve being on this level, the everbeacons brightened ever so slightly ahead, leading to one final cell before the tunnel came to an end.

Certain this was it, Viri took a steadying breath, squared her shoulders, and marched forward until she stood before the glass-fronted cell. Like all the others on this level, it was reasonably sized, with enough room for a thin mattress atop a stone slab, and even a small area for personal hygiene. The general layout was the same as that of the cells on the higher prison levels, including the lack of metal bars, eliminating the risk of corrosion from the damp earth. Instead, there was just a large, clear barrier separating her from Reeve Ashton as she set eyes on him for the first time in seven long, life-changing years.

Dressed like midnight, he leaned casually against the rock wall, seemingly without a care in the world. His black hair was still a familiar tousled mess, as if being windswept was its natural state, and his eyes were still like starlight—or storm clouds, depending on his mood—but that was where any similarities to the boy she'd once known ended. With his clothes fitted like ink against his body, all it took was a quick, betraying glance for Viri to note how much he'd changed, all his soft childhood edges now sharpened and sculpted into what could only be called a work of art.

He wasn't pretty—there was something too dark and dangerous

about him to be called that—but he was without a doubt beautiful to behold. He'd been cute seven years ago, but now . . .

Now he was devastating.

Unable to stop herself, Viri's gaze wandered over him again, taking in his tall form, broad shoulders, and narrow waist. His arms were crossed at his chest, making his biceps strain against the dark material of his shirt, the sleeves rolled up to reveal corded forearms and golden-tanned skin. Long, lean legs met well-worn boots, the latter being the only part of him that Viri felt safe looking at until she collected herself enough to meet his eyes. The moment she did, she scowled fiercely at the cocky amusement in his impossibly silver gaze.

"Like what you see?" he asked, smirking.

The *audacity*—Viri couldn't believe it. Couldn't believe *him*.

"What I like seeing is you behind bars," she returned coldly. "Exactly where you belong, reaper."

His mouth quirked upward. "Reaper? So formal, Little Shadow?"

Pain slammed into Viri at the once-familiar nickname, something he alone had used. But she didn't reveal the sudden squeezing of her heart, only thinned her lips and said, "Don't call me that."

Reeve's gaze dropped to her feet, moving slowly, leisurely, back up again, humor brightening his eyes—along with numerous other things Viri refused to acknowledge.

"I suppose you're not so little anymore," he admitted. His voice was deeper than she remembered, soft with intimacy and heady with appeal. "And it's been a long time since you followed me around like a shadow. But I can't help myself. It still suits you, Viri."

At the sound of her name on his lips, a shiver rippled through her. Revulsion—nothing more, since she firmly stomped down everything else that dared so much as try to break free.

Counting to five, she quickly regained control, determined to treat this like any other interrogation. "You're going to be locked down here for a long time, but you don't have to be miserable—you'll be given certain privileges if you cooperate. Books, exercise, visitation rights. I heard you'll only speak to one person, but that's evidently not the case, so—"

"Oh, it's definitely the case," Reeve said.

Viri pointed to herself. "Clearly not."

He just looked at her, arching a brow, until realization barreled into her.

She was the person he'd said he would speak to.

Viri wasn't a fool—she could see the trap for what it was, a cat-and-mouse game where he toyed with her emotions for his own sick entertainment. He knew enough about her past to make her hurt more than anyone else. Hell, he'd *lived* it with her, witnessing every horrifying second and then abandoning her when she'd needed him most. If he wanted to play that hand, then fine, she would endure whatever he threw at her—but she was damn well going to get what she needed in return.

"In that case, let's cut straight to the chase," she said. "How do I find your master?"

"My *master*?" He laughed darkly, the sound like a caress against her skin, making her fight another shiver. "I bow to no one, Little Shadow. Never have, never will."

Viri ground her teeth at his repeated use of her old nickname but yielded that battle for the larger one. "The Reaper Priest—where is he? How do we—"

Reeve interrupted by yawning loudly and pushing off the

wall. "I've been waiting hours for you, you know." He stretched his arms over his head, his shirt rising just enough to show a glimpse of abdominal muscles contracting in the dim light. "I'm not sure who was more furious when I made my request—the revered captain of the Nox Custodia or your equally intimidating hunter boss. What do you call her, by the way? Chief? General? Madam Overlord?" An edged smile. "Oh, wait, I forgot that last one's reserved for your precious Magistratus."

Viri ignored the dig at Sarielle. "My 'boss' is Commander Roth to you," she said shortly, the words sounding strange to her ears. While Darik preferred the Nox to address him by his title, Meera kept things more casual among the hunters. "Now answer my questions."

Reeve huffed out an amused breath. "Where's the fun in that?"

Her patience thinning, Viri gritted out, "This isn't meant to be *fun*, Reeve."

His eyes flared as she said his name for the first time in years, but he quickly returned to his cavalier amusement. "I'll make you a deal," he said smoothly, walking over to the glass until he stood right before her.

"No deals," she said, her voice firm.

He ignored her. "We'll play a game. An answer for an answer."

"I said no—"

"I'll go first: Who hurt you?"

"I'm not—" Viri stopped abruptly, blinking as his words processed. "What?"

He gestured toward her cheek and repeated, the words more clipped this time, "Who. Hurt. You?"

A storm of emotion flooded through Viri, too overwhelming

and confusing for her to control, so she settled on the most dominant feeling: *rage.*

"*You* did, Reeve," she snarled, relieved that her fury kept her voice from cracking.

A muscle feathered in his jaw as he understood her meaning, but his tone remained light as he said, "I think I'd remember that. I keep a pretty strict no-hitting-girls rule. Call me old-fashioned, but casual violence doesn't appeal to me."

"No, just killing kids to steal their magic," Viri spat. "There's certainly nothing casual about *that.*"

Reeve said nothing, his silence telling. His veins might not be streaked with black at present—nor was the hunter's mark on Viri's palm searing with his proximity—but that only meant he hadn't siphoned recently enough for there to be any stolen ellixen left in his body. It didn't change what he was. What he *did.* Reapers were addicts—once they had a taste of power, they never stopped hungering for it. Reeve was no different from the rest of them.

"No comeback?" Viri taunted. "You're not going to defend your choice to prey on children?"

Reeve unfolded and refolded his sleeves, taking his time before responding. "Reapers can siphon from adults, too." His eyes captured hers. "You know that better than anyone."

Grief burned through Viri like fire, but she stifled it as fast as she could, shoving more bricks into her mental wall and refusing to let any memories surface. "It's not a matter of if you *can*, but if you *will*," she retorted. "People older than fourteen don't have enough ellixen left to tempt your interest."

"Maybe you can speak to someone about that, *hunter*,"

he goaded. "Get them to change the laws, raise the age of Impartation, and reapers will have more of a range to sample from. If it's only kids you're worried about, then you should have a solid argument up your sleeve."

Viri sent him a disgusted look, making it clear how she felt about that idea. The Impartation—a ceremony where children, on or before their fourteenth birthday, surrendered their magic to fuel the obelisks warding the city from blackmist—was the only thing that all but guaranteed protection from reapers. The human body required a mere drop of ellixen to survive, so that was all that remained after the sacrifice, the reduced power not enough to entice reapers and therefore eliminating the threat of being attacked. It was also what kept the reaper population in check, since they had to be willing to prey solely on children—to *murder* children—in order to start down the dark, addictive path of siphoning. Very few could stomach it, but for those who did . . .

Reapers were monsters.

All of them.

And as much as Viri wanted to look at Reeve and see the innocent boy she had once known, it wasn't possible. Because that boy was gone.

Forever.

"Enough stalling," Viri said, stepping closer to the glass. "I answered your question, now it's your turn. Where's the Priest?"

Reeve cocked his head to the side. "You didn't actually answer *my* question. I think we both know you answered a different question. That means it's still my turn."

Viri slammed her hands against the barrier, ignoring the sting of ellixen-suppressing magic beneath her palms—a standard requirement in all Underlock cells. "I'm not playing your games,

Reeve. Tell me what I want to know, or I'm gone. It's of little consequence to me."

"You always were a terrible liar." He grinned. "Nice to see some things haven't changed."

Eager to put a dent in his confidence, Viri spun on her heel and began walking away, praying he wouldn't call her bluff. She nearly wilted in relief when she heard his soft "Wait," and paused to look back over her shoulder.

"Are you finally going to cooperate?" she asked. "Or just keep wasting my time?"

"Time is a construct, so 'waste' is a matter of interpretation." When she started walking again, he quickly added, "But yes to your first question. The one about cooperation. Lucky for you, it's my word of the day."

Certain she would regret it, Viri returned to his cell, tapping her foot as she glared at him in expectation. "Well?"

Reeve placed his hands in his pockets and rocked back on his heels, looking way too comfortable given his circumstances. "You want to know where the Reaper Priest is?"

"Yes," Viri hissed. "I've only asked about a thousand times."

His lips twitched. "So dramatic. I missed that about you."

Viri felt a stab of pain, but it was quickly replaced by anger. "Three seconds and I leave again. This time for good. One. Two—"

"You used to be so much more patient," Reeve said, as if *she* were the one being difficult. "But fine. You want the answer? I'll tell you everything I know about the Priest. I won't even make you finish our game—just you asking the questions, and me revealing all. Is that what you want?"

Viri didn't dare get her hopes up, not as she caught the calculating look on Reeve's annoyingly handsome face.

"There's just one small condition," he said, removing one hand from his pocket to inspect his nails. The move made the dim light glint across a ring on his middle finger, the band as black as onyx and etched with silver runes. He'd never been one to wear jewelry when they were kids—yet another of the million things that had changed since then.

"Look around," Viri said, repressing the urge to step through the barrier and shake some sense into him. "You're not in a position to make demands."

"Let's call it a new game, then." Reeve dropped his hand to look straight at her, his eyes like thunderclouds as he declared, "Get me out of here, and I'll tell you anything you want. That's my offer, Viri—my freedom for your answers."

For a long moment, she just stared at him, but then she couldn't help laughing. It was a bitter, humorless sound.

"Enjoy life in a cell, Reeve," she said, turning away. "Or don't. I really don't care."

Without giving him a chance to reply, she strode off down the tunnel, not stopping this time. But she couldn't keep from hearing the words he called after her as they bounced off the rocky walls and echoed in her ears:

"We both know I'm your only hope of finding him. When you change your mind, I'll be waiting."

Viri clenched her jaw and forced herself to keep walking. She wouldn't give him the satisfaction of knowing how much their encounter had affected her—or how tempted she was by his offer. But she knew better. He was a reaper, and reapers were liars. No matter what he said, she couldn't trust him.

Angry at herself for thinking their reunion might have gone differently, for the sliver of hope she'd been unable to quash—

a sliver that was now fully extinguished—Viri was lost in her head by the time she reached the elevator and began speeding upward. It was clear that Reeve had never intended to cooperate. Instead, from the moment of his arrest, he'd been working on a plan to escape—and that plan was to use Viri.

Cursing him viciously under her breath, Viri was in a foul mood by the time the elevator slowed at the Nox administration level—foul enough that she decided she would let Soren know she was safe, then head straight out to the surface to blow off steam by doing what she did best: reaper hunting.

Her plans, however, were derailed as soon as the elevator doors opened.

Because standing in front of them was Meera, her hands on her hips, her dark face frowning as she spoke directly to Viri's mind and ordered, *"My office. Now."*

4

The Hunters' Guild was located directly above the Nox Custodia—close enough that they shared the same elevator and wayportal—so Viri didn't need to leave the lift. Meera joined her in it, the tension so thick that Viri loosed a relieved breath when the doors finally opened to the Guild's familiar dark-green-marbled corridor.

Unlike the Nox, hunters didn't have individual workstations, since they were almost always out searching for reapers and only visited the Guild for training, meetings, and mentor check-ins. Whenever they captured a reaper, they delivered them to the Nox to finalize the arrest and handle the paperwork. It worked perfectly for Viri, who hated being chained to a desk. She needed to be up and moving, not trapped in place—in every aspect of her life.

Right now, she felt *very* trapped as she followed Meera down the everbeacon-lit corridor, walking past tunnels that led to the sparring chambers, the theater-sized conference room, and a cluster of offices used for casual meetings. Meera, of course, had her own permanent office as head of the Guild, carved into the side of the mountain and boasting a sealed window wall that overlooked the eastern cliffs of Elverdine Isle and the roaring sea hundreds of feet below.

As Viri stepped into Meera's office, her gaze jumped straight to the window, a shiver traveling down her spine as she took in the deadly blackmist hovering over the ocean. But her focus shifted at the sound of a clearing throat, and she spun to find Darik standing beside Meera's mahogany desk at the back of the room, his frown as fierce as the one Meera still wore.

Both leaders were tall and strong and undeniably intimidating, but that was where their similarities ended. Somewhere in her mid-thirties, Meera had dark skin, wavy brown hair, and wore tight-fitting leathers. Darik was a good twenty years older, with salt-and-pepper hair and pallid skin beneath his buttoned-up Nox uniform. Meera's jade-green eyes were sharp and alert, while Darik's black gaze was severe and bordered on hostile—though that look was usually only reserved for Viri.

It was widely known that the captain of the Nox Custodia resented her, even if he was professional enough not to let it affect their interactions. *Mostly.*

Everyone knew the reason, tragic as it was:

He blamed Viri for his daughter's death.

It wasn't her fault—she'd never even *met* Istrid Farrow. But they did share history. Because sixteen and a half years ago, Istrid had been a young hunter mentored by none other than Viri's parents, Jorth and Amity Solace. Meera, too, had been under their mentorship, both her and Istrid fresh out of training. As a newly engaged couple, Meera and Istrid had always hunted as a pair, with Jorth and Amity supervising—until one night, without warning, Viri's parents didn't show up. That same night, a reaper caught Meera and Istrid by surprise, slashing a blade through Meera's throat and leaving Istrid to fight alone.

Istrid managed to kill the reaper—but she didn't survive the attack.

Meera obviously did, though her throat was so damaged that she'd had to rely on a magical amulet from that day on, an artifact left by the ancient mages that allowed her to speak mentally. Its reach was limited to line of sight and her listeners still had to respond audibly, but at least she was able to communicate.

At least she was *alive* to communicate, unlike her beloved fiancé.

Ever since Istrid's passing, Darik had hated Viri's family—first her parents, for not protecting his daughter, and then Viri, after their deaths.

She understood his heartache. She could even relate to it. But her patience for his misplaced grudge had its limits. If Meera, who had loved Istrid beyond measure, could get past what had happened, then Darik could, too.

He, however, refused to let go of his enmity. Even now, Viri could see it in the shadows of his eyes and the firm set of his jaw. But she met his gaze unflinchingly, and when he pointed an angry finger at the chair in front of Meera's desk, she trudged over and slumped onto it, bracing for the scolding she was about to receive.

Deciding her smartest move was to go on the offense, Viri waited for Meera to take her seat before she jumped in first to ask, "Anything either of you would like to tell me?"

Meera's brows shot up as she mentally repeated, *"Anything* we *want to tell* you?"

"Mm-hmm." Viri brushed lint off her cloak. "I'll give you a hint: When the Reaper Priest's right-hand man is arrested and says he'll only talk to one person, maybe, just *maybe*, that person should be made aware of it."

A flash of guilt from Meera, but Darik's black eyes were stern.

"There are protocols to follow, Solace," the Nox captain said. "You know that."

Viri looked to her mentor and was heartened—slightly—by the hint of frustration on Meera's face. Darik was a rule follower and instilled that trait in his guards. Meera had a hunter's heart and recognized that some rules were made to be broken.

"Reapers don't have rights," Darik went on in his deep, gravelly voice. "Just because Ashton wanted to speak to you doesn't mean we had to agree. We followed procedure and took his request to the council; if they'd voted yes, *then* we would have brought you in."

"They voted no?" Viri was surprised. Reeve's proximity to the Priest was enough that even Sarielle would see the value in getting him to talk, no matter what—or *who*—it involved. The Magistratus might be Viri's guardian, but protective or not, she had a moral obligation to put the good of the many before the good of the few.

"They haven't voted yet," Meera answered for Darik. With a dry look, she added, *"And there's no need to now, is there?"*

Viri squirmed in her seat.

"We know Archer took you to see Ashton," Darik said, disapproval lacing every word. "He hasn't admitted to anything, but there's no point denying it." His tone shifted with warning. "Your friend's loyalty is going to get him in real trouble one day."

"It wasn't his fault," Viri said quickly. "I made him do it."

Meera snorted. *"Soren Archer doesn't do anything he doesn't want to. Try again."*

Before Viri could reply, Darik interjected, "We can discuss your blatant disregard for the rules later. For now, we only have two questions."

Just two? Viri wondered. Her head was buzzing with thousands, all of which remained unanswered thanks to the arrogant reaper imprisoned beneath her feet.

Darik's hands moved to his hips. "Why did the Reaper Priest's most loyal servant request to speak to you"—his gaze was shrewd, suspicious even, as he emphasized—"*only* you, and what did he say?"

Viri hesitated, knowing she needed to be careful. Darik and Meera hadn't become captain and commander by chance. Both were perceptive enough to sense deceit—Meera especially, when it came to Viri.

Keeping as close to the truth as possible, she answered, "Ree—Ashton didn't say why he wanted to speak to me." True. "If I had to guess, it was so he could taunt me." Also true, just not in the way Meera and Darik would think.

Sure enough, Meera's features softened. She rubbed the thick, jagged scar across her throat as she said, *"Because of your parents?"*

Darik's expression darkened at the mention of Amity and Jorth, but then he turned thoughtful. "Of course—Ashton would know all about what happened to them. And your reputation is growing among reapers, so it makes sense that he'd target you."

He paused. "But it still seems very personal. Why not another hunter? Or a Nox? Or a council member?"

Viri found herself wishing Darik were just a little less adept at his job—or at least less intuitive with his line of questioning.

"He didn't say," she repeated, unwilling to offer more.

"What did *he say, then?"* Meera asked, steepling her hands on her desk. *"Did he tell you anything about the Priest?"*

This answer was easier for Viri, if still infuriating. "I tried to get him to talk, but he was toying with me. Playing games." In a mutter, she added, "He's so full of himself that it's a marvel his head can fit in his cell."

"Think hard, Solace," Darik urged. "Are you sure he didn't give anything away?"

Viri shook her head. "There was nothing. He was very clear that he would only answer my questions if—"

"If what?" Meera pressed, leaning forward into her palms.

"He tried to make me a deal," Viri admitted. "His freedom for my answers."

Their reactions were predictable: Meera sighed with annoyance, and Darik's lips thinned.

"Hardly unexpected," Meera said, *"but still, disappointing."*

"I can try again," Viri offered, albeit reluctantly. It had been seven years since she'd last seen Reeve; she'd much prefer to wait another seven—or more—for their next encounter.

"We'll consider it," Darik said, though his frown said otherwise. "For now, we'll keep him isolated. Once he comes to terms with his new living situation, he might be more inclined to share what he knows."

Viri doubted that, but she nodded anyway and stood, eager to venture outside and start her hunt. Reapers dwelled in the mountains and undercity, too, but today, she needed fresh air and sun on her skin. She needed to feel *alive.*

"If that's all—" she began, moving toward the door.

"It's not," Darik said, making Viri pause. He didn't continue immediately, instead taking his time to straighten his black leather gloves, something he was never seen without. Meera wasn't the only one with scars—no one knew where Darik's came from, just that they were grisly enough for him to keep them concealed at all times. "There's still your punishment to address."

Viri spun to Meera, hoping to find an ally in her mentor. Instead, there was an apologetic yet unyielding expression on Meera's face as she stated, *"You visited a high-security prisoner without clearance."*

She knew Viri well enough to understand *why*, but even so—

"I'm sorry, Viri," Meera went on, *"but actions have consequences."*

Viri couldn't help asking, "Would you still be saying that if I'd learned anything of use?"

"You didn't," Darik said, never one to pull his punches, "so that's irrelevant."

Ouch. Viri felt the sting of failure all over again. She turned to the window, watching the blackmist drift over the crashing waves like an ominous, dark cloud. "Fine. What's my punishment? Extra sparring sessions? Training the novices? Cleaning weapons?" She'd been tasked with all of those before, none of which were pleasant, but they were still better than—

"Desk duties," Meera said, making Viri whirl back around in horror. *"You'll report directly to the Nox archives. One week. No hunting."*

Viri gaped. "A whole *week*?"

"Be grateful it's not more," Darik cut in, giving his gloves one last tug before returning his hands to his hips.

"But—"

"I'll still expect you at training every morning," Meera said, halting Viri's objection with a warning look. Viri knew that look—it wasn't a warning not to argue; it was a warning not to push her luck. If she fought the punishment, especially with Darik there, she could be locked out of the Guild for the full week—or longer. At least this way she would still see Meera daily and keep up with any hunting news. It was a compromise, one Viri knew few of her colleagues would be granted.

Swallowing her protests, she asked, "When do I start?"

"Straight away," Meera said, causing Viri's shoulders to drop. *"Head Archivist Thornton has already been notified of your arrival."*

"We don't tolerate laziness in the Nox, nor do we abide disrespect," Darik cautioned. "For the next seven days, you're an archivist's assistant, not a hunter. Don't forget that, or you'll remain there for longer."

Viri bit back her retort. She might not like the punishment, but she also wasn't a delinquent child who was going to slack off, no matter how tedious she found the work.

"It goes without saying that you're not to visit Ashton again," Meera said, watching Viri closely, as if anticipating an argument. But Reeve was the last person she wanted to see.

"That won't be a problem," Viri said firmly enough to satisfy Meera. Darik, too.

"Good." Meera dipped her head toward the door. *"We're due back at the council, but you know where the archives are, so head on down. And Viri?"* Her jade eyes narrowed. *"Don't be late to training tomorrow. I won't be forgiving if it happens again."*

Viri mumbled her agreement and hurriedly left the office, her tension easing at the sight of Soren resting against the wall, waiting for her. His hair was still perfectly coiffed, his uniform still immaculate, but there was a trace of worry in his brown eyes that only faded when he saw she was in one piece.

"Next time I say 'be quick,' maybe consider listening," he drawled as she approached.

"Lesson learned," Viri said, scrunching her nose. "Are you in much trouble?"

"Me? The Nox's golden boy?" He smiled wryly and gestured for her to follow him back through the Guild toward the elevator. "Nah. A slap on the wrist and some extra shifts patrolling the undercity. Nothing I can't handle. You?"

"A week of desk duties." Viri sounded as miserable as she felt. "Effective immediately."

"Elders save you." Soren chuckled. "Your worst nightmare."

Viri only grumbled in reply.

"Was it worth it?" he asked as they continued along the green-marbled corridor. "Did Ashton tell you anything useful?"

"No, and no," Viri said, annoyed all over again.

"I warned you that he wouldn't speak," Soren said, albeit gently.

"He did speak, just nothing that was worth hearing."

Soren's sandy brows shot upward. "You got him to talk?"

"It was getting him to shut up that was difficult," Viri muttered, before remembering herself. Thankfully, they reached the elevator then, just as the doors opened and three hunters walked out, one of whom hailed Soren to ask about a recent arrest they'd shared.

Judging by the coy look on the attractive young man's face, that wasn't all they'd shared, and Viri barely hid a smirk as she told Soren she'd see him later.

Alone in the elevator, Viri just stood there for a moment, wishing she had time to go outside and clear her head, especially after her worthless visit with Reeve. But she couldn't afford to risk Darik's threat, so with a deep exhale, she pressed the down button, ignored the prickle of ellixen as the lift began to move, and prayed to the Elders that she would get stuck between floors and have a valid excuse to skive off the rest of the day.

Unsurprisingly, the Elders weren't listening—the gods of old apparently had better things to do with their time—and all too soon the doors were opening at the Nox archives.

A single step into the cavernous white-walled space was all it took to remind Viri why she hated the archives so much. It wasn't just the piles—and *piles*—of paperwork. Nor was it the floor-to-ceiling bookcases that traveled farther than she could see, all overflowing with ledgers and reports covering everything from small crimes to serial killers. It wasn't even the stuffy desks crammed together in one corner and the weary-looking archivists sitting behind them. None of those things were appealing, but nor were they bad enough to make Viri want to leave as quickly as she'd arrived. Instead, it was the air itself that made her struggle not to flee—because she'd forgotten how strong the archives' preservation wards were, the ellixen so powerful that it was like a physical attack on her senses.

Usually, Viri didn't mind being more sensitive to magic than most, but at times like this, when it was concentrated enough to feel like an overstimulating assault, she wished she could be more normal. Not even the Underlock cells used this much magic—but they also didn't need to protect flimsy records from being destroyed in the moist inner-mountain air.

Standing still, Viri closed her eyes and breathed in the calming aroma of paper and ink as she waited for her body to adjust. Only when the feeling shifted from lightning bolts zapping her nerve endings to a soft humming beneath her skin did she shake off the sensation and reopen her eyes—to find every archivist in the room staring at her.

Clearing her throat, Viri started toward the group in the corner, but was intercepted by a short, bald man who appeared from between a set of bookcases.

"Viridia Solace?"

"That's me," she confirmed, realizing he wasn't short so much as hunched, no doubt from years of bending over a desk.

"I'm Head Archivist Thornton," he said with an imperious sniff, then turned and headed back into the bookshelves. "Come with me."

Viri hadn't had much experience with archivists, but Soren and his Nox friends always joked about the record keepers being a serious bunch. "Prickly" was the word they used. Thornton was already living up to the description.

Swallowing her pride, Viri followed like an obedient dog, her boots clicking on the pristine white floor as they passed row after row of bookcases, then finally reached a pale wall with an open door cut into it.

"This is where you'll work while you're with us," Thornton said, gesturing for her to precede him into the room.

Viri nearly hissed as she stepped through the doorway and

encountered another strong ellixen ward. She gritted her teeth until the feeling passed, then looked around the small, sterile office that had paperwork covering every surface, including the sole desk and chair.

"We've been understaffed for the last few months," Thornton said, explaining the mess. "Certain things have been neglected so we could prioritize more urgent cases." He moved to the desk and picked up a pile of papers. "Everything in this room is a crime, a complaint, or a concern that has been reported to the Nox. Noise disturbances, theft, graffiti, trespassing, assault, possession of illicit substances—you name it, and it's here." He set the pile back down. "Your job is to sort through all this so it can be filed away."

Viri gulped at the sheer amount of work ahead of her. "How?"

Thornton grabbed a page and pointed to the top, where the number seven was written in green ink, then reached for a different page that showed a blue number eleven, before he indicated the rest of the chaos so Viri could see all the various colors and numbers. "Everything is coded into offense categories. All you have to do is put them into piles by color and arrange them by number."

"Sounds idiot-proof," Viri commented.

Thornton looked straight at her. "It is."

Viri almost laughed. *Prickly, indeed.*

"I know you hunters are used to working at all hours," the archivist went on, "but this week you're on a strict day shift with me: eight a.m. to six p.m., with two ten-minute breaks plus a half hour for lunch."

Viri sighed quietly at the unexciting daily structure, already missing the freedom of her hunting job.

"I'll be back in a few hours," Thornton said, heading for the door. "You're only to leave this office for your breaks or if you have questions. Understood?"

He didn't wait for her answer before vanishing from the room, leaving Viri alone with her mammoth task. She doubted she would sort through even half the piles before her week was up, but she silenced her misgivings, straightened her shoulders, and got to work.

The first hour passed slowly.

The second was glacial.

The third and onward were borderline torture.

But still, Viri sorted paper after paper, going one step further than the colors and numbers to also arrange them by date—partly because she was bored to tears and it gave her an added distraction, and partly because she didn't want Thornton telling Darik she'd done a half-assed job.

Over the course of her shift, the Head Archivist returned a handful of times to see if she had any questions before quickly leaving again. When one of his midafternoon check-ins arrived, Viri had finally cleared a section of the desk large enough to notice a pattern that piqued her curiosity.

"There's a lot of red here," Viri commented to Thornton, who stood half in and half out of the doorway, eager to return to whatever he'd been doing.

He nodded. "Red is something reported as missing. It's a common complaint."

Viri reached for the small pile she'd sorted into that color. "Many of these are numbered 'three,' especially over the last six months. Before that, there were hardly any, maybe a couple each year—"

Thornton cut her off by saying, somewhat impatiently, "I told you not to worry about the filing code. That's not your job."

"What does the number three mean?" Viri pressed, unable to decipher the shorthand used in the reports. "What's going missing?"

"Children," Thornton said curtly. "And they're only *reported* as missing, not necessarily *actually* missing or even *still* missing. Every case has been followed up by the Nox, who either resolved it or ran out of leads."

Viri gaped at him. "These are missing *children*?" Her voice was pitched higher than normal. "*All* of them?"

The archivist shrugged, showing no sign of how disturbing the news was.

"Why haven't you told the Hunters' Guild?" Viri demanded. "If children are going missing, then it's most likely reapers who are—"

"It's not reapers," Thornton interrupted again, his tone still impatient but now condescending, too. "Reapers don't steal children—they kill them. The reports in your hands are for *missing* children, not *dead* children. Reapers leave bodies. You're a hunter—you know that better than anyone."

An image from last night flashed across Viri's mind, the young boy who had been siphoned to death by the time she'd arrived in the cellar. He wasn't the first child she'd found dead by the hands of a reaper, nor would he be the last. Everything Thornton had said was true—they abducted to kill, not to keep.

"And as I said before," the archivist continued, "these cases have all been followed up by the Nox and, after investigation, deemed nonurgent. Most missing children are back with their families within hours of their disappearance. So you can stand down, Hunter Solace, and focus on the job you're here to do."

With that, he left again, and there was enough warning in his final words that Viri fought her urge to chase after him. Thornton was right about kids going missing all the time and panicking their parents, only to be found with their friends eating candy in the market district or exploring the uncharted tunnels of the undercity. Just because there were so many reports in the last six months, that didn't mean anything nefarious was afoot. Indeed, given the piles of paperwork still to be sorted, the numbers could be similar to the previous years and Viri just hadn't gotten to those cases yet.

Resolved to ignore her concerns, Viri continued sorting, and whenever she added a new red three to the growing pile, she told herself it was nothing to worry about. The Nox were good at their jobs, these cases were marked nonurgent for a reason—and if there *was* anything troubling going on, then Darik and Meera would know about it, as would the rest of the hunters and Nox. Everything was fine.

But despite trying to convince herself, Viri's instincts were screaming that something more was happening here.

She just didn't know what.

THE JOURNAL OF CELESTIAL MAGE KADMUS CASTRO

Forty-First Sun, Fifth Cycle, Twelfth Age

Elverdine Isle is beautiful.

I was told it would be—warned, in fact, about its splendor, and how easily it distracts from the danger all but humming in the air. It's hard not to be enthralled, though, when half the island is covered in lush, verdant forests and the other half with rolling fields that lead to three majestic mountains rising high above the clearest lake I've ever seen. Even Zeranthe is impressed—something she grudgingly admitted as we circled the island upon our arrival, inspecting our new home from every angle.

The flight across the Ametrine Sea took eight hours, but my loyal companion's wings never failed, her energy never waned, and while she remains cantankerous as always, I know she's as eager as I am to begin our new lives here. She's already found the perfect place to roost in one of the mountains with the other dragons, while I've settled in nicely to my lakeside cottage in the quaint township of Aravell, nestled at the base of the three peaks.

Magistratus Garrin Solace, elected leader of Elverdine's inhabitants, welcomed me with open arms on my first day, telling me how honored they are to have a Mage Priest in residence. He's a shallow, like everyone else who has ever lived on the isle—until recently—so I know his reverence is genuine. The few mages who arrived just before me, however . . . Much like on the mainland, my calling isn't appreciated by my magical brethren here, who roll their eyes and openly scoff at me.

But no matter—I'm used to their mockery. Those who suffer scorn reap integrity. And besides, I didn't come here for them. It's the shallows who need me, having never had access to a Mage Priest before. Oh, the wonders they'll experience at my hands. They'll soon see for themselves the kind of power I can grant, especially with the first celestial event of the season on the horizon: a lunar eclipse. I'll be performing a rite of blessing at the Midnight Festival, assuming my magic acclimatizes to the island in time—though that in itself is a peculiar uncertainty, something I've never had to navigate before.

Now that I'm here, I'm fascinated by how my ellixen is reacting to the raw power saturating the isle. It's common knowledge that magic is alive, but it's much more temperamental here than anywhere else I've ventured. Back on the mainland, magic is easier. It's more flexible, more willing to please, more obedient. Here, it's none of those things. It's almost . . . wild. Today alone I nearly burned my cottage down when lighting my fireplace, while yesterday I could barely manage a spark, my ellixen resisting me at every turn.

I was warned this would be the case. It's the reason mages have avoided visiting Elverdine over the ages, and never before lived here. The magic . . . it's volatile. Dangerous. Until recently, no one understood why, just that it wasn't safe for us. But now we have an answer: Somewhere on this isle is a lost Hallow Stream. It's astounding—for so long we believed there were only two sacred pools fueling our world with magic, when really there were three. The scholar mages were in raptures when they translated the Elder texts unveiling the third's existence, all of them desperate to travel here, find it, and study it, risks be damned.

And there are risks. The two other Hallow Streams are both on the mainland and surrounded by natural wards that protect the populace, but the one here . . . there's no barrier between us and the ellixen flooding out of it, nothing forcing all that power to submit to our demands.

The magic—it's so strong I can almost taste it. I can't yet tell if it's playful or spiteful, if it wants to help or to hurt. What I can tell is that it's intoxicating, perilously so. Mages throughout history have been right to avoid this place, even to fear it, because that kind of power . . . if there were ever a way to tap into it, to control it . . .

To yield to such temptation would only end in death.

I, however, am unconcerned, since I have no intention of risking my life over anything as meaningless as a lust for more magic. I'm here for one reason: to act as a representative of the Celestial Order—chosen by His Eminence, the Celestial Mage Lord himself—to offer my services as a Mage Priest to the shallows. I will enlighten them. I will empower them. And they will love me for it.

Unfortunately, as the only celestial mage willing to travel here, I find myself alone in having to tolerate the rest of my brethren arriving from the mainland—not just the scholar mages fixated on finding the Hallow Stream, but also the fabricator mages, enchanter mages, elemental mages, healer mages, augmenter mages, and many others, all with grand ideas for the isle's evolution, including expanding the tranquil town into an elaborate city. Part of me loathes their arrogant supremacy, but . . . while I might not like the domineering ways they utilize their magic, even I can acknowledge that our being here will improve life for the shallows. The things we can do . . . It's a simple fact that we mages are the superior species. Magistratus Garrin accepts this, as do many of his people. They are grateful for our appropriation of their isle and eager to see how we can help them advance. As for the rest of Elverdine's inhabitants . . . well, the sooner they accept us, the happier they'll be.

And for their sake—and <u>mine</u>—at least there are no alchemist mages here yet, with their inquisitive minds and reckless experiments. Elders help us all when one of <u>them</u> arrives. I know it's only a matter of time—the raw magic of the Hallow Stream will be too great a temptation for them to resist, along with the intrigue of this new land and its people. I can attest to that myself.

One thing is sure: Elverdine Isle is a blank page, full of uncertainty—and overflowing with opportunity.

What a grand adventure this shall be.

5

When Viri finally made it back to her apartment after a full day of sorting, she felt as if three hundred years had passed.

Fortunately, there had been only a handful more reports of missing children during her last few hours, all cases older than six months, making her wonder if she'd invented the threat just to occupy her mind. Her lingering concern had faded upon leaving the ellixen-warded office, with only the smallest niggle of unease remaining—just enough for her to keep monitoring things in the coming days.

For now, however, Viri didn't even want to *think* about the archives, not when there were much more pleasant things on the agenda for tonight. Because it was Friday, and that meant—

"Family night!" Wynter screeched, already dressed in fluffy purple pajamas and pouncing on Viri as soon as she walked in the door. "You're nearly late!"

"'Nearly' being the key word," Viri returned, removing her scarlet cloak and working the kinks out of her neck and shoulders.

"Hurry up and get changed." Wynter prodded Viri in the

direction of her bedroom. "Soren and Jessy are already here. Mom's getting the games out. I'm on snacks."

Viri halted mid-step and turned to give her friend a warning look. "Nothing weird, Wyn."

"Weird?" Wynter's face was a mask of innocence. "Me?"

"I mean it," Viri said. "No experimenting. Not like you do with"—Wynter's eyes rounded in alarm, until Viri rolled her own and finished—"coffee."

It wasn't the first time they'd used the word "coffee" in place of "alchemy," especially when Sarielle was nearby. She was rarely in hearing range, though, with her Magistratus duties often keeping her away from home. Friday nights were the exception, something she carved out time for despite her busy schedule, making sure they knew family came first, always.

"I've had a rough day," Viri went on, "and I need comfort food, not indigestion. Promise me."

"No indigestion, promise," Wynter agreed quickly.

"No *experimenting*," Viri corrected, her voice firm. "Fruit. Nuts. Cheese. Crackers. The basics, that's it."

Wynter sighed at Viri's serious expression. "Fine. Whatever." She stepped closer to whisper, "But only because I have something new for you to test later. Deal?"

"Deal," Viri said, trusting Wynter's risky alchemy experiments considerably more than her food experiments.

Satisfied, Wynter skipped off in the direction of the kitchen, leaving Viri to continue to her bedroom and change into her favorite blue pajamas. Comfort was a requirement of their weekly family nights and had been since they'd begun the tradition, back when Sarielle had opened her home to Viri after the deaths of her parents. Originally, Viri had been meant to stay for only a few days while the High Council investigated the tragedy, but Sarielle's heart had bled for the grieving Viri—a child barely a year older than her own daughter—and when the inquisition finally ended, Sarielle had refused to send Viri off to the orphanage and instead arranged to become her legal guardian.

Viri had been so numb that she'd hardly spoken for weeks, not even to Wynter, who she'd never met until moving into the bedroom next to hers. But neither Sarielle nor Wynter gave up on Viri, their relentless love slowly mending the gaping wound inside her. While Sarielle would never take the place of Viri's parents, and Wynter was more often a sisterly pest than best friend, the two of them—and Soren, after Viri met him months later—were the reason she'd survived the darkest time of her life. For that, she would forever be in their debt.

It was with those nostalgic thoughts swirling in her mind that Viri left her bedroom and sought out the family she'd been gifted after losing her own, finding them waiting in the spacious lounge area, seated around a circular table piled high with food. An everbeacon chandelier lit the cream-colored room, its brightness increasing as the sky purpled into dusk beyond the sealed windows, the moon steadily rising over the lake resting far beneath them.

"Finally," Wynter said as Viri approached the table.

"It's been five minutes," Viri said.

"Wars have been won in less time."

"Name two."

Wynter opened her mouth and then closed it again just as fast.

A soft giggle had Viri turning to take in the rest of the table, the sound having come from Jessalyn, though Soren and Sarielle weren't hiding their mirth.

It was obvious where the blood relations were among them

all. With hair as dark as Wynter's and eyes just as blue, Sarielle was undeniably Wynter's mother. Viri had never met Wynter's father—nor had Wyn, for that matter—but whoever he was, there was little of him in his daughter. Her lawbreaking tendencies, though . . . Viri did sometimes wonder if they might have come from him, since they certainly didn't come from her mom.

As for Jessalyn, she looked like a younger, female version of Soren, with long, sandy-blond hair that was slightly curly and brown eyes a shade lighter than his. Her yellow pajamas suited her sunshine personality perfectly, but it was Soren's bright pink set that brought a smile to Viri's face—a punishment his sister had gleefully doled out when he'd lost last week's game.

"Nice jammies, Sor," Viri teased, bumping his shoulder as she moved past. "The color really brings out your eyes."

The rude gesture he sent her—hidden from Sarielle's sight—only made her smile grow.

Had anyone other than Jessy dictated what he wore, Soren might have ignored them, but he'd move the stars for his sister if she asked—a consequence of his becoming her sole caregiver three years ago, when their self-centered parents had left them to fend for themselves. Their love for each other was deeply rooted, with Soren taking pains to make sure Jessy was happy, and her in turn knowing what it cost him and doing her best to return the favor—when she wasn't causing mischief, which, admittedly, was most of the time.

"Now that Viri's here, can we eat?" Jessy asked, jiggling in her seat.

"Go ahead," Sarielle invited. She patted the chair beside her for Viri to take, her silky peach pajamas shimmering as she leaned in to ask, "All right, darling?"

Peering into Sarielle's comforting blue eyes, Viri knew what her guardian was really asking. There was a firm no-work-talk rule at family night, but Sarielle had undoubtedly heard about Viri's unsanctioned visit to Reeve—and her week of desk duty as a result.

"I've been better," Viri replied. "But I only have myself to blame."

And Reeve—she could blame him, too.

For so many things.

"The time will pass before you know it." Sarielle squeezed Viri's arm in reassurance. "Then you can forget everything about today, like it never happened."

That was unlikely, but Viri offered a weak smile in agreement, determined not to give Reeve any more mental space tonight. Grabbing a handful of popcorn, she asked, "What are we playing?"

"We couldn't decide, so you're the tiebreaker," Soren said, sliding a bowl of melted chocolate across the table, knowing Viri liked to drizzle it over her popcorn. She refused to think of the silver-eyed boy who had first introduced her to the sweet-and-salty creation, and the fact that he was rotting in a cell at this very moment.

"It's between Mage Quest and Dungeon Escape," Jessy said around a mouthful of berries.

After the day she'd had, Viri grimaced at the idea of playing Dungeon Escape—a game that would require her to help free her teammate from prison—so she said, "Let's go with Mage Quest. I'm in the mood for magic and treasure."

Within minutes, the table was cleared and the board set up. They'd all played enough times to know their preferred characters:

Jessy, an elemental mage; Soren, a nature mage; Sarielle, a glamour mage; Viri, a warrior mage; and Wynter, an alchemist mage.

As they began rolling the dice and moving their characters across the board, completing quests for treasure rewards, Viri's mind wandered to the mages of old and the world they'd lived in—a world that could very well still exist beyond Elverdine Isle. The blackmist was so isolating that no one knew whether magic flourished elsewhere, or if there were any mages left. In ancient times, their numbers had been few, with most of the population made up of shallows—people who, upon reaching puberty, maintained shallow enough levels of ellixen to keep them from using all but the smallest of magics. Only those whose ellixen continued to grow after age fourteen were considered to have enough power to train in the magical arts, and thus became mages.

It had been many generations since such a person had lived on Elverdine Isle—indeed, it was impossible for any of them to be mages now, not when they surrendered all but a drop of their ellixen to fuel the obelisks.

Viri didn't mind; it seemed a fair trade, given that doing so protected them from reapers and the blackmist, and also from burnout—the painful death or, perhaps worse, mindless existence that came with a buildup of unstable ellixen, and befell anyone who didn't yield their magic by age fourteen. Long ago, the shallows and mages had all been taught how to control their ellixen—no matter its strength—and so avoided any risk of burnout, but that knowledge had been forgotten in time, leaving all those who remained on the isle no choice but to rely on the obelisks to absorb their magic and keep them safe.

Again, Viri felt it was a fair trade. Death by reaper, death by blackmist, death by burnout—none of those things appealed to her. At all.

"You're quiet tonight, Viri," Jessalyn said, jolting Viri from her thoughts. "You didn't even notice when I stole your dragon to overthrow the Malevolent Queen."

Viri frowned down at the board, seeing Jessy was right. "Sorry. Long day."

"I hear you." Jessy blew out a dramatic breath. "We studied reapers in school. Talk about boring."

"Boring?" Soren raised his brows. "I think you mean 'important' and 'potentially lifesaving.'"

"No, I meant boring," Jessy repeated, rolling her eyes. "I already knew everything."

"Is that so?" Soren's expression turned challenging. "Where do reapers live?"

Jessalyn groaned. "Really?"

"I'd like to hear the answer," Sarielle interjected, looking amused as she sipped her herbal tea—something she had no idea was one of Wynter's concoctions, intended to help with relaxation and stress relief. "It's important for me to know that the Scholars' Guild is maintaining a high standard of education."

Jessalyn saw right through Sarielle's ploy, but with a long-suffering sigh, she recited, "Reapers can live anywhere they want—the uppercity, the undercity, the inner-mountain—just like anyone else."

"How do they stay hidden?" Wynter jumped in, nibbling on a wedge of cheese.

"They don't need to," Jessy said. "They look just like us." When Soren opened his mouth to correct her, she quickly added, "Their veins turn black after they siphon and stay that way until the magic fades, but only reapers and hunters can see them. No one else."

"And why is that?" Sarielle asked.

"The reapers, we don't know, though it's probably because the stolen ellixen heightens their senses. But the hunters—" Jessalyn gestured to Viri's palm. "It's because of their marks. The ink used is magical and comes from a stylus gifted to the first hunters by the ancient mages. It lets them recognize reapers and also feel when they're near."

"Why just hunters?" Soren asked. "Why not the Nox"—he pointed to himself—"or the general public? Why limit who's allowed to see them?"

"Because we don't know how much ink is left in the stylus," Jessy said, "and we can't risk it running out. Without hunters, it'd be a lot harder to catch reapers, and way more kids would die."

As dark as the discussion was, Viri was impressed by how much Jessalyn knew.

"How do people become reapers?" Soren asked, moving his nature mage into a copse of trees to guard his dwindling pile of treasure.

"They siphon ellixen from kids who haven't Imparted and still have enough—"

"But *how*?" Soren pressed. "And why?"

Jessalyn crunched on a cracker, spraying crumbs everywhere. "The why is simple—they want power. Speed, strength, healing, longer life. Some just want to feel like they're high all the time, since stolen ellixen is like a drug to them. It's why they get addicted." She reached for another cracker. "As for the how, if you mean the actual *process*, then they need to be touching someone, skin to skin, and they just"—she made a slurping sound that caused Viri's stomach to turn—"suck it right out of them. Like pulling out a splinter."

"As easy as that, huh?" Wynter asked, looking as disturbed as Viri felt.

Jessy's normally bright face turned solemn. "Well, no. A taste is never enough, so they have to be willing to kill kids to steal all their magic. That's a choice they make before they siphon for the first time—to become murderers. Nothing about that should be easy."

With Jessalyn's bubbly, youthful personality, Viri often forgot that she was quickly growing from a child into an adult. Her answer showed a depth of maturity that filled Viri with pride.

She wasn't the only one. Soren was also smiling softly at his sister. But then he schooled his features, used his character to summon a river as a defensive barrier, and asked, "Where did the first reaper come from?"

Jessy shrugged. "No one really knows. The most popular theory is that there was a weak shallow who was angry at the ancient mages for having all the power, so they messed around with magic they shouldn't have and it corrupted them." She shrugged again and used her elemental mage to take control of Soren's river. "They probably used some kind of alchemy. We've all heard how dangerous that is. *And* we know it transforms one thing to another. A shallow to a reaper? Makes sense to me."

Viri was careful to keep her eyes on the game. Wynter, at her side, did the same, though she squirmed slightly in her seat.

"It's a shame we have no way of knowing what happened in the past," Sarielle said, sipping more tea, "but what about today? Now that reapers exist, who controls them?"

"Not who—*what*," Jessalyn answered. "I said before that they're addicted to ellixen, so they're controlled by their need for more of it." She paused. "But if this is a trick question and you're asking about a person, then throughout the ages, their leader has always been known as the Reaper Priest."

Viri's body tightened automatically.

"They follow him—or her—as much as they'll follow anyone," Jessy went on. "The current Priest is male, and he's held the title for around seven years."

"That's a long time," Sarielle mused. "Why haven't the hunters caught him yet?"

We're trying, Viri thought begrudgingly, though she knew her guardian was well aware of that.

Jessalyn shook her head. "They've been searching, but no one knows his name or what he looks like or where to find him, and the other reapers who are caught never share anything useful. They're protective of their leaders, which would be honorable if they weren't . . . you know . . ."

"Soulless, child-murdering psychopaths?" Wynter suggested lightly.

Jessalyn pulled a face. "Yeah. That."

A grim silence fell, until Soren chomped loudly on a carrot and said, "Last question: How many reapers are out there? Dozens? Hundreds? Less? More?"

Jessalyn blinked. "I—uh—Our teacher didn't—" She looked at Viri. "It can't be too many, right? Because not a lot of people are willing to kill kids just for the sake of power. The cost isn't worth the reward." Somewhat anxiously, she repeated, "Right?"

Viri wanted to reassure her, but she couldn't lie, not about this. "Reapers are like rats—no matter how many we catch and throw in the Underlock, they just keep appearing."

She wished it weren't true, wished there were an end point in sight for eradicating reapers entirely, but as long as people lusted for power, there were always going to be those willing to pay any price for it.

The mood around the table plummeted in the wake of Viri's words, but then Sarielle cleared her throat and said, in a deliberately bright voice, "Well, I think it's safe to say the Scholars' Guild is keeping our educational system strong." She smiled proudly at Jessalyn. "But let's move on to something a little more cheerful, shall we?" She winked at the young girl. "Perhaps a certain someone's upcoming birthday? Fourteen is a very special day."

"Two more weeks!" Jessy's face shone with excitement, all thoughts of reapers forgotten. Viri resolved to do the same. "Soren's letting me have a party to celebrate my Impartation."

"That reminds me," Soren said, turning to Viri and Wynter. "How would you like to plan a party for a group of hyperactive kids?"

Viri snorted, and Wynter choked on a laugh, both knowing just how far Soren was out of his depth.

"I'm happy to help," Sarielle offered, rolling the dice and moving her mage forward. "An Impartation only happens once in a person's life—we need to give it the attention it deserves." Glancing thoughtfully around the room and at the now fully dark view outside, she beamed at Jessy and announced, "We'll have the party here. There's plenty of space, so invite whoever you want."

Jessalyn looked like she might burst. *"Really?"*

"Really," Sarielle confirmed. "We'll have music and games. I'll even ask my theater friends in the Entertainment Guild if they'll come and do a quick show. Or—" She snapped her fingers together as an idea came to her. "The Incendio Illusionists are performing in Encore Alley until the end of the month. I'll call in a favor."

"The Incendio Illusionists?" Jessy shrieked, wonder clear in her eyes. "The *acrobats* who juggle *fire*?"

"Elders help me," Soren muttered, rubbing a hand over his face.

"I doubt even they can help you now," Wynter said, her shoulders shaking as Sarielle continued suggesting party ideas and Jessalyn became more starstruck with each new possibility.

"Sure, find amusement in my demise," Soren grumbled.

"Aww, is the big, scary Nox afraid of a few little kiddies?" Wynter teased. "Or is it the fire acrobats? We all know you're scared of clowns. Don't worry, this is a safe space."

Soren used his middle finger to scratch his nose, prompting Wynter to snicker and respond in turn. Viri hid her smile at their antics, relieved they were back to behaving like best friends after their brief—but disastrous—attempt at dating a few months ago.

"As for the Impartation itself, I assume you have a day in mind, Soren?"

Sarielle's question made Soren start, his focus having drifted from the party conversation. "Uh—yes." He sat up straighter. "We're doing it on her birthday, first thing in the morning."

"Wonderful," Sarielle said. "I'll clear my schedule."

Viri had already told Meera she'd need that morning off. It was customary for loved ones to attend Impartation ceremonies, partly for support but also to honor the sacrifice being made when children yielded their magic to the obelisks—not that kids had a choice. Imparting was the most sacred law on Elverdine

Isle and had been ever since the ancient mages flew away on their dragons, taking their wisdom and knowledge but leaving the four obelisks behind as a parting gift. Protection from the blackmist. Protection from the reapers. Protection from burnout.

Some people considered it a tragedy. Viri understood why, but her hunter mind was still relieved that she lived in a time when the only citizens with notable levels of ellixen were those younger than fourteen, since at least that meant there wasn't an entire population for reapers to siphon from. Some didn't even wait until fourteen—Viri herself had been ten when she'd given her magic to the obelisks. She could barely remember her Impartation ceremony now . . . but that was only because it had been overshadowed by her parents dying that same day.

"Everything all right, V?" Wynter asked. "You're looking pale."

Realizing it was her turn to play, Viri rolled the dice and used her warrior mage to save a village from marauders, then collected the bountiful reward. "Just tired. *Someone* woke me up this morning."

Wynter grinned shamelessly.

"How is it that even when tired, you still manage to beat me?" Soren asked, indicating his pile of treasure cards that was half the size of Viri's.

It was only then that she saw they'd reached the end of the game, and the others were counting their cards. She didn't need to, given how visibly large her pile was.

"Viri won, Soren lost," Jessy declared with no small amount of glee. "That means she gets to choose his penalty."

"I will never understand why the winner's reward is to punish the loser. What are we, sadists?" Soren complained. His grouchy attitude was an act, though—of them all, he was the least likely to hold a grudge or be a sore loser.

"What's a sadist?" Jessy asked, her head tilted curiously to the side. "Isn't that some kind of sex thing?"

Wynter, having just taken a sip of her sparkling elderberry juice, nearly spat it all over the table.

"It absolutely is not," Soren said firmly.

"I mean, it *can* be," Wynter murmured, dabbing juice from her chin. "Crack a book, Sor."

The look he leveled at her had Viri coughing to cover a laugh.

"This isn't the most age appropriate of topics," Sarielle said mildly, her words belied by the humor in her eyes. "Let's move on, shall we?"

"I'm nearly fourteen," Jessalyn argued. "You don't have to treat me like a child."

"You'll always be a child to me, sweet girl." Sarielle glanced around the table. "That goes for all of you."

"Ugh, we've reached the *feelings* part of the night," Wynter said with a comical shudder. "Quick, Viri—give Soren his penalty before Mom lets loose with the emotions."

Viri was too tired to think of anything creative, so she went with something useful. "You'll owe me a favor," she told him. "Anything of my choosing."

Soren was gracious enough not to mention the favor he'd already granted her that very morning. "Just don't make it anything weird," he warned. "And remember, what goes around, comes around. Next time I win and you lose, watch out."

Viri couldn't remember the last time Soren had won a game at family night. But she said nothing, only smiled to herself and helped Sarielle pack up the board while the others cleared away the food, until the room was immaculate once more.

"Time to get this one to bed," Soren said, slinging an arm around Jessalyn's neck.

She elbowed him in retaliation. "Only one of us needs beauty sleep, and it's not me."

"She's got you there," Viri said, yawning. "With that face, you need all the help you can get."

Soren didn't miss a beat. "Fortunately for you, there's more to life than looks."

Viri laughed. "Such a charmer."

"I save all my best lines for you, Solace."

And with that, he offered a cheeky goodnight wave and led his sister out the door.

Turning to Wynter and Sarielle, Viri jokingly asked, "Remind me what we see in him again?"

"He has a very nice backside," Wynter said seriously. "His front side isn't bad, either."

Viri choked. "Wyn!"

"What?" she said, all innocence. "Objectively speaking, it's true."

"That's our best friend you're talking about."

"Yes, and we both have eyes. Hell, I *dated* the guy, so trust me when I say that he is beautiful *every*wh—"

"La-la-la, not listening." Viri spoke over her, plugging her ears.

Sarielle looked as if she wasn't sure whether to laugh or cringe. "On that note, I think it's time we all retired for the evening."

"I couldn't agree more," Viri said emphatically.

"Same here," Wynter said. But despite her agreement, she moved toward the front door. "I just have to grab some notes I forgot to bring home earlier. I need them for a weekend assignment."

Sarielle's forehead wrinkled. "Can't that wait until tomorrow?"

"Procrastination is the killer of dreams, Mom. But don't worry, I'll take Viri with me for company."

Viri was about to protest until she caught the look on Wynter's face and realized her friend wasn't heading to the Healers' Guild, but instead to her secret lab to practice alchemy—something Viri had forgotten she'd promised to help with.

Regretting the deal she'd made earlier, Viri didn't have time to come up with an excuse before Wynter started dragging her away.

"Don't wait up, Mom," Wynter called over her shoulder.

And with no say in the matter—and many mental curse words aimed at her friend—Viri was yanked out the door.

6

"*I know I told you not to miss training today,*" Meera said the next morning, her communication amulet gleaming against her scarred neck, "*but I also expected you to be* awake *for it.*"

Viri grunted as her mentor landed yet another blow, this time a firm kick to her abdomen that stole her breath and made the dark green walls of the Hunters' Guild sparring chambers spin around her.

"I'm awake," Viri wheezed, raising a hand to say she needed a moment.

Meera didn't give it to her, launching another attack that sent Viri scrambling backward across the large gray mat while trying valiantly to refill her lungs.

"*You're like a newborn fawn stumbling around on fresh legs,*" Meera said, her dark features set in a frown. "*I haven't seen you fight this poorly since you were a novice.*"

That was harsh, Viri thought, though not untrue.

It was Wynter's fault—Wynter and her stupid alchemy.

All too vividly, Viri recalled what had happened the previous night after she'd been dragged to Wynter's lab in the undercity, the memory playing out in quick flashes:

"I call it 'zingzest.' It's an elixir to boost energy," Wynter declared, shoving a vial of shimmering orange liquid into Viri's hands. "The name works two-fold: increased vitality and a citrusy taste. Zing and zest—get it?"

"What's wrong with coffee?" Viri asked, swirling the vial suspiciously.

"When I say energy boost, I mean boost,*" Wynter emphasized. "No coffee in the world will hit you as hard and fast as this will."*

Despite herself, Viri was intrigued. It was dangerous to hunt reapers with depleted energy, but sometimes unavoidable. An elixir like this could be the difference between life and death.

Even so . . .

"How long does it last? I want to get some *sleep tonight, Wyn."*

"I'm still refining the formula, but it should fade fast," Wynter assured her. "It's only meant to be a quick hit, like for a surprise attack. Swallow this, and BAM! An instant shot of adrenaline straight to the veins."

Viri had trusted her friend and downed the vial, with Wynter's words proving true almost immediately—both the citrusy taste and the violent awakening of every nerve in her body. Pure energy had slammed into her, making her believe she could take on all the reapers in the world without breaking a sweat.

However, while it *did* fade after a few minutes, as promised, Viri had been left with a jittery feeling for *hours*, her heart beating rapidly, her head pounding, her body shivering and feverish, almost like a drug withdrawal. Her symptoms had eased with just enough time for her to manage an hour of sleep before she'd had to leave for dawn training. And to add insult to injury, Wynter's only comment upon Viri bursting furiously into her bedroom that morning had been, "Interesting. I'll adjust the formula for the next time you try it."

Viri had wanted to throw something at her. Instead, she'd stormed off to meet Meera, fueled solely by irritation, but that had long since burned away, leaving her barely conscious as she sparred sluggishly with her mentor.

On the plus side, they were only practicing unarmed combat today, so she didn't have to worry about bleeding out from a stab wound. A small mercy.

"If you were going to waste my time, you could have at least had the decency to tell me beforehand," Meera said when Viri failed to dodge another easy attack—a quick leg hook behind her knee that sent her sprawling onto the mat.

"Time is a construct, so 'waste' is subjective," Viri panted from the ground, wincing when she realized she was semi-quoting Reeve, of all people. She winced again at the look on Meera's face. "I mean"—Viri scrambled back up to her feet and hurried to correct her mistake—"you're right. I'm sorry, I'm not at my best today."

Meera's hard expression softened a fraction. She didn't renew her attack, but instead squared her stance and crossed her arms. *"Talk to me. What's going on?"*

"Nothing. I just didn't sleep well."

"Is this about you being stuck on desk duty?" Meera asked. *"If we'd been alone yesterday, I would have been more lenient."*

"It's fine. I get it."

Meera continued as if Viri hadn't spoken. *"You're one of my best hunters—I'd much rather have you out saving lives than cooped up with paperwork. But the Underlock falls within Darik's purview as captain of the Nox. My hands were tied."*

"I know that," Viri said, though she didn't have to *like* it. "It's tedious, but no one has ever died from boredom. I doubt I'll be the first."

"Then what's bothering you?" Meera pressed, her jade eyes pinning Viri in place. *"You're not just tired—you're distracted. I know the difference."* She cocked her head to the side. *"Is it Ashton?"*

Viri gave a slight jerk, and Meera pounced on the reaction.

"I didn't push you to talk yesterday when Darik was with us, since you've always been a little scared of him—"

Viri spluttered. "I'm not *scared* of him!" She just didn't like him, and only because *he* didn't like *her.*

"—but you and I are close enough that you can be open with me. Argue all you want, but I know it must have been hard confronting someone so loyal to your parents' killer."

"Of *course* it was hard," Viri said, still smarting over Meera thinking she was afraid of Darik. "But as unpleasant as it was to talk with Ree—Ashton, that's not the thing about yesterday that's bothering me."

The words left her before she could stop them, but that didn't make them any less true. Her sleepless night had given her time to mull over the hours she'd spent in the archives, specifically all the missing children she'd tried to convince herself weren't a cause for concern, despite her gut telling her otherwise.

"I'm listening," Meera said, settling her weight back in her heels.

Viri hesitated, not having planned to say anything yet. "It's probably nothing."

"Let me be the judge of that."

It was enough of a command that Viri blew out a breath and shared, "Something happened in the archives yesterday."

Meera blinked in surprise—and disbelief. *"Now I know you're lying."*

The dry retort coaxed a reluctant smile out of Viri. "I didn't say it was something *exciting.* Just . . . something."

Meera's attention sharpened. *"Go on."*

As succinctly as she could, Viri told her mentor about her sorting task, explaining the color and number allocations and the growing pile of red threes, especially in the last six months.

"Like I said, it could be nothing," Viri repeated. "Thornton was adamant that the Nox have looked into all the cases, but something he said came back to me overnight, and I can't get it out of my head."

Meera's face was impossible to read, as it had been the whole time Viri had been talking. *"Tell me."*

"He said that for every case, the Nox 'either resolved it or ran out of leads,'" Viri recounted. "Those are two very different outcomes."

"They are," Meera agreed, still giving nothing away, though there was a furrow in her brow. *"Did he say anything else?"*

"Only that the disappearances can't be connected to reapers, because reapers don't abduct kids, they kill them outright." Viri scratched her jaw. "He's not wrong."

"But you're still worried?" Meera asked.

Viri looked down at the mat, uncertain. "I don't know. Maybe? I know the Nox are always diligent, just as I know those kids are probably all back with their families, their cases closed. But I have this—this *feeling* I can't shake."

"Your instincts have never failed you before," Meera stated, her mental voice filled with reproach. *"Don't start doubting them now."*

Viri's eyes shot back up. "What are you saying?"

"Are you a hunter or not?" Meera sent her an arched look. *"Most of your job is investigation. So, investigate."*

"But—my punishment—the archives—"

"You have breaks, don't you? And there's always after hours."

"Do you think there's something in this?" Viri's stomach flipped at the thought.

Meera considered her reply. *"Normally, I would say no. If there was a concern, surely Darik and I would be aware of it."* She shuffled her feet, her leather boots leaving indents on the spongy mat. *"But I chose you as my protégé for a reason, Viri. I trust your intuition. So look into this, if only to give us both peace of mind that there's nothing to worry about."*

Viri nodded, heartened by her mentor's belief in her and relieved to have a plan, even if it—hopefully—led to nothing.

Agreeing to keep Meera informed, Viri left the sparring chambers to freshen up and visit her favorite bakery for breakfast before heading to the archives. The ellixen wards wreaked havoc on her fatigued body, making her stumble after Thornton to her office, the mountains of paperwork waiting for her seeming even higher than yesterday.

With a sigh, Viri got to work, her hours passing much as they had the previous day, with the only difference being the plummeting feeling she experienced whenever she found a new red three from the last six months. She soon became jittery enough that she took an early lunch to follow Meera's advice, using her break to visit two of the addresses on the files—where both families quickly confirmed their children were safe and sound. False alarms, the parents claimed, embarrassed that they'd bothered the Nox for no reason.

Viri felt a weight lift off her shoulders. She knew better than to give up after checking only two addresses, but it was nevertheless reassuring.

The next day continued in the same way: training, filing, and visiting more families, all of whom reported that their children were no longer missing. Viri even met some of the kids, witnessing for herself that they were alive and well.

By the third day—Viri's fourth in the archives—she'd checked on twelve different families spread across the undercity, uppercity, and inside Mount Tembris, and all their children were fine. Viri almost abandoned her mission, and would have, if not for the continually growing pile of red threes—and if not for what happened on her fourth day of investigations.

Because that was when she visited another family during her lunch break, one whose eleven-year-old daughter had gone missing over a month ago . . . and still hadn't been found.

It was as if the floodgates opened after that, with each new family Viri sought out revealing—with tears in their eyes—that their children were still missing.

Thirteen-year-old Avelin, missing for two months.

Nine-year-old Dale, missing for six weeks.

Twelve-year-old Makir, missing for fifteen days.

Ten-year-old Lilly, missing for three months.

The list continued, the ages ranging from seven to thirteen years old, all children young enough not to have undergone the Impartation ceremony yet, their ellixen strong—and ripe for siphoning.

Viri felt sick every time she knocked on a new door to find another teary-eyed parent looking at her with hope, only to see that bleed away when she had no news. As the numbers passed into the tens, then continued into the twenties and beyond, the gravity of the situation became clear. Someone was abducting children. The question was: Who? And *why*?

Meera didn't know the answer, nor did Darik, the two of them grim when Viri reported her findings on Thursday night after her final shift in the archives. She'd been updating Meera daily, but her mentor had wanted the Nox captain to join them in her office at the Hunters' Guild so they could pick apart everything Viri had discovered during her week of investigating.

"At my count, thirty-two children are missing, but I only made it through half the case files," Viri said upon finishing her debrief, the moon well and truly risen above the sea cliffs visible through Meera's window wall. "Elders know how many more red threes might be in those piles."

"I'll assign some Nox to go through the rest as a matter of priority," Darik said, his black eyes flinty as he stared down at Viri's notes spread across the desk. "I'll also have them confirm your numbers, since I struggle to believe the extent of what you're saying."

Viri bit her cheek to hold in her response. She had no reason to lie, and Darik knew that.

"If it *is* true," he went on, "then it's alarming that this slipped by unnoticed until now. The archivists have never made such a grave mistake before."

"I don't think it was their fault," Viri said. "Thornton told me they've been understaffed for months, and everything in the room where I worked was deemed nonurgent."

"And *that* is something I'll be looking into as well," Darik said tightly. "Not just because it doesn't make sense."

Seeing Viri's confusion, Meera explained, *"Files don't get sent for sorting unless they've been signed off by me, Darik, someone in the Legal*

Guild, or someone on the High Council. That's how the cases get color- and number-coded—we *make those notes—after which they're sent to the archives with an urgent or nonurgent classification."*

"So you're saying somebody screwed up, multiple times," Viri realized, before a more alarming thought hit her. "Or they did it deliberately."

"Maybe more than one person," Darik said, fiddling with the cuffs of his black gloves. Pointedly, he added, "Assuming, of course, this is all true."

Viri had to bite her cheek again, and this time she tasted blood.

"For the sake of this conversation, we're assuming it is *true,"* Meera said, just as pointedly, *"and that means our priority should be the children, not the negligent paperwork. We'll ask the Magistratus to launch a cross-Guild inquiry to determine who signed off on the cases, but our focus needs to be on finding the kids and bringing them home."*

"If they're still alive," Darik muttered. "Reapers aren't known for their mercy."

"We don't know for sure that reapers are responsible," Meera said, then continued over Darik's objections. *"With children being the targets, the likelihood is high, but this kind of large-scale kidnapping doesn't match any known reaper behavior. Most of them don't have the self-control to keep their victims alive for minutes, let alone months. And yet, we don't have any corpses."*

"*Most* of them," Darik repeated, his dark eyes locked on Meera's, sending a silent message that caused Viri's mentor to still.

Viri froze as well. She didn't need to read their thoughts to know what they were thinking—or rather, *who* they were thinking about.

Because there was one reaper who had shown time and again

that he had self-control in spades. He wouldn't have been able to stay hidden for so long without it.

"You think the Priest has something to do with this?" Viri rasped out.

Meera turned quickly to Viri. *"We don't know anything. It's guesswork at best."*

"But we have to entertain the possibility," Darik asserted. "It's the most likely scenario, after all."

Viri's fingers dug into the velvety armrests of her chair, her skin turning clammy at the mere *thought* of the Priest being involved with the abductions. If that was true, those children were as good as dead.

"We can't do anything else tonight, not until we've notified the council," Meera said soothingly, likely noting the way Viri was clenching her seat. *"I'll head up to the Summit now and call an emergency meeting to share what we know."*

Viri's grip tightened as she thought about how Sarielle would take the news, her soft heart a curse when it came to matters such as these, even if her professional mask never slipped when she was acting as the Magistratus.

"I'll meet you there after I send a team of Nox to the archives," Darik said, smoothing the front of his uniform. "If they find more red threes, I'll have them contact the families to see if their children are still missing. We'll have confirmed numbers within hours."

The way he emphasized *confirmed* made Viri grit her teeth, since it was clear he wasn't fully convinced of the threat. But he would know the truth soon enough.

"And I'll—" Viri began, intending to say she'd start searching for leads, but she was interrupted.

"You'll go home."

Viri gaped at her mentor. "You can't expect me to just—"

"I'll make it an order if I have to," Meera warned.

Viri opened her mouth to argue, but she was halted with a look.

"The entire Guild will be summoned for a meeting first thing tomorrow," Meera said. *"Every available hunter will be on this. If we're going to find these kids, I need you at your best—and that means I need you rested. You've done well investigating these cases, but now the real work begins. Are you up for it?"*

It was a rhetorical question, so Viri didn't answer. Instead, an idea came to her. "What about Reeve?"

Darik leaned forward, his gaze narrowing. "Ashton? What about him?"

"He might know something, especially if the Priest is involved," Viri said. She'd tried not to think about Reeve since she'd seen him last Friday, but he'd crept into her thoughts unbidden every day. Each time, she'd wanted to scrub her mind with one of Wynter's experimental cleaning potions just to get rid of the image of his smirking face and stormy eyes. But now . . . he could be the key to solving this mystery.

"He's still not cooperating," Darik shared, which, while frustrating, didn't surprise Viri.

"But you're right that it's worth a try," Meera added, locking eyes with the Nox captain until he sighed and relented.

"Fine," he said. "I'll head down to his cell and see if I can coax anything out of him."

For the greater good, Viri dredged up the words, "I could go—"

"No." Both Darik and Meera spoke at the same time, their expressions like steel.

Viri straightened her shoulders. "If his offer to talk to me still holds, then we can use that. Use *him*."

"And how far did that get you last time?" Darik asked, eyebrow raised.

Viri flushed, her failure still fresh.

"For now, you need to trust us," Meera said, albeit gently. *"You said yourself that Ashton likes playing games. Sending you to him will only give him another chance to toy with you, and I can't risk you being distracted from what's ahead. The missing children need you as focused as possible, as do your fellow hunters. That means—"*

"I go home and rest," Viri said, resigned.

Meera nodded approvingly, then rose to her feet. Darik did the same, leaving Viri little choice but to follow.

"We'll skip training tomorrow so I can prep for the Guild meeting," Meera said, walking Viri to the door, *"but I'll send for you if there are any updates in the meantime."*

With nothing left to say—or do—Viri was shuffled out of the office.

It was only as she was heading back to her apartment that she recalled Reeve's parting offer from last week, something she'd firmly evicted from her brain in order to uphold the most sacred rule of hunting: Never bargain with a reaper. And yet, as his words returned to her now, Viri couldn't so easily ignore them:

"Get me out of here, and I'll tell you anything you want. That's my offer, Viri—my freedom for your answers."

7

Reeve's smooth voice repeated in Viri's mind for her entire journey home, his offer like a chant—*my freedom for your answers; my freedom for your answers*—until she finally managed to banish the words upon reaching her apartment.

He was a reaper, and reapers lied. Even if his offer was genuine, he might not know anything about the missing children. He might not even know where the Reaper Priest was, regardless of whether the Priest had anything to do with the kids. Reeve might know nothing at all, and just wanted an easy escape. Viri couldn't risk that. *Wouldn't* risk that.

But despite her resolve, her thoughts remained turbulent as she entered her apartment and found it empty, with Sarielle likely on her way to the emergency council meeting and Wynter no doubt off creating something illegal. Viri would have given anything for a distraction, even if it meant being her friend's test subject, but she'd told Meera she would stay home, so she made herself keep her promise. Rest didn't come easily, though, and after eating a late dinner—grilled cheese that she barely tasted—she paced up and down the living room, the normally tranquil view of the moonlit lake doing nothing to ease her tension as she waited for her guardian to return.

It took longer than expected, but Viri finally heard the front door open, followed by Sarielle's familiar heels clacking through the entryway. But the Magistratus didn't appear; instead, her footsteps faded down the hallway, until the next sound Viri heard was Sarielle's bedroom door quietly clicking shut.

Viri winced, realizing her guardian must be more upset by the news than she'd anticipated. She considered bringing her a cup of Wynter's relaxation tea, but decided against it. Sarielle would leave her room when she was ready, and Viri would respect that, even if it meant she now had no option left but to try to sleep.

Predictably, that task was impossible. After hours of tossing and turning, Viri gave up, leaving her bed for some warm milk, which had always comforted her as a child. Wynter's bedroom door was open—not unusual, as she often spent late nights in her lab—but Viri was surprised to find Sarielle's open, too, and even more surprised to find her guardian standing in their dark living room, staring out the window. Clouds had formed since Viri's earlier pacing, a storm now brewing on the horizon, as if the weather were perfectly in tune with her mood.

"I guess you couldn't sleep, either," Viri said quietly as she approached.

Sarielle didn't jolt, indicating she'd been aware of Viri's arrival. "I doubt I will as long as those children are missing."

Viri moved closer until they were standing side by side before the stormy view. "Every available hunter will be working this case. We'll find them. It's what we do."

Whether the children would still be alive was the question, but neither of them gave voice to their fears.

"Have you considered how you'll keep your emotions under control, especially with the Reaper Priest's involvement?" Sarielle asked. At Viri's startled inhalation, she continued, "I know you want him to pay for what he did to your parents, but you already take so many risks while searching for him." She rubbed her chest, right over her heart. "I've already lost one child. I wouldn't be able to bear it if something happened to you, too."

Viri sighed inwardly at her guardian's overprotective nature. She understood where it stemmed from, aware that Sarielle had lost her first child, a son, years ago, and had never fully recovered from her grief. The boy would have been Wynter's half brother, both he and his father having died tragically from magefever—a rare illness with no known cure—before Wynter was born.

But . . . while Viri felt deeply for Sarielle, her job as a hunter was dangerous, regardless of who she was hunting. Sarielle knew that better than most—she'd been a hunter herself before turning to politics. All Viri could do was offer reassurance, so she adopted a soothing tone and said, "We don't know for sure that the Priest has anything to do with this. Let's not worry about that until we—"

She stopped when an unreadable look rippled across her guardian's face, visible even in the darkness.

"What?" Viri asked, turning more fully toward her. "Do you know something?"

Sarielle didn't answer for a long moment, then slowly said, "If it came down to a choice between saving the children or getting your revenge, can I trust you to make the right decision?"

Viri's stomach roiled at the thought of having to make such a choice. "I told you, we don't know that the Priest is—"

"He is."

Two words, and Viri felt the room tilt around her. Hoarsely, she said, "Meera and Darik said it's just a guess."

"Neither Commander Roth nor Captain Farrow are the Magistratus," Sarielle returned. "They deal in facts, not rumors. It's my job to listen, even to the most outlandish of speculation. But I never thought—" Her voice cracked, keeping her from finishing.

Viri's pulse began to quicken. "What rumors?"

Sarielle closed her eyes, her features pale in the dim light. "About six months ago, I started hearing whispers about the Reaper Priest planning something." She ran a shaky hand through her dark hair. "Something big."

Viri's insides clenched.

"I thought it was fearmongering—it's not the first time that kind of gossip has spread." Sarielle reopened her eyes, staring somberly at the view once more. "But the nature of these whispers was different. Before, there were always specifics involved—the Priest had targeted someone, or made an enemy of so-and-so, or was tempting certain people into becoming reapers—all information that was passed on to the Nox and hunters for investigation. But this rumor was vague, only a warning."

The hairs on the back of Viri's neck prickled. "What warning?"

"That it would involve children—lots and lots of them." Sarielle's voice was barely audible, but it rose again as she continued, "I brushed it aside, since it was hardly news that reapers target the youth. It was only tonight, when I learned of the mass abductions, that I realized the warning hadn't been about *individual* children, but a *group* of them, *together*." Her troubled eyes caught Viri's. "The Reaper Priest has been collecting children. Exactly as the rumor warned."

"But . . . *why*?" Viri asked, failing to see any motive. "It's not like he's keeping them close just to have a ready stockpile to siphon from, otherwise we'd still find their corpses afterward. There has to be a reason he'd go to this trouble—and hide it for so long."

Sarielle wrapped her arms around herself. "There was another rumor, something I heard only once. It haunted my nightmares for so long that I convinced myself I'd imagined it. But now . . . I'm not so sure."

"Tell me," Viri said.

"Have you heard of the Aurora Comet?"

Viri frowned at the unexpected question. "No. Should I have?"

"It's a comet that appears above Elverdine Isle once every two hundred years," Sarielle said. "The ancient mages called it a 'celestial event,' something that could increase the strength of their ellixen to untold levels, making them nearly invincible. But in order to channel from Aurora as it passed by, they needed three things: enough magic of their own to draw down the comet's power, a pure heart, and—"

Viri interrupted by snorting incredulously.

"If you're worried about the Reaper Priest trying something like that, you can rest easy. He has the opposite of a pure heart, and any ellixen within him was stolen from others. There's no way he meets the requirements."

Sarielle didn't look reassured. If anything, her features turned even more strained. "You don't understand, Viri. That rumor I heard wasn't that the Priest would use his *own* heart and his *own* magic. It was about him using *someone else*." Her throat bobbed. "Or in this case, *multiple* someones. Because the third thing that's needed for the ceremony . . . is blood."

Ice flooded Viri as she realized what her guardian was saying.

"You think the Priest is going to—to *sacrifice* the children? That he'll use them to—" She thought back to what Sarielle had said, horror washing over her as she stuttered, "—to make himself invincible? Is that even *possible*?"

"Anything is possible when it comes to magic as ancient as this. Even the mages of old forbade the use of sacrificial rituals, and for good reason," Sarielle said. "Think about it. If all the Aurora Comet needs is a pure heart and strong, untainted ellixen, can you imagine how much power the Priest might obtain if he were to sacrifice fifty innocent children? All at once?"

"Fifty?"

Sarielle nodded solemnly. "Captain Farrow sent word an hour ago after receiving final numbers. It makes sense," she added, sounding hollow, "since fifty is considered a number of power in ancient numerology. The Priest is covering all his bases to ensure the sacrifice works."

Viri knew nothing about numerology, but fifty children were missing—*fifty!*—and if Sarielle's rumors proved true, then the Reaper Priest was planning to slaughter them all.

"When's the comet due?" she asked, her voice ragged.

Sarielle shook her head. "The Scholars' Guild is looking into it, but the mages left us with so few ancient texts, and even fewer that speak of magical events such as this. We might not get an answer, let alone in the time we need it."

"So we have to assume it could be any day," Viri said, her dismay growing.

"And if we don't find the children in time," Sarielle said, "not only will they be killed, but the Priest will have access to magic unlike anything we've ever seen."

A weighty feeling hit Viri, as if there were rocks in her stomach.

But her mind kept spinning ahead. "For what purpose?" she wondered aloud. "What does the Priest actually *want*?"

"What does anyone with ill intent want?" Sarielle asked wearily. "Power."

"There has to be more to it than that," Viri argued. "Let's say he succeeds in drawing magic from the comet—what then? What does he plan to use all that power for?"

"If only there was someone who could give us those answers." Sarielle sighed. "All we know for sure is that we need to find him before the comet arrives. Because if we don't . . . Elders help us all."

Viri barely heard the second part of what her guardian said, having stilled after the first sentence. A now-familiar voice whispered in her mind, more insistent than ever:

"My freedom for your answers."

Slowly, ever so slowly, Viri asked, "If there was a way to get the answers we need, maybe even learn where the Priest is hiding, but the cost was . . . steep . . ." She swallowed, and made herself finish, "Would it be worth it?"

A flash of lightning in the distance revealed the dark circles beneath Sarielle's eyes. "Honestly, darling," she said, sounding as exhausted as she looked, "there's no cost too steep if it means finding the Priest in time to stop him."

A lump lodged in Viri's windpipe as her thoughts began to scream at her. She barely noticed when she remained quiet for too long, barely heard Sarielle say something about sleep, barely felt it when her guardian kissed her cheek and left her alone before the coming storm. All she could hear was Reeve's voice replaying in her mind—but this time, it wasn't just his offer. It was also the final words he'd taunted her with:

"We both know I'm your only hope of finding him. When you change your mind, I'll be waiting."

"Elders, don't let me regret this," Viri breathed into the darkness, before spinning on her heel and hurrying to her bedroom, unable to believe what she was about to do, but knowing it was her only option.

She had to at least *try*.

Even if it cost her everything.

THE JOURNAL OF CELESTIAL MAGE KADMUS CASTRO

Forty-Eighth Sun, Fifth Cycle, Twelfth Age

My ritual at the Midnight Festival was a roaring success.

Magistratus Garrin attended, along with other curious Elverdine shallows, all of whom were astounded when I drew power from the eclipse to amplify their normally limited stores of ellixen. Temporary or not, the magical boost will aid them in many ways, from increasing their strength and energy to swifter healing for their illnesses and injuries. It's nowhere near the amount of power we mages have, but for shallows, the difference is substantial, even if it lasts only a few days.

To say they worship me is an understatement, though I've made it clear that, as their Mage Priest, I am merely their humble servant. That is my calling, my purpose, my honor in life—to help those less fortunate than me. Hopefully word will spread and more shallows will come to the next ritual, one that falls in a fortnight upon the arrival of the Draconis meteor shower.

I must admit, being here on Elverdine is a breath of fresh air. The residents haven't yet developed magical prejudice, which means they don't consider celestial magic a "useless" or "lesser" craft, unlike those on the mainland. Back there, only the major celestial events are celebrated by the populace anymore: both equinoxes and solstices, the twilight sun, the advent moon, and the rare comet or conjunction. But even those are more about jollification than sanctification these days. It hasn't always been this way, though. In ages past, celestial magic was so revered that my Priest forebears were performing rituals every month, sometimes every week, with shallows attending in droves to reap the favor of our blessings and purifications. But now . . . it's not only the mages on the mainland who reject the power of the heavens, but also the shallows, as if they've resigned themselves to a feeble—*shallow*—existence.

On Elverdine Isle, however, there's a thrilling hunger for more. The residents have been secluded for too long, isolated from mages and the vast possibilities of our magic. Their desire for what I can offer as their Mage Priest only rouses my commitment toward them.

Zeranthe says I need to be careful not to let their adoration go to my head. She also keeps reminding me of how capricious magic is here, something the native dragons have cautioned her and the other magebonded dragons about, given our proximity to the unwarded—and still unlocated—Hallow Stream. But their warnings are unnecessary. Despite my initial concerns, I had no trouble controlling my ellixen at the lunar eclipse. Indeed, it was almost too easy. And while I did feel different after the ritual was complete, it wasn't a bad different. Just . . . different.

Better.

Stronger.

More powerful.

I haven't told Zeranthe. I know she can sense something unusual through our bond, but she already acts like a grumpy mother hen, and I don't want to incite a worried lecture. It's likely what I'm feeling is simply the residual power drawn from the eclipse. It'll fade from my body, just as it'll fade from the shallows I bestowed it upon. Celestial magic is fleeting; it always has been.

Though . . . I can't help wondering if maybe it doesn't have to be.

Perhaps things will be different on Elverdine. Perhaps my closeness to the Hallow Stream will change everything I've ever known about celestial magic. Maybe even about *all* magic.

It seems as if anything might be possible here.

8

The headquarters of the Nox Custodia were always quiet during the late-night hours—something Viri was counting on as she made her way there, questioning herself with every step. She almost *wished* there were more guards around, someone to ask what she was doing, to tell her how very foolish she was being, to stop her. But as always, most on-duty Nox were out patrolling the city, with only a skeleton crew remaining for emergencies.

The guards manning the reception desk were used to Viri coming and going at odd times, so all they did was wave tiredly when she breezed past in her hunter attire and vanished into the elevator.

Her heart was racing, her plan—if it could be called that—having so many holes that she wondered if she was mad. Part of her desperately wanted to return home and act like the conversation she'd had with Sarielle had been nothing more than a vivid nightmare, one she'd laugh about in the morning. But she couldn't just ignore what she'd learned and hope the problem would go away on its own. There were fifty missing children who were counting on her to find them, and an entire city that might be at risk if the Reaper Priest gained the power of the Aurora Comet. Viri couldn't let that happen, even if it meant breaking the most fundamental rule of hunting.

She was about to bargain with a reaper.

It went against everything she believed in, everything she *was*, and yet, Sarielle had said there was no cost too steep if it led to them getting the answers they needed.

Viri just had to hope that was true, since there was no going back now, the elevator descending fast beneath the mountain. As usual, the ellixen powering it made goosebumps prickle her flesh—or maybe they were from the trepidation she felt, which only deepened when she came to a halt and used a shaky hand to pull a vial of black powder from her cloak. It was another of Wynter's experiments: an ellixen disrupter that could briefly interrupt the flow of magic, created for Viri to use against reapers with enchanted artifacts or weapons. But that wasn't why she'd brought it with her tonight.

Without Soren's Nox clearance granting her access through the elevator's door—something Viri couldn't ask for again—the powder was her only hope of getting to Reeve.

"Please work," she whispered, tipping half the vial onto her palm and blowing it at the command panel.

She waited what felt like a lifetime, but finally, the powder took effect and the doors opened, prompting Viri to slump with relief and send a mental thank-you to Wynter.

Time was of the essence now, with every moment counting if Viri wanted to avoid discovery. Even tired, the two Nox guards at the reception desk would notice if she took too long to reappear. She and Reeve needed to be long gone before anyone started asking questions.

Hurrying down the dimly lit tunnel, Viri didn't allow herself to second-guess what she was about to do. She wasn't going in blind this time—she knew Reeve liked to play games, but she could play them, too. His offer demanded freedom in return for answers, so she would help him escape, ask her questions, get the information she needed—

And then drag him straight back to the Underlock.

Reeve thought he was smart, but Viri was smarter. There was no way she was letting him loose just so he could scurry back to his master. Contingencies upon contingencies—that was what she needed in order to win games against a reaper.

Channeling confidence, Viri turned the final bend in the tunnel and approached the cell at the end, anticipating having to rouse Reeve from sleep. But when she halted before his glass-fronted prison, she found him wide-awake, lying on his thin mattress and tossing a stone into the air. Up, down, up, down, he repeated the motion, the muscles in his tanned forearm rippling with the move, the onyx ring on his finger gleaming in the low light. He didn't so much as twitch when she cleared her throat to announce her presence, almost as if he'd been expecting her.

"I need to talk to you," she said.

"I'm busy. Come back later."

Five words, and Viri could already feel her blood pressure rising. "I'm here about your offer."

Reeve's quicksilver eyes flicked her way, but otherwise he didn't move, just continued to toss his rock—up, down, up, down. "What offer would that be, Little Shadow?"

"You know what offer," Viri ground out. "Get your ass up. If you want your freedom, we need to move."

His lips twitched, but he still didn't budge. "So polite. Did they teach you those manners at hunter school?"

Every part of Viri wanted to snap back at him, but with so much at stake, she swallowed her pride—and her tongue—and said, "Please, Reeve. We don't have long."

Whether it was her plea, the urgency in her tone, or the possibility of escape, something finally got through to him enough that he dropped the rock and rose to his feet. Impossibly, he looked no worse for wear after a week in prison. If anything, he seemed *rested*, which was hardly fair. His dark clothes were somewhat rumpled, and his black hair more tousled than usual, but otherwise he looked—he looked—

Don't think about how he looks, Viri scolded herself, hating that someone so evil could be so physically appealing. He was like one of Wynter's experimental poisons—beautiful, but deadly.

"Hands," Viri said as he approached the barrier. She gestured to the small square cut into the fortified glass that was just large enough for objects to pass through, things like food—and wrists.

He did as ordered, not even flinching as the ellixen-suppressing wards bore down on him, indicating he'd done this in recent days, likely numerous times. But while his other visitors would have slapped him with nullicuffs—magic-nullifying handcuffs—Viri had something else in mind.

"Do you remember this?" she asked, uncoiling her golden weapon from her forearm.

"Your parents' fillium," Reeve said, eyeing it thoughtfully, a slew of emotions playing out across his face before he schooled his features once more. "How could I forget?"

"Do you remember what it does?"

"Which part? The magic suppression, or the truth detection?"

"Both," Viri said, satisfied with his memory. If she'd been less unbalanced during her last visit, she would have thought to use it on him then, if only to find out how much of what he'd said was a lie and how much the truth. It couldn't force answers out of him, so it wouldn't help her get the information she required, but it *could* offer the reassurance she needed to risk going through with her plan tonight.

Binding one end of the golden cord around Reeve's wrists in a figure eight, she looked straight into his silver eyes and asked, "Is your bargain genuine? If I free you, will you answer my questions? All of them?"

He didn't hesitate. "Yes to the first, yes to the second, and yes—within reason—to the third."

She frowned. "Within reason?"

"I'll answer your questions about the Priest, as promised," Reeve said, before a trace of a smirk touched his lips. "But if you want to know about anything else, including my personal life, you'll have to earn it."

"Good thing I don't care about your personal life," Viri said.

His smirk grew. "Still lying, I see."

She indicated her own hand touching the fillium. "This proves I'm not."

A dark laugh left Reeve. "It proves nothing."

Viri stilled, before forcing herself to relax. He couldn't possibly know the golden weapon had never worked on her—she wouldn't have been able to wear it long-term otherwise. While she might have yielded almost all of her ellixen during her

Impartation as a child, the fraction she'd kept would object to being constantly suppressed, leaving her in a perpetual state of exhaustion—something Reeve would soon start to feel himself, though the fillium's draining power wouldn't hit him as hard or as fast as it would a reaper who had recently siphoned. Still, it wouldn't be long before he began to feel its effects. Viri, however . . . her immunity was a mystery. Despite the fillium being a family heirloom, neither of her parents had been impervious to its magic, so they'd always limited their contact and taken turns using it during their hunts. Viri didn't have that problem, something she was eternally grateful for.

"We don't have time for this," she said, moving them on. "One more question before I decide if this is worth it."

"For you or for me?"

"Me, obviously." Viri arched a brow. "Did you sell your brain along with your soul when you became a reaper?"

"Is that your question? Because would you believe I never actually—"

"No—just—ugh, shut up," Viri cut him off, angry at herself more than him for wasting precious seconds. "My question is: Do you *actually* know where the Reaper Priest is and what his plans are, or are you just using me to escape?"

"I know more than you do," Reeve answered. Before Viri could demand a better response, he added, "And what I know, you're going to want to hear. That's all I'm saying until you get me out of here." A slash of a grin. "Time to choose, Little Shadow. Will you bargain with a reaper?"

Half certain she was making the biggest mistake of her life, but also aware that she didn't have time for doubt, Viri pressed her free hand against the panel embedded in the tunnel wall beside the barrier. Normally, that was all that was needed to open the Underlock cells, her hunter's mark being recognized by the wards and allowing her to release any inmates, but Reeve's prison apparently required more than that. Thankfully, she still had half of Wynter's powder left, and she used the last of it to disrupt the magic, just like in the elevator.

It took mere seconds for the transparent barrier to dissolve, the glass vanishing along with the magic that had kept the ellixen ward in place.

And then, suddenly, there was nothing but air between Viri and Reeve.

He stepped forward, and she instinctively stepped backward, before giving herself a mental slap.

His lips quirked, his voice low as he asked, "Scared?"

Viri tugged on the fillium, making the cord tighten around his wrists. "The only person who should be scared is you."

A soft laugh. "No one has ever scared me more than you, Viri."

She almost scoffed before remembering that he couldn't lie while touching the fillium. "When have I—"

"Uh-uh," he *tsk*ed. "No personal questions, remember?"

"You said I could earn them."

"And you said you weren't interested."

"I—" Viri snapped her mouth shut, if only to keep from putting her foot in it. She hated the amusement lighting his eyes—it was even more devastating up close—and spun on her heel, yanking him after her. "Come on. We need to hurry."

His long legs kept pace easily with hers as they headed in the direction of the elevator. "I take it you have a plan?"

She tried not to think about the fact that she was walking side by side with a reaper—one she'd willfully broken out of a prison cell—just as she tried not to think about the fact that the reaper was Reeve. She honestly wasn't sure which was worse.

"Of course I have a plan," Viri lied as they moved quickly through the tunnels, thankful yet again that the fillium didn't work on her. "You just have to tell me where we're heading once I get us out of here."

Reeve's surprise was clear in his voice. "You're letting me choose?"

"The bargain is for your freedom, isn't it?" Viri didn't intend to let him go for real, but a false sense of security never hurt anyone. As long as her weapon remained around his wrists, he wasn't going anywhere without her, nor could he siphon any magic to help him flee. At the end of this night, he would be right back where he started—locked in a cell.

"In that case, there are so many options," Reeve mused.

"Just figure it out before we reach the wayportal," Viri told him, not caring where they went as long as she got the information he'd promised. "If you want to cut some questions from my list, feel free to take me straight to the Reaper Priest or the missing children. Preferably both." She knew there was no chance of him doing that, but still, it was worth asking, if only for what he said next.

"So you know about the kids." An unreadable look flashed across his face. "You've been busy."

Viri's jaw clenched. Some small, secret part of her had hoped he might be ignorant of the abductions, but that had been foolish. Reeve was the Priest's most loyal follower. As disgusted as she was by the role he must have played in the kidnappings, at least that meant he would be able to answer her questions about the approaching sacrifice.

"How long do the kids have left?" she asked, figuring she might as well get a head start on her interrogation.

Reeve, however, disagreed. "No cheating, Little Shadow. I'm not free yet."

"You're no longer in a cell."

"But still in prison."

"Some say life is a prison," Viri returned. "That's not something I can free you from."

"I'm sure you could think of a way." He sent her a sideways look as they rounded the final bend in the tunnel, the elevator in sight up ahead. "Don't tell me it hasn't crossed your mind."

Viri bristled at his implication. "Unlike you, I don't fantasize about killing people. And even if I did, I wouldn't waste the mental space on you."

"Just the Reaper Priest, then?"

Tension flooded Viri, but she forced her limbs to keep moving, the elevator now only steps away. "He deserves what's coming to him."

Another sideways look from Reeve. "Are you sure about that?"

Before Viri could respond, the elevator arrived with a soft *ding*—but it hadn't come at her request.

Panicking, she looked around for somewhere to hide, a shadowy corner, *anything*, but it was no use. The tunnel was dim but not dark enough to conceal her and Reeve.

She cursed under her breath. "Get ready. We're about to be ambushed."

"All part of your plan, right?" Reeve said dryly.

Viri shot him a glare. "I take back what I said about not fantasizing about your death."

He winked. "Just add it to the other fantasies you have about me."

For a moment, Viri genuinely considered letting Reeve get locked up again, bargain be damned. But then she came to her senses and remembered why she was helping him in the first place.

"Just keep your mouth shut and stay out of my way," she ordered as the elevator doors began to open.

Reeve raised his bound wrists. "I can help you fight if you free me."

"If you think for one second that I'd trust—"

She didn't get to finish before the doors opened wide enough for a black-uniformed guard to rush through, nor did she react in time to stop Reeve from leaping between her and the threat, moving so fast he was a blur as he spun behind the Nox and enclosed his bound hands around the young man's neck.

A very familiar young man.

"No—Reeve—*stop!*" Viri cried as Soren coughed and bucked against Reeve's choking grip. "Let him go!"

She yanked on her fillium for good measure, but Reeve was already backing away.

"Elders, are you all right?" Viri asked, hurrying to her friend's side as he sucked in heaving gulps of air. "What are you doing here?"

"What the hell do you *think*?" Soren rasped, rubbing his reddened neck and glaring at Reeve before turning that glare on Viri.

"You're not supposed to be here," she said quickly. "I didn't want—"

"*You're* not supposed to be here," Soren interrupted, his glare intensifying. "I just got back from patrol, ready to head home to my nice, warm bed, only to hear the reception guards mention how you must have been busy with 'hunter paperwork' since you'd arrived but never left." He leaned in angrily. "Paperwork. *You.* It didn't take a genius to figure out why you were really here."

Viri bit her lip. "I—"

"How the hell did you even get past the elevator?" At the look on her face, his own darkened. "Wynter. Of course."

"Sor—" Viri started, but he cut her off again.

"Do you realize how much trouble you'd be in if someone other than me had come down here?" Soren's brown eyes were furious. "How much trouble *I'd* be in, if they thought I helped you again? If anyone finds out—"

Viri spoke over him. "I wouldn't be here if it wasn't an emergency."

Soren shook his head. "That's not good enough." He jabbed a finger toward Reeve. "Explain to me why this scumbag is out of his cell. Right now."

"This 'scumbag' has a name," Reeve drawled.

Viri sent him a warning look, willing him to be silent.

"I know exactly who you are," Soren said, drawing himself up to his full height. For most, that would be intimidating, but Reeve was equally tall, and all he did was roll his eyes and yawn in response. Viri wanted to kick him.

"There are things you don't know, Sor," she answered her friend. "Life-or-death things. Reeve has the answers I need to stop something terrible from happening."

"Captain Farrow has briefed me about the missing kids," Soren said, his face still hard. "The Nox are teaming up with the hunters on this—everyone's getting orders in the morning. We'll find them. We don't need help from some reaper filth to do it."

"First 'scumbag,' now 'filth'?" Reeve sounded amused. "What's next—you insult my mother? Go ahead, I'll join you."

"Shut *up*, Reeve," Viri hissed. To Soren, she said, "Darik doesn't know everything, not yet."

Quickly, she summarized her conversation with Sarielle, watching Soren grow paler with each word she uttered.

"How long do we have until the sacrifice?" he asked, his expression no longer hard but instead pinched with worry.

"That's one of the many things I intend to find out," Viri said, gesturing to Reeve. "We made a bargain. If I help him escape, he's promised to answer everything I want to know about the Priest and his plans."

"I have a better idea," Soren said, taking a menacing step forward. "How about he answers your questions right here."

Reeve had the audacity to chuckle. "You're plucky for a city guard, I'll give you that. But you should know better than to break a bargain with a reaper. Careful, Archer. You don't want me as your enemy."

Soren stilled upon hearing his surname.

Reeve's mouth curled into an edged smile. "You think I don't know who you are? Soren Archer, friend to Viridia Solace"—he waved his bound hands lazily toward Viri—"and Wynter Starling. Brother and guardian to Jessalyn Archer. Revered member of the Nox Custodia and on a career path toward captaincy one day. You hate your parents, you love your sister more than anyone in the world, and you'd do anything to protect the people you care about. Shall I go on?"

"Is this your attempt at threatening me?" Soren asked through clenched teeth. "Telling me you know about my life?"

Reeve's smile turned dangerous. "If it was, you wouldn't have to ask. You'd know."

When Soren took another angry step toward Reeve, Viri leapt forward to place her body between them. "That's enough. Need I remind you both that we're sitting ducks down here? We could be caught at any minute, and then we'll *all* end up in cells." Her blood chilled at the thought, but then she reminded herself of the stakes, stomped down on her unease, and turned to Reeve. "You and I need to get out of here." She spun back to Soren. "And you need to create a distraction so no one sees us sneaking out through the wayportal."

Soren spluttered. "Why the hell would I do that?"

"Because you're my friend and you love me?" Viri suggested innocently. At his flat look, she sighed. "Fine. Consider this me calling in the favor I won at family night."

Disbelief splashed across Soren's face. "Are you *kidding* me?"

"You told me not to make it anything weird," Viri reminded him. "You didn't say it had to be legal."

Soren's disbelief only grew. "I figured it was *implied* by the fact that we *both* work in *law enforcement*."

"This is fun," Reeve observed, shifting to lean against the tunnel wall. "If you two ever get sick of public service, you should consider joining the Theater Guild."

"I swear, Reeve," Viri grated out, "one more word, and I'll throw you back in your cell myself." She turned to Soren with a pleading expression. "Please, Sor. I know this isn't ideal—I hate it more than you do, trust me—but we need answers. And I need your help to get them."

Soren dragged a hand through his sandy-blond hair, looking torn. "If you do this, V, you'll be painting a target on your back. You know that, right? If you take off with Ashton, every available guard will come after you. You won't be the hunter—you'll be the hunted. Can you handle that?"

"It'll be worth it," Viri said, even as her stomach dropped. "It has to be."

If all went to plan, Reeve would be locked away again before anyone realized he was gone. But if worse came to worst, Viri was counting on the fact that everyone would be too busy trying to locate the children to waste resources finding her. And if it turned out she was wrong, if she was caught harboring a fugitive . . .

"There's no cost too steep if it means finding the Priest in time to stop him."

Sarielle's words repeated in Viri's mind, giving her the courage she needed to stay the course.

"I know what I'm doing, Sor," she said softly. "I need you to trust me."

"*You're* not the issue." He shot an angry look at Reeve.

"If you're concerned for her welfare, you needn't be," Reeve said smoothly, still leaning against the wall, his hands bound in front of him and legs crossed at the ankles. "If there's anyone Viri can trust with her life, it's me."

The fillium meant he wasn't lying, but Viri knew better than to lower her guard. There were plenty of ways he could hurt her that didn't leave a mark—he'd taught her that lesson himself.

"Forgive me if I have trouble believing the word of a murderer," Soren stated acidly.

"You're forgiven," Reeve returned. He cocked his head to the side. "Since we're saying nice things about each other, has anyone ever told you that you have hero hair? I've never seen anything so perfectly coiffed."

A startled, choked laugh left Viri without her permission. She quickly stifled it at the look Soren sent her, and staunchly ignored the pleased light in Reeve's eyes.

Adopting a serious expression, she said, firmly, "Stop antagonizing each other."

"He started it."

Both Soren and Reeve spoke at once, making Viri cough against another poorly timed laugh. But she fought it down and asked, "Sor, are you in?"

A long-suffering sigh. "Do I have a choice?"

Making sure the fillium was still tight in one hand, Viri used the other to squeeze her friend's arm. "Of course you do. But I'm really hoping you'll choose to help."

He sighed again, louder this time. "What kind of a distraction do you have in mind?"

9

The plan they came up with was almost alarmingly simple, especially after Soren pointed out that the easiest way for Viri and Reeve to sneak past the Nox reception guards would be if no sneaking was necessary.

"The best deception is always the most obvious one," Soren said as they entered the elevator. With nimble fingers, he unfastened the polished silver buckles of his dark trench coat, shucked it off, and handed it to Reeve. "If you don't look out of place, no one will think you're not meant to be there."

"Clever," Reeve hummed, motioning for Viri to release his bindings—which she did, but only after sending him a cautionary look—and then he donned the uniform over his black attire, transforming instantly into a Nox guard. "In another world, we might have been friends, Archer."

"Pity the only other world you're likely to see is the underworld, and I don't intend to meet you there," Soren replied without missing a beat. He ignored Reeve's snort to wave toward his coat and warn, "I expect that back. If I find out you've been posing as a Nox, not even Viri will be able to protect you."

"Trust me, I can't think of anything more miserable." Reeve's nose wrinkled as he inspected his reflection in the smooth wall of the swiftly rising elevator. "Black suits me, honor doesn't."

It was the first time since their reunion that Viri agreed with something he'd said. But she didn't comment, only focused on retying his bindings. She wasn't worried he'd escape while inside the elevator, but once the doors opened, she wouldn't risk him fleeing before he'd fulfilled his side of the bargain.

"Call me paranoid, but what happens if someone notices you walking me like a dog on a leash?" Reeve drawled, lifting his hands and gesturing to the length of golden cord stretching from him back to her.

Viri frowned, realizing he was right. The guards on the night shift might be tired, but they weren't blind. Even with Reeve playing dress-up, it would be a dead giveaway that he wasn't a real Nox if his bindings were spotted.

Thinking fast, she freed one of his wrists and wrapped the remaining length of cord around her own before grabbing his still-bound hand and twining their fingers together.

She felt his surprise—saw it, too, as his dark brows shot upward—but she was too busy trying not to think about his warm, callused skin against hers to explain how their hand-holding would keep any eagle-eyed guards from noticing the bindings.

Reeve, it seemed, didn't need an explanation, not when he was so obviously entertained by her discomfort.

"Careful, I might be contagious," he said, his silver eyes dancing. "Watch out or I'll grow on you."

Not missing his meaning, Viri deadpanned, "I guarantee I'm immune."

A soft chuckle, and a gentle squeeze of his fingers around hers. "We'll see."

Soren cleared his throat sharply and sent Viri a *What the hell is going on between you two?* look that she skillfully ignored. He still knew nothing of her history with Reeve, and while she was beginning to regret keeping such a big secret, it worked in her favor tonight, preventing Soren from questioning her motives for the jailbreak. Reeve was a means to an end, nothing more, but she couldn't risk Soren doubting that.

Fortunately, the slowing of the lift diverted his attention. "We're nearly there," he said. "Everyone ready?"

Viri nodded as the doors opened, then followed Soren into the Nox's white-marbled reception area, Reeve striding confidently at her side. Her grip on him tightened as the two guards at the front desk looked up, both different from the ones who had been on duty when Viri had arrived and looking much fresher than their predecessors.

Sensing her unease, Soren touched the back of Viri's free hand reassuringly and headed straight for the guards to play his role perfectly.

"Jost, Estrin, everything quiet up here?" he asked, leaning casually on the desk to limit their view of Viri and Reeve walking past.

"As dead as the necropolis," the male guard—Jost—said. "You three done for the night?"

"Yeah," Soren said, shifting slightly to keep blocking Viri and Reeve as they continued toward the wayportal nestled in the far corner of the room. "Hoping to catch a few hours' sleep before Captain Farrow's meeting in the morning."

The female Nox—Estrin—fluttered her eyelashes. "We're

covering for Caz and Hutton while they take a break, but my shift ends once they're back, in case you don't feel like sleeping just yet."

Elders spare me, Viri thought, mentally gagging at the blatant proposition. Reeve was no help—his body shook with humor against hers. She crunched his fingers hard in warning, but that only prompted him to release an audible snicker.

Thankfully, they were now far enough away from the desk that the guards couldn't hear—nor did Viri have to endure Soren's reply—and only a few steps from the shimmering magestone arch that would whisk them to their next destination, safe from imminent arrest.

While part of Viri couldn't believe their ruse had worked—indeed, Soren was still chatting with the guards, who were oblivious to the criminal escaping under their watch—another part was beginning to regret telling Reeve he could choose where they headed next. He'd had plenty of time to think about it, and that could mean anything for her—including being delivered straight to his murderous reaper friends.

Unwilling to risk falling into a trap, Viri yanked on his hand when they reached the wayportal, preparing to step through first and pick their destination herself.

Only, she didn't get the chance before someone arrived through the arch, appearing directly in front of them.

And not just anyone—

It was Darik.

The Nox captain's black eyes widened in surprise at seeing Viri, then narrowed just as fast at the sight of Reeve, whose borrowed uniform did nothing to conceal his identity up close.

Panic blared through Viri, freezing her in place. Her mouth

opened, an excuse ready on her tongue—but before she could get a word out, Darik rushed forward, yelling orders to his guards.

What happened next was a blur. Instinct kicked in, and Viri moved to intercept Darik, only for Reeve to rip his hand from hers and beat her to it. He moved so fast that his actions were impossible to follow, but somehow, in the space of a heartbeat, the captain was crumpling to the ground, unconscious.

Viri gaped at Darik, before screeching at Reeve, "What did you *do*?"

"Incoming," was all he said, using the fillium still connecting them to tug her out of the way just as Jost and Estrin reached them.

Though her mind screamed at her to stop, Viri defended herself automatically, and within seconds, the two reception guards were on the ground beside their captain.

"So much for sneaking out," Reeve murmured, taking in the three prone bodies and pulling a face. "What a mess."

Viri's glare could have burned him alive.

"I *told* you freeing Ashton would paint a target on your back," Soren growled, marching their way. He knelt beside Darik, checking the captain's pulse. "There's no coming back from—"

Before he could finish, Reeve struck him on the back of his head hard enough to make him collapse beside his fellow Nox. "You can thank me later, Archer."

Viri stared down at her friend in horror, before turning to Reeve and all but shouting, *"Why the hell did you do that?"*

He looked at her like she was an idiot. "I thought you didn't want him involved?"

"I *didn't*—"

"Don't you think it'd be suspicious if he was the only one

still standing *and* he let us get away?" Reeve waved his unbound hand toward Soren and the other unconscious guards. "I did your friend a favor."

Viri ground her teeth so hard they hurt. She hated that Reeve was right—that the best way to protect Soren was to make it look like he'd been attacked, just like the other guards.

Just like Darik.

"Elders, we're dead," Viri breathed, her eyes locked on the captain, but imagining Meera's irate face instead. Her mentor was *not* going to be pleased when she learned of what had happened tonight. "*I'm* dead."

"Not yet," Reeve said, "but there's a high chance we will be if we don't get moving."

Viri's gaze shot back to him as she hissed, "You just brought down three trained Nox *and* their leader without breaking a sweat. How—"

"Actually, *you* brought down that guy." He pointed to Jost. "And I'm pretty sure you did most of the work with her, too." He indicated Estrin. "But we can argue over who's the better fighter later. You promised me freedom, and I promised you answers. Eyes on the prize, Little Shadow." He jerked his chin toward the wayportal. "Let's get out of here before more of your Nox friends arrive."

Yet again, Viri hated that Reeve was right, almost as much as she hated the idea of leaving Soren helpless on the ground. She even felt bad about Darik—albeit to a lesser degree. But if she waited for them to awaken, then everything they'd done to escape would be for nothing.

Soren would forgive her.

And Darik . . .

Well, she would just have to find a way to explain things to the Nox captain after the danger had passed. Given his lifelong resentment toward her, she doubted he would *believe* her, but that was a problem for her future self. Right now, the only thing that mattered was stopping the Reaper Priest.

"Come on," she muttered, dragging Reeve toward the way-portal. She looked back just once, sending a silent apology to Soren—and Darik and Jost and Estrin—before stepping through the arch, mentally guiding it to the first connection point that came to mind.

"I thought you were letting me choose our destination," Reeve said as he arrived behind her, though he didn't sound surprised. He did, however, look bewildered as he peered around the shadowy inner-mountain alley before them and asked, "Why are we in the market district? It's the middle of the night—everything's closed."

"I can't exactly take you back to my apartment with the Magistratus sleeping down the hall," Viri returned, tugging on the fillium. "Follow me. I know a place where we can talk."

It was almost eerie, walking through the sleeping alley located halfway up Mount Verta, past closed shops carved into the rock wall and canvas-covered stalls lining the lane. Come morning, the spiraling mountain thoroughfare would be teeming with people buying everything from fruits and vegetables and meats—all fresh from the farms located just outside the uppercity—to clothes and crafts and jewelry. As the commercial hub of Aravell, the market district boasted the city's best tearooms, bakeries, perfumeries, florists, confectioneries, boutiques, bookstores, and more. If it could be bought, sold, or traded, then it could be found right there in the heart of the mountain.

Normally, Viri could happily lose time wandering around the stores, or just people-watching from the railing that overlooked the hollow center of the mountain. As the midpoint in Mount Verta, glancing up afforded a spiraling view toward the Entertainment Guild, the Scholars' Guild above that, then the Summit, where the High Council convened. Glancing down found the City Services Guild, the Healers' Guild, then the base of the mountain, where the hunters and Nox presided. Seven main levels, covering everything the citizens of Aravell needed to survive and thrive on Elverdine Isle.

While the inner design of Mount Verta had always fascinated Viri, tonight she paid it little heed as she led Reeve along the darkened alleyway, past familiar cafés and market stalls, all locked up tight for the evening. There were plenty of after-hours businesses in the Entertainment Guild that Viri could have taken him to—eateries, theaters, taverns, gambling houses—but she didn't want to be around crowds right now, constantly looking over her shoulder in fear of being caught. As soon as Darik woke, he would send out his Nox—there was no doubt about that. What Viri needed was a discreet place to hide while she obtained the answers she'd been promised.

"We're nearly there," she said, seeing lights coming from a shop carved into the mountainside ahead.

"Don't rush on my behalf," Reeve replied. "I've always enjoyed a good nighttime stroll." He patted his stomach. "Aids digestion."

"Elders forbid you show the slightest hint of concern about being on the run," Viri muttered.

"I've been on the run for seven years." He gave a careless shrug. "From you, mostly."

"I haven't been chasing *you*."

"No, but you've been chasing—"

"We're here," Viri cut him off, not needing a reminder of all the years she'd been trying—and failing—to catch the Reaper Priest. As his closest follower, Reeve might have interpreted that as her searching for him as well, but *he* wasn't the one who had killed her parents, so her vendetta hadn't been focused on him. Nevertheless, he was a reaper, so it was inevitable that she would have hunted him eventually.

"Betty's Bakes," Reeve said, reading the sign above the door where she'd halted them. "You brought me to a bakery?"

"Not just any bakery—the best bakery in Aravell," Viri said loyally, waving to the mouthwatering assortment of cakes and pastries displayed in the window.

Reeve tapped the CLOSED sign. "Are we breaking and entering? Barely an hour together and I'm already a bad influence on you. That's a new record."

Viri rapped her knuckles against the wooden door. "It's only closed to customers."

"What are we? Fish?"

Inhaling slowly, Viri sought patience and explained, "The owner—Betty—always stays late to prepare orders for the next day. She's used to me dropping by during my hunting shifts, so she won't think it strange that I'm here tonight."

"And me?" Reeve asked.

Viri flicked his borrowed coat. "You're my Nox friend."

"'Friend'?" He smirked. "How scandalous."

"Not *that* kind of friend," Viri gritted out. She heard footsteps hobbling toward the door and quickly warned, "Betty's old and kind, but she's also nosy. Be careful what you say in here. And for Elders' sake, behave yourself."

"For Elders' sake, or for your sake?"

"For *your* sake," Viri said, but the menace in her tone only made him chuckle.

Before she could tell him exactly what she would do if he said anything inappropriate, the wooden door opened, releasing a delicious wave of baking aromas that instantly made Viri's stomach rumble. Light flooded out from within, revealing Betty's short, rounded figure, her hair as white as the flour that dusted it, her wrinkles like aged parchment. Large, circular glasses sat over cloudy brown eyes that squinted into the darkened alleyway, but then a wide smile stretched across her face as she lunged forward, arms open in welcome.

She wasn't, however, reaching for Viri.

"Sugarplum!" Betty cried, pulling Reeve to her ample bosom. "I've missed your visits!"

Viri's mouth dropped open as she watched Betty embrace Reeve tightly, then release him to pinch his cheeks.

"Handsome as always," the elderly woman said. "Just like your father."

"But less of a scoundrel," Reeve said with a roguish grin.

Betty wheezed out a laugh. "I doubt that. But what's life without a little mischief?" She turned to Viri, sending her a wink. "Good thing hunters know how to have fun. Right, sweets?"

Viri couldn't respond, her brain struggling to process what was happening. Not only did Betty know Reeve, she'd also known his *father*, who, if Viri recalled correctly, had died from an untreatable blood infection shortly after Reeve's fifth birthday. His mother had abandoned him as a babe by running off with another man, so his father's passing had left Reeve bouncing between group homes and orphanages until he'd finally been adopted by an elderly couple—Viri's childhood neighbors. That was how she'd first met him all those years ago. He'd been, quite literally, the boy next door.

"I'm sorry," Viri said weakly, waving a hand between Reeve and Betty, "but how do you two know each other?"

"This is the best bakery in Aravell," Reeve said, repeating Viri's earlier words almost mockingly. "I've been coming here for years."

"I thought I was being haunted by the ghost of his father," Betty said with a tender look at Reeve. "Jude Ashton was always a sweetheart, so it's no surprise that his son is, too."

A sweetheart? *Reeve?* Clearly Betty was turning senile in her old age.

"Gracious, look at me, yabbering away." Betty flapped her hands, sending flour everywhere. "Come in, come in. I've just made a fresh batch of custard tarts." She beamed at Reeve. "Your favorite."

"You're an angel," Reeve said, returning her smile. "You wouldn't believe how bland prison food is. I've been hungry for a week."

Viri's eyes widened at what he'd just revealed, but Betty barely reacted.

"We can't have that," the old woman *tsk*ed as she turned and hobbled back into her shop, gesturing for them to follow. "You're a growing boy."

Boy was hardly the word Viri would have used. Despite Reeve being only eighteen, there was nothing boyish about him—not the way he looked, not the way he acted. And certainly not the way he killed innocents for his own gain.

The reminder sent a cold rush of reality over Viri, and she stomped into the bakery, jerking on her fillium to drag Reeve after her. There were plenty of wooden tables for them to choose from, all decorated with flowers and candles and doilies, making the inside of the store look almost as good as it smelled. But Viri didn't appreciate it as much as she usually did, her focus narrowed on getting what she needed, then sending Reeve back where he belonged.

"Take a seat anywhere, honeybuns," Betty invited as she shuffled behind the counter and toward the kitchen. "I'll be right back with your treats."

Viri dragged Reeve to the farthest corner of the room and sat opposite him, sliding the decorations aside so the only thing between them was her fillium extending across the table.

"Time for some answers," she said without preamble. "I gave you what you wanted. Now it's your turn."

10

Reeve made himself comfortable, stretching his legs beneath the table and ignoring Viri's kick when he encroached upon her space. "A deal's a deal, Little Shadow. Where would you like to begin?"

"You can start by not calling me that," Viri said. "Then continue by telling me what I've already asked countless times: Where's the Reaper Priest?"

"Why don't you ever use his real name?"

Viri's vision turned red. "Because when he became the Reaper Priest, he forfeited his humanity, and therefore his right to have one." She leaned forward and hissed, "And this isn't your time for questions—it's mine. So answer, or I'll take you straight back to the Underlock."

Reeve huffed out a laugh. "As if you're not planning to do that anyway."

Viri stilled, then forced the tension from her body. "I don't know what you're talking about."

"To be fair," he continued, as if she hadn't spoken, "I'd be disappointed if you *didn't* have some kind of double-cross in mind.

You've earned a reputation for being a ruthless hunter, Viridia Solace. It'd be a shame to find out it wasn't true."

Before Viri could think of a response—or come up with a believable lie—Betty reappeared from the kitchen and placed a tray in front of them, loaded with enough cupcakes and cookies and custard tarts to feed a city. She left again, only to return moments later with a steaming teapot and two mugs painted with gold hearts, setting them down on the table with a flourish.

"A romantic feast for my two favorite people," Betty said. "You cuties enjoy your date." She sighed wistfully. "Oh, to be young and in love."

Viri made a strangled sound. "No—That's not—*We're* not—"

But Betty was already hobbling away, disappearing into the kitchen once more.

"We'll be sure to invite her to the wedding," Reeve said, lips twitching as he poured their tea. "If we ask nicely, maybe she'll make the cake."

Viri scowled. "Stop laughing. This isn't funny."

"I'm not laughing."

"Your eyes are."

"My *eyes*?"

"Just—ugh! Never mind." She snatched up one of the custard tarts and bit angrily into it, but her pique dissolved instantly as a rush of sweetened vanilla flooded her senses.

"Amazing, right?" Reeve said, reaching for his own tart and taking a bite. He moaned, the sound unforgivably suggestive. "Mmm. Delicious."

Viri took a scalding sip of tea in the hope that it would hide the flush rising to her cheeks.

"But back to what we were saying," Reeve continued, licking

his fingers, which only made Viri's flush deepen, "I don't care about your intention to double-cross me, since it's not going to happen."

Viri's gaze narrowed. "It's not?"

"You need me," Reeve said simply. "As long as I have information about the Priest and the kids, you can't risk letting me out of your sight."

"Information you *owe* me, per our bargain."

"You're right, I do," Reeve agreed, sipping his own tea. "There's just one slight problem." He raised his free hand, pressing his forefinger and thumb together. "A teeny, tiny issue." He paused. "Or, well, *three* issues, if we're being exact."

Something about his tone had Viri bracing. "What kind of issues?"

He drank more tea, then set his mug down. "You want to know where the Reaper Priest is? Where the children are? When the sacrifice is happening?"

Viri nodded stiffly. "Yes."

"Then those are your three issues," Reeve said. "Because I don't have the answers."

Viri stared at him for a beat, then started laughing. There was no humor in the sound. "Nice try. Now tell me what I want to know."

Reeve raised his hands. "I swear, I'm telling the truth. But before you skewer me with your glare, it's not all bad news. I know how to *find* the information. We just have to go somewhere else to get it."

Viri laughed again, incredulous this time. "You're joking, right?"

"Do I look like I'm joking?"

His serious expression made Viri sober.

"Why would I go anywhere with you?" she demanded. "You already know I was planning to betray you—"

"Past tense? That's encouraging."

"—so why would I risk my life following a reaper?"

"Because we want the same thing," Reeve stated plainly.

"And what's that?" Viri asked, doubt clear in her voice.

"To stop the Aurora sacrifice."

Viri reeled backward in shock, but then she frowned. "You're the Priest's most loyal follower—why would you want to stop his plans?"

Reeve's expression blanked. "No personal questions. That was our deal."

"A deal you've *broken*," Viri fumed. "And how is that a personal question?"

"I haven't broken our deal—I literally just told you how we can get your answers. You're the one arguing about logistics."

"I'm not *arguing*," Viri argued.

Reeve looked at her pointedly.

Viri wouldn't have been surprised if steam began to shoot from her ears. She took a moment to breathe deeply, inhaling the calming scent of vanilla and custard, hating that her plan had gone so awry. Reeve had played her—*again*—but if there was a chance he was telling the truth . . . if he had a way to get the answers she needed . . . if he really *did* want to stop the Aurora sacrifice from happening . . . then that meant they shared the same goal. She wasn't deluded enough to think *all* their goals were aligned, not while he was faithful to the Priest—and a reaper, at that—but in this single instance, it might be worth the risk of going with him, especially if it meant saving the children.

Viri's instincts had never led her wrong before, and she prayed they weren't about to start now as she looked Reeve squarely in the eyes and said, "Where do we need to go?"

In answer, he downed another custard tart and rose to his feet. "It's not far. A quick trip through the wayportal."

Pressing her lips together, Viri stood as well, wondering if she was making a terrible mistake. But her gut was saying this was the right thing to do. She didn't trust Reeve as far as she could throw him, but she'd long since learned to trust herself, and she wouldn't stop now.

"Thanks for the midnight snack, Betty!" Reeve called into the kitchen as he began to lead the way toward the door. "Catch you next time!"

"Bye, loves!" the old woman yelled from somewhere out of sight. "Don't do anything I wouldn't do!"

Viri cringed at the implication but focused on following Reeve around the decorated tables, her fillium shining between them. Seeing it, something began to niggle at her, growing into confusion and then alarm as she watched Reeve stride comfortably forward—*too* comfortably.

"Why aren't you stumbling?" she asked.

He looked at her over his shoulder, one eyebrow raised. "Because I learned how to walk as a child?"

"No—why aren't you tired?"

His eyebrow rose higher. "Because I've been locked in a cell with nothing to do but nap for a week? And because I just ate my body weight in sugar?"

Annoyed, Viri said, "Stop answering my questions with questions."

Bemused, Reeve returned, "Stop asking vague questions and just say what's on your mind."

Viri waved her hand holding the fillium. "You've been wearing this long enough that you should definitely be feeling its effects by now. You should be exhausted, not . . . perky."

"Perky?" Reeve's mouth curled upward. "I've certainly been called worse."

Viri halted just before the bakery door, tugging on the cord to make him stop. "Answer me."

He shrugged. "I haven't siphoned in a while. Maybe that has something to do with it."

Viri flinched at the reminder of what he was, what he *did*. "That only means it wouldn't affect you as fast. You still have your own drop of ellixen for it to suppress—it would've taken more time, but you should be as weak as a kitten by now."

He shrugged again. "Maybe it's broken."

Dread flooded Viri at the thought. But . . . she could still *feel* her weapon, her heightened sensitivity picking up a low-level thrumming of ellixen that told her it held as much power as it always had. So that meant—

"It doesn't work on you," she gasped out. "Does it?"

A devilish grin stretched across Reeve's face. "Took you long enough."

"You *asshole*." Viri shoved his chest, then shoved him again when he unwound the cord from his wrist and dangled it tauntingly in the air, something that would have been impossible for any normal captive.

"It's not my fault you didn't ask," he said, still grinning. "You of all people should have noticed the signs, especially since it doesn't work on you, either."

Viri gaped at him. "How do you know—"

"Because I *remember*, Viri. Just because you chose to forget our past doesn't mean I did."

"But—I—" Viri didn't know what to say, having no memory of a time when they might have both realized they were immune to her parents' fillium. But Reeve was right about her choosing not to recall so many things from back then, the pain too raw to handle, her grief easier when kept at a distance.

Now wasn't the time to wonder what else she might have swept into the depths of her subconscious, so she held on to her anger and said, "You've been able to lie all night. Has *anything* you've told me been true?"

Sobering, Reeve said, "I haven't lied to you. Not once."

"You told me you knew about the Priest and his plans."

"No, I told you I know more than you do, and that you're going to want to hear it. That's still true. In more ways than you know."

"Then *tell* me," Viri said.

"I will—just not yet."

Viri wanted to stomp her foot like a child. Instead, she coiled her weapon around her arm while grumbling under her breath about infuriating reapers, then reached for Reeve and began checking the pockets of his dark coat.

He jolted back in surprise, bumping into a chair, but Viri didn't pause her search.

"What are you doing?" he asked in a *What the hell?* tone.

"Stand still," she ordered, patting him down.

"If you wanted to feel me up, you only had to ask."

"Let me restate," Viri bit out. "Stand still, and *don't speak*."

There was nothing in his outer pockets, so she unbuckled the front of his coat and began to rifle through the insides, her fingers skirting lightly over his sides as she sought to find what she knew had to be in there somewhere.

Reeve's frame stiffened and then jerked slightly as her fingers shifted between pockets, a noise escaping his lips that had Viri looking at him in disbelief as she realized—

"Are you *ticklish*?" When he didn't answer, she continued, almost accusingly, "You can't be. You're a reaper."

"Why do you make it sound like there's a rulebook I'm meant to be following?" Reeve asked. "Should I be taking notes?"

Viri shifted her hands upward, deliberately grazing his sides, and this time, an audible squeak left him.

"You *are* ticklish!" she cried. She nearly laughed at how ridiculous the thought was, but before she could make that mistake, she finally found what she was looking for. "Aha! Thank you, Soren!"

When Reeve caught sight of what she'd been searching for—a standard accoutrement carried by all Nox guards—he sighed. "Nullicuffs? Are those really necessary?"

In answer, she slapped one around his wrist and the other around her own, wincing at the sting of ellixen as the nullification effect set in. Unlike her fillium, there was no cord dangling between the cuffs, just two separate bracelets that were linked intangibly, both intended to stop magic from being used rather than suppressing and draining it. While less powerful than her own weapon, at least Reeve wouldn't be able to siphon. Plus, there was one more benefit.

"Since my fillium doesn't work on you, this will ensure you don't try to run away." Viri touched the glittery black cuff. "Move more than ten paces from me, and every nerve in your body will feel like it's on fire."

"Yours, too," Reeve warned.

"It's worth it for my peace of mind."

There was a hint of frustration in his tone as he said, "I told you before, we have the same goal. I'm not going anywhere without you."

"I know you're not," Viri said, touching her cuff again. "Now take off your coat. You've played Nox long enough tonight. Betty will make sure it gets back to Soren."

"You didn't think to have me take it off *before* you went all handsy on me?" Reeve asked dryly, removing the uniform and laying it over the back of a chair. "If I didn't know better, I'd say you enjoyed—"

"Finish that sentence and I'll walk ten paces away myself," Viri threatened, willing the heat from her cheeks. She hadn't even *thought* to ask him to take it off first, much to her embarrassment. "Now get moving. You have a bargain to keep."

11

Neither Viri nor Reeve spoke as they retraced their steps through the darkened market district back to the way-portal, the silence oddly peaceful. But by the time they reached the shimmering magestone arch, any sense of calm Viri felt was replaced by unease.

"For what it's worth, I promise I'm not leading you into a trap," Reeve said, noting her trepidation. "You have my word."

Viri straightened her scarlet cloak, surreptitiously making sure her hunter daggers were within easy reach, two strapped to her belt and one hidden in her boot. She preferred using her fillium—it was much less messy—but she'd long since learned not to be picky. "Forgive me if the word of a reaper doesn't count for much."

"How about the word of an old friend?" Reeve asked. "Does that count for anything?"

Pain swept through Viri at the reminder of what he'd once been, but she kept her features blank.

"If I wanted to hurt you," he went on, "I could have done it at any point tonight." Viri started, realizing he was right. "I told Archer you'd be safe with me, and I meant it."

Viri struggled to come up with a response, her feelings too confusing, so she focused on her memory of Soren lying unconscious back at Nox HQ and gestured tersely to the wayportal. "Let's just get this over with."

Reeve watched her for a beat, looking as if he might say more, but he stopped himself with a slight shake of his head and turned to the wayportal. Just as he was about to step through, he held his hand out to her. "Better safe than sorry."

Wayportal magic had been heavily researched by Aravell's top scholars for centuries, but so much about the magestone arches remained a mystery. They were part of daily life on Elverdine Isle, with citizens only needing to envision the location of a connected portal to be transported there instantly, along with any companions. Physical touch wasn't required—the portal remained open until a new destination was envisioned—so while Reeve had to go first since only he knew where they were heading, Viri didn't need to be holding his hand to follow. But when he saw she was about to object, he jiggled the glittery cuff on his wrist, reminding her of the agony they would suffer if they were separated more than ten paces, and she begrudgingly twined her fingers with his for the second time that night.

"Don't get used to this," she muttered.

Mirth touched his eyes. "Maybe you should take that advice for yourself."

Before she could tell him she'd rather hold hands with a corpse, he stepped into the wayportal, pulling her after him. Seconds later, they appeared out the other side of an arch Viri had never ventured through before, but the inner-mountain design revealed they were deep within the residential Mount Tembris. There was no way to tell what level they were on, but the filtered air felt thinner and drier than she was used to, so they must be close to the tapering peak. There were only a handful of doors placed along the short tunnel—more proof of how high they were, as less space meant fewer apartments—one of which Reeve halted in front of. He didn't knock before reaching for the handle, but as he moved to open it, Viri froze.

Because her hunter's mark began to burn.

"Wait!" She slapped Reeve's hand from the door, then snarled, "You swore this wasn't a trap!"

He looked at her in bewilderment. "It's not."

Viri pinned him with her fiercest glare. "Then why is there a *reaper* in there, Reeve?"

He glanced toward the interlocking circles inked onto her palm, his expression clearing with understanding. But instead of reassuring her, he only said, "Hopefully there's two. It'd be a pain in the ass if we have to track down the other one."

Before Viri could stop him, he opened the door, grabbed her hand—*again*—and dragged her through with him.

As she crossed the threshold into the apartment, Viri forgot all about the burning in her palm—not because it faded, but because agonizing pain assailed the rest of her body, like a million lightning bolts were zapping her nerve endings. If Reeve weren't still holding her hand, she would have thought they'd accidentally triggered their nullicuffs. But this pain was familiar enough that she knew exactly what had happened, even if she couldn't fathom *why*.

"An ellixen ward?" she rasped out as her body adjusted to the surge of magic she'd passed through. "What the *hell*, Reeve?"

He peered at her as if intrigued. "Most people can't feel them."

Viri breathed deeply through the last of the pain, her jaw clenched as she stated, "I'm not most people."

"Believe me, I'm well aware," Reeve said, his tone and expression unreadable. "I didn't realize you were so sensitive to magic. Interesting. Though it makes sense, given your history."

"What hist—" Viri cut herself off when her palm burned again, her hunter training overriding any curiosity she felt as her survival instincts kicked in.

Uncoiling her fillium, she balanced her weight on the balls of her feet and quickly took stock of her surroundings, noting that she stood in the living room of an apartment similar to her own, only smaller and with darker décor. The view was different, too, with large sealed windows looking straight across to Mount Mort, the jagged, imposing, northernmost peak in the Tridus Mountain range. Unlike Tembris and Verta, Mort was inaccessible to humans, sitting beyond the protection of the obelisks and covered in a near-constant cloud of blackmist, even during the day. No one in Viri's lifetime had dared venture there—or no one who had lived to tell about it.

Viri shivered at the sight of the deadly mountain, then shivered again when a flash of lightning barely penetrated the dense blackmist surrounding it, the distant storm from earlier now much closer, nearly upon them.

"Where are we? And why?" she demanded, glancing warily around the dimly lit living room, seeing no sign of the reaper her palm told her was nearby.

"You can relax," Reeve said, moving toward what looked like a small, rectangular house resting on the floor near the window. "The ellixen ward ensures we're safe here."

"From what?" Viri asked. "Or who?"

"Both," Reeve said nonsensically, before crouching down and fiddling with a metal latch near the top of the little house.

Annoyed by his lack of answers, Viri inspected the apartment again, taking in the gray walls and dark leather couch, all decidedly masculine colors. "Is this—Do you live here?"

Reeve was too distracted to reply, his attention on lifting the lid of the house and reaching in to pull something out—something that made Viri step closer to make sure her eyes weren't playing tricks on her. Sure enough, there was a small rabbit cupped in Reeve's hands, easily the most adorable thing Viri had ever seen, with fluffy, light brown fur that darkened over its nose and droopy ears.

Unable to comprehend what she was seeing, Viri asked, somewhat stupidly, "What is *that*?"

"What does it look like?" Reeve said, snuggling the little furball against his chest and patting its long, soft-looking ears.

Viri wondered if she was having a stroke.

"You can't have a pet *bunny*," she spluttered. "Bunnies are cute and sweet and—and—*floppy*, and you're evil incarnate. This goes against the laws of nature."

"Firstly, thank you for implying I'm not floppy. I'm flattered you noticed." He winked, causing Viri's cheeks to warm even as she scowled in response. "Secondly, 'evil incarnate' is a step up from 'asshole,' so I'll take it. And thirdly, Walnut isn't mine. He just likes me more than most."

Viri was certain her brain was exploding. "You named him *Walnut*?"

"No, *I* named him Walnut, because he's mine," came a new voice, causing Viri to whirl around in time to see a boy her age appear from the hallway. He had an innocent look about him, his blond hair a mess of curls, his blue eyes guileless behind rectangular glasses, his smile bright and seemingly genuine. He even wore a checkered sweater-vest, something Viri had never seen on anyone under the age of fifty.

By all accounts, he seemed harmless, but appearances were deceiving. Viri didn't need to feel the now-searing heat in her palm to know that a reaper had just entered the room—she could see it in the darkened veins crawling all the way up his forearms, offering undeniable proof of what he was.

Bracing her feet and gripping her fillium tighter, Viri was ready to meet the reaper's attack. But he barely glanced at her, instead striding straight for Reeve and carefully taking the rabbit from his hands.

"And just to add," the boy continued, stroking Walnut gently before placing him in the front pocket of his vest, where the bunny quickly shifted to poke his little head out, watching them curiously, "he only likes you most because you feed him all the carrots. Or maybe it's because of how you smell, like apples and sandalwood—his two favorite things."

"I doubt that's how he smells right now," came another voice, female this time, as a second reaper appeared from the hallway, waving a hand in front of her nose. She was striking, with short purple hair and sharp hazel eyes, and wore beige fighting leathers that showed enough skin to make it impossible to miss the blackened veins spidering along her flesh. "Have you been wearing the same clothes for a week, Reeve? Gross."

"I had a washbasin." He crossed his arms. "I'll have you know that my personal hygiene is exemplary."

"Exemplary or not," the purple-haired girl said, "a week without a fresh change of clothes is ick by anyone's standards. Were they trying to torture you?"

"They offered me another outfit." Reeve paused. "It clashed with my hair."

The girl smirked. "By that I assume you mean it wasn't your preferred color."

Brushing invisible dirt from his shoulder, Reeve said, "I look best in black. Some people say it matches my soul."

"You're a reaper," Viri said without thinking. "You don't have a soul."

All eyes turned to her, and she suddenly remembered she was the only person in the room who *wasn't* a reaper. Her grip on her fillium tightened even more, but none of the killers seemed the least bit bothered by the sight of a scarlet-cloaked hunter standing in their midst.

"I suppose introductions are in order," Reeve said, waving a lazy hand between them. "Sage D'alia, Jonas Flynn, this is Viridia Solace. Careful, she bites. And not in a good way."

The girl—Sage—snorted, but the boy—Jonas—sent Viri a cheerful smile, adding a goofy wave for good measure.

"I've heard so much about you, Viri," Jonas said, straightening his glasses. His gaze homed in on the weapon she held and lit with pleasure. "Ahh! The legendary fillium! Can I touch it? Please?"

Viri blinked. "What?"

Before she could stop him, Jonas moved close enough to press a finger to the golden cord, his face instantly paling as a shudder rippled through him. He quickly jumped backward, shaking his hand. "Oh, yes, that's awful. Zero out of ten, would not recommend." He shuddered again, but if anything, his smile only widened. "How amazing is magic?"

Viri stared at him, lost for words.

"You'll have to forgive Jonas," Reeve said, amusement clear in his voice—along with affection. "He has a scholar's heart, particularly when it comes to anything to do with the ancient mages and their use of ellixen."

"If not for, you know, *this*"—Jonas indicated his blackened veins—"I'd spend every waking hour studying at the university. But with hunters popping in and out on a whim, it'd be too hard to avoid their notice. That, and the Scholars' Guild has pretty firm rules about who they let enroll."

Viri continued to stare at him. "You don't say."

"No, really, I've tried," Jonas said, missing her sarcasm. "I even wrote a strongly worded letter to Chancellor Reginald, bringing to light the rampant discrimination and emphasizing the need for diversity among students and peers. I never heard back." He sighed wistfully. "Bigots."

"It's their loss," Sage said, nudging Jonas. "And our gain. What would we do without you and your books and your cleverness helping us to—"

Reeve cleared his throat, and Sage immediately stopped speaking.

"Helping you what?" Viri probed.

Sage ignored her, turning instead to look at Reeve with accusation in her eyes. "What's she doing here, anyway? I assume there's a good reason you brought a hunter to Jonas's apartment?"

"Viri's not a hunter right now," Reeve said.

"Um, yes, I am," Viri corrected, frowning. "I'm always a hunter."

Jonas was unperturbed, but Sage tensed and shifted her weight, prompting Viri to do the same, her heartbeat quickening as she prepared for an imminent attack.

Reeve stepped smoothly between them. "Easy, we're all friends here." He placed a calming hand on Sage's shoulder. "Let me rephrase: Viri's a hunter, but she's not hunting right now."

"I should be." Viri's frown deepened. "And we're absolutely not friends. If I wasn't at risk of being thrown in a cell beside you, I'd drag you all straight to the Underlock."

"Congratulations, Reeve," Sage deadpanned. "She's a real catch."

Eyes narrowing, Viri said, "He didn't catch me. He was the fool who got himself caught."

A snort left Sage. "Funny. I could have sworn—"

"Sage," Reeve said in a low tone, but before he could continue, three loud knocks sounded on the front door, and it swung open just far enough for an attractive young man to poke his head through. His physique was similar to Reeve's—broad and tall and radiating confidence—but his skin and eyes were both brown, his hair dark, shoulder-length, and unbound with a wave to it, and there was a wicked scar slashing through one eyebrow that somehow only added to his overall appeal. Or it would have, if he weren't another Elders-damned reaper, his blackened veins crawling up his arms and disappearing beneath his cloak.

"Hey, Ardin," Jonas greeted him with a friendly smile. "We weren't expecting—"

"We've got a transfer," Ardin interrupted, not moving from his position at the door.

"When?" Reeve asked, transforming before Viri's eyes. Gone was the smirking amusement and nonchalance he'd maintained for most of the night, replaced by squared shoulders and a serious expression that made him seem much older than his eighteen years.

"Any minute," Ardin answered. "The news reached me late—we need to move."

Sage leapt into action, sprinting down the hall at reaper speed, with Jonas at her heels.

"What's going on?" Viri demanded, moving closer to Reeve. "What's a transfer?"

He cursed and ran a hand through his midnight hair, a flash of lightning outside highlighting the frustration on his face. "Of all the rotten timing."

The words had barely left him before Sage returned, her arms full of weapons.

Viri tensed, about to cast her fillium, but the purple-haired girl strode straight past her, directly to Reeve.

"Here," she said, shoving half of her collection into his arms, then securing the rest to her body.

Reeve did the same, sheathing numerous daggers in his belt and finishing by strapping a gleaming black sword to his back.

Seeing so many blades in the hands of reapers, it took everything in Viri to resist lunging forward to disarm them.

"The storm is getting close out there," Jonas said as he reappeared, carrying two hooded black cloaks, which he handed to Reeve and Sage. "Be careful. It looks like a nasty one."

"A storm is the least of our worries," Reeve said, throwing the cloak on over his clothes.

"Reeve." Viri grabbed his shoulder. "Talk to me. What's happening?"

"Deal with your hunter pet, Reeve," Sage said, her hazel eyes hard as she looked at Viri. "We don't have time to waste."

Patience gone, Viri took a menacing step toward the purple-haired girl, ready to bring her down, but Reeve's arm circled her waist like a steel band and he dragged her backward toward the dark leather couch.

"Let me go!" Viri ordered, and he instantly did so. She spun around, intending to lay into him for manhandling her, but he spoke first.

"I'm sorry about this," Reeve said. "Jonas will watch over you while we're gone, and I'll explain everything once we're back, but for now, just know this is for the best."

Viri was about to spit fire, but her rage turned to incredulity when Reeve reached for his nullicuff, and with a tap of his finger, the magic-nullifying bracelet *dissolved*.

A stunned inhalation was all Viri managed before Reeve shot forward like lightning, his hand coming to the side of her neck, just beneath her ear. There was no force behind his attack, his fingers gentle against her skin, but despite that, a wave of ellixen slammed into her, a thousand times more potent than anything she'd ever experienced.

"What—" Viri gasped, but she couldn't utter more than that, her world suddenly spinning, her knees buckling, her vision darkening at the edges.

"Shh," Reeve said, catching her as she fell and carefully lowering her onto the couch. "You're safe. Don't fight it."

Viri wanted to scream at him, to claw at him, to know what the hell he'd done to her—and *how*—but her surroundings were quickly fading, Reeve's apologetic face blurring above her as she lost her battle to unconsciousness.

Just before her eyelids fluttered shut, she saw something else—something impossible.

She saw Jonas hold his hand out to Sage and offer, "Take as much as you need."

And then she saw Sage siphoning from her reaper friend, the transfer of power making Viri's hunter's mark sear.

That pain was the last thing she felt before everything went black.

THE JOURNAL OF
CELESTIAL MAGE KADMUS CASTRO

Fourth Sun, Seventh Cycle, Twelfth Age

Another group of mages arrived this week.

I sincerely hope they're the last newcomers we'll see for some time, though I know that's wishful thinking, especially with the Hallow Stream still undiscovered and our magic remaining volatile enough to pique the interest of more and more mages willing to risk the journey for the sake of their studies. It's not my field of expertise, but even I continue to be intrigued by the way ellixen works here. One day, it'll be quiet, pensive, submissive, and the next—chaos.

I overheard one of the nature mages, Saskia Cilla, offering a theory. She proposed that, while it's widely known that the three Hallow Streams generate and release magic into our world—into the air, into the earth, into every space and creature in between—here on Elverdine Isle, the lack of warding around the Stream means there's a polarity about the way it flows. She used a gravity metaphor, saying it's like dropping a stone and expecting it to fall swiftly downward, but instead, the raw, unwarded magic acts like a magnetizing force that causes the stone to fly in numerous different, unpredictable directions.

As mages, most of us draw from our own inner stores of ellixen to perform magical acts, so if Saskia's theory is correct, then the moment we summon it for a task, it immediately meets and clashes with the Stream's erratic, polarizing power. Our stones aren't falling, they're flying—and we have no control over where they go.

I think her idea holds merit, but I also believe it goes beyond that, to the amount of raw power the Hallow Stream emits. Without any natural wards, there's no limit to how much magic it releases across the isle.

Polarized or not, it's becoming harder to ignore just how potent it is—and how *good* it feels—especially when it's in a cooperative mood.

Unfortunately, it remains too fickle to rely upon. While frustrating, I can't help finding it amusing sometimes, like when I'm conjuring water for my morning cup of tea and I end up soaked from head to toe. It's almost as if the magic is mischievous. But then it will take a turn toward spite, and entire buildings will implode.

Literally.

That happened yesterday, right in the heart of the swiftly expanding town. Mercifully, there were no casualties, but still . . . it seems inevitable that something disastrous will eventually occur, with so many mages now here and so much magic being used—particularly by the fabricator mages performing their architectural augmentations. Thanks to them, the once-quaint settlement of Aravell is becoming more like a city every day. They've even begun to carve out space beneath the lake and inside the mountains, their innovative vision for citywide expansion as awe-inspiring as ever.

Magistratus Garrin and most of Elverdine's shallows continue to be grateful for our presence here and the advancements we're providing, but while I know we are improving their lives, a small part of me hopes the population never grows enough to need all the space the fabricator mages are creating. This isle has been left alone for so long that its beauty has remained largely untouched. It's a haven. A sanctuary.

And maybe we're at risk of ruining that.

It's only going to get worse now that a meddlesome alchemist mage has arrived. Tephryn Alemedes. She graduated from ICOMA a few years behind me, and though we've never met, everyone knows that only the most elite mages are invited to study at the Imperia College of Magical Arts. I'm already dreading what her plans are for her time here and the experiments she intends to attempt.

May the Elders help us all.

12

A sharp *crack* of thunder startled Viri awake, and she sat up with a jolt, feeling foggy and disoriented until the events of the night came crashing back to her.

Leaping to her feet, she spun once, twice, searching Jonas's living room for any sign of a threat, but it seemed she was alone. A glance out the window showed the storm now raging outside, with rain lashing the glass and lightning streaking every other second—good news, she told herself, since it meant she hadn't been unconscious long.

Unwilling to wait around and hope Reeve would return and explain all the things he owed her answers to—including how he'd used actual *magic*—Viri sprinted toward the door. She had no clue where he might be, but he couldn't have had much of a head start, and her hunter skills would have to be enough to find him.

Or maybe not just her skills, because the warmth in Viri's hand told her she *wasn't* as alone as she'd thought. Instead of running straight out the front door, she forced her steps to slow and turned to walk softly down the hall, deeper into the apartment. Her ever-warming mark led her to an open door, which she carefully, quietly, peeked around.

Inside was an office, or perhaps a small library, judging by the number of books lining the walls and cascading to the floor in haphazard piles. There was no desk, just a coffee table and a set of plush green armchairs facing the window, one of which showed the back of Jonas's curly head as he sat there, hunched over a book.

Cautious of his heightened reaper senses, Viri inched forward on silent feet, barely breathing, the only sounds being his page turns and the rumbling thunder outside. He was oblivious to her presence, something that changed only when she slipped her fillium around his neck from behind.

"Don't move," she ordered, though it was unnecessary, given that her weapon would keep him from retaliating—or even standing.

"Yep, definitely unpleasant," he said, grunting at the feeling of his magic being drained. "But still fascinating."

Viri shifted around the armchair to face him, making sure her golden cord remained touching him—not just to keep him incapacitated, but to ensure he told the truth. She didn't expect to find Walnut dozing on his lap, but she also didn't let the fluffy bunny distract her as she demanded, "Where's Reeve?"

Jonas closed his book, his blue eyes wide with curiosity behind his glasses. "How did you wake up so fast? He hit you with enough ellixen to keep you down for hours."

As determined as she was to find Reeve, Viri couldn't resist asking, "What *was* that?"

Jonas shook his head, his shifty look making it clear it wasn't because he didn't know, but because he didn't want to answer. "It's best if you ask him."

"Then where is he?" Viri asked again, impatience threading her tone.

"He's—" Jonas groaned in response to whatever he'd been about to say, the fillium preventing him from lying. Despite his discomfort, his eyes lit with glee at the new experience, and he touched a finger to the golden cord. "So it *does* make you tell the truth. I'd heard rumors, but still . . . remarkable. I'd give anything to study how it works. Would you mind if I—"

"Jonas," Viri barked. "Answer the question."

"I can't tell you." He made a helpless gesture with his hands, careful not to disturb Walnut. "If I do, you'll go after him. And that's a very bad idea."

"Why?"

"Because then you'll see—" Jonas clamped his mouth shut.

Viri leaned in. "See what? What's Reeve doing? What's this 'transfer' thing your friend Ardin mentioned?"

Jonas looked alarmed. "It's noth—" He broke off with a pained gasp as the fillium stopped another lie, then repeated, through panting breaths, "I can't tell you." Quickly, he added, "I promise it's for the best."

"Those were Reeve's exact words before he attacked me," Viri said bitterly. "Forgive me if I don't believe you."

"He didn't *attack* you." Jonas's eyes rounded with disbelief. "What he did was to *protect* you."

Viri scoffed. "I don't need protection, but if I did, it would be from *him*."

A startled but genuine laugh left Jonas. "Reeve's the last person who would ever—"

"I'm not arguing about this," Viri cut him off, unwilling to hear a reaper defend another reaper. "Tell me where he is, or I'll find him on my own."

"I'm sorry," Jonas said, his face—and the fillium—revealing he meant it. "I can't help you. But you can sit with me and watch the storm while we wait for him to come back. You can even hold Walnut if you want." He lifted the dozing bunny toward her. "He's soft and very cuddly."

Viri made a frustrated sound and began to back away, intending to follow through on her threat to hunt Reeve down herself. But just before she released Jonas from her fillium, she caught sight of the veins along his forearms, the darkness more faded than earlier, almost unnoticeable. Out of nowhere, she recalled the hazy image she'd seen before passing out, something that must have been a hallucination, because it shouldn't have been possible. And yet, even knowing that, she couldn't stop herself from asking, "Did Sage siphon from you?"

Jonas stilled. "What would you say if I told you yes?"

Viri answered instantly, "I'd tell you reapers can't siphon from each other. If you could, then you wouldn't murder innocent children to get your ellixen fix."

He flinched—actually *flinched*—at the mention of children, causing Viri's brows to shoot upward. A reaper with a conscience? Unlikely.

"There's lots you don't know about us," he said. "But the short answer is yes, Sage did siphon from me. It's not a common practice; there's a cost involved for the giver"—he gestured to his faded veins, proof that his magic had weakened—"and the ellixen transferred through to the receiver isn't as strong as what would come from—from—"

"From a child," Viri said flatly.

Jonas flinched again, but also nodded. "Because of that, most reapers won't even consider it unless they have no other choice. They'd rather steal straight from the source."

Viri could hardly believe what she was hearing: that reapers were able to *choose* how they stole ellixen and yet they *still* preyed on children. She hadn't thought it was possible to feel more disgust toward them, but apparently she'd been wrong. "So tonight, Sage needed a magic boost for whatever she and Reeve are off doing, and since there were no kids here for her to murder, she stole your ellixen instead?"

For the first time since she'd met him, Jonas looked almost angry. "It's not like that. *We're* not like that."

"No?" Viri challenged. "You've never killed someone?"

He dropped his gaze to stare at Walnut, his silence telling.

"Did Reeve siphon from you, too?" Viri asked, needing to know what she'd be facing when she found him, how strong he might be if he had a fresh dose of ellixen in his veins.

"Of course not," Jonas said, as if her question were ridiculous.

Another thought hit her, and she gasped, "Did he siphon from *me*?"

She realized the moment the words left her lips that he couldn't have. She didn't have enough ellixen to tempt a reaper, and if any of them were ever desperate enough to try, the limited amount she had would be sucked dry in seconds, her life along with it. She'd seen it happen before.

To her parents.

"You have an incredibly poor opinion of the person who once saved your life," Jonas muttered, yanking Viri from her memories and prompting a disbelieving laugh from her.

"Reeve never saved my life. If he said otherwise, he lied. That's what he does."

Jonas just shrugged, but Viri had wasted enough time with this conversation, and she wasn't going to sit around and listen to one of Reeve's reaper buddies singing his praises. She could admit that Jonas was the most amiable monster she'd ever encountered—almost unnaturally so, given what he was—but that wasn't saying much considering all the others had tried to kill her. The verdict was still out on whether Reeve and Sage planned to do the same.

"Last chance to tell me where he is," Viri said.

"You're making a mistake by going after him," Jonas returned, looking at her pleadingly. "Trust me."

Viri released him from her fillium and strode for the door, confident he was too drained to get up and follow. "I don't trust reapers," she said without looking back. "And if I did, I wouldn't start with a friend of Reeve's."

With that, she took off down the hallway and out the front door. She didn't feel the ellixen ward this time—it must only affect people entering the apartment, not leaving it—but even if she had, she wouldn't have stopped, her focus single-minded on finding Reeve. He could be anywhere, but as she sprinted along the inner-mountain tunnel, she was counting on the late hour to mean the other inhabitants of this level would be sleeping—and therefore Sage, Reeve, and Ardin would have been the last people to use the wayportal. Viri would be delivered straight to wherever they had traveled, and from there, her hunter's mark should be able to guide the way. If not . . .

She didn't let herself finish the thought as she reached the wayportal and leapt through, praying to the Elders that it would take her exactly where she needed to go.

She should have prayed harder—or at least added some specifics, like *not* arriving outside in the middle of the raging thunderstorm.

Rain and wind instantly pummeled Viri, causing her to gasp as cold water soaked through her scarlet cloak and into her leathers. That was the least of her concerns, though, given where she'd landed. A quick scan showed the wayportal had delivered her close to the Northern Obelisk, right by the bank of River Mort, the winding tributary that flowed from Lake Mirtis to Mount Mort before disappearing into the blackmist-covered mountain.

Viri rarely ventured this close to the northern edge of the uppercity, and never at night, the mist far too near for comfort. With the added wind from the storm, the danger was perilously high. But before she could convince herself to leap back through the wayportal, she felt it—the warmth in her hand, telling her there was a reaper nearby. Or reapers.

Reeve, Sage, and Ardin.

Ignoring the threat of the mist and the violence of the storm, Viri focused on her mark, following it west, away from the mountain and along the riverside path toward Elders' Grove. She shuddered at the thought of entering the small woodland, where the creepy, ancient trees cast shadows that moved as if alive. But to her relief, her mark led her away from the river just before it reached the grove, sending her along well-lit streets filled with lavish houses owned by those who preferred to live on the surface rather than beneath it, all carefully sealed during the unsafe night hours. She barely spared the homes a glance, concentrating only on her heated mark as she left the affluent part of the uppercity behind and headed into the dark, narrow alleyways of the slums.

The wind was fiercer here, the rain coming down hard enough to make visibility difficult, coupled with the flashing lightning that distorted Viri's vision and the repeated thunder booms that left her ears ringing. But still, she pressed on, hurrying past crumbling, abandoned buildings, her palm becoming so hot that she knew she had to be close.

Turning a corner into an even narrower lane, Viri saw shadowy movement up ahead and swiftly ducked down behind a pile of rickety wooden crates. She swiped water from her face and pulled her hood up to shield her eyes, but the wind kept tearing it back, leaving her to squint through the rain as she peered out to see what Reeve and his friends were doing so far from anywhere.

Only, it wasn't Reeve she saw.

Her mark hadn't led her astray—there *were* reapers in the alley, over half a dozen of them, which was more than Viri had ever seen in one place. Reapers rarely worked together—they didn't need to, their strength and speed making it easy for them to abduct and kill their targets without assistance. Plus no two reapers would ever share the ellixen they stole, not when they could take it all for themselves. Before tonight, Viri had never encountered more than one in any single location, with the combination of Reeve, Jonas, and Sage—and then Ardin—having been an anomaly. But seeing *seven* together in this alley . . . Viri's stomach tightened with dread at what they might be doing.

And then she saw it—something that stole her breath and made her heart slam against her rib cage. Because the reapers weren't the only ones in the alley.

There were also children.

Viri slapped her hand over her mouth to stifle her gasp as she did a quick head count, finding twelve in total, bound together by ropes and standing in three lines of four, their clothes and hair soaked from the rain, their little bodies shaking with fear.

The group was small enough that Viri doubted they were the kids who had been abducted in the last six months—or not all of them—but she'd still never seen anything like this in all her years of hunting. The reapers weren't siphoning from their captives, nor did they seem poised to do so. If anything, it looked like they were *moving* the children, with three of the dark-cloaked killers holding the ropes and ruthlessly tugging them forward.

Viri suddenly recalled what Ardin had said upon arriving at Jonas's apartment—*"We've got a transfer"*—and her blood turned cold as she realized he'd been referring to whatever she was witnessing right now. *This* was what Reeve and Sage had come to help with—they were out there in the alley, moving these children to Elders-knew-where.

Bile rose in Viri's throat as she watched a young boy slip on the wet ground and fall to his knees, accidentally pulling the three others in his line down as well. A reaper was at their sides in seconds, hauling them up and snarling into their faces, a monster from their nightmares come to life. Their terror was so tangible that Viri swore she could feel it from her hiding spot halfway down the alley. She wanted to leap to their rescue, but no hunter could take on seven reapers at once, especially with the fillium-immune—and magic-wielding—Reeve among them.

No, Viri's only option was to stay hidden and follow where they went. Once she had their location, she would return to the Hunters' Guild, admit to the colossal mistake she'd made in freeing Reeve, and beg Meera and Darik to send out a team of hunters and Nox to bring the reapers down. Until then—

Viri's mental planning screeched to a halt when two new figures appeared from the shadows, their blades glinting beneath the lightning. Immediately, the four reapers not holding ropes shouted at their three companions—words Viri couldn't hear over the rain and thunder but instinctively knew were orders to flee with the kids—and then they rushed forward to meet the two attackers.

Taking in the dark clothes of the newcomers, Viri wondered if they were city guards, but she couldn't make out Nox uniforms through the pouring rain, just hooded black cloaks. As with the children and the reapers, the stormy gloom made it impossible to see any identifying features, but whoever they were, they were fools if they thought they could defeat seven monsters alone. But then another figure joined them, bringing their number to three against seven, the odds more favorable, though still sorely lacking.

The danger was high, but Viri couldn't ignore the opportunity before her. She shoved down her trepidation and sprinted out from her hiding place, fillium in one hand, dagger in the other, her boots splashing through puddles as she raced toward the skirmish.

An earsplitting crack of thunder sounded as she neared the fighting group, the cries of the resisting children audible now, blending with the clash of steel as the newcomers fought their ellixen-heightened opponents. Impossibly, they weren't struggling to hold their own against the strength and speed of the reapers, but were instead meeting them strike for strike, their movements so fast they were like blurs.

The next flash of lightning gave Viri a better look at the newcomers, revealing *why* they weren't struggling—and causing her to stumble to a shocked halt in the middle of the alley.

Because they were reapers, too.

And not just any reapers. With their hoods blown back by the wind, it was all too easy to recognize Reeve, Sage, and Ardin.

They weren't abducting the children—they were fighting *against* the abductors.

Viri had no time to make sense of what she was seeing, not when one of the reapers who had been tugging at a line of kids released his rope and charged her way. She acted on instinct, ducking as his fist flew at her face, then leaping backward when he slashed a dagger toward her abdomen. She didn't have any of Wynter's impedidust on her, nor any other handy alchemical experiments, just her weapons and her wits—but that was enough. Because when the reaper came at her again, instead of avoiding his attack, she rushed forward and pivoted at the last second, hissing when his dagger sliced through her cloak and grazed her forearm—a calculated sacrifice that allowed her to grab his arm and yank him off-balance. The slick, wet ground did the rest, his slipping feet giving her an opening to slap her fillium around his wrist, instantly incapacitating him. With a swift kick to his torso, she sent him crumpling to the side of the alley, a moan leaving him as he tried—and failed—to rise again.

Confident he was down for good as long as her golden cord was touching him, Viri whirled to meet her next opponent, frustratingly aware that she had only one fillium, and there were still six reapers left. No—five, she amended, watching as Reeve finished one off and spun in time to meet two others, rain cascading off his sculpted form. For a moment, she could only stare as he battled in the storm, his sword slashing in one hand and dagger slicing in the other, his midnight hair plastered to his head, his eyes flashing like the lightning overhead. He was death incarnate, parrying and striking against his two opponents at an impossible speed, relentless in his assault. Viri had never seen anything so beautiful, so mesmerizing . . . so deadly.

With effort, she tore her gaze away, remembering where she was and the threat that remained. Sage was holding her own against a reaper, as was Ardin, but that still left one more, a woman who had been trying to single-handedly haul all twelve children away but had now abandoned them and was lunging for Viri, her dagger raised.

The woman's speed was alarming—as was the strength of her attack when Viri stopped the blade with her own, every bone in her body jarred by the impact. She forced the weapon back with all her might, gaining just enough space to unsheathe her second dagger and stab it forward, straight after her first. But the reaper merely twisted at the waist before slashing with her own blade again, causing Viri to jump to the side to avoid being gutted.

"Not so powerful without your shiny little cord, are you?" the reaper sneered, her eyes dark with malice. "Let's see how long you last without it."

And then she lunged again—or tried to. But before she could make it one step, she gasped and stumbled, looking down incredulously at the black blade piercing her chest from behind.

Reapers could heal fast, especially when they were full of elixen, but all the stolen magic in the world couldn't save them from a death blow. There was nothing this woman could do against the sword spearing her heart, and the light quickly faded from her eyes as she crumpled to the ground—revealing the furious form of Reeve standing in her place, his weapon dripping blood, his thunderous gaze pinned on Viri.

"What the *hell* are you doing here?" he demanded over the torrential rain, stomping forward. It was only then that she realized the sounds of crashing steel had faded, with all seven reapers down for the count.

"Me?" she cried, panting hard and swiping wet hair out of her eyes. It was almost cathartic, having to shout to be heard. "What are *you* doing here? Why are you fighting your own kind?"

"You're meant to be unconscious!" he returned angrily. "And I told you I'd explain everything when I got back!"

Viri's knuckles tightened around her daggers, her anger easily as strong as his. "Because you've done *such* a great job of explaining things so far! Did you really think I'd just twiddle my thumbs with your babysitter until you returned?"

His gaze slitted. "If you'd just *waited*—"

"REEVE!" Sage screamed over the rain, her voice full of warning.

But his widening eyes revealed he'd already seen what she had, and he was instantly in motion, leaping toward Viri as eight new reapers appeared out of the shadows, one of whom flung an eerie red dagger with impossible speed—

Straight at Viri's heart.

13

Reeve tackled Viri just in time, knocking her to the ground and landing on top of her with bruising force. His weight pushed all the air from her lungs, but it was his pained groan that kept her from shoving him away and instead made her freeze beneath him.

"Reeve?" she wheezed out, then gasped when she caught sight of the red dagger embedded in his side—the dagger that had been meant for *her*. "You're hurt!"

"Get your ass up or we'll both be dead," he grunted, rising to his feet and yanking the blade from his body with a sickening *squelch*.

Viri's stomach roiled at the sound, then roiled again when she saw the amount of blood gushing from his wound. But the renewed clashing of steel told her Reeve hadn't been exaggerating—Sage and Ardin were holding back the reapers, but there were too many for them to handle alone. Reeve was already rushing forward to help, and Viri didn't delay in leaping up after him, automatically moving into position at his back. They were immediately targeted by four of the reapers, their blades slashing hard and fast, while three others continued their assault on Sage and Ardin. Where the eighth was, Viri couldn't see, the chaos of the fight and the violence of the storm making it impossible for her to focus on anything other than trying to stay alive.

"Duck!" Reeve bellowed, and she instantly dropped, feeling the *whoosh* of his sword overhead as he spun in a circle, slicing straight through the middle of one of the reapers.

"Look out!" Viri shouted, and jumped back up to block a different reaper whose blade was on a trajectory for Reeve's neck. She staggered against his strength, but it didn't stop her from bringing her knee up to strike him in the groin, and when he doubled over, she sent her dagger straight into his chest.

"On your left!" Reeve yelled, but Viri was already being tackled to the ground for the second time that night, this time by a woman who snapped her teeth like a feral beast and clawed at Viri's face with long fingernails.

Viri hissed as her cheek tore open, the rain adding to the sting, but she ignored the pain and bucked violently until the woman lost her grip and slipped off to the side. Shifting quickly, Viri only just managed to get one of her daggers up between them before the reaper was upon her again, not seeing the weapon until it was too late.

A gargled sound left the woman's lips as she impaled herself on the blade, leaving Viri to crawl out from under her dying body while swallowing the urge to be sick. She was no stranger to death—she'd killed before while hunting, but when possible, she always tried to bring reapers in alive. Tonight, she'd already taken two lives . . . and those were just two of the many bodies surrounding her, lying in puddles of blood.

As much as Viri longed for a moment to catch her breath and

center herself after what had just happened, the fight wasn't over yet, so she forced herself back to her feet, tugged her final dagger from her boot to replace the one trapped beneath the woman, and reentered the fray.

The storm raged on above them, as merciless as the reapers, but Viri, Reeve, Sage, and Ardin were just as fierce, battling side by side and back-to-back as if they'd been fighting together for years. They began to take ground, the monsters falling one by one, until, finally, only the four of them remained standing, panting hard over the slain bodies and covered in so much blood and mud that not even the rain could wash it all away.

As if the weather knew that their skirmish had ended, the violence of the storm began to ease, the wind quieting, the torrent slowing to a drizzle, the thunder and lightning fading into the distance.

"Typical," Sage said, scowling up at the sky, her beige leathers stained with enough filth to make her look like a walking corpse.

"Everyone good?" Reeve asked, his silver eyes scanning each of them, lingering on Viri's clawed cheek and the rip in her cloak where her arm had been grazed by the first reaper's dagger.

"'Good' is relative," Sage answered, prodding a swelling bump on her head, her purple hair almost black from the rain. "But I'm alive."

"Me too," said Ardin, his dark gaze alert as he peered into the shadows of the alley, making sure there were no more reapers lying in wait. "I think we're clear."

"Viri?" Reeve pressed. "You good?"

She nodded her lie. Physically, her wounds were superficial. But mentally, she was reeling—not just from the fight, but from whom she had fought *with*. She had so many questions that she didn't know where to begin, but before she could figure it out, a soft sniffling noise had her whipping around and remembering the reason for the reapers being in the alley in the first place.

The children.

Ardin stood closest to where they were huddled beneath the half-collapsed awning of a derelict building, and he slowly approached them, his hands raised in a calming gesture. "You're safe now," he told them. "Don't be afraid—we're here to help."

A few of the children started sobbing—whether from relief or as a delayed reaction to the trauma of what they'd witnessed, Viri wasn't sure. But as much as her heart went out to them, there was something she needed to know with urgency, so she moved cautiously their way. She was aware of how terrifying she looked, covered in muck with blood dripping from her scratched face, but she pasted a comforting smile on her lips as Ardin began sawing through their bonds and asked, "Does anyone remember where you came from tonight? Were there any other kids with you there?"

Headshakes met her question, but a young boy around Jessalyn's age spoke up and said, his voice wobbling, "It was just us, but they said they were taking us to be with others."

Viri cursed inwardly, but outwardly she kept the smile on her face. "Did you hear them say anything else?"

A girl around the same age whispered, "They called us spares. I—I don't know what they meant."

This time, Viri's inward curse was much more profane. The Reaper Priest was apparently covering his bases, making sure he had more than enough children to guarantee the fifty he needed for the sacrifice.

"All right," Viri said gently, "thank you for—" She stilled as Ardin cut through the last of the ropes, her face draining of color as she realized there were only two lines of children, not three. Eight kids in total.

There should have been twelve.

Whirling around, she caught Reeve's eyes, seeing the moment he noticed it as well.

"The eighth reaper," she gasped out, recalling the one she'd lost track of in the fight. "They got away." And they'd taken four of the children with them.

Reeve swore, then swore again, swiping an aggrieved hand over his face and swaying on his feet.

It was the sway that broke through Viri's horror, but she didn't have a chance to question it before a furious voice hissed, "This is all *your* fault!"

Viri spun at Sage's words, finding the purple-haired reaper glaring daggers at her.

"*My* fault?" Viri repeated, incredulous. "What did I—"

"You're not meant to be here," Sage said, closing the distance between them and jabbing a finger at Viri's face.

Indignation rose within Viri like fire blazing in her chest. "What are you talking about? I *helped* you!"

"You only got in the way!" Sage spat. "If Reeve hadn't wasted time saving your ass, we would have taken down that second group before any of them could slip away." She jabbed her finger again. "*You're* the reason we lost those kids!"

Viri rocked backward at the accusation, part of her wanting to scream her defense and the other part whispering that maybe Sage was right. But before she could decide between rage or remorse, Reeve moved forward to break them apart—only to stumble and fall down on one knee. A groan left him as he curled over himself, pressing a hand to his side.

His *heavily bleeding* side.

"Reeve!" Sage cried, rushing toward him, with Viri right on her heels.

His dagger wound—Viri had forgotten all about it, especially since he'd fought so effortlessly that it was as if he'd never even been injured. She'd assumed his enhanced reaper healing must have helped him, but now . . .

Now she wasn't so sure.

"I'm fine," he grunted, trying to rise again, but unable to support his own weight.

"Let me see." Sage shoved his hand away, then sucked in a sharp breath at what she found. *"Elders!"*

Viri leaned in to look and nearly retched. It wasn't just the depth of the wound that was alarming, it was also the skin around it, which had turned an unnatural green color beneath the still-gushing blood.

"Why does it look like that?" she breathed, worried she already knew the answer.

Poison.

Sage didn't confirm her fears, only ordered, "Grab his other arm." To Reeve, she said, "We need to get you to Jonas. Right now."

"The kids—" Reeve gritted out.

"I'll see them all safely back to their homes," Ardin said, having appeared at their sides without Viri noticing.

She was about to protest—the thought of leaving the children in the care of a reaper went against everything she believed in—but when Reeve groaned again, the sound flooded her with guilt. He'd taken that dagger for *her*. She owed him her help, even if that meant trusting someone whose very nature was untrustworthy. Ardin had risked his life that night to save the kids—as had Reeve and Sage, to Viri's unending confusion—so she had to hope his protective act meant he wouldn't turn around and hurt them now.

"Swear to me that they'll be safe with you," Viri said, her voice low to keep the children from hearing. With the storm gone, the alley was nearly silent, the only sounds being the drip of rainwater and the quiet sniffing of the kids.

"Any oath I offer will mean little since you don't know me," Ardin said, his dark eyes steady on hers. "But on my life, I swear no harm will come to them while they're in my care."

Viri's gaze dropped to the veins along his hands. He didn't try to cover them, didn't hide what he was, didn't *deny* what he was, and that more than anything gave her a strange kind of reassurance.

"We need to move," Sage told Viri. "Help me get him up."

"One second," Viri said, sprinting over to the reaper still incapacitated by her fillium to ask where he and the others had been taking the kids. But when she reached him, he wasn't half conscious and spitting curses, as she'd expected.

Instead, he was dead.

Viri blanched at the sight of his slashed throat, then tensed as Ardin stepped up beside her.

"The reaper who got away must have done this," he observed grimly, nudging the body with his boot. "They couldn't free him from your weapon, not without suffering the same effects, so they silenced him to keep him from being interrogated by it."

Ruthless but effective, Viri thought, disgusted anew by the merciless nature of reapers.

"We're not all like that," Ardin said quietly, reading the revulsion on her face.

Viri didn't bother responding, just reclaimed her fillium and hurried back to where Sage was holding Reeve upright, his head drooping and his face so pale it was nearly gray. She hesitated only a beat before slinging his free arm around her shoulders, buckling slightly as she took half his weight.

"I've got him," Viri said. "Let's go."

14

The trek back to the wayportal was long and laborious, with Reeve nearly a dead weight by the time they stepped through the magestone arch and made it to Jonas's apartment.

As they burst through the front door, Viri's discomfort from the ellixen ward was second to her aching neck and shoulders, with relief coming only when they lowered Reeve onto the couch she'd passed out on earlier that night.

"Hey, guys," Jonas said, appearing from the hallway with a smile on his face and Walnut peeking out from his vest pocket. "Did you save the—"

He halted abruptly at the sight of their soaked, filthy forms, his smile faltering and nose scrunching at the water dripping onto his carpet. But then his gaze traveled to the pallid, bloodied Reeve, and his blue eyes widened in alarm.

"What happened?" he asked, hurrying over.

"Grimblade," Reeve forced out, sounding like the effort cost him. "I don't know what kind."

Viri sucked in a shocked breath. Grimblades were extremely rare weapons used by the ancient mages, each infused with a specific kind of magic. She'd heard rumors of grimblades that left untreatable wounds, others that could turn people to stone, or could track anyone whose blood they'd drawn, or could cut through the thickest of armor. There were even whispers of ones that could nullify magic, like Viri's fillium. Whatever power they held, grimblades were all created and used with a single purpose: to bring suffering and death to their victims.

"Elders," Jonas breathed as he bent closer and saw the green tinge spreading across Reeve's side. "That's not good." He prodded the wound, ignoring Reeve's pained grunt. "How long ago did this happen?"

Reeve rattled off a time, causing Jonas's normally cheerful face to turn grave.

Sage tensed at his reaction. "You can help him, right?" she asked. "It's obviously some kind of poison, but you're good with poisons. You've studied them. You know how to cure them."

"Not *magical* poisons." Jonas waved a hand at Reeve's wound. "I wouldn't know where to begin with treating something like this. I'm just as likely to make it worse."

"But you can figure it out, can't you?" Sage pressed. When he said nothing, she leaned in and said, "You're the genius here—there has to be something in one of your books that can help him."

"Nothing on magical poisons or ailments, making them *or* curing them," Jonas returned. "You know how limited that kind of knowledge is. I can't heal something I don't understand."

"You could at least *try*—"

"Both of you, calm down," Reeve interrupted Sage, but his authority was lessened by how weak his voice sounded. "I'm fine. I just need to sleep it off."

Viri snorted, and all eyes turned to her. She flushed, but said, "You're obviously not fine."

"And whose fault is that?" Sage's worry shifted to anger as she pinned Viri with her hazel glare, her hands fisted by her sides. "If he dies, it's on *you*."

Viri's indignation rose anew. "I didn't ask him to jump in front of that dagger."

"You ungrateful little—"

"And I don't know what you're all so worried about," Viri continued over Sage. "He's a reaper. It wasn't a death blow, so grimblade or not, he'll heal. He just needs to siphon and the magic will clear the poison from his blood." She felt sick saying it, but that didn't make it any less true.

"Are you volunteering, hunter?" Sage asked, her voice filled with menace.

Viri paled but stood her ground, knowing the other girl was only trying to intimidate her. "He'd hardly get enough from me to heal a paper cut."

"No one's siphoning from anyone," Reeve said as firmly as he could, trying to stand. "And no one's dying. I told you, I just need to—"

He wasn't able to finish before he tipped forward, and only kept from tumbling off the couch because Jonas caught him in time.

"Easy, Reeve," the blond boy said, pushing him down again. "The more you move, the quicker the poison will spread."

Too late for that, Viri thought, recalling the strenuous fight in the alley, most of which had taken place after Reeve had been impaled by the dagger. She still didn't understand why Sage and

Jonas were so concerned about him, but at the same time, despite what she'd said about not asking him to save her, guilt clawed at her. If not for Reeve, Viri would be the one infected with grim-blade poison right now—and that was only if the eerie red blade hadn't killed her on impact, as their attacker had surely intended. The sooner Reeve was healed, the quicker she could let go of any debt she owed him.

"I saw Sage siphon from Jonas earlier," Viri said, looking straight at Reeve. "If you're worried about me learning that reapers *don't* have to prey solely on children, then that ship has sailed. So just"—she waved a hand between him and his friends—"do what you need to do."

"That's not an option," Reeve said mildly, his body beginning to shiver.

Viri threw her arms out to the sides. "Why the hell not? You're a reaper—siphoning is second nature to you."

"Are you really that dense?" Sage said cuttingly. "Look at him. Look at his veins. Does he *look* like a reaper to you?"

"Just because he hasn't siphoned in a while—"

"A while?" Sage repeated incredulously. "Try *seven years*."

Viri jerked backward in disbelief, but then she came to her senses and said, directly to Reeve, "You're the right hand to the Reaper Priest. If you expect me to believe you don't siphon—"

"I'm not sure I have the energy to care what you believe," Reeve said, leaning back against the couch and closing his eyes, sweat now dotting his brow as he clenched and unclenched his hands, as if trying to shake feeling back into them.

His vulnerable posture should have alarmed Viri, but if anything, it just made her madder. "What's next?" she demanded.

"Are you going to tell me you've never siphoned from anyone, *ever*?"

Reeve's eyes shot open, the silver suddenly blazing. "I didn't say that. I've siphoned before. But as Sage said, it was seven years ago, and just the once." In a mutter, he added, "That was enough."

Viri blinked, caught off guard by his rare moment of honesty, and somewhat stunned that he'd managed to fight the addictive nature of ellixen and only siphoned once in all the years he'd been with the Priest. But even so—

"And what, pray tell, happened to your innocent victim?" she asked scathingly. "Did they miraculously survive?"

There was a pause as Reeve stared into her eyes, but then he dropped his gaze to look past her shoulder and admitted in a tight voice, "No. She died."

Viri's lips thinned with disgust, along with an unexpected dose of disappointment. But she pushed aside what she was feeling and said, "So there it is. You've siphoned before, you know how to do it, so just"—she waved toward Sage and Jonas again—"*do it*."

Reeve shook his head. "I told you, it's not an option. I don't siphon anymore, end of discussion." Before Viri could object, or ask how in Elders' name he'd destroyed the nullicuffs and knocked her out with magic if he didn't have access to stolen ellixen—not that he could have used it for that anyway—he turned to Jonas and asked, "What should I expect as the poison spreads?"

"I can't say for sure," Jonas said, looking anxiously between Viri and Reeve, "but if it works like nonmagical poisons, then it could induce any number of symptoms before it starts to shut down your internal organs and then, ultimately, kills you." He straightened his glasses and continued, as if reciting from a book, "It could be fast acting or slow spreading. It could cause tingling in your extremities, numbness, fevers, chills, dizziness, abdominal cramping—"

"Let's say I already have most of those," Reeve said, wiping his brow and pressing his hand to his stomach—not his bloodied side, his *stomach*. "Is there a way to slow it down?"

"It's not just the poison that's the problem," Jonas said, indicating his red-splattered couch. "Whatever magical toxin was in the grimblade, it seems to be stopping your wound from clotting. You're bleeding out. If the poison doesn't kill you first, that will."

"Fabulous," Reeve muttered, and then, before any of them could react, his face lost what little color had remained and he lurched forward to vomit all over the floor.

Sage cursed and jumped backward, but Viri froze at seeing the unnatural blackish bile Reeve had spewed out.

"That *really* isn't good," Jonas said, sounding panicked. "Reeve, can you tell me exactly what you're feeling—"

Jonas didn't finish before Reeve's eyes rolled to the back of his head and he slumped over on the couch, unconscious.

"Reeve? *Reeve!*" Sage cried, avoiding the puddle of sick to reach out and shake his shoulder, but he remained unresponsive. "Jonas, talk to me," she said urgently. "What are our options?"

Jonas ran his fingers through his blond curls, making them look even wilder. "We need someone who knows about these kinds of things. Someone with medical knowledge *and* magical knowledge. But that person doesn't *exist*."

Viri's heart began racing, not just at the sight of Reeve looking like he was at death's door, but also because of what Jonas had said. She licked her lips and shared, "Actually . . . they do."

Sage and Jonas spun toward her, and for a moment, she wondered what the hell she was thinking. Then she looked at the unconscious Reeve again, seeing his sweating, shivering, bleeding form, and suddenly, he wasn't an eighteen-year-old reaper, but instead the eleven-year-old boy she'd once considered her closest friend. He'd saved her life tonight—she couldn't ignore that. But even if he hadn't, he was still *Reeve.* She couldn't let him die, no matter what kind of monster he'd become.

"I know someone who might be able to help," Viri said. "Quick—get him up, and follow me."

THE JOURNAL OF CELESTIAL MAGE KADMUS CASTRO

Seventeenth Sun, Tenth Cycle, Twelfth Age

The fabricator mages have built wardstones.

"Obelisks," they're calling them—four obsidian pillars, placed toward the north, south, east, and west of the now fully formed city. Or uppercity, as it's known, with many residents having relocated inside the mountains and to the undercity beneath the surface. I don't understand the appeal—I'd much rather feel the sun on my skin and the breeze on my face, but to each their own. I can, however, acknowledge that the underground and inner-mountain design is a marvel, even by fabricator standards. For shallows who have never experienced magic-made architecture, let alone our wayportals and ellixen-infused elevators, I understand why they might be charmed enough to want to live in such places.

But the wardstones—the "obelisks"—I'm not sure how I feel about those.

Because they've suppressed the power of the Hallow Stream.

What was once a flood of unruly magic is now a trickle. Submissive, subdued, silent. Just like back on the mainland.

Part of me is relieved, since it means my ellixen is no longer reacting in unpredictable and temperamental ways. It's nice not to wonder whether I'll heal a bruise or accidentally turn it into a broken bone, summon a book or have it burn to ash, unlock a door or trap myself in a sealed room. But another part of me is . . . grieving.

I never told anyone—I've barely even admitted it to myself—but I'd secretly hoped I might one day be able to use the raw magic emanating from the Stream to increase the power I draw from celestial events. I think I already <u>was</u> to a degree—I think the Stream was helping me, that it *wanted* to help me. Because unlike on the mainland, the strange, residual power I've experienced with each new ritual has stayed with me for hours afterward. Sometimes days.

I've never felt anything like it before, not in all my years of practicing celestial magic.

It's addictive.

And I want more.

But with the wards from the obelisks taming the Stream's magic, I already know things are going to change. More and more shallows have been attending my ceremonies over the last few months, hungry for my blessing rites that amplify their ellixen, but now the celestial power I summon will no longer be as strong or as lasting—for them or for me. They'll eventually stop coming to my rituals, stop needing me, stop *wanting* me. It'll be just like on the mainland, with my role as Priest slowly but surely becoming obsolete.

I blame Tephryn Alemedes. She's the reason the fabricator mages decided to build the obelisks—she came up with the idea, taking inspiration from the natural wards that surround the two Hallow Streams on the mainland, then infusing the towering obsidian pillars with her own experimental suppression magic. Of course she did—only an alchemist mage would be so reckless. Transformational magic is dangerous, and infusions, especially, can be deadly. There's a reason why alchemy is so carefully supervised during training, and why so few mages choose it as their specialty. The discipline it takes, the *sacrifice* . . . not to mention the risks and consequences when it goes wrong . . .

I'm not sure if I abhor Tephryn or admire her. I think it's a combination of both—though I'm also self-aware enough to know her physical appeal is swaying my bias, since it would be much easier to dislike her if she weren't so beautiful.

It would also help if she weren't one of the only mages here who doesn't openly ridicule me. She came to my moonfall ceremony a few nights ago, as impossible as that is to believe. A mage—and an alchemist mage, at that—attended one of my rituals.

I'd have thought she was mocking me if not for how many questions she asked afterward and the genuine curiosity that shone in her starlit eyes. She even suggested we meet later this week to discuss the upcoming arrival of the Adastrum Devotis comets. It's been two hundred years since they last graced our skies, but while the power they emit is unparalleled, she's not a celestial mage, so I'm unsure why they would interest her.

Zeranthe says I'm being obtuse, that Tephryn doesn't want to meet about the comets but instead has romantic inclinations. I'm not sure I can trust a dragon's judgment on such matters, nor am I sure how I'll proceed if it turns out she's right.

All I know is that I need to be careful. I can't allow myself to fall for Tephryn's allure—or any other part of her.

Nothing good would ever come of it.

15

Unsurprisingly, Sage wasn't thrilled by the idea of blindly trusting Viri, but after Jonas pointed out their lack of options, the purple-haired reaper grudgingly helped drag Reeve out of the apartment—but not without first warning Viri that there would be hell to pay if she was leading them into a trap.

Viri would have laughed at the irony if she hadn't been so anxious about where she was taking them and the line she was about to cross. But Jonas had said Reeve needed someone with medical *and* magical knowledge, and there was only one person she knew who fit that description.

As quickly as they could manage while bearing Reeve's unconscious form, their small group hurried to the wayportal. Viri stepped through first, guiding it not to the surface this time, but into the heart of the undercity.

"This way," she told the reapers, sending up a prayer to avoid any Nox patrols—or worse, hunters—while she ushered them along a tunnel almost identical to those in the inner-mountains, its magically filtered air cool and slightly damp.

Like Mount Tembris, the undercity was mainly used for

residential purposes, with levels upon levels of apartments. But there were also communal areas, like Mount Verta's market district, as well as recreational spaces similar to the Entertainment Guild's renowned Encore Alley, and an assortment of businesses dotted throughout the labyrinthine tunnels. It was frustratingly easy to get lost, and not just because there were many paths carved by the ancient mages that had yet to be fully explored.

Viri, however, knew exactly where she was going, and she didn't hesitate to lead the reapers into a narrow passage off the main walkway, stopping at a dead end.

"Did we take a wrong turn?" Jonas asked, panting under Reeve's weight.

Instead of answering, Viri reached for the rocky wall and ran her hand down it three times. On the third stroke, a *click* sounded, and the entire surface shifted inward, revealing a hidden door.

"Whoa," Jonas breathed.

Sage looked at it with suspicion. "Warded?"

"No." Viri pushed the wall-door fully open. "Just hidden from anyone who doesn't know it's here."

"And how did *you* know it was here?"

"Because this is my best friend's lab," Viri said, gesturing for them to follow her into the large, circular workroom. "It was a gift from her dad—a present for her fourteenth birthday." It was also the only thing the mystery man had ever given Wynter, his letter arriving just before her Impartation ceremony with instructions on how to find the place, a warning to keep it secret, and an unhelpful sign-off saying, *Use it well. With great affection, your father.*

Before Sage could ask, Viri confirmed, "Yes, I'm talking about Wynter Starling, the Magistratus's daughter. No, her mother doesn't know about this lab. Only Wyn, me, and our friend Soren. That's it." She paused. "And now you."

"Is there a reason it's so secret?" Sage asked with an arched brow.

Viri arched her own in return. "Look around."

As soon as Sage stepped fully into the lab, all it took was one sweep of her widening hazel eyes to see exactly why Wynter wouldn't want her mother to know this place existed. Or anyone, for that matter.

"Whoa *again*," Jonas repeated as he gaped around the brightly lit room, his gaze roving from the domed glass ceiling that offered a view straight up through Lake Mirtis—dark now, but when the sun rose, it would reveal all kinds of aquatic creatures drifting by—and then lowering to take in the rest of the space. His eyes glazed with wonder as he spotted the shelves full of ancient leather books, many written in the runic language of the mages, but while his attention stayed there, Sage continued to peer around the rest of the lab, unable to hide her shock.

Viri understood her reaction. The room was teeming with too many illegal alchemical items to count, almost all of which had been included as part of the "gift" from Wynter's dad. There was the large terrarium full of magical plants and flowers—some of which were *glowing*. Then there was the cabinet that housed a rare assortment of precious metals and gemstones—with some of those glowing, too. And then, of course, there was the long workbench covered in vials of various colors and states, from liquids—like the zingzest elixir—to solids—like the impedidust—to smoky gasses in stoppered flasks—which Viri had yet to be subjected to. She eyed those warily, but she was more concerned by the foul-smelling brown sludge oozing out of the hot furnace, and she made a mental note to not volunteer for that particular experiment, regardless of how much Wynter begged.

Casting her gaze around, Viri tried to see the lab through Sage and Jonas's eyes, noting the hundreds of potions shelved along the walls and the unfamiliar ingredients interspersed among them, the plethora of tools for crushing and grinding powders and pastes, the collection of measuring glasses, pitchers, and vials, the numerous distillation vessels and tubes, and the pages and pages of parchment full of Wynter's scrawled notes. If the room hadn't been so tidy, it would have been overwhelmingly chaotic. Instead, it was—

"Magical," Jonas whispered, looking as if he might cry. "This place is *magical.* Walnut and I want to stay here forever."

Peeking out from Jonas's pocket, Walnut didn't seem nearly as enchanted by their surroundings, though his nose did twitch adorably as he took in the foreign scents of the lab.

"There's a couch over here," Viri said, leading them to the far side of the room, then helping lower Reeve onto it. It was strange to see him lying there, especially since Viri had spent so many hours on that couch herself, keeping Wynter company while she worked, or, less enjoyably, fighting off side effects caused by Wyn's experiments. There was even a first aid kit at the foot of the couch for just that purpose, full of forbidden magical remedies all made by Wynter: a soothing gel for burns, an anti-itch cream, a warming potion, an anti-nausea tonic, a morphenine painkiller, and a healing salve—though the latter was more often used to treat Viri's hunting scrapes than anything Wynter's tests put her through.

As helpful as the supplies were for minor wounds and ailments, there was nothing that would cure Reeve of a magical poison, and by the look of him, he didn't have time for guesswork.

My fault, my fault, my fault. Viri heard the words in her mind, replaying the moment when he'd tackled her away from the dagger and yanked it out of his side with a sickening *squelch.* Saliva filled her mouth at the memory, and she knew—*she knew*—she would never forgive herself if he died from saving her life.

"All right, you got us here," Sage said, breaking into Viri's spiraling thoughts. "Now where's your friend? I assume she's the one you think can help Reeve?"

"Wait here," Viri said, moving back toward the door. "I'll go wake her."

But Viri barely made it halfway across the lab before the hidden entrance echoed with a clicking sound and the wall shifted inward again.

Sage reacted instantly, unsheathing two blades and raising them in a defensive stance. Jonas also reacted instantly, uttering a squeak of fright and leaping behind the couch—making Viri belatedly realize why he hadn't been out fighting with his friends that night. He was, without a doubt, the strangest reaper she'd ever met. But with a quick shake of her head, Viri's attention turned to Wynter, who appeared through the hidden doorway and came to a stuttered, wide-eyed halt at the small group assembled in her secret laboratory.

"I can explain," Viri blurted, all too aware that she stood there with a clawed face and filthy, wet clothes, and was in the company of three strangers, one of whom was unconscious, and all of whom were covered in blood—mostly Reeve's. On the plus side, Wynter couldn't see Sage and Jonas's darkened veins, though it wouldn't take long for her to guess what they were. "I promise to tell you everything, but first, we need your help."

"Are you *crazy*?" Wynter shrieked, pushing through her shock and marching forward, her glossy black hair swaying behind her. "Do you know how many people are looking for you? I'm only awake because Darik barged into our apartment and woke Mom and me, claiming you attacked him. He has half the Nox out searching for you. And, I assume, *him*." She jabbed a finger in Reeve's direction. "That's Ashton, isn't it? The right hand to the Reaper Priest?" She then pointed to Sage and Jonas. "Are they his reaper buddies?"

Viri winced, wishing her friend wasn't so clever. "I hoped we'd have more time before they came for us."

Wynter's sapphire eyes flooded with disbelief. "I'm all for bending the rules, you know that." She indicated the magical contraband surrounding them. "But *what the hell*, V?"

"I needed Reeve's help with something," Viri said. "It's important."

"It'd better be life and death for what you did. Do you have *any* idea how much trouble you're in?"

"It *is* life and death. He has information that could—"

"Yo!" Sage interrupted, a fierce scowl on her face. "Can you two maybe play catch-up when our friend *isn't* dying?"

Viri winced a second time, knowing Sage was right. "Please, Wyn," she begged. "He's been poisoned by a grimblade."

At the mention of the rare magical weapon, Wynter's eyes rounded with surprise, then narrowed again just as fast. "Why should I help a reaper?"

The answer rasped out of Viri. "Because the blade he took was aimed at me." She held her friend's gaze and whispered, "He saved my life. Now I need to save his."

There was a pause while Wynter stared at Viri, weighing her decision, but then she sighed. "Tell me what happened. The weapon, the poison's effects, everything."

Relief surged through Viri, and she hastily shared what she knew, from her memories of the dagger's appearance to the symptoms Reeve had shown before passing out. When she was done, Wynter gave a solemn nod, pushed the sleeves of her cobalt sweater up to her elbows, and strode off toward where Reeve lay.

"You, purple-haired angry girl," Wynter said, snapping her fingers. "Roll him over so I can see the damage."

"That's Sage," Viri quickly introduced. "And Jonas is behind the couch."

Hearing his name, the blond boy came out of hiding and gave a little wave.

Wynter blinked. "Is that a *bunny* in your pocket?"

"His name is Walnut," Jonas said, petting the rabbit on his head. "He gets separation anxiety if I leave him alone for too long." He paused. "And he's technically a lop-eared dwarf rabbit—they're much smaller than the standard size. Like baby bunnies, but for life."

Wynter blinked again. "That's . . . oddly precious," she muttered, before returning her attention to Reeve, now resting on his good side with his wound facing upward.

Seeing the extent of it, Wynter made a gagging sound. "Ugh, blood. Disgusting."

Sage's eyes speared to Viri. "I thought you said she had medical knowledge?"

"She's training to be a physician," Viri replied. Quieter, she admitted, "She's just not very good at it."

"Excuse you." Wynter frowned. "I'm *very* good at it. Or I would be, if they'd let me heal people the way I want."

"By that, she means she'd prefer to use magic to treat her patients," Viri clarified to Sage and Jonas. "Which, in the case of alchemy-created cures, is forbidden."

"It's a stupid law," Jonas said, pushing his glasses up his nose. "The ancient mages used magic for everything, *especially* healing."

"They also knew what they were doing," Sage pointed out. "They had years of training and generations of knowledge at their disposal." She looked at Wynter, who was prodding Reeve's wound while visibly trying not to heave, and flatly added, "Something tells me that's not the case here."

"Unfortunately for you, I'm all you've got," Wynter said, stepping away from Reeve and heading to the nearest bookcase. Scanning the spines, she pulled out two thick, leather-bound tomes, then carried them to her workbench and dropped them on it with a heavy *thud*. "Bunny boy, get over here. You look like you know your way around a book."

Jonas practically ran to her side. "What do you need?"

She held up one of the tomes, the cover embossed with golden symbols. "Can you read runes?"

He shook his head. "Basic letters only."

Wynter reached for the second book—this one with the words *Potente Toxicum* written across the front—and shoved it toward him. "Then you take this one. Look for anything that mentions green flesh and sluggish coagulation. If you can't find those, then search for any of the other symptoms your friend experienced."

Jonas got straight to work, as did Wynter with the runic

book—a language she'd taught herself in the years since she'd first discovered the secret laboratory and its ancient literary collection.

"What can we do?" Viri asked, indicating herself and Sage.

"Here." Wynter tossed her a vial of shimmery orange liquid. "Get that into him."

Viri hesitated at the familiar elixir in her hands. "Um, this is your zingzest."

"Don't worry, I modified it since you tested it," Wynter said distractedly, skimming the page before her. "All the adrenaline, none of the withdrawal."

Viri wasn't worried about the withdrawal—she was worried about the fact that it was an *energy booster*, and Reeve was out cold. Elders knew what effect it might have on him.

Seeing her uncertainty, Wynter used a finger to mark her place and took the time to explain, "Magical ailments are complicated, V. His best chance at surviving this is if he's conscious enough to fight it." With gravity, she added, "His pulse is already too slow—he doesn't have much time left. It's a risk, but it's a calculated one, and I wouldn't suggest it if I thought it would cause more harm than good. He saved your life, so we save his, right?"

Viri's throat clogged with gratitude for her friend, and she gave a quick nod before unstoppering the vial and pressing it to Reeve's lips, gently tipping his head back. His midnight hair was like silk against her fingers as she coaxed the citrusy elixir down his throat with one hand and supported his neck with the other, all while Sage watched protectively from a few feet away.

Just as it had for Viri, the zingzest worked almost instantly, prompting Reeve to sit up with a gasp and launch into a coughing fit.

Being closest to him, Viri lowered herself onto the couch and patted his back. "Deep breaths, Reeve."

"Hurts," he gritted out.

Viri felt the pain of that one word piercing her chest. "I know," she murmured. "Just breathe through it. It'll ease in a second."

It wouldn't, though. Not while the grimblade poison flooded his veins. But at least he was awake again, and the zingzest had brought color back to his cheeks. His eyes, too, were more alert as he finally stopped coughing long enough to look around, his body tensing as he took in their unfamiliar surroundings and only relaxing again when he caught sight of Sage and Jonas.

"Where are we?"

"Wynter's lab," Viri answered, then gestured to her friend. "Wyn, meet Reeve Ashton. Reeve, Wynter Starling."

"The pleasure is all yours," Wynter muttered.

"The Magistratus's daughter has been keeping a naughty little secret," Sage told Reeve in a drawl. "She's been practicing alchemy under her darling mommy's nose for years."

Wynter didn't look up from her reading as she drawled back, "She also knows enough of that alchemy to cover you in boils and give you an embarrassing rash." Her tone lowered in warning. "Don't mess with me, reaper. You won't like the results."

Reeve was staring at Wynter, his face a mask of shock and something else, something unreadable—wariness, perhaps—but then his features turned pained again as another coughing fit struck, ending only when he leaned forward and spewed up more of the unnatural black bile.

Wynter immediately dry retched. "Ugh, people are so gross," she moaned, then threw a vial of white powder to Sage. "Pour that on it. The whole vial."

Sage did as ordered, and the vomit evaporated as soon as the dust hit it.

"Impressive," Sage murmured, inspecting the empty vial in the light of the nearest everbeacon.

"Scrubbydust," Wynter said. "Instantly cleans liquid spills of all kinds. One of my first experiments."

"Successful," Viri corrected, thinking of all the failed alchemical attempts before it. "One of her first *successful* experiments."

"Semantics." Wynter waved a hand, but paused mid-motion to lean closer to the page she was reading. "Wait—I have something." She turned to Jonas. "Is there an entry in there on Wraith Tears?"

"I'm only up to the Ns," he said. "Hang on, I'll skip ahead." Pages rustled, then slowed. "There's nothing that translates to that exact name, but there's a mention of *Weepus Wraithos*—Weeping Wraith—and the etymology is nearly identical." He squinted as he read the entry aloud: " 'Weeping Wraith is a poison derived using a combination of wraith blood and dragon tears. Its liquid form is sufficient to bring a swift death, but greater suffering can be achieved by imbuing it into objects, particularly weapons, as the effects become longer-lasting and more torturous. Symptoms include green flesh around the wound, black bile, fever, chills . . .' " He rattled off the list, with Reeve nodding weakly to each mention.

"That's it," Sage said, sounding surprised. "Does it say how to cure it?"

Jonas shook his head and tapped his book. "Not here." He looked at Wynter. "You?"

Wynter was already lost in her runic tome again, mumbling under her breath and scrawling on a piece of parchment. There was a furrow in her brow as she concentrated, but it cleared when she looked up. "I think I've got it." She reread her handwriting, the furrow returning. "It's actually a simple antidote, though I suppose it does need rare magical ingredients and someone who can read runes, so 'simple' might not be the right—"

"Not to rush you," Reeve rasped, one hand holding his stomach and the other pressed to his wound, "but unless you have a whole barrel of that cleaning powder, you're going to want to hurry up with the cure."

The threat of him vomiting again had Wynter leaping into action, pulling colorful ingredients from the shelves and hastening over to her terrarium to pluck an assortment of plants, including two angelrose petals that continued glowing even after they left the vine. A strong floral aroma flooded the room, sending Jonas into a sneezing fit, but watery eyes or not, he watched on with visible awe as Wynter got to work.

It wasn't true alchemy she was doing, since that involved the magical transfiguration of matter and would require her to tap into the small amount of ellixen she'd retained after her Impartation—something that was not only incredibly dangerous but also *beyond* illegal. But regardless, potion making was still a perilous art, particularly when it used unstable magical ingredients. Wynter had taught herself everything she knew, and while she claimed to be a novice, Viri couldn't imagine trusting anyone else with her life—or in this case, Reeve's.

"Done," Wynter declared, stoppering a glass vial and giving it a shake. The liquid within was pink and glowed slightly from the angelrose petals. "Which of you two has known Ashton the longest?"

She looked between Sage and Jonas, oblivious to Viri turning solid on the couch.

"Why?" Sage asked cagily.

"Wraith blood is nasty stuff," Wynter said. "It goes beyond the physical—much like how wraiths themselves attack not just the body, but also the mind and spirit. According to legend, at least." She shrugged. "Point is, to keep the wraith blood from lingering in Ashton's psyche even after the poison is purged from his body, the cure needs to be administered by someone with a strong emotional connection to him, forged over as many years as possible. The longer you've known each other, the deeper the connection, which will ensure the potion is powerful enough to expel all traces of the wraith blood from his system."

There was a beat of silence, before Sage said, "That makes no sense whatsoever."

Wynter shrugged again. "Magic rarely makes sense. That's why it's so interesting."

"I couldn't agree more," Jonas said, bouncing excitedly at her side.

"So, who is it?" Wynter pressed, holding the pink vial out toward the reapers.

Neither of them moved, their eyes flicking instead to Viri, whose heart had begun to pound in her ears.

Reeve cleared his throat beside her, and the slightest turn of her head caused their eyes to lock. As unwell as he looked, he was still impossibly handsome, but there was something in his gaze now, a challenge and a question, as he waited to see what she would do.

She, however, had limited options. She'd already started down this path—it was too late to turn back now.

"It's me," Viri admitted, standing shakily and walking toward her friend. "I've known Reeve the longest."

Wynter's dark eyebrows shot upward. "What are you talking about? You only met him after he was arrested last week."

Viri shook her head. "I've known him since I was four."

A sharp breath from Wynter. "You *what*?"

"Thirteen years," Viri confirmed, feeling an odd sense of relief at having the truth finally out there. Or one truth. The other was coming—she could feel it.

Wynter leaned forward and hissed, "How is that possible? He's the Reaper Priest's most loyal follower!"

Viri winced. "I know."

"The Reaper Priest who *murdered your parents*!"

Viri winced again. "Yes."

"The Reaper Priest who you've sworn to hunt down and make pay for everything he's done!"

This time, Viri just nodded, though from the corner of her eye she saw Sage take an angry step forward, halted only by Reeve's restraining arm. Even Jonas had his hands clenched by his sides, as if upset to hear anything against their monstrous leader.

Wynter's face suddenly turned white as she stared at Viri in dawning horror, her quick brain putting the pieces together. Slowly, as if afraid to give voice to what she'd just realized, she said, "If you've known Ashton that long, then you must know how and when he became the Priest's right hand."

A reluctant nod from Viri.

"That means . . ." Wynter said. "That means . . ." Her throat bobbed, but she forced herself to ask the question Viri had been dreading for seven years—her greatest secret, her most devastating truth. "You know who the Reaper Priest is, don't you?"

Viri couldn't resist looking back at Reeve, finding his silver gaze unexpectedly soft, full of compassion. She closed her eyes, unable to bear the sight of him looking at her like that as she answered her best friend, her voice little more than a breath.

"His name is Braedan Solace." A tremulous pause. "He's my brother."

16

For a moment, there was nothing but silence in the laboratory. But then—

"The Reaper Priest is your *brother*?" Wynter shrieked. "I didn't even know you *had* a brother! How—Why—What—*I don't understand!*"

"How about we cure Reeve and *then* have question time," Sage suggested tightly, gesturing to the vial clutched in Wynter's white-knuckled grip. "It's a miracle he's still alive with how chatty you lot are."

"I can wait a bit longer," Reeve said, watching Viri carefully, his eyes still full of compassion. But it was clear he was in a great deal of pain, too, the color leaching from his face as the zingzest left his system. It wouldn't be long before he lost consciousness again, and this time . . . he might not wake up.

"Sage is right." Viri held her hand out to Wynter. "I'll answer anything you want in a minute. Just tell me how to help him first."

Wynter's mouth opened and closed like a fish as she stared between Viri and Reeve, shock still splashed across her features, but she pulled herself together and handed over the pink vial. "Thirteen years should be more than enough."

"I haven't seen him for the last seven," Viri said. "Will that matter?"

Wynter stared between them again, likely calculating what that meant in the timeline of Viri's life, her eyes widening with realization. But she only said, "No. Magic isn't fickle like that. It'll still count as thirteen years."

Viri turned the vial between her fingers. "Do I just shove it down his throat, like the zingzest?"

"I vote we come up with an alternative word to 'shove,'" Reeve murmured, groaning as he leaned back against the couch, unable to keep holding his body upright without support.

"He can swallow it himself this time," Wynter said. "You just need to be touching him while he does it." Seeing Viri's expression, she quickly added, "Holding hands is fine. Anything skin to skin."

"Ahh, of course," Jonas said gleefully as he skimmed Wynter's notes. "Essence transconveyance."

"Essence what?" Sage asked, squinting at her friend.

Wynter looked at Viri and explained, "When Ashton takes the cure, the poison will be forced to leave his body, and it's going to do that through his connection to you. The magic demands a cost, and you'll be the one paying it."

"No, we're not doing that," Reeve said, his words stronger than any he'd uttered since being stabbed. "Come up with something else."

"Easy, Ashton," Wynter said, waving him down when he tried unsuccessfully to stand. "She wasn't stabbed by the grimblade, so the poison itself won't infect her. She'll only feel the metaphysical essence of it, a fraction of what you're experiencing, and for barely a second. Think of her like a wayportal—a one-way transit point. The cure sends the poison from your body into the 'portal,' and your connection to her pushes it out the other side, never to return. Understand?" When she received blank looks from everyone but Jonas, she threw her hands in the air and pointed to her runic book. "Fine, you don't need to understand. Just do it because the instructions say so, all right?"

Not thrilled by being referred to as a human wayportal, Viri decided the best thing to do was to get it over with, and she moved back to Reeve's side, passing him the vial and holding her hand out to him.

"You, uh, might want to sit down," Wynter warned.

Viri looked back at her friend. "I thought you said I'd barely feel it?"

"I did." Wynter shifted uneasily beside her workbench. "But, you know, just in case."

Sighing, Viri lowered herself beside Reeve again, then held out her hand once more.

He didn't take it.

"Go on," she urged, and when he still refused, she rolled her eyes at the concern she saw in his expression and grabbed his hand herself. "Swallow the cure, or I'll make you."

His voice was quiet, just for her, as he said, "I don't want to hurt you."

She braced herself against everything those words made her feel and bluntly said, "I've survived worse than this from you. Just do it already."

Reeve held her gaze for a long moment, then tightened his

grip and obediently threw back the contents of the vial, shuddering at the taste.

One second passed.

Five seconds.

Ten.

Still, nothing happened.

"Well, that was anticlimactic," Viri said, frowning from the empty vial to their joined fingers. "Wyn, are you sure it—"

She broke off in a gasp as pain slammed into her, her temples pounding, her body freezing and boiling, her stomach cramping, her skin feeling like it was being peeled away layer by layer. She clenched Reeve's hand so hard it must have hurt, but it was that or scream loud enough to pierce his eardrums. The pain—the *pain*—

Just when she was sure she couldn't stand it another moment, the agony vanished, leaving her collapsed and panting on the couch with Reeve leaning over her, his free hand cupping her uninjured cheek, his silver eyes edged with worry.

She pushed him away and sat up again, but did so while croaking out, "If that was only a *fraction* of what the poison made you feel, how the hell did you last so long?"

Immediately, Reeve's face shuttered. He rose to his feet, stretching his limbs and rolling his shoulders, evidently as good as new. "I'm no stranger to pain," he answered, avoiding her gaze. "The more you feel it, the less it hurts."

Unease rippled through Viri, the feeling unexplainable—and unwelcome. "What do you—"

Reeve didn't let her get the question out, instead walking over to Wynter and saying, "Thank you for your help. I'm in your debt."

Wynter handed him a jar of healing salve. "Put some of that on your wound. You've lost a lot of blood, but with the poison gone, it'll fix the damage in no time."

Reeve followed her instructions, causing Wynter to gag and turn away as he lifted his shirt to reveal the wound in all its grisly glory. Viri turned away for a different reason, though not in time to stop the image of his tanned, chiseled torso from being burned into her brain. A flush hit her cheeks, only growing when he strode back over and sat beside her once more, reaching for her hand.

"What—" She cut herself off when he moved her scarlet cloak aside to smear some of the salve over the dagger gash on her forearm. His gentle ministrations caused a lump to lodge in her throat, but a strange, urgent fear took over her when he scooped up more and raised his fingers toward her clawed cheek.

"I've got it," she said quickly, her voice hoarse as she took the jar from him and leapt to her feet, slathering the ointment on herself and wincing at the sting. Somehow, she knew that if she'd let Reeve do it, it wouldn't have hurt at all.

"Here." Viri passed the salve to Sage, gesturing to the bump on the purple-haired girl's head. "It'll bring the swelling down."

"Incredible," Reeve murmured, and when Viri swung back to him, his shirt was lifted again—Elders help her, she was never going to get that image out of her mind now—and he was staring in amazement at how fast his wound was healing.

"That's alchemy for you," Wynter said with a humble shrug. "Magic can do anything. The only limit is your own imagination."

"And a lack of accessible knowledge and training. Those are limitations, too," Jonas said, staring longingly at the books lining

Wynter's shelves. "I'm so jealous that you've had all this at your fingertips for years."

"Speaking of years . . ." Wynter glanced pointedly between Viri and Reeve. "He's not dying anymore, so it's time for answers."

Viri swallowed at the firm expression on her friend's face and resisted the urge to say she was in desperate need of answers herself—from Reeve. But Wynter had just saved his life, so Viri could spare a moment to fill her in.

"I mentioned before that we met thirteen years ago—that's when he was adopted by my next-door neighbors," Viri said.

"Adopted?" Wynter looked at Reeve. "No parents?"

Viri bit her cheek, feeling a pang of discomfort for Reeve at the personal question, but he casually answered, "My father died when I was five—a few months before I met Viri—and since I didn't know who or where my mother was, I was declared an orphan."

"I'm sorry," Wynter said, softening slightly toward him.

He just shrugged. "I loved my dad. He was a kind, honest man, and I miss him every day." Something shifted in his eyes as he looked away from Wynter and stared up through the glass-domed ceiling. "But my mom can go to hell for the selfish choices she's made."

His fierce declaration made Wynter soften even more. "I'm lucky to have a great mom, but my dad . . ." She paused, then quietly finished, "I know what it's like to be abandoned by a parent. I wouldn't wish it upon anyone."

Reeve said nothing, a muscle clenching in his jaw as he continued staring into the gloomy lake.

Viri cleared her throat and picked up her story. "When Reeve moved in, he quickly became close with my family. His adoptive parents were old—so old they're no longer with us—and mine were always off hunting, so it was just us kids around for most of the time. He and—and Braedan"—Viri choked on her brother's name, having not said it aloud in seven years until today—"they hit it off right away. Brae's four years older than me, three years older than Reeve, but the age difference didn't matter—they became best friends. And where they went, I went."

"My Little Shadow," Reeve murmured, a smile tugging at his mouth, though he kept looking up through the water.

Viri pressed her lips together in annoyance, but only said, "That's how we know each other—we were childhood friends. End of story."

Wynter placed her hands on her hips. "End of story, my ass. You said you haven't seen him in seven years. It's been seven years since your parents died. Your parents who were killed by the Reaper Priest—which means your parents were killed *by your brother*." She leaned forward. "Those are some pretty big plot holes, V. How did I not know you had a brother? What happened seven years ago? Why did—" She stopped herself, her voice gentling. "Please, V. Help me understand."

Viri hugged her elbows, refusing to look at Reeve, though from the corner of her eye she could see him frozen. Sage and Jonas had also tensed now that Braedan—their leader—had come into the conversation.

"You don't have to answer," Wynter said softly when Viri remained silent. "I won't force you to. I just—I'm here if you want to talk about it. I've been here for seven years."

It was the hurt in Wynter's voice that broke through to Viri, making her realize she *wanted* her friend to know everything.

With a fortifying breath, Viri said, "It happened on the day of my Impartation ceremony. You already know that—your mom took me in that day, and you saw what a mess I was for months afterward."

Reeve flinched, but Viri ignored him and kept going, "What you don't know is that it was Braedan's Impartation as well. It was his fourteenth birthday, and he wasn't looking forward to it—he'd always liked the idea of having magic, even if the law said he couldn't keep it forever. To make it easier on him, our parents decided we would both yield our ellixen at the same time. I could have waited another four years, but they were worried about my magic being prematurely unstable—I heard them whispering about it in secret, so I knew they feared me burning out early. And unlike Brae, I didn't mind giving up my ellixen, especially if it meant I could do it with him."

Viri's mind traveled back to that dreadful day, sifting through the hazy memories she normally kept locked away. "My parents chose the quieter Southern Obelisk for our ceremony, so it was just the five of us out there by the edge of the necropolis, with nothing but farmland and forest in sight—Mom, Dad, Braedan, Reeve, and me."

"Reeve was with you?" Wynter asked quietly, saying his given name for the first time.

"He was family," Viri answered just as quietly, seeing him flinch again, this time more violently. "Brae gave his magic to the obelisk first, and everything seemed fine. Then it was my turn, and maybe it was because I was younger, or maybe my parents were right about me being close to burnout, but I fainted when I yielded my magic. I was only out for a moment, but that was all it took, because when I came to . . ." Viri had to swallow against the tightness in her throat, her voice rough as stone as she finished, "Mom and Dad were dead."

Wynter was pale, her question hesitant. "Are you sure it was your brother?"

"Positive." Viri swallowed again. "Braedan killed our parents. I know what I saw."

Reeve spoke up then. "You don't, though. You said it yourself—you were unconscious."

Viri whipped around. "So I just *imagined* Mom and Dad on the ground, their ellixen drained from their bodies, and Braedan standing over them with newly blackened veins?" Her heart felt like it was breaking all over again, her grief raw and timeless. "There was no one else with us, Reeve. He *siphoned* from them. He *murdered* them. And then you *left* with him before the hunters and Nox arrived. You *chose* him."

And with that choice, he'd abandoned her, right when she'd needed him the most. The pain of that would never leave her, the hurt a scar that would never heal.

Viri was breathing heavily, her eyes burning as she turned back to Wynter. "I was so horrified by what Braedan had done that I lied to the council about it, telling them he'd been killed with my parents and dragged away by the reaper, leaving no body for the hunters to find. Your mom could see how upset I was, and even though she was wrong about the reason, it was a relief when she promised we'd never talk about him again. That's why you didn't know about him—and why anyone who ever did thinks he's dead."

Wynter's face revealed her shock, but also her understanding. "That's a lot for you to have carried by yourself, V. I wish you'd told me."

Viri didn't know how to explain that she hadn't *wanted* Wynter to know. She hadn't wanted *anyone* to know. The pain, the shame . . . they were too much—then, and now.

Steadying herself, Viri forced the last part out. "When whispers of a new Reaper Priest started circulating soon after my parents' deaths, along with mentions of him being young—*too* young—and powerful—*too* powerful—I knew then that what Braedan had done hadn't been an accident, or some awful mistake that he'd instantly regretted. It had been calculated. Premeditated, even. He hadn't wanted to let go of his magic, so he'd found a way to make sure he never had to, not just choosing his dark path, but also setting himself up to be a merciless leader revered by all other reapers. I don't—" She sucked in a raspy breath. "I don't know how that part happened, how he got so powerful, especially since he was only fourteen. But he'd always been mature for his age, and ambitious—so ambitious." Another raspy breath. "And he wasn't the only one."

She turned to Reeve, swiping angrily at a tear dribbling down her healing cheek as she locked eyes with him and declared, "You stood by him as he became a monster—and in doing so, you became one yourself."

Reeve said nothing in his own defense, just held Viri's watery glare.

Sage, however, bit out, "You know nothing, hunter. If you had *any* idea—"

"Sage," Reeve murmured. "Let it go."

"No, please, I'd *love* to hear your thoughts," Viri said cuttingly, her grief hardening to rage as she gestured to Sage's blackened veins. "Was Braedan the one who convinced you that killing innocents would be a winning life choice? Has your dear Reaper Priest lived up to your expectations as a murderous leader?"

"V." Wynter looked nervously at Sage, whose hands were clenching her sheathed daggers. "Maybe we should go for a walk. Take a breather."

"I don't need a breather," Viri all but snapped at her friend, her blood boiling at the thought of anyone defending her brother's decisions. Reeve's, too. Her fury was such that she almost *wanted* Sage to attack, if only so she could have an excuse to fight back.

"Well, I do," Wynter insisted, grabbing Viri's arm and dragging her away.

Viri barely kept from snarling. *"Wyn—"*

"Two minutes," Wynter said firmly, hauling Viri not just across the lab, but out of it entirely, into the darkened dead end of the tunnel. Only when the door was sealed behind them did she release Viri and say, "I meant the breather part literally. What you just shared was heavy—let it settle, take a second to regain some control. Then we'll go back in there."

"I don't need—"

"Yes, you do."

Viri ground her teeth together, hating that her friend was right. She'd let her emotions take over, and now she had to find a way to reel them in again before she stormed back into the lab and did something she'd regret.

Forcing herself to stay in the tunnel, Viri closed her eyes and filled her lungs with the damp underground air, its earthy scent reminding her of the calming smell of rain. She inhaled once, twice, three times, allowing the anger to cool from her veins, the tension to ease from her muscles. Her grief, though . . . that stayed with her. It always had, and always would.

"Better?" Wynter asked after a moment.

Viri slumped against the wall. "A little." She bit her lip and met Wynter's eyes. "Are you mad at me? For the secrets?"

"Everyone has secrets." An unreadable look crossed Wynter's face, but it quickly turned into a guilty smile as she gestured to her illegal lab. "I know that better than anyone."

Viri huffed out a laugh. "Yeah, I suppose. But still—"

"I'm not mad," Wynter promised. "Disappointed that you didn't tell me, yes. But I also get it. That kind of betrayal, especially from someone you love . . ." She shook her head. "I'm so sorry you went through that. That you're *still* going through it."

Viri wasn't sure if Wynter was referring to Braedan or Reeve—or both. Either way, she rubbed a weary hand over her face and said, "I hate this." She speared a glare at the closed door. "And I hate that it means I'm stuck working with *them*."

"I'll admit to being unsure of the whys, but you never do anything without reason," Wynter said, smoothing her cobalt sleeves. "I'm assuming this is one of those 'the enemy of my enemy is my friend' kind of deals."

Viri grimaced. "'Friend' is too strong a word. But . . ." She sighed. "We're allies, I guess. In the loosest definition of the word."

"Any chance you feel like explaining that?" Wynter jerked her chin in the direction of the lab. "You said before that Reeve has information you need, something about life and death?"

The reminder was like a bucket of ice water crashing into Viri. As much as she wanted to walk away and leave all her problems behind—*especially* the three reapers waiting beyond the door—the missing children were counting on her. She refused to let them down.

"I'll explain inside," Viri said, taking one final, calming breath and pushing off the wall. "Let's go interrogate some reapers."

17

When Viri stepped back into the lab, Reeve and Sage immediately halted what looked like a tense conversation. Jonas, on the other side of the room, jumped guiltily away from the magical terrarium, wonder splashed across his features—as well as angelrose luster, indicating he must have touched the petals and then wiped his fingers under his glasses. Walnut, too, was glowing slightly, his brown coat dusted with pink speckles, his whiskers twitching.

"Everything all right?" Reeve asked Viri as she and Wynter approached, his tone hesitant. Wary.

Viri understood his caution, but she was back in control now—and ready to finally get some answers. She launched straight in with the first thing that came to mind. "Why were you out in the alley tonight? Why did you save those kids from your own kind?"

If Reeve was surprised by her opening questions, he didn't let on, his features unwaveringly calm as he replied, "I promised you answers, so ask anything you want. But keep in mind, I already told you we have the same goal."

Viri couldn't keep the doubt from her voice. "To stop the Aurora sacrifice."

Wynter held up a hand. "I'm sorry, the what-now?"

Reeve ignored her to tell Viri, "We"—he indicated himself, Jonas, and Sage—"have been working for months to foil as many transfers as possible, ever since we first heard whispers about the children being taken, and why. Ardin has a vast network of connections within the reaper world, so whenever he learns about kids being shuffled around or relocated, he finds out the route they'll be taking, and we intervene. Usually it's only one or two at a time—not enough for your Nox friends to investigate, since the kids we help are returned safely without ever knowing the real reason they were taken in the first place. They rarely even realize it was reapers who took them—or reapers who saved them."

Viri thought of all the red threes she'd visited who had already found their way home and wondered how many of them had Reeve and his friends to thank for it.

"But tonight was different," Reeve went on, his tone lowering with concern. "I've never seen a group as big as that."

"You know what that means," Sage said, her face grim. "If they're taking that kind of risk, with that many reapers as a guard . . . *and* those kids were considered 'spares' . . . then there can only be one reason."

Jonas paled. "The comet must be nearly here."

"What comet?" Wynter frowned. "And what's this about kids?"

"So tonight," Viri said, her focus solely on Reeve, "when you knocked me out with magic—and you'd better believe we'll be talking about that later—it was so you could go and *save* the children? All to keep them from being included in the Aurora sacrifice?"

"More to slow things down," Reeve said. "The timing of the comet isn't something we can control, but the kids . . . with fifty of them needed, every one we saved meant another had to be abducted in their place." His shoulders rose and fell. "We did what we could with the limited information we had."

Viri could hardly believe what she was hearing, but there was one thought screaming across her mind. "Why didn't you just *tell* me?"

Reeve looked steadily at her. "Would you have believed me?"

"I—"

"Don't lie."

Viri rocked back on her heels, annoyed that he was right. She never would have believed that a reaper would protect children rather than siphon from them—not if she hadn't seen it with her own eyes.

Frustrated at Reeve, at herself, at the fact that they'd saved eight kids but lost four—something that might not have happened if she'd known what was going on—Viri couldn't help saying, her tone bitter, "Sage blamed me earlier, but most of this is *your* fault. I don't think I've ever hated you more than I do right now."

"No," Reeve said, still unmovably calm. "You hate who you think I am. There's a difference."

Before Viri could respond, or even fully process what he'd said, Wynter shouted, "EXCUSE ME!" All eyes turned to her as she demanded, "Can someone explain what the hell you're all talking about? *What* sacrifice?"

With an apologetic grimace, Viri brought her friend up to speed. She kept the details brief, finishing with how they didn't know when or where the Aurora sacrifice was taking place, nor what Braedan intended to do with the comet's power if he succeeded.

Wynter's face was a sickly green color by the time Viri was done, but she wasn't the only one exhibiting strong emotion. Sage looked like she wanted to take a swing at Viri for what she'd said about Braedan's deadly intentions, and Jonas had pulled Walnut out of his pocket to cuddle the bunny against his chest for comfort. Reeve alone was composed, staring up through the glass dome again, the water a shade lighter as dawn approached.

"Aurora . . . Aurora . . ." Wynter repeated the name, her eyes glazed in thought. "Why does that sound so . . . ?" She blinked, gasped, and rushed across to her bookcase, pulling down another thick tome, this one covered with shooting stars and lustrous planets.

"The Aurora Comet—I'm sure I've read about it before," Wynter said, flicking frantically through the pages as she moved to sit on the couch, then making a triumphant sound. "Got it!"

She lowered the book onto her lap and tapped a finger on the opened page, prompting everyone to crowd around her, with Viri sitting at her side and Reeve, Sage, and Jonas standing shoulder to shoulder and leaning in for a closer look. The text was written in indecipherable runes and had a shimmering gold illustration in the corner: two radiant beings sharing a passionate embrace.

"The comet is part of the Adastrum Devotis—the star-crossed lovers," Wynter said, translating the runes for them.

"Part of?" Reeve repeated, examining the drawing.

"Aurora is one of a pair—the first of *two* comets that appear once every two hundred years," Wynter said, skimming the page. "The story goes that she and her lover, Orion, were two mages of such incredible power that, whenever they touched, the world trembled on its foundations. The destruction they caused was a danger to all living creatures, so the Elder mages banished them to the heavens, ensuring they would be separated for all time, with Orion forever straining for his lover but never able to reach her." Wynter ran her hands over the embracing couple. "The Aurora Comet and the Orion Comet—where one goes, the other follows, for all eternity."

"That's a very depressing story," Jonas said, cuddling Walnut closer. "Why do so few legends have happy endings?"

"Depressing or not," Wynter said, still reading the runes, her brow scrunched in concentration, "I have good news, bad news, more bad news, and then some *very* good news."

"I can guess some of the bad news," Reeve said, his body lined with tension, as it had been ever since Wynter had begun sharing the star-crossed tale. "A second comet means there's a second opportunity for a sacrifice, even if we manage to stop the first."

Viri froze, realizing he was right.

"Yes," Wynter confirmed. "But the good news about that is, according to this"—she pointed to the ancient writing—"the Orion Comet requires a different kind of sacrifice than Aurora. There aren't many details here—I'll have to do more research—but there's a reference to something called *ellixen abyssus*, which, roughly translated, means 'void magic.' I'm not sure what that is, just that it's apparently very rare. So even though both comets require the same baseline things—purity of heart, magical strength, and bloodletting—this addition for Orion is good for us, because whatever it is, it's unlikely to be found in one child, let alone many."

"So Aurora is still the main threat," Viri surmised, with no small amount of relief.

"I'd go as far as to say she's the only threat you need to worry about at this point," Wynter said. "Which leads me to the other good news and bad news—the bad being that I don't know how much time will pass between Aurora's arrival and Orion's. It could be days, it could be weeks. I'll look into it, but for now, at least we know the second comet isn't the main concern, not if it needs this unique *ellixen abyssus* magic."

Viri's relief grew at her friend's confidence. They still had one sacrifice to stop, but one was *much* better than two.

"If that's the bad news, then what's the good?" Sage asked.

A victorious light touched Wynter's eyes as she pointed to a set of runes at the bottom of the page. "I might not know about Orion, but I can tell you when Aurora will be appearing."

Viri's heart skipped a beat. "How long do we have?"

The light left Wynter's eyes as quickly as it had come. "According to this, Aurora will pass over Elverdine Isle this Sunday night." She traced the runes. "That means you have until then to find the Reaper Priest and stop the sacrifice."

Horror slammed into Viri. "That's *three days* from now."

Reeve cursed and pinched the bridge of his nose, but then his expression steeled with determination as his eyes locked with Viri's. "We need to get to Brae. I know where he is, but you're the only one who can find him."

Viri's brow furrowed at the convoluted words. "What do you mean?"

"It's why I sought you out in the first place," Reeve went on. "I can't get to him without you."

"Hang on." Viri raised her palm in a stop motion. "I was the one who came to you—in *prison*, remember?"

He held her gaze. "Didn't you ever wonder why I let myself get arrested?"

An incredulous laugh left her. "You were caught. There's a difference."

"Was I, though?"

Viri stilled at the look on his face—part proud, part calculating, all confident. A knot formed in her stomach as she belatedly recalled that no one had come forward to take credit for his capture.

"It's like he just . . . appeared *here,"* Soren had said.

But if what Reeve was saying was true, then that meant . . .

"What are you playing at?" Viri demanded.

"I needed your attention," Reeve said without a hint of shame. "So I found a way to get it." He looked ruefully around the lab. "Granted, I didn't expect it to take a whole week, but here we are."

Viri wasn't sure what she felt more acutely: disbelief or anger. "There were a million ways you could have reached me that didn't involve a prison. Or a prison *break*." She thought of what they'd done to Soren—and Darik—and scowled fiercely. "You made me an accomplice for no reason."

"You'd be surprised how few options I had," he replied, an odd, bitter tinge to his voice. "This was the only way to do what needs to be done without watching eyes."

"Whose eyes? What needs to be done?" Viri's scowl deepened. "What the hell is going on, Reeve?"

He looked at Jonas and Sage, just a brief glance, as if to bolster himself, then said, "I need to tell you something—it's the reason I wasted a week in a cell just to get to you, so when I say it's important, I mean it."

Viri braced, sharing her own look with Wynter, who was watching with rampant curiosity.

"I know how you feel about me—you've made yourself perfectly clear," Reeve continued, that odd bitterness returning to his voice again before it vanished once more. "I'm not asking you to trust me. I'm not even asking you to believe me. I'm just asking you to listen. Can you do that?"

Whether it was the way he was looking at her—earnest and pleading—or the desperation in his words, Viri couldn't deny his request. But before she could tell him as much, a *click* sounded as the door to the lab opened and Soren burst through, looking more panicked than Viri had ever seen him.

"Thank the Elders you're here," he panted, running over to where they were clustered around the couch.

Viri and Wynter leapt up at his wild-eyed entrance, but he barely glanced at them, moving straight to where Reeve stood beside Sage and Jonas.

For a brief moment, Viri wondered if Soren was going to pay Reeve back for knocking him out earlier, but he didn't attack. Instead, he said the last four words she ever expected to hear from her rule-abiding best friend.

"I need your help," Soren rasped to Reeve.

Reeve's eyebrows shot upward—as did everyone else's.

"What's wrong, Sor?" Wynter reached for his arm. "What's happened?"

"It's Jessalyn." Soren's voice shook so hard that goosebumps rose on Viri's skin.

“What about her?” Wynter asked. “Is she hurt? Sick?”

Realization slammed into Viri the second before Soren answered, along with a wave of dread, stronger than anything she’d felt that night.

“Worse,” Soren croaked out. “She’s missing.”

THE JOURNAL OF CELESTIAL MAGE KADMUS CASTRO

Twenty-First Sun, Tenth Cycle, Twelfth Age

Zeranthe was right.

Tephryn didn't want to meet about the Adastrum Devotis comets. Or not *just* about the comets. Mostly, she wanted to get to know me, not as a celestial mage but as a person—a novel concept.

It was . . . nice. I felt surprisingly comfortable in her presence, and the only time that became less so was when she asked about the rituals I perform and whether it's true they all require three things: a pure heart, strong enough ellixen to connect with and draw from the celestial bodies, and blood. The blood is my own, of course, and just a drop for the blessing and purification rites I practice, though the idea of using blood at all makes many mages uneasy, given some of the sacrificial rituals used—and forbidden—long ago.

Fortunately, Tephryn was fascinated rather than appalled. But then she started asking whether there has been anything unusual about my ceremonies on the isle compared to the mainland, and I skillfully evaded her queries. Instead, I turned the conversation around onto her and, specifically, the obelisks, hoping I might glean a way to counteract their power before my next ritual.

Our conversation, held at her favorite lakeside teahouse, went like this:

"I'm not sure how the wardstones themselves are made—the enchantments the fabricator mages use to create them have always been a well-guarded secret—but I came up with the idea to infuse them with suppression magic," Tephryn said, her dark skin gleaming in the sun-dappled space as she looked at me over her teacup. "All I did was capitalize on the protective nature of the wardstones, and instead of their usual form of shielding, my infusion altered them to suppress the Hallow Stream's uncontrollable flood of magic." She shrugged. "Simple, really."

Simple wasn't the word I would use.

"That said," she added, her pretty teal eyes shining with intelligence, "it was tricky not knowing where the Stream is. That's why we had to build enough wardstones to cover the whole city, which was a hassle, but it was worth it since our magic is working normally now. And when the mage scholars *do* finally locate the Stream, at least we know the suppression wards will keep them safe while they study it."

I tried to appear curious rather than desperate when I asked, "But how did you make the suppression part work? I've never understood alchemical infusions. All I know is that they're dangerous."

Her head tilted thoughtfully as she considered my question. "Your celestial magic—it works by you siphoning power from ellixen-rich astronomical events, yes?"

Siphoning. That was a good way to describe my rituals, so I nodded.

"And the power you draw down is absorbed by the shallows in attendance?"

I nodded again, saying nothing about how I also absorb some of that power, at least here on Elverdine.

"Well, think of infusion as the opposite of what you do. You siphon magic from an outside source to acquire more power, like reaping a harvest grown by someone else. Or in this case, some*thing* else."

"I'm sorry . . . harvest reaping?"

"*Magical* reaping," Tephryn clarified. "When you siphon ellixen, you're essentially stealing it. Reaping it. What alchemists do with infusion is the opposite—instead of pulling magic from elsewhere, we push our own magic into things. Potions, weapons, talismans, and the like."

"But other mages push their magic outward, too," I argued. "Fabricator mages, elemental mages, enchanter mages, healer mages, nature mages . . . Elders, even the shallows who have enough ellixen to perform small tasks like conjuring and cleaning and—"

"Yes, yes." Tephryn waved an impatient hand, nearly spilling her tea.

"I know most ellixen is used like that, with it leaving us for an action or creation of some kind. But infusion is different. Alchemists transform preexisting matter into something new, something magical, and it remains that way—*forever*. Because of that, infusion goes against the natural law. And depending on the complexity of the task, it can require us to push the boundaries of our ellixen for it to actually *work* and not just be temporary, or become something else entirely. *That's* why it's dangerous. Because if we use too much of our ellixen, or if it doesn't replenish fast enough, then we risk burning out."

Before I could ask if she'd ever come close to the deadly threat of burnout, she went on to share more about the experimental infusion she'd used on the obelisks, and then began hypothesizing about the secret enchantments the fabricator mages used during their construction. I could barely follow what she said, though it left me feeling disheartened with the realization of how strong and permanent the four obsidian pillars are. Nothing short of a miracle could destroy them, and even then, Tephryn and the fabricators would just build new ones.

I have to be smart if I want to find a way to regain access to the full, unrestrained power of the Hallow Stream. And I *do* want that. No—I *need* it. The shallows here depend on me. I will not lose their devotion. I *cannot* lose their devotion.

And the magic . . . I need more of it.

More to siphon. More to reap.

Those two words Tephryn used keep replaying in my mind. *Siphoning*. *Reaping*. There's something in them, something whispering to me, taunting me, like an idea just out of reach.

I will figure this out.

I *will*.

18

Viri couldn't stop trembling as Soren shared the few details he had about Jessalyn's disappearance, starting with how he'd awoken from Reeve's knockout punch to be questioned by an irate Darik before being ordered home. Once there, he found a note left by Jessalyn's babysitter saying she'd gone for a sleepover with her friend Mia, something she often did when Soren had late-night patrols.

"With the news about the missing kids and the sacrifice fresh in my mind, I needed to see for myself that she was safe, even if it meant waking Mia's family," Soren said, pacing back and forth around the lab, running his hands through his hair until it was an uncharacteristic sandy mess. Even his black uniform was untucked and rumpled, proving just how distraught he was. "When I got there, her parents were already awake, so I knew something was wrong. They told me Mia and Jessy went to meet some schoolmates for ice cream after dinner, but they—" His throat bobbed. "They never returned."

Viri wasn't sure if she was breathing as her friend continued his tale. She was aware of Wynter shaking on her left side, of

Reeve standing rigid on her right, of Sage and Jonas a few steps away, all of them listening intently.

"I hurried back to work to raise the alarm, but the reception guards told me eight kids had just been saved and returned home, including some of Jessy's friends. So I rushed back to our apartment to see if she was there, but she—she wasn't."

A sound left Viri's lips, part gasp, part moan, all horror. She swayed on her feet and only kept from falling because Reeve's hand curled around hers, his touch grounding her. She didn't even consider ripping her arm away. Instead, she held on tight and turned to him, seeing the same realization in his stony features.

The four kids they'd lost in the alley—Jessalyn had been one of them.

"This is all your *fault!"* Sage's voice raged across Viri's memory. "You're *the reason we lost those kids!"*

Soren kept speaking, explaining how he'd sought out his sister's friends and begged for information about where she might be, but they'd known nothing. Viri barely heard him, a tightness pressing against her chest so hard that she was beginning to see black spots at the edges of her vision, Sage's words still screaming in her mind.

"Breathe, Little Shadow," Reeve whispered into her ear, interrupting her shrieking thoughts. He leaned so close that the warmth of his body was almost enough to melt the ice encasing hers. "Breathe, or you'll pass out."

At the authority in his voice, Viri sucked in a painful breath, then another, her vision returning, the tightness in her chest easing, the enraged words quieting. But her horror remained, more acute than ever.

"And then finally I spoke with a boy, Mateo, and he told me they were saved from a group of reapers by a red-cloaked hunter and three people who moved so fast they could only be reapers themselves," Soren said. He glanced at Viri, taking in the now-dry alley filth and crusted blood covering her, then cast his gaze over Reeve, Sage, and Jonas. "It was you, wasn't it? You saved those kids?"

Viri was still struggling to breathe, let alone speak, so she didn't correct him about Jonas and only nodded.

Reeve, however, said, "We did. But unfortunately, there was a small group that disappeared while we were fighting."

"Mateo told me that as well." Soren's face was pale as he stared at Reeve. "It's why I came looking for you. Please, I have to find my sister. I can't—" His voice broke. "I can't lose her. I'll do anything. Just—Just tell me what to do."

Viri felt as if a knife were stabbing her heart. It was unheard of, a Nox asking a reaper for help, and yet, here they were.

For a long moment, Reeve and Soren just looked at each other, silver eyes meeting brown, but then Reeve turned to Sage and said, "Viri and I need to go after Brae, but in case things don't go as planned, we still need boots on the ground to find those kids. Track down Ardin, get him to work his connections, tell him we only have until Sunday before the comet arrives."

"Sunday?" Soren turned alarmingly paler. Wynter was at his side in an instant, wrapping an arm around him and murmuring in comfort.

Reeve continued to give Sage orders. "If we can't find the kids, then we need to know where the sacrifice is taking place. But keep in mind, the Nox and hunters will be searching as well, so be careful not to cross paths with them since they won't know we're allies."

There was that word again—allies. Viri never would have thought it possible before tonight, but all evidence suggested Reeve and his reaper friends were doing exactly what they'd claimed: helping. She didn't have to like them—Elders knew that would never happen—but it was time she put aside her misgivings and at least tried to trust that they were all on the same side. For Jessalyn's sake, if nothing else.

"Understood," Sage said with a solemn nod.

Reeve nodded back, then gestured between her and Soren. "Archer, this is Sage D'alia, a fierce warrior and loyal friend. If you can stomach working with reapers, then she'll take you to our other friend, Ardin Avarni, and they'll do everything they can to help find your sister."

Seeing the uncertainty on Soren's face, and still feeling guilt over Jessalyn's abduction, Viri said, "Maybe I should go with—"

"No," Reeve interrupted, his hand squeezing hers. She'd forgotten he was still holding her, and hastily unwound their fingers. "I can't stress enough how important it is that we find your brother."

Viri was aware of Wynter whispering to Soren—filling him in about the Reaper Priest's identity and Viri's history with Reeve—but despite the shock she could feel coming from her friend, Viri's gaze remained locked on Reeve as she said, "Soren needs me. *Jessy* needs me."

"This whole *city* needs you more," Reeve countered. "If we don't stop Braedan from what he's about to do, then everyone on this island is going to die."

His words were like a thunderclap, leaving a ringing silence in their wake.

But then Viri realized exactly what his dramatic declaration meant, and she said, with clear accusation, "You know what he plans to do with the comet's power, don't you?"

A muscle feathered in Reeve's jaw as he debated whether or not to answer. It took a moment, but with a long, resigned sigh, he finally revealed, "If the sacrifice goes ahead, the power drawn from Aurora will be strong enough to destroy the obelisks."

Viri stared at him, certain she must have heard wrong.

She wasn't the only one, since Wynter asked, her words choked, "But—if the obelisks are destroyed, then the wards around the city will be destroyed with them. There'll be no protection from the blackmist."

Soren pressed a hand to his temple, looking queasy. "There'll also be no way for kids to Impart—which means reapers will have an unlimited siphoning range to choose from."

"They won't, though. If kids don't yield their magic, they'll burn out," Wynter argued. "Without knowing how to avoid it, they'll die. Or if they survive, they'll become living shells."

"Do you think reapers will care if the person they siphon from is cognizant or not?" Soren argued back. "They don't give a damn where their ellixen comes from, just as long as they get it." He glanced at Reeve, Sage, and Jonas and grimaced, as if belatedly remembering he'd come to them for help, and grudgingly added, "No offense."

Viri spoke up then, her voice trembling. "There's a bigger problem. If there are no wards to keep the blackmist away, then the surface will become uninhabitable, and we'll all be stuck inside the mountains and in the undercity. That means—"

Wynter clutched her throat. "The farms. The docks. We won't be able to get to them."

Viri nodded grimly. Without protection from the blackmist, it would be impossible to access their food sources—grains, vegetables, fruit, meat, fish, *everything* would be gone. They'd have only what was in storage, eventually leaving the entire population to starve to death.

"But . . . wait," Wynter said, her forehead creasing. "It won't benefit the Reaper Priest if we all die. Reapers are human. They need food, too."

Sage gestured to her blackened veins. "Actually, we can survive on ellixen alone if we must."

Wynter blinked at that revelation. "You still need people to siphon from. And if everyone's dead, there goes your source of ellixen."

Viri glanced between Sage and Jonas, recalling how reapers could also siphon from each other. But Jonas had said it was a detestable practice to most, since they preferred their ellixen fresh from the source. She was about to ask if Braedan would really damn the innocents of the city just to be left with a group of disgruntled, hungry reapers when Jonas spoke up first.

"Um, actually, ellixen doesn't leave the body after death." He clutched Walnut nervously. "Not unless it's been siphoned, which therefore is the cause of death."

A beat of silence passed, before Wynter said, slowly, "Correct me if I'm wrong—and please, Elders, let me be wrong—but it sounds like you're implying that reapers don't require people to be *living* in order to steal their magic." When Jonas said nothing, her voice pitched a full octave higher. "Are you saying you can siphon from *corpses*?"

Hesitantly, Jonas nodded. "It's gross, though," he added quickly. "I would never disrespect the dead like that. *We* would never." He indicated himself and Sage. "And Reeve doesn't siphon at all, so he'd definitely never do that."

Both Wynter and Soren looked at Reeve in surprise. He just shrugged in response.

"The point is," Jonas continued, "if the obelisks fall, and people are trapped underground, and the food runs out, and everyone dies . . . then reapers can still live on."

"With full control of the city," Soren said tightly, cursing at the scope of the threat. "If the Priest succeeds in destroying the obelisks, then reapers will have complete freedom. No more fear of arrest, no hunters or Nox to contend with. And they'll have a whole population's worth of people—dead or alive—to tide them over for years until they run out of bodies."

"But they *will* run out eventually," Viri noted, her brow furrowing. "And when that happens, they'll be as trapped as the rest of us. The blackmist is just as dangerous to them—it absorbs the ellixen of anyone it touches, *including* reapers, which makes it a death sentence to *everyone*. That leads us right back to the reapers being stuck underground, where one day, they'll have no more magic left to steal. And since Jonas told me earlier that most of them refuse to siphon from each other—"

"Wait, reapers can siphon from *each other*?" Wynter exclaimed.

"—then this doesn't seem like a strategic long-term goal," Viri finished over her friend. She chewed her lip and looked at Reeve. "Are you sure this is what the comet is being used for? Brae's never been shortsighted. Even as a boy, everything he did was calculated. This seems almost desperate, not something he's been planning for months, maybe years."

"I'm absolutely certain that the power of the Aurora sacrifice will be used to destroy the obelisks," Reeve confirmed. Something about his wording tugged at Viri, but she was distracted when he scratched his neck and acknowledged, "But there could also be more to it. Something else we haven't factored in."

"Like Orion," Viri guessed, recalling how the second comet had been a surprise to them all. "Brae might have plans for it as well, something that supports a longer-lasting goal for reapers once the city falls to the mist."

"I still don't think Orion's a concern," Wynter said. "But I'll comb through every book I own for any references to it and its *ellixen abyssus* requirement, just to be sure."

"I can help!" Jonas offered, his eyes bright behind his glasses at the idea of inspecting more ancient magical tomes.

"That would be appreciated," Reeve told them both, "but there's actually a different reason why we need to be worried about Braedan. Something much more time-sensitive."

"More time-sensitive than the *three days* we have until he tries to kill us all?" Viri asked incredulously.

Reeve's face was grave. "If he succeeds in what he's planning, he won't need those three days. It's what I began telling you before we were interrupted. And speaking of . . ." He turned to Sage and Soren. "You should go find Ardin, see if there's a chance of tracing Jessalyn while her trail's still hot. But if not—"

"Find the other kids, or worst case, the location of the sacrifice," Sage recited. She eyed Soren, a challenge in her expression. "What do you say, Nox? Are you willing to work with a reaper?"

"I'm here, aren't I?" He shook off his horror over what they'd just learned and returned her look with a challenging one of his own. "Help me find my sister, and I might not even arrest you afterward."

Sage barked out a laugh. "You could try." Her teeth flashed in a devilish grin. "But you'd fail." She marched away without giving him a chance to reply, calling over her shoulder, "Haul ass, Archer. We've got kids to save."

Soren looked at Wynter, who nodded in encouragement, then turned to Viri, his features flooding with uncertainty.

"Go. Find Jessy," she told him. She made herself add, "Sage is rough around the edges, but she's good to have in a fight and seems to have a decent moral compass." For a reaper, at least. "That goes for Ardin, too. If you can resist killing each other, I don't think they'll let you down." It went against Viri's instincts to say the words, but surprisingly, she meant them. "Be on your guard, but—as strange as this is to say—I think you can trust them."

"And you?" Soren asked, his gaze flicking between her and Reeve, then down to where they'd been holding hands earlier, something he hadn't missed even in his panic. "Are you still on your guard?"

Reeve chuckled darkly and answered for her. "Don't worry, she still hates me. Apparently more than ever—her words."

"That's not what I asked," Soren said, before pointedly adding, "And it's clear to anyone with eyes that she doesn't."

"Anyone with eyes needs to get their vision checked," Viri stated flatly. "And I'm a hunter—I'm always on my guard." She pushed Soren toward the door, where Sage was impatiently tapping her foot. "Now go, before she leaves without you."

Soren was clearly waging an inner war, wanting to stay with

Viri and Wynter and hear what Reeve was about to share, but also needing to save his sister. Reason won out, and, with a warning look to Viri, a silent reminder to be careful, he strode off after Sage, the two of them vanishing from the lab.

Viri spun back to Reeve. "Time to talk. What's this new time-sensitive threat?"

19

Much like Soren had earlier, Reeve began to pace around the workroom, his agitation more concerning than the stillness he'd maintained for most of their discussion.

"Do you remember the story your parents used to tell us when we were kids?" he asked. "The one about the Guardian of Elverdine Isle?"

Viri blinked at him. Blinked again. Then threw back her head and laughed. "Elders, you can't be serious?"

Reeve halted his pacing to cross his arms over his broad chest. "I told you earlier that I don't need you to trust me, but I do need you to listen. Laughing isn't listening."

"Don't worry, I heard you loud and clear," Viri said, still chuckling. "I also know that whatever you're about to say is going to be ridiculous. The Guardian of the Isle? *Really*, Reeve?"

"What do you remember about it?" he pressed.

Viri's laughter faded. "This is hardly the time for fairy tales."

He shot her a look. "Humor me."

Baffled, Viri glanced at Jonas and Wynter, both of whom

seemed to be on Reeve's side—Jonas likely because he already knew what Reeve was going to say, and Wynter because she was dying of curiosity.

"Do you want the full bedtime story," Viri asked dryly, "or will a summary do?" She couldn't believe she was indulging him when it felt as if the whole island were burning around them.

"A summary is fine," Reeve said.

"No, the full story," Wynter requested. "What's the Guardian of Elverdine Isle?"

"Not what, *who*," Jonas corrected. "He's part of an ancient legend, one not widely known."

Wynter's brows rose with intrigue, and she looked at Viri in expectation.

Giving in, Viri sighed and said, "You might as well sit back down for this."

Wynter returned to the couch, and when Jonas sat beside her, she held her hands out for Walnut. "I sense I'm going to need bunny snuggles for this."

"It's not a scary legend," he assured her.

"I didn't think it would be. I just want an excuse to pet the floof."

Jonas grinned and handed the rabbit over. "I can't fault you there. Walnut snuggles are the best snuggles."

"Elders save me," Viri muttered, looking up through the glass dome in search of divine patience, only to become alarmed by how much lighter the lake was now, with dawn swiftly turning into sunrise somewhere above the water. No wonder her tolerance was gone—she'd missed an entire night's worth of sleep.

"I'm only going to say this once, so pay attention," Viri warned, starting her own pacing around the lab. "There had also better be a damned good reason for this waste of time." She speared a look at Reeve, who remained in the middle of the room, his feet planted, his arms still crossed, but he gave a dip of his head to indicate there was.

"I'll explain when you're done," he promised. "But I need to know what you remember first."

Viri's eyes narrowed. "I'm seventeen, not seventy. My memory's as good as it's always been."

Reeve said nothing to that, though there was an odd tension about him, as if he was restraining himself from snapping back. Instead, all he said was, "Fabulous. Now prove it."

Viri gritted her teeth, then started at the beginning, just like her parents used to. "Once upon a time there were three young hunters: a husband, his wife, and their best friend. All of them were skilled, the husband especially so—until he was injured in a reaper attack and siphoned almost to death, leaving him weak and unable to do the one thing he felt he was born to do: hunt."

She tucked a strand of hair behind her ear and continued, "Miserable and without purpose, he began to fade away, so his concerned wife and friend suggested they seek out the mythical Guardian of Elverdine Isle—a mage who had chosen not to depart with his ancient peers and instead stayed behind to watch over the island from his tower beyond thc Mistwood."

"*Beyond* the Mistwood?" Wynter repeated, wide-eyed. "But . . . there's nothing beyond it. There's no way through the blackmist—it covers the entire forest."

Viri pinched her forehead. "Please, Wyn, no interruptions. This is painful enough."

"Sorry, sorry." Wynter smiled apologetically. "I'll wait until the end."

Grateful, Viri went on, "Legend claimed that anyone who found the Guardian would be granted a magewish—a treasure of incomparable worth, powerful enough to fulfill any request. It was assumed that no one would be able to reach him to claim such a prize, because even without the threat of the blackmist, the Mistwood was ever-changing and the path to the tower was always shifting. But what the Guardian didn't know was that one of his fellow mages had left behind a magical map that could lead to his location, along with a set of talismans that could ward against the blackmist saturating the wood. He also didn't know that this map and one of the talismans had found its way to the family of the wife, handed down from generation to generation, providing the means for her husband to get his life back."

Viri kept pacing as she continued, "Guided by the map and protected by the talisman, the three hunters ventured through the Mistwood to the Guardian's tower, and when they found him there, he was honor bound to gift them their magewishes—one each, no more, no less. The husband used his straightaway and was instantly healed. But his wife and their friend wanted to save theirs, so the Guardian gave them each a token and said that when they were ready, they could return the tokens and make their requests."

"I've never even *heard* of magewishes," Wynter whispered to Jonas. "I *love* this story."

Viri shared a beleaguered look with Reeve, whose lips

twitched in response. She scrunched her nose up at him—which only made his lips twitch more.

"Time passed." Viri spoke quickly now to hurry things along. "The husband and wife had a child and longed for another, but the young mother found she couldn't conceive again. So she returned to the Guardian and used her wish. Her womb opened and a second child arrived, their little family happy and complete." Viri's tone lowered as the tale darkened. "But disaster struck less than a year later, when their second-born was touched by the blackmist. The husband and wife knew there was only one way to save their precious babe—they needed their friend's unused magewish. And so, in an act of desperation, they stole the token and hurried back to the Guardian with their dying infant."

Wynter was at the edge of her seat, clutching Walnut so close that Jonas seemed tempted to pull his bunny back to safety.

"The Guardian wasn't pleased," Viri said. "The wishes were meant to be one per person, but since they had their friend's token, he reluctantly agreed to grant their request. Unfortunately, while they were debating it, the blackmist infecting the babe finished its work, absorbing the final speck of ellixen, and the child passed away."

A gasp from Wynter. "No!"

"Calm down, Wyn, it's just a story," Viri said, rolling her eyes. "And don't worry—the babe survived. The magewish had already been spoken, so the Guardian was bound by the laws of magic to fulfill the request. He did warn that there would be a steep cost to bringing a life back from death, and that he would need to bind the child to the magic of the island to do so, but the parents didn't care what that meant as long as their babe was saved. And so the Guardian granted their wish, the child was purged of the blackmist and filled with ellixen straight from the isle . . . and their little family lived happily ever after."

Viri stopped pacing right in front of Reeve. "Did I remember everything to your satisfaction, oh doubting one?"

He ignored her sarcasm. "I'm very impressed. Gold star."

"Wait—what happened to the friend?" Wynter asked. "Weren't they angry about their magewish being stolen?"

"The story always ended at the 'happily ever after' part," Viri answered. "I don't know what happened beyond that. And just to reemphasize, it's a *story*."

Wynter's face was contemplative as she stroked Walnut's ears. "All stories come from somewhere."

"I'd be guessing the friend was furious," Reeve said, his eyes on Wynter, not Viri, as if looking for something in her reaction, but she only nodded.

"Same here," Wynter agreed. "Talk about the ultimate betrayal."

"Again, it's a *story*," Viri said firmly.

"How did you even hear it?" Wynter tilted her head to the side, her hair flowing like ink over her shoulder. "The Guardian, the magewishes—these aren't common lore, and yet, you heard it as a bedtime story. How? *Why?*"

Viri knew she was going to regret answering before the words even left her mouth. "Because my family is supposedly descended from the husband and wife."

Wynter's eyes bugged out. "You're related to the was-dead child who was revived with special magic?"

Viri shook her head. "No." She bit her cheek. "Well, technically yes. But it could just be through the line of the wasn't-dead firstborn."

"*Or* it could be—"

"Either way," Viri cut Wynter off before she could get ahead of herself, "it doesn't matter, since it happened a long time ago—if at all—and even if I *am* a direct descendant of the was-dead babe, none of that special magic is in me." Or if it had been, it would have been given to the obelisks during her Impartation. "Stop gaping at me like that, Wyn."

"Oh, I'm sorry," Wynter said with attitude, "but it's not every day that I learn my best friend is part of an *ancient legend*."

"I'm not. My great-great-great-whatever grandparents are. That's hardly newsworthy—we're all related to someone with a story. Mine just happens to involve Guardians, magewishes, and unorthodox resurrection magic."

"Don't forget betrayal," Reeve said, still watching Wynter, but his features lost their tension at whatever he saw. "That one's important, too."

"You'd know," Viri said under her breath.

Bemused, Wynter asked, "How can you not have more questions about this? I'd want to know *everything*. Like—" She gasped again and sat up even straighter. "The map. The talisman. If they're handed down from generation to generation—"

"And now we've come to why we're here," Reeve interjected smoothly. He was still standing in front of Viri, his attention returning to her fully as he asked, "Why do you think I wanted you to remember that story?"

Viri groaned. "Reeve, I'm tired. I missed a whole night of sleep thanks to you, so instead of playing guessing games, just tell me. But if you're going where I think you're going with this, then don't bother."

He just looked at her, waiting for her to say it.

Viri groaned again. "No. *No.* Braedan isn't looking for the Guardian of the Isle. It's impossible. The legend is a myth, and even if it *wasn't*, the Guardian would be long dead by now. The ancient mages were powerful, but they weren't immortal."

"The Elder mages were," Wynter put in. "But regardless, 'Guardian' could be a title that gets passed along each generation to someone new."

Through clenched teeth, Viri said, "Fine. If by some miracle a Guardian does exist, then Brae would still need—"

"The map and talisman that your parents had?" Reeve asked, cocking an eyebrow. "The ones they kept locked in a warded chest behind the hidden wall in their closet?"

All the air left Viri in a rush. "What?" she breathed.

"We found it by accident," Reeve said. "Brae and me—we were messing around, looking for a place to hide the next time we played Seeker with you." Ruefully, he added, "You were always so quick to find us. We needed all the help we could get."

Viri pushed through a stab of pain, shoving the memories away.

"The ward was keyed to your bloodline, so I couldn't open it, but all Brae had to do was touch the lock on the chest and it opened instantly," Reeve went on. "We didn't know what we'd found at first—the map was obviously a map, but we didn't realize it was special, not until we saw that it covered the whole island, going beyond the city into what should have been uncharted territory. But what really clued us in was the dotted line leading through the Mistwood, because it *moved*. From one blink to the next, the path changed, though the end point was always the same: a location at the northwest edge of the island called Nevarnost Tower."

"Nevarnost . . ." Wynter whispered. "It even *sounds* magical. Definitely somewhere an ancient mage would live."

Viri still had her doubts. "So you claim you found the map—"

"We *did* find the map."

"—but what about the talisman? What makes you so confident about that?"

Reeve met her smug tone with his own. "Because we tested it."

"Nice try," Viri scoffed. "That would mean—" She broke off, paling. "Tell me you didn't."

He offered a one-shouldered shrug. "We were young. Fearless."

"You were *stupid*," Viri corrected.

Jonas coughed to hide his snicker. Wynter didn't bother to hide hers.

"We had to find out somehow," Reeve defended. "We'd heard the story from your parents so many times that we knew it by heart, and the map was clearly magical, so it wasn't a huge leap to trust that the talisman would work. Which it did, obviously, since we took it into the mist and we're both still alive."

Viri didn't know what to say. The risk they'd taken . . . her stomach turned just thinking about it.

A teasing smile touched the corner of Reeve's mouth. "Is that concern I see in your eyes, Little Shadow?"

Viri wiped her face clear. "No. Just disappointment that it worked."

Reeve huffed out a laugh. "And we're back to lying." He shook his head, amused, but then returned to his story. "Brae and I wanted to seek out the Guardian for our own magewishes, but your parents discovered we'd been snooping, and the next time we went looking for the chest, it was gone. We searched everywhere but never found it again."

Relief slammed into Viri. "So Braedan *doesn't* have the map and talisman?" Annoyance set in. "Why are we even talking about this, then? He can't reach the Guardian without them."

"The talisman was part of a set, remember?" Reeve said. "Brae mightn't have the one belonging to your family, but that doesn't mean he hasn't located another."

"I doubt they're growing on trees," Viri countered sarcastically.

"Look around." Reeve indicated the colorful alchemy lab. "You two aren't the only ones in this city to possess rare magic."

"He has a point," Wynter said, shifting on the couch. "Speaking from experience, people go to great lengths to hoard—and hide—enchanted artifacts. It's not a huge stretch to think your brother might have been able to source one of these talismans from a discreet collector, especially when he already knew what he was looking for."

Viri didn't want to agree, if only because she feared what it might mean. "For the sake of your argument, let's assume Brae does have a talisman. He still doesn't have the map."

"No, but he's seen it," Reeve said. "It might have been years ago, but he's always had near-perfect recollection, even after his Impartation. He could draw a replica in his sleep."

"But it wouldn't be magical."

"It doesn't need to be. The magical map shows the most direct route to Nevarnost Tower, one that changes as the forest moves. But I told you before, the end point we saw always remained the same. The trek would be a lot slower for someone who doesn't know how to navigate the shifting Mistwood, but Brae would still be able to find his way there eventually."

Viri's pulse picked up speed as dread began to set in. It was impossible—*surely* it was impossible—and yet . . .

"Let's say I believe you, that Brae can get safely through the blackmist, and his childhood memory of a map he saw years ago is all he needs to find the tower," Viri said, wishing she sounded cynical but instead swallowing against the dryness in her throat. "Let's say he's making his way to the Guardian as we speak. What happens when he gets there? He'll get one magewish—how does he intend to use it?"

"I already told you." Reeve held her eyes. "I said earlier that if we don't stop him in time, everyone on the island will die."

"You were talking about the sacrifice."

"No, you just thought I was."

Viri reeled backward, suddenly understanding. "So this is a backup, then?" She quickly corrected herself. "Or . . . if he's already on his way to the Guardian, then the sacrifice is actually the backup, something he's put in place in case he doesn't reach the tower before Aurora arrives. Either way, he'll use the magewish or the comet to destroy the obelisks and doom us all."

Reeve said nothing, but Viri knew she must be right, her heart now pounding as she whispered, "We need to stop him."

"I mentioned that before, too," Reeve said dryly. "Numerous times."

Viri had *also* mentioned it numerous times—hell, she'd been trying to stop her brother for *years*—but now more than ever, urgency thrummed within her. If Braedan found the Guardian . . . if he was granted a magewish . . .

She forced herself to take a breath. Right now, the obelisks were still in place, the city was still protected, and that was all that mattered. Worrying about the future wasn't going to change it. She needed focus, not fear. That was the only way she would survive this.

"So what's the plan, then?" Wynter asked, looking pale as she jumped up from the couch to join them, Jonas following behind her. She reluctantly handed Walnut back, and the bunny settled contentedly inside Jonas's vest pocket once more.

"The plan is for Viri and me to go after Braedan," Reeve said. "He's had a solid head start, but he'll have trouble navigating a path to the tower. If we get our hands on the map, we should be able to beat him to the Guardian." To Viri, he added, "The map belongs to your family line, so the magic only works for someone with Solace blood. Aside from Brae, you're the only one who can use it."

"I know where he is, but you're the only one who can find him." Reeve's earlier words returned to Viri, along with sudden clarity about why he'd sought her out in the first place. He *needed* her. She wasn't sure if that made her feel powerful . . . or disappointed.

"And how do you propose we *find* the map?" Viri asked.

For the first time that night—now morning—Reeve looked uncomfortable. "I was hoping you could tell me."

Viri started. "How would *I* know? I didn't even know it existed until a few minutes ago."

Reeve ran his fingers through his hair, the reason for his discomfort becoming clear as he answered, "It would have been left for you with your parents' belongings. Just like your fillium."

Viri's stomach hollowed. She touched the golden cord around her wrist as she replied, "I wasn't given this until I finished my hunter training. Nothing else came with it—definitely no map.

And no talisman, either." Which they would also need to survive the mist themselves.

"I didn't say it was given to you—I said it was *left* for you," Reeve said. "You were young when your parents died. Someone would have taken possession of their things on your behalf—most likely the same person who kept your fillium from you."

Viri turned to Wynter, both of them realizing at the same time.

"Mom," Wynter breathed.

A flicker in Reeve's silver eyes made Viri suspect he'd already known the answer and had just been waiting for them to figure it out.

"Sarielle gave me my fillium when the time came," Viri confirmed aloud. "But she only kept it from me because I didn't need it before then. If she has anything else in storage from my parents, I can just ask her, and she'll hand it over."

"That easy, huh?" Reeve's skepticism was clear.

Viri shrugged. "She wants to stop the Reaper Priest as much as anyone."

An oddly dark chuckle left Reeve. "More, I'd say, given everything at stake." His expression cleared as he went on, "Regardless, you're currently on the run from the law."

Viri's lips pressed together. "Thanks to *you*."

"And Sarielle Starling is the Magistratus," he continued, ignoring the bite in her voice. "No matter how close you two are, she has a legal obligation to report you. If you approach her about this—or about *anything*—she'll have no choice but to call for the Nox."

"She's the one who told me there was no cost too steep if it meant finding the Reaper Priest," Viri argued. "She all but gave me permission to break you out of the Underlock."

"That's probably a stretch," Wynter murmured. "You know how Mom is."

Viri opened her mouth to object but then closed it just as quickly. Sarielle loved Wynter and Viri more than anything, but her life and career were both rooted in her integrity. If push came to shove, Viri wanted to believe her guardian would protect her, and she knew that was what Sarielle would *want* to do, but the truth was, Viri couldn't be entirely confident.

Sighing, she asked, "What do we do, then? If Sarielle does have more of my parents' things, she doesn't keep them in our apartment."

"Mom has an entire storeroom attached to her office," Wynter said thoughtfully.

"That's for files and legal reports and other council-related stuff," Viri returned, having visited Sarielle during work hours plenty of times.

"I'm pretty sure it's also where she kept your fillium," Wynter shared, a pensive look on her face. "If she's safeguarding anything else, that's the first place I'd search."

"I can't exactly walk into the Summit at the moment, Wyn," Viri said, frustration leaching into her tone—not at her friend, at the situation. "And before you offer to go for me, if the map only works at my touch, then I'll need to be there in person to identify it."

"And I'll need to be there to identify the talisman," Reeve said, fiddling with the onyx ring on his finger.

Viri laughed incredulously. "You *definitely* can't walk into the Summit. You'll be arrested on sight."

He arched a challenging brow. "Then we'd better come up with a plan, hadn't we? Because we can't stop Brae without those two things, and in order to get them . . ." He trailed off, his brow arching higher as he waited for Viri to finish his thought.

She sighed again, louder this time, as she realized there was only one path forward. "We need to break into the Summit."

"Great idea." Reeve flashed a winning grin. "I've always loved a good heist. Now here's what I'm thinking . . ."

20

The plan they devised was relatively straightforward, especially once they realized they could infiltrate the Summit without anyone ever seeing them.

It wouldn't have been possible on any other day, but the High Council held a weekly meeting every Friday at midday, which guaranteed a full hour when Sarielle and her colleagues would be holed up in their conference chamber. Her assistant, Galen, would still be a problem, since his desk was right outside her private office, but Wynter was confident she could tempt him away for lunch with the help of a little flirting from her "new friend" Jonas. That would leave the path clear for Reeve and Viri to sneak in, get what they needed, and sneak out again—hopefully without being arrested in the process.

When the plan was as solid as they could make it, enough time had passed that the glass dome overhead showed sunbeams trickling into the lake and an assortment of creatures swimming by, proof that morning had well and truly arrived. Viri was almost relieved that they couldn't do anything until midday, since it meant she was able to curl up on Wynter's couch and rest her tired eyes. She'd planned to only take a short nap, but everything from the previous night caught up to her the moment she lay down—fighting the reapers, Reeve's poisoning, Jessalyn's abduction, the star-crossed comets, Braedan's desire to find the Guardian, and the imminent destruction of the obelisks—and she ended up sleeping for much longer than intended. She only startled awake when Wynter shook her shoulder and handed her a pile of clothes, nudging her in the direction of the lab's adjoining bathroom.

Still half asleep, Viri scrubbed away the filth covering her from head to toe, then donned the outfit Wynter must have retrieved from their apartment while she'd been dozing—a fresh set of black hunting leathers and a clean scarlet cloak. A quick look in the steamy mirror revealed her lavender eyes to be bright and more rested than she'd expected, her red-and-silver hair wet but clean and braided over her shoulder once more, and the claw marks on her cheek completely gone thanks to Wyn's healing salve.

Feeling somewhat human again, Viri left the bathroom to find that Reeve and Jonas had also washed and changed while she'd been sleeping. Jonas now wore a different sweater-vest—this one checkered pink and purple, with another front pocket for Walnut—while Reeve was in his usual black, minus the blood and grime and dagger-slashed fabric. His hair was still damp from bathing, his eyes clear and alert enough that he must have curled up for his own nap sometime that morning.

"It's nearly time," Wynter announced. Her trainee-physician robes were nowhere in sight, but Viri decided not to comment, especially given the looming deadline for Braedan's plans and their need for Wyn to be researching the comets in what little time remained.

"Here," Jonas said, shuffling over to Viri and handing her a brown paper bag identical to the one Reeve held. "I grabbed this for you when I went to get Reeve's clothes."

Viri opened it warily, only to be hit by a delicious smell that instantly made her mouth water. "Egg-and-bacon wrap. My favorite."

Jonas beamed, his eyes flicking to Reeve, who was concentrating almost too intently on pulling a blueberry muffin out of his own bag. "I heard."

Viri could have let it affect her, the knowledge that Reeve remembered her favorite breakfast from seven years ago and had shared it with Jonas. She could have felt moved or annoyed or sad or elated or any other number of emotions. Instead, she chose to ignore everything but her rumbling stomach and bit into her wrap. Only, as she did so, an image of Jessalyn flashed across her mind, making it difficult to swallow. Had Jessy been given food since her abduction? Were she and the other children being taken care of? Were the reapers—

No, Viri told herself. *Stop.*

Soren was out searching for his sister. Sage and Ardin were with him. Viri had her own mission, and her concern for the young girl would only distract her. *Focus, not fear,* she reminded herself. Jessalyn would be all right—she had to be.

"I have something for you as well," Wynter interrupted Viri's thoughts, dragging her away from Reeve and Jonas and over to her workbench, where she'd lined up a small collection of vials. "If everything goes to plan and you head straight from the Summit to your brother, I'll feel better if you have these with you." She pointed to the vials in turn. "Impedidust and zingzest—you already know how to use those. The healing salve and morphenine, too. But this one is new." She picked up a scarlet powder in a stoppered glass. "I haven't had a chance to test it yet, but it might come in handy."

Around a mouthful of food, Viri asked, "Do I swallow it?"

Wynter blanched and all but shouted, *"No!"*

Viri jumped and nearly choked on a piece of bacon.

"Sorry," Wynter said, clutching the vial close. "But you definitely don't want to ingest this. Don't inhale it, either. Don't even *touch* it if you can help it."

"Then what—"

"It's an explosive," Wynter blurted, then winced at the look on Viri's face. "Or it *hopefully* is. Like I said, I haven't been able to test it yet. But I've been working on a new formula from one of my books, and I'm pretty confident I got it right."

"On a scale of *it doesn't work at all* to *be careful not to blow yourself up*, how confident is your 'pretty confident'?" Viri asked dubiously, finishing off the last of her breakfast and tossing the bag into the trash.

"When I say 'explosive,' I don't mean the incendiary kind, so you won't blow yourself up—or anyone else, for that matter," Wynter assured her, placing the vial back on the bench. "It's more that it works *explosively*, in the sense of it having a larger range than, say, the impedidust. If you find yourself attacked by a group of reapers—like you did last night—then smash the vial wherever they're the most concentrated. If the dust touches their skin, or they breathe it in, they should feel its effects almost immediately."

"What will it do?"

"If I made it right, it should block their ellixen-heightened abilities," Wynter answered. "Speed, strength, healing—all of that will be inaccessible. It won't drain them like your fillium, but it'll put you on even footing in a fight, at least until the effects wear off."

Viri stared at the scarlet powder in awe. "Like temporary nullicuffs, but in alchemical form."

Wynter grinned. "Precisely."

"You're a genius, Wyn," Viri said—something she'd told her friend many times, but that never made it any less true.

"Don't thank me yet," Wynter warned. "It might not work."

"Doesn't make you less of a genius."

Wynter's eyes warmed. "Love you, V," she said softly. "Promise you'll be careful?"

"Always." Viri reached out to squeeze her friend's hand. "And love you back. You're the Orion to my Aurora, you know that, right?"

Wynter mock-pouted. "Why can't I be Aurora?"

Viri chuckled. "Works for me. I'd happily chase you anywhere."

"Speaking of chasing . . ." Wynter said slyly, her gaze drifting over to where Jonas and Reeve were talking quietly on the other side of the room. "We only have a few minutes left before we need to go, so you'd better spend *every second* explaining how you kept such a juicy secret from me for so many years."

The breakfast wrap turned sour in Viri's stomach. "Braedan—"

Wynter waved a hand. "I'm not talking about your brother—we've already covered that. I want to know about Reeve."

Viri jolted. "What about him?"

"What about him?" Wynter repeated incredulously. "Have you *seen* him? He's not my type—it doesn't take an alchemist to know that mixing charm, intelligence, and confidence that borders on

arrogance is a recipe for disaster—but, Elders, even I can admit that he's beautiful to look at."

Humor quirked Viri's lips at the understatement, but then she sobered. "Beautiful or not, he's a reaper. I won't deny that there's . . . something between us, some kind of spark, or attraction, or maybe just nostalgic feelings left over from the friendship we once shared. But it doesn't matter, because like I said—he's a *reaper.* That overrides everything else."

Wynter's head tilted thoughtfully to the side. "He's not, though. Not really."

"He mightn't siphon now, but he did once," Viri said, refusing to forget what he'd done. "He killed someone. A girl. He told me so himself."

Wynter didn't have a comeback for that, but she lowered her voice to say, "I had a chance to speak with him and Jonas while you slept, and I have to admit, I like them. Did you know Jonas and Sage and their other friend—Ardin, right?—they only siphon from each other and other reapers? They don't target children. They haven't for a long time."

Viri peered across the room at Jonas, watching as he petted Walnut's head peeking out of his pocket. "I knew they could. But I didn't know they did it exclusively."

"It's quite remarkable, really," Wynter said. "They can never stop siphoning entirely because of their addiction, but the way they do it means allowing themselves to be stronger or weaker depending on who needs the ellixen more. It's almost selfless, if you think about it." Seeing Viri's expression, she added, somewhat carefully, "They're not like other reapers, V. I'm not saying they haven't made mistakes, or that I condone what they've done in the past—we both know how they became what they are, and how steep the cost was. All I'm saying is . . . it sounds like they've been trying hard to make up for their choices. And that's admirable, if you ask me."

Unsure how to respond, Viri swallowed and looked away from her friend's probing eyes. Part of her agreed with Wynter—it *was* admirable that the reapers were going against their ellixen-motivated natures and choosing a redemptive path instead of more violence. But on the other hand, no one had forced them to become what they were. At one point in time, they'd *chosen* to take innocent lives, and while it was commendable that they were trying to make amends, the hunter in Viri couldn't forgive their crimes so easily. She could work with them, even trust them to a degree, but that was where she had to draw a line.

"I know this is hard for you, especially after what happened to your parents," Wynter said quietly. "But just . . . maybe try to keep an open mind. Something tells me there's a lot more going on here than we know. *Especially* with Reeve."

"Reeve can keep his secrets," Viri said, wishing she meant it. "I'll be glad when all this is over and I never have to see him again." She wished she meant that, too.

Unfortunately, Wynter saw right through her lies, judging by the amusement lighting her features. But all she said was, "If the way he stares at you when you're not looking is any indication, I doubt he feels the same."

Viri couldn't help glancing back in Reeve's direction, finding him still engrossed with whatever Jonas was saying. But as if he felt her gaze, he looked up and met her eyes, arching a brow in question. She hurriedly turned away, willing the heat from her cheeks at having been caught.

"Seven years is a long time," Wynter went on, a smirk teasing her lips, "and you know what they say about absence and the fondness of hearts. As much as I love being one half of your star-crossed comets, I think your real Orion might just be—"

"Oh, look, it's time to go!" Viri said loudly, causing Wynter to snicker but effectively keeping her from finishing her sentence. "Is everyone ready?"

Reeve and Jonas approached the workbench as Viri pocketed the alchemy vials, both confirming they were all set.

"I'm a little concerned about the flirting part of this plan," Jonas said, removing his glasses to polish them nervously on his vest. "Walnut gets jealous when he sees me with other men."

Viri had to bite her cheek to keep from reacting to that, and an ill-timed look at Reeve showed he was doing the same, his eyes bright with mirth as they locked with hers, which only deepened her urge to laugh. But just as quickly, her humor dissolved, turning bitter. She wished things were simpler, that she and Reeve could laugh together as they once had. But that wasn't possible anymore. He was a reaper, and she was a hunter. They couldn't be what they once were—or anything else.

Allies for now. Enemies forever.

That was the way it was. The way it had to be.

"Don't worry," Wynter said to Jonas, patting his shoulder, "after I introduce you to Galen and get you both settled with lunch, I'll take Walnut on a nice, long stroll around the market district. He'll never know."

Jonas still looked torn, but he sighed and told Viri and Reeve, "I'll keep Galen away for as long as possible, but don't linger in the Magistratus's office if you can help it."

Viri was acutely aware that she and Reeve would be risking

capture with every passing second, but they weren't the only ones the plan might endanger. In a place as busy as the market district, it would be difficult for any roaming hunters to sense Jonas or see his darkened veins—especially since Sage had siphoned most of his stolen ellixen last night—but it wasn't impossible. The Hunters' Guild was small compared to the Nox, but what they lacked in numbers they made up for in skills, one of which was constant vigilance. Jonas might be able to blend into the crowd, but he'd still need to stay on his guard.

"We'll be quick, in and out," Viri promised him. "And then you can come back here and bury yourself in books."

Her words had the effect she'd been hoping for, replacing his nerves with excitement. "I can't wait. Wynnie's already said she'll teach me some more runes. We're going to have the best time researching the comets."

Viri looked at her friend and mouthed, *Wynnie?*—to which Wynter just coughed and shook her head as if to say she didn't have the heart to tell the unnaturally sweet reaper what nickname to call her. Or *not* call her.

Eyeing them all, Reeve spoke up to say, "We only have a small window while the Magistratus is with the High Council, so we need to make the most of it." With a devious grin, he finished, "Let's go break some laws."

21

The first part of their plan went as well as it could, starting with them leaving the lab and heading along the undercity tunnel back to the nearest wayportal. The thoroughfare was much busier than it had been in the early hours of the morning, the lunch rush surging in both directions, but Viri was grateful for it, since it lessened the risk of any passing Nox or hunters spotting or sensing them in the crowd. Wynter could walk freely, and Jonas could, too, as long as he didn't cross paths with anyone bearing a hunter's mark, but both Viri and Reeve were fugitives with targets on their backs. As difficult as it was, Viri resisted the urge to keep looking over her shoulder all the way to the magestone arch, knowing it would only draw attention.

Once they reached the wayportal, Wynter led the way into it. Per their plan, they didn't head directly to the Summit, instead arriving through the same arch Viri and Reeve had used for their stopover in the market district last night. The inner-mountain alleyway was the opposite of dark and lifeless now, bustling with sights and sounds and smells. It was even busier than the undercity tunnel, enough that the four of them had to scramble to the side of the wayportal to keep from being trampled as hordes of people came and left through the shimmering arch.

"Here's where we part ways," Wynter said, drawing Viri into a deep hug. "Hopefully the next time I see you, you'll have kicked your brother's ass and we can celebrate you saving the city."

"No pressure," Viri said dryly.

"I'm having shirts made while you're gone," Wynter said, straight-faced. *"Viridia Solace: Savior of Aravell."*

"Do that, and I'll make some of my own: *Wynter Starling: Ex-Best Friend.*"

Wynter laughed, but her humor faded as she hugged Viri again, whispering into her ear, "I know I said it earlier, but I'm saying it again. Love you, V. Please be careful."

Viri squeezed her friend just as tightly. "I'll be back before you know it." She nudged Wynter in the direction of the wayportal. "Now go help Jonas flirt up a storm."

Jonas took that as his cue to step closer to Viri, removing Walnut from his pocket and holding him out. "Walnut wants to wish you luck."

A lump lodged in Viri's throat as she petted the bunny's soft head. "Thanks, Walnut," she said quietly, but her gaze was on Jonas as she uttered the words. "Right back at you."

Jonas smiled, his blue eyes misty behind his glasses. He launched himself at Reeve, careful to keep Walnut held safely out to the side of their embrace.

"You'll be fine, buddy," Reeve said, patting Jonas on the back. "It's just lunch."

A laugh bubbled out of Jonas, and he pulled back to punch Reeve in the arm. "I'm not worried about *lunch.*" He made a face. "I mean, I don't *want* to go on a fake date, but it's nothing compared to what you're doing. Come back safely, all right? And bring—" He cut himself off, his eyes shifting to Viri, almost fearfully. But he quickly coughed and finished, "Bring good news back with you."

"That's the plan," Reeve said, giving Jonas a gentle push toward where Wynter was standing. "Now go. We're on the clock."

Jonas nodded and trailed obediently after Wynter, the two of them disappearing into the wayportal.

Viri blew out a breath. "And now we wait."

"Always the worst part," Reeve said, before gesturing to a set of fruit stalls bustling with customers a short distance away. "Let's head over there. We'll be able to see when they come back through, but we'll blend in better and keep them from noticing us."

Since the next part of their plan relied on Galen *not* being aware of what was happening, Viri followed Reeve to hide among the fruit-buying crowds, keeping her eyes peeled every time the wayportal activated. It was too noisy to hold a conversation—not that she had anything to say—so they wandered around the stalls and inspected the produce as if debating what to purchase. Soon enough, though, they were able to drop their acts, because Wynter and Jonas reappeared through the magestone arch with the tall, gangly Galen following close behind.

"That's our cue," Viri said once the three of them vanished deeper into the market. "Let's go."

Hurrying back to the wayportal, Viri leapt through first and guided it straight to the Summit, arriving outside the cold, clandestine walls of the Legal Guild. From there, it was only a short walk to the High Council offices and their glass-doored entry—something Viri normally appreciated for how transparent it implied the city leaders were, but today the see-through entrance just increased the risk of discovery. Thankfully, the councilors were already sequestered in their midday meeting, and since their assistants worked farther along the crisscrossing Summit tunnels, the risk was low that Viri and Reeve would run into anyone. Even so, they made sure the coast was clear before opening the glass doors, then dashed directly past Galen's vacated desk to Sarielle's office beyond it.

There, they encountered the first hiccup in their plan.

"It's locked," Viri whispered, jiggling the doorknob a few times to be sure. "Help me look for a key in Galen's desk, or find something thin and sharp so I can pick it."

"As much as I would love to watch you pick a lock—and trust me when I say I mean that"—Reeve's expression was both curious and intrigued, with a hint of something else that made Viri fight a blush—"I have a better idea."

He reached for the handle, and as he did so, Viri's skin prickled as ellixen saturated the air. A second later, the door clicked open.

"You just—You just used magic," she choked out, belatedly realizing she'd forgotten all about him knocking her out last night and her intent to interrogate him sooner—though in her defense, a lot had happened since then.

Reeve raised his hand and pressed his forefinger to his thumb. "Only a little."

"You shouldn't be *able* to—"

"Let's discuss this inside, shall we?" he suggested, opening the door fully and looking pointedly around to remind her of where they were standing, and that anyone could see them.

It cost her, but Viri bit her tongue and hurried into Sarielle's office, finding comfort in the familiar space, from the soft-carpeted floor to the polished oak desk to the picturesque sight out the large, sealed window wall. Given how high up they were, the view was unparalleled, showing Aravell's entire uppercity, the vastness of Lake Mirtis glistening in the midday sun, and even the shadowy Mistwood fading on the horizon. Viri shuddered as she realized her brother was out there somewhere, and that she would soon be venturing after him into the deadly forest, but she shoved the thought away and focused on the task at hand.

"Over here," she said, heading to the door carved into the mountain wall to the left of Sarielle's desk. This one wasn't locked, but it was only when she opened it and was about to step into the storage room beyond that she realized Reeve wasn't with her.

Turning back, she found him staring at a portrait on the wall, a gift from one of Aravell's most renowned artists. The man had painted Sarielle with her arms around a much younger Wynter and Viri, the three of them smiling brightly. Viri had always cherished the depiction of their little family, their love for each other shining through the talented artistry, but a glance at Reeve revealed a strange, almost resentful look on his face. She couldn't tell what he was thinking, whether he was upset at seeing her happy with Sarielle and Wynter, or whether it was his own demons he was battling, the fact that he, too, had found a second family—Viri's—only to lose them along with his first, leaving him alone and on the run for seven years.

Part of her ached for him, but another part, a stronger part, remembered that *he* was the one who had left. He could have stayed with her; they could have found their way together. Instead, he'd chosen Braedan. Whatever he was feeling now, he only had himself to blame.

"Reeve," Viri called, her voice like a whip in the silence of the room. "Get your ass over here."

He jolted from his thoughts and moved obediently toward her, his expression wiped clear of emotion as he followed her into the storeroom. But then a low whistle left his lips as he took in the multiple rows of floor-to-ceiling shelves bursting with boxes and files and haphazardly stacked papers, all illuminated by dim overhead everbeacons. It was nothing compared to the size of the Nox's archives, but the room was still large and chaotic enough to present a time challenge.

"I didn't expect it to be this spacious," Reeve admitted. He peered around with a calculating expression. "Let's go row by row—I'll take the left side, you take the right. If the map and talisman are here, they're probably still in the warded chest, maybe boxed up, so look for anything bulky."

Viri nodded and followed him down the first row, trying not to think about what they were doing, the crime they were committing just by being there. The fear of discovery made her skin turn clammy, but she shoved away all thoughts of Underlock cells—and Sarielle's disappointment—and got to work.

The aisle between the shelves was narrow, their elbows bumping as they stood back-to-back, inspecting anything that fit Reeve's description. Soon enough, Viri realized she could ignore the filing cabinets to focus on the storage boxes alone, but most of those still contained paperwork, some marked confidential, others little more than accounting ledgers or stationery orders. The task was tedious and time-consuming, but she continued opening and closing boxes until finally she couldn't contain her curiosity a moment longer.

"Tell me about the magic," she said, not pausing what she was doing.

Reeve, too, continued reaching for new boxes, his tone unconcerned as he asked, "What do you want to know?"

"You know what I want to know." Viri resisted the urge to turn and glare at him. "How did you do it? Destroying the nullicuffs, knocking me out, unlocking the door . . . none of those things should have been possible."

"The ancient mages were able to use magic for everything," Reeve said. "What I did was nothing compared to what they could do."

"You're not an ancient mage."

"No, but I suppose I'm what you'd call a current one."

Viri stilled in the process of opening a new box and whirled around in the narrow aisle to look at him. "That's not possible. Mages don't exist anymore. Not on Elverdine Isle."

"The reason they don't exist here is because children yield their ellixen to the obelisks, which stops them from being able to access and develop it," Reeve said, taking the box from her hands, peering inside, then placing it back on the shelf. "If they didn't, then some of them would find themselves powerful enough to become mages—assuming, of course, that they could keep from burning out in the process."

Viri could only gawk at him as he nudged her around the corner into the next row.

"Are you—Are you saying what I think you're saying?" Her voice croaked with disbelief.

"I never Imparted," Reeve confirmed. "And because of that, I found out I had enough ellixen to technically make me a mage."

At the look on her face, he added, "I was eleven when I left with Brae. When my fourteenth birthday arrived, I was already known to the Nox and hunters as the Reaper Priest's right hand. I couldn't exactly stroll to the nearest obelisk and yield my ellixen, not without chancing capture."

"But the *risk*—"

"Was limited," Reeve said with a dismissive wave. "I had a teacher of sorts, someone who taught me how to control my ellixen, which protected me from burnout." Despite his easy words, there was a darkness to his tone as he spoke of his teacher, a bitterness Viri couldn't ask about because she was too distracted by the impossibility of everything he was claiming.

"The knowledge you're speaking of doesn't *exist*. If it did—"

"More people would defy the Impartation laws?" Reeve finished for her, brows raised. "Funny you should say that, given that your own best friend never went through with the ceremony."

Viri froze in the act of reaching for a new box. "What's that supposed to mean?"

"Wynter," Reeve said. "She never Imparted—and like me, she ended up with the power level of a mage." Seeing Viri's shock, he chuckled. "Come now, Little Shadow, you're smarter than that. How do you think she practices alchemy without using ellixen?"

"I know she uses bits of it in her more potent experiments." Viri's mind screamed that he was *wrong, wrong, wrong*. "But they don't require much—just what she kept after she Imparted."

Reeve cocked his head to the side. "Did she tell you that?"

Viri was about to say yes, but then she realized Wynter had never claimed anything of the sort. Viri had just assumed she was accessing the small amount that remained after she'd sacrificed the rest to the obelisks.

"I would know if Wyn never Imparted," Viri said, wishing she sounded more confident. "And I'd definitely know if she was a mage. We tell each other everything."

Reeve made a humming noise. "Like you told her about your brother being the Reaper Priest, you mean?"

Viri winced, but said, "I went to her ceremony, Reeve. I was *there*."

He shrugged as he searched through another box. "Ask her yourself the next time you see her. I don't think she uses her elixen for anything other than alchemy, but I'm guessing that's because she doesn't know how—which makes her no less a mage, just an untrained one. She's lucky that whoever left her that magic laboratory explained how to avoid burnout, even if they didn't share anything else."

"Her dad left her the lab," Viri said, "but he didn't explain how to—"

She broke off as she remembered the letter Wynter's mysterious father had sent—the one that had arrived on the morning of her Impartation, mere minutes before they'd left for the ceremony. Viri had only seen one page, thinking that was the extent of it. But . . . if there had been more . . . if it had included instructions . . .

"Everyone has secrets," Wynter had said in the undercity tunnel just last night. *"I know that better than anyone."*

Viri cursed and closed her eyes as she thought of her too-curious-for-her-own-good best friend. If Wynter *had* known how to avoid the danger of burnout, then it wasn't a stretch to believe she might have caved to the temptation of faking her Impartation to practice magic, even if it meant breaking the law. Hell, *especially* if it meant breaking the law, given that she already did that every single day.

Groaning loudly, Viri said, "Her mother will die if she ever finds out the truth."

A dark laugh left Reeve. "If only it were that easy."

Viri's eyes shot back open to narrow at him. "That's my guardian you're talking about."

"I'm well aware," Reeve said, his focus still on the shelves—as Viri's should be. "Elders forbid anyone says anything against the great Magistratus."

"What's your problem with her?" Viri demanded. "Everyone loves Sarielle."

Reeve snorted. "No one is loved by everyone. It's a statistical impossibility." He closed a box harder than he needed to, crumpling the edges. "And my grievances with the Magistratus are none of your concern, but let's just say she hasn't always been there for *all* of her beloved citizens, no matter what she might like you to think."

"You're a *reaper*, Reeve," Viri returned hotly. "She was a hunter before she became the Magistratus—it's in her nature to despise you and your kind." That was long ago, before Wynter was born. But still . . . "Can you blame her for drawing the line at helping murderers?"

"Maybe not, but I can blame her for—" Reeve stopped suddenly, his body tensing as he spun in the narrow aisle toward the entrance to the storeroom. It wasn't visible from where they stood, but it might as well have been for how intensely he was focusing in that direction.

"What—"

With lightning-fast reflexes, Reeve pressed his hand over Viri's mouth, muffling her question. Not a second later, a *click* sounded and the door to the storeroom opened, followed by heavy footsteps echoing unevenly throughout the space—*clack-clunk* . . . *clack-clunk*.

The blood drained from Viri's face as she realized they were about to be discovered. Not only had they failed to find the map and talisman, but they would be thrown into the Underlock for the effort, leaving Braedan free to find the Guardian *and* carry out the Aurora sacrifice. It couldn't end like this. It couldn't—

Clack-clunk . . . clack-clunk.

The footsteps were coming closer, but something about the uneven gait niggled at Viri's memory. When recollection hit her, she shoved Reeve's hand away and carefully peeked past him around the corner of the row where they were standing. All she could see was a shadow of the person slowly hobbling their way, but their outline was enough to confirm their identity, allowing Viri to form a quick, desperate plan.

Facing Reeve again, she blurted, "Kiss me."

For the first time since she'd known him—now or in the past—he gaped at her and stammered out, "Excuse me?"

There wasn't time for her to explain, and she didn't waste the few seconds they had by asking again. Instead, she fisted her hands in the material of his shirt and yanked him close, rising up on her tiptoes as she drew him down to her.

"Viri—*what*—"

She silenced him by slamming her lips into his, her heart pounding as she prayed her plan would work.

But then it began pounding for a different reason.

She'd intended the kiss to be brief, just long enough for them to be caught in their embrace. She'd also intended it to be dispassionate, little more than a closed-mouth peck. What she hadn't factored in was how slowly the newcomer was hobbling—or just how good Reeve's lips would feel against hers.

He was like a solid wall, frozen with shock—

Until, suddenly, he wasn't.

From one second to the next, any control she'd had over the kiss fled as Reeve's arm banded around her waist to haul her closer, his other hand cupping her cheek and tilting her face to the side, his tongue sliding along the seam of her lips. Her mouth opened in a gasp, and he instantly deepened the kiss, taking it beyond anything she'd intended, anything she'd *imagined.* A moan left her against her will, echoed by his own, the sound rumbling in his chest beneath her now-trembling fingers.

There was nothing gentle about his touch—it was fierce and possessive, her legs turning to jelly as his tongue devoured her, giving, taking, demanding, yielding, each stroke fanning the flames simmering within her, making heat pool in her core and spread across her nerve endings like wildfire. When she moaned again, his arm tightened until there was no space left between them, her hands shifting upward to tangle in his midnight hair, drawing him even closer.

More, she needed *more*—

"Good gracious!"

Viri jumped backward, hitting the shelf behind her with enough force that an entire box of unbound files tumbled to the ground in a shower of paper. A quick, stolen glance at Reeve revealed his mussed hair and dazed features—no doubt identical to her own—before she spun on weak legs toward the hunched-over woman standing in the aisle before them.

"Viridia Solace, is that you?" the elderly lady asked, squinting through thick glasses that Viri knew did nothing to improve her vision. "I see that red cloak—don't try to fool me."

"Judge Muriel," Viri panted, her words both hoarse and breathy, neither of which were feigned. She could barely string a thought together, her body still on fire, but she reclaimed her wits enough to say, "We, uh, thought we were alone."

"You thought wrong, young lady," Muriel said sternly, though there was a mischievous twinkle in her nearly blind eyes. "This is the second time I've caught you here in a compromising position. One might think you make a habit of it."

"We were just . . . um . . . doing some filing," Viri said, crouching down and deliberately fumbling for the fallen papers. Or not so deliberately, given her still-trembling fingers.

"Filing?" Muriel raised a bushy white eyebrow, the deep wrinkles in her dark-skinned forehead creasing further with the gesture. "Is that what you kids are calling it these days?"

Acting or not, Viri couldn't keep her cheeks from heating as she rose again, papers in hand. She forced herself to sound anxious—which wasn't difficult—as she begged, "Please don't tell Sarielle that you found us here. She'd never let me live it down."

Muriel sniffed loudly, offended. "I may be a judge, but I'm no snitch. And as I told you last time, I was young once, too. I enjoyed plenty of 'filing' myself, back in my day. We called it something else then, mind you."

Elders kill me. Viri wanted the ground to swallow her whole—

a feeling that only worsened when Muriel winked in Reeve's general direction, her unfocused gaze fixed slightly past his ear as she said, "Good seeing you, Soren, dear. Nice to know you're looking after our girl."

Reeve made a choking sound, which turned into a muffled oath when Viri stomped on his foot, hard.

"What was that?" Muriel asked, cupping her ear.

"He said he definitely is," Viri answered for him. The old woman's sight might be failing her, but she was too familiar with Soren's voice not to recognize it. The moment Reeve spoke, their ruse would be up.

"Good man," Muriel said approvingly, then waved the papers in her age-spotted hand. "I'll leave you two lovebirds to it and come back later to deal with these. Best finish up soon—the next person who catches you might not be so sympathetic to your lustful yearnings."

Chuckling to herself, Muriel turned and hobbled away, the *clack-clunk . . . clack-clunk* of her limp fading as slowly as it had arrived, every uneven step making Viri's heart rate speed up all over again as mortification set in.

Only when the sound of the closing door echoed around the room did she finally summon the courage to look at Reeve. His hair was still mussed from her wandering fingers, but his dazed expression was gone, replaced by guarded features, crossed arms, and eyebrows raised in question.

"Judge Muriel," Viri said quickly, clearing her throat when her voice came out embarrassingly husky. "She was meant to retire a decade ago but keeps refusing to, claiming she's still as smart as a fox, even if she can barely see more than two feet in front of her these days."

Reeve's features cleared with understanding. "That's why she thought I was Archer."

"She can see colors and shapes—my red cloak was enough for her to identify me, and your black clothes can easily be mistaken for a Nox uniform, which was all she needed to make an educated guess."

"Educated, perhaps . . . but there was also her implication that she's caught you in here with him before."

It was a leading statement, but it gave Viri the reprieve she needed, her embarrassment shifting to nostalgic amusement as she explained, "Soren and I were doing some filing for Sarielle a few months ago—*actual* filing, not the euphemism kind." She grimaced, realizing she would never be able to hear that word again without thinking of Reeve. "I tripped over a stack of boxes, and he caught me just as Muriel walked in. With her poor eyesight, all it took was our arms around each other for her to think we were full-on making out." Clearing her throat again, Viri shared, "That's what gave me the idea today. Once I realized she was the one walking toward us, I figured . . ." She trailed off, not needing—or wanting—to put words to what they'd done.

A beat of silence passed before Reeve said, "It was a clever plan. But I have one question." He moved a step closer, making the narrow aisle seem even smaller. "If Muriel saw your innocent embrace with Archer as the two of you making out, why did you *actually* make out with me, when you could have just re-created what you did last time by putting your arms around me?"

Viri's mouth turned dry, every defense eddying from her mind as she realized with painstaking clarity that Reeve was right. They *hadn't* needed to actually kiss in order to sell the deception.

She cleared her throat—*again*—and bluffed her way through

an answer. "Wynter says medicine is improving every day, so I didn't want to risk that Muriel might have sought a new treatment for her vision." Elders, that was pathetic. "Besides," Viri hurried on, waving a flippant hand, "that was hardly what I would call making out. We did what we had to do, and we'll never speak of it again, since we obviously both hated it."

"Obviously," Reeve repeated, humor now lacing his tone. "Because I'm a reaper, and you're a hunter, and the only thing that will ever be between us is hatred."

Viri nodded stiffly. "Precisely."

His humor grew, his silver eyes dancing as he moved another step forward, right into her space. He didn't touch her, but his closeness was enough that she fought the urge to melt into the shelf pressing against her back.

"There's just one problem," Reeve purred as he dipped his face toward her, his mouth stopping a mere breath away. "I didn't hate it." Viri stilled at the admission, but he wasn't done, moving even closer, his lips whispering against hers and prompting a traitorous shiver to travel down her spine. "You can lie to yourself all you want, Little Shadow, but the next time you ask me to kiss you, we both know it'll be because you want it as much as I do."

Full-body tingles scrambled Viri's mind, making it nearly impossible for her to scrounge up the self-control needed to keep from leaning forward and pressing her mouth to his again. Instead, she somehow managed to rasp out, "That will never happen."

A huff of laughter against her lips. "We'll see."

His eyes held hers in challenge, a knowing smile curling the edges of his mouth—

But then he suddenly stepped back again, the unexpected loss of him making Viri feel unbalanced enough that she swayed forward before she could get a grip on herself.

"We're nearly out of time," Reeve said, straightening his sleeves, all business once more, as if their intimate exchange had never happened. "We need to speed this search along before we get caught for real." He glanced around, brow furrowed, then turned back to her with a thoughtful look. "The magic you feel—your heightened sensitivity—how strong is it?"

Viri was still reeling, struggling to catch up—and to catch her breath—after what had just occurred between them, both physically and verbally, but she gave herself a mental shake and answered, "I have nothing to compare it to, but I know it's not normal."

"Is it specific only to wards?"

"No, it's any ellixen, but wards affect me the most."

Reeve's thoughtful look deepened, even as he said, somewhat oddly, "That makes sense." His face cleared as he focused on her again. "I have an idea. If the map and the talisman are still inside the warded chest and they're somewhere in this room, you should be able to feel them out and guide us straight to them."

"I can't feel anything," Viri objected.

"That's because I haven't told you how yet," Reeve said. "Just close your eyes and trust me."

"I don't trust—"

"You do. Now shut up and close your eyes."

Viri's gaze slitted. "Don't tell me to shut up."

"Don't tell me you don't trust me when you just had your tongue in my mouth."

Face instantly searing, Viri hissed, "I thought we agreed not to speak of that again."

"We agreed to no such thing," Reeve said. "Now close your eyes and concentrate, unless you want the Magistratus to find us—which could happen any second, given how long we've been in here."

Viri wanted to argue more, if only on principle, but Reeve was right about them running out of time. Shooting him an annoyed look, she slammed her eyes shut and said, with clear skepticism, "What now?"

His next words were entirely unexpected.

"Remember when we were kids, how you, me, and Brae would go out to the surface on clear, warm days and dip our feet in the shallows of Lake Mirtis?"

Viri's stomach clenched. "Reeve, what—"

"Do you remember?"

"Of course I do," she said tightly, her eyes still closed. "What does that have to do with—"

"In the springtime, there were those flowers that grew along the shore—the purple ones with the yellow centers." He spoke over her. "You were obsessed with them, picking bunches at a time and forcing Brae and me to wear crowns and necklaces and bracelets that left us covered in sticky sap that dried like snot on our clothes."

A bittersweet smile tugged at Viri's lips. "Mage blossoms. I still love them."

"I want you to think of those, picturing them in your mind," Reeve instructed, his voice quieting. "Think of how they close up at night, their petals drawing in to shield themselves from the elements. Now think about your sensitivity to magic, how you keep it reined in to protect yourself from what it makes you feel. Can you see the similarities?"

Viri swallowed and nodded. She didn't actively stifle it—mostly because she didn't know how—but she did shove it down and ignore it as much as she could when she was around magical objects or in ellixen-saturated areas, like warded rooms and elevators.

"Good," Reeve said. "Now think of the mage blossoms again, but this time, picture them at sunrise when they unfurl petal by petal, opening up to greet the day. That's what I want you to do—I want you to imagine yourself unfurling like a mage blossom under the first rays of sunlight, expanding your senses outward, letting go of any fear you have and just *feeling* the space around you. Don't try to focus on anything in particular, just see if something calls to you."

His voice was so lulling, so hypnotic, that Viri followed his instructions without thinking, releasing whatever instinctive leash she kept on her heightened sensitivity, allowing it to flood outward unrestrained, like a river breaking through an embankment. A startled breath left her at the freeing sensation, before anxiety took hold from how powerful, how *uncontrollable* it felt. But she didn't wrestle it back in just yet, searching, searching, until she felt it: the prickle of an ellixen ward nearby, faint but unmistakable.

Her eyes shot open. "The chest," she gasped, smothering her flooded awareness until it was safely behind the embankment once more. "It's two rows over, on the left."

A proud smile stretched across Reeve's lips. "I knew you could do it."

Feeling embarrassed for no logical reason, Viri didn't reply, just rushed over to where she was certain the chest was waiting, finding it where she'd said, hidden halfway up the shelf. The bloodline magic warding the ancient wood prompted another tingle of ellixen that intensified when she pulled it closer, but then it eased again, almost as if it recognized her. Sure enough, the moment her finger pressed against the lock, it opened effortlessly, revealing two items inside: a familiar-looking onyx ring and a blank piece of parchment that came to life at Viri's touch, lines bleeding outward from the center to form a map showing the entirety of Elverdine Isle—with a dot labeled "Nevarnost Tower" right there in the upper left-hand corner.

"We found it," Viri breathed, turning to Reeve, unable to keep the wide, disbelieving grin from her face.

"Told you it was real," he said smugly, tapping a line that tracked out of Aravell—a line that moved before her very eyes but always began south of the city, where the necropolis bled into the Mistwood. Reeve tapped that spot, too. "There's our starting point."

Viri's insides somersaulted at what they had to do next—venture through the deadly forest to reach the Guardian before her brother did—but she stomped down her trepidation and tucked the map into her cloak, watching as Reeve grabbed the ring and held it out to her.

"One blackmist talisman, as promised," he said.

Seeing it in his open palm made her realize why it was familiar: because it was identical to the one he wore on his middle finger, right down to the silver runes etched into it.

Viri's eyes narrowed as they bounced back and forth between the two black rings.

Before she could demand an explanation, Reeve said, "There was a set of talismans left by the ancient mages, remember? Emphasis on *set*." He wiggled his middle finger, almost tauntingly. "I told you Braedan had likely located one of the others—let's just say my confidence wasn't unfounded and leave it at that."

Viri's gaze slitted further at the knowledge that Reeve had been wearing his own blackmist talisman all along, which meant he'd probably been with Braedan when the two of them had procured their rings.

"How—*Where*—"

"No time for questions," Reeve said, sliding the second ring onto her finger. "There. Now you'll be protected from the mist, too."

"But—"

"Ticktock, we're on the clock," he interrupted in a singsong voice. "You can interrogate me later."

Viri ground her teeth together to keep from arguing, telling herself she could ask how and where—and *why*—he got his ring once they were safely away from the Summit.

"Whatever," she grumbled, striding forward and leading him out of the storeroom. "Let's just get out of here."

But they barely made it two steps into Sarielle's office before Viri came to a stumbling halt.

Because standing in the middle of the room, dressed in a smart white pantsuit and gaping at them with shocked disbelief—

Was the Magistratus.

THE JOURNAL OF CELESTIAL MAGE KADMUS CASTRO

Fifty-Third Sun, Thirteenth Cycle, Twelfth Age

The first of the Adastrum Devotis comets is due to appear tonight. Aurora, she's called. Her lover, Orion, will follow later, as he always does, but I haven't yet consulted my sky charts to calculate his arrival date. I've been . . . preoccupied of late. Distracted.

Mostly by Tephryn.

I told myself I wouldn't fall for her, knew no good would come of it.

She made it impossible.

After our meeting in the teahouse—our first date, she later told me, though I didn't know it at the time—I began to see her everywhere. For a while, I thought it merely a pleasant coincidence that we were always bumping into each other. It was only when Tephryn laughed and rolled her eyes one day, mumbling under her breath about me taking too long, and then kissed me, that I comprehended—belatedly—that we'd been courting all along. Or rather, she'd been courting me, since I'd been oblivious.

Zeranthe has never said "I told you so" as much as she has of late. She was already arrogant for a dragon—now she's near insufferable. But I find I don't mind it as much as I normally would. Because Tephryn . . .

I've never had anyone look at me the way she does, like I summon the stars one by one each night and make them twinkle across the sky, just for her.

~~It makes me feel~~

~~She makes me feel~~

She told me she's in love with me. Said she has been since she first saw me months ago, walking through the town square with my nose in a book and indifferent to the mockery coming from the other mages. She liked that I didn't care what they thought of me and my magic, liked that I was passionate about helping the shallows despite the ridicule I receive for it. She liked <u>me</u>.

And it turns out, I like her, too.

Maybe even love her.

No—I <u>do</u> love her.

But therein lies my problem.

Because a heart divided is a heart unfaithful.

I have a calling, a purpose. I am a Mage Priest, bound by the oath I gave upon choosing my celestial path, sworn to serve my congregation of shallows. And of late, I haven't been able to do that. Not for lack of trying, but because of the obelisks.

The vernal equinox was last week. It should have been a powerful event that left the shallows giddy with ellixen. Instead, without the Hallow Stream augmenting my ritual, I was only able to draw down a fraction of what I could prior to the obelisks' construction.

The shallows on the mainland are used to such paltry offerings—it's the reason why so many have stopped attending celestial events altogether. But here on Elverdine, the residents have become used to receiving a flood of magic from me, and now . . .

I haven't been able to deliver that in any of my recent ceremonies.

But I will.

I've made them a promise. I told Magistratus Garrin that I know how to fix this, that he and the other shallows can count on me—and it's true. Because I've figured it out, thanks to the Adastrum Devotis comets. Aurora is coming tonight, her celestial power matched only by that of her lover, Orion.

I've known for weeks that a miracle would be needed for me to get past the suppression magic of the obelisks.

Aurora is my miracle.
Tephryn won't be pleased, but I can't let that stop me.
My shallows need this too much. *I* need it too much.
A heart divided is a heart unfaithful.
My heart is not divided in this.

22

A thousand swear words screamed across Viri's mind as she looked at her stunned guardian, panic instantly rising within her.

"This isn't what it looks like," she blurted, then winced, because it was exactly what it looked like. She and Reeve had been caught red-handed inside the Magistratus's locked office—there was no way to deny that.

Viri wasn't sure what she expected to happen next, though a large part of her was certain Sarielle would have no choice but to follow protocol and call for the Nox.

That, however, wasn't what Sarielle did.

Instead, she unfroze and strode straight over to Viri, wrapping her in an embrace.

"Elders, I've been so worried," Sarielle said into her ear.

Viri nearly wilted with relief. "I'm sorry—I never meant for you to find us here. I know what a difficult position this puts you in."

"Never mind that," Sarielle said, drawing away. Her blue eyes flicked to Reeve, her features tightening as she realized who—and what—he was, but she quickly returned her attention to Viri. "Everyone is looking for you. Captain Farrow has his Nox out in force, half ordered to find the missing children, the other half ordered to find you."

Viri grimaced, but said, "They won't be able to find us where we're going."

That was one benefit of traveling into the deadly wood, at least.

Sarielle held Viri's eyes for a long moment, before she quietly said, "I won't tell you not to do whatever it is you're doing. I know better than that—just as I trust there's a reason you're here with him."

Sarielle's gaze flicked to Reeve again, and this time, Viri turned as well, finding him as tense as stone, his features completely blank as he stared unflinchingly at the Magistratus. There was no indication of the animosity he held toward her, thank the Elders, but it was obvious he didn't want to be in her presence. That was hardly surprising, given who they both were: the right hand to the Reaper Priest and the city's highly moral leader who had once been a hunter, two people who would never be on the same side of anything.

Except, right now, they *were*.

"There's a reason," Viri confirmed. "You told me last night that there's no cost too steep if it means finding the Reaper Priest." She dipped her chin toward Reeve. "This is the cost of me being able to do that. I don't have time to explain, but I promise everything I'm doing is with the aim of stopping him."

Sarielle's lips pressed together, as if she were fighting the urge to say that hadn't been what she'd meant *at all*, but then she sighed. "Whatever your plans are, just be careful."

"Always," Viri said, knowing it was what her guardian needed to hear and praying she could keep her word.

Sarielle was about to say something else—maybe ask what Viri and Reeve were doing in her office to begin with—but she was interrupted by a knock on the door. Before any of them could react, Meera walked in, her focus on the papers in her hands as she said, *"We forgot something at the meeting—"*

The head of the Hunters' Guild stopped abruptly when she caught sight of Viri and Reeve, her dark features slackening with shock.

Viri's heart leapt to her throat, but it wasn't just because of her mentor's unexpected arrival.

It was because two Nox guards appeared directly behind her.

A single glance was all it took for them to recognize who they'd just walked in on, with both lunging forward at the same time, making Viri realize she and Reeve were going to have to fight their way out of the room.

Only, that wasn't what happened.

Because Meera leapt in to intercept the Nox, her papers flying everywhere, and in less than four moves, she had them both on the ground, unconscious.

Her jade eyes skewered Viri, her mental voice curt with warning as she said, *"You have five seconds before I raise the alarm. Make them count."* Her eyes slitted. *"And don't make me regret this."*

Gratitude swept through Viri at the gravity of what her mentor had just done, at the trust Meera was showing without demanding any answers. "Thank you," she croaked out.

"Thank me by saying nice things at my funeral. I might be able to accept that you're following some half-baked plan to save the kids, but Darik is going to kill me for letting you get away," Meera said flatly, then jerked

her head at the door. *"Now go. And be prepared to face the longest debriefing of your life once this mess is over."*

Viri nodded and couldn't resist rushing forward to hug her mentor, never before so grateful that Meera had a hunter's heart and was willing to bend the rules—and the laws—to do what had to be done. Or in this case, to allow Viri to do it.

There was so much Viri wished she could tell both Meera and Sarielle—so much they needed to know about the comets and the sacrifice and the plan to destroy the obelisks—just as she wished she could spare a moment to make sure Sarielle knew about Jessalyn and reassure her that Soren was already out searching. But every minute Viri delayed was another Braedan could use to reach the Guardian first, dooming them all. So as hard as it was, she forced her feet toward the door, turning back just once to blow a kiss at Sarielle, who caught it and pressed it to her heart.

That was the last Viri saw of them as she and Reeve hurried from the room, their pace increasing to a run as they passed Galen's still-empty desk and headed toward the glass-doored exit. People were milling about now, councilors and Guild heads who had finished with their meeting, some crying out in startled recognition as Viri and Reeve rushed by—which in turn drew the notice of two waiting Nox guards, likely the partners of those Meera had knocked unconscious.

Viri cursed as the Nox sprang forward in pursuit, yelling at her and Reeve to stop. She pushed her legs harder toward the exit, her heart hammering in her chest as she sprinted through the doors with Reeve at her heels, both of them barreling along the Summit's inner-mountain tunnel toward the wayportal as the Nox's yells continued ringing out behind them.

But Viri and Reeve were too fast, their desperation too strong, and with an extra burst of speed, they made it to the magestone arch, where Viri leapt through first and guided it straight to the still-bustling market district. She waited only as long as it took for Reeve to appear before grabbing him and jumping back into it again, confident that one of the many busy shoppers would activate the portal next—which would keep the Nox from following them to their actual destination: the uppercity's southernmost wayportal.

The moment Viri hurtled out the other side, bright sunlight seared her vision, causing her to hiss with pain. Reeve's arrival was less dramatic, though he quickly shielded his eyes from the glare, both of them breathing hard from their mad dash.

That was close, Viri thought, knowing that a few more seconds and those Nox might have caught them. If not for Sarielle being so understanding . . . If not for Meera helping them get away . . .

Viri didn't want to think about what might have happened, had the timing or circumstances been any different.

"Let's not do that again," Reeve panted, rolling the tension from his shoulders.

"Agreed," Viri murmured, assuming he was talking about being chased by the Nox, though he could have been referring to any part of their Summit infiltration. Everything they'd done . . . There would be repercussions, she was sure of it. But she would deal with the fallout later. For now, their mission was all that mattered.

Inhaling deeply to steady herself, Viri peered around to get her bearings, taking in the vast farmland stretching out to the east—the animals all safely inside the wards—and the ancient white mausoleums peeking out from within the craggy trees to the west. There was something else, too—something resting in between the farms and the necropolis, standing tall and proud beneath the sunshine.

The Southern Obelisk.

Viri shivered at the sight of it in the distance, unable to forget the last time she'd been this close to the tapered obsidian stone that rose as high as any building. It might have been seven years, but the tragedy of her Impartation day was still fresh enough that a lump formed in her throat, and she hastily tore her gaze away.

"This way," she said hoarsely, avoiding Reeve's probing eyes as she strode west toward the necropolis, pulling the map out to confirm their magical path began at the farthest border of the ancient cemetery.

Keeping pace at her side, Reeve glanced from her to the shadowy obelisk and asked, hesitantly, "Do you want to talk about—"

"No," Viri said sharply. He was the last person she would ever want to talk to about what happened that day.

He let it drop, almost as if he didn't want to discuss it either, though that was unsurprising given the choices he'd made in the wake of her parents' deaths.

Viri's pain and rage rose so swiftly that she could taste them, like a bitter, coppery film coating her tongue. She couldn't bear to look at Reeve as they stepped through the pillared entrance into the necropolis, needing space, needing *distance*, hating that neither would be possible until they stopped her brother and could go their separate ways.

Digging her fingernails into her palms, Viri used the sting to ground herself, then forcefully pushed her emotions—and memories—away. Only when the urge to lash out at Reeve had passed did she take the time to look around, her boots crunching over rocks and dirt as they moved quickly through the eerily quiet necropolis.

It had been over a decade since Viri had last visited, but her surroundings were just as unnerving now as they'd been then, the sunshine struggling to trickle through the twisting canopy of trees, creating shadows that were often mistaken for wandering spirits. Once known as the City of Tombs, the expansive burial grounds contained a variety of vaults and crypts and catacombs both above and beneath the earth, all carved out of pure white stone. Many of the structures were so old that they were little more than crumbling monuments—some as large as houses, others mere grave markers small enough to trip over—and at the heart of them all was a towering cathedral sitting atop a grassy knoll, said to be haunted by the ghosts of the ancient mages.

Viri wasn't afraid of ghosts, but even she couldn't keep from shivering as they passed the rusted gates at the base of the small rise, the spired white cathedral looming over them like something straight out of a nightmare. She could almost swear she heard screams coming from within, the cries of the ancient dead calling from beyond the sealed front doors. Goosebumps prickled her skin, but she gritted her teeth against her unease, refusing to be spooked by what was surely a combination of creaking branches, whistling wind, and all-around creepiness of the necropolis.

"I hate it here," Reeve murmured, visibly shuddering as he stared up at the spooky cathedral. "My dad used to say they buried people alive in there—the White Tomb, he called it. He said anyone who dared pass through the doors never came out again." A sad smile touched his lips. "I'm pretty sure he was just trying to scare me away from exploring. Probably worried I would disturb the dead and end up cursed or something. He was superstitious like that."

Viri was surprised to hear him speak about his father, since he rarely had when they were young. "Parents tell their kids all kinds of stories to keep them from sneaking around out here," she said. "Not just to respect the dead, but because we're so close to the Mistwood." She indicated the trees surrounding them, which were becoming denser as they neared the far edge of the necropolis, where the Southern Obelisk's wards ended. "One step too far, and that's it. There's no coming back from black-mist exposure."

"Not without a magewish," Reeve said wryly, reminding her of the Guardian legend and her supposedly revived-from-the-dead ancestor.

"I still find it hard to believe that happened," Viri said, picking her way around a crumbling staircase that led to an underground crypt.

Reeve shrugged, the gesture strangely stiff. "We can ask him ourselves soon enough."

The very idea was surreal, but it prompted Viri to pull the map out again as they passed the last of the white mausoleums and approached a set of rusted iron gates similar to those that had led up to the cathedral—a flimsy barrier between the necropolis and the deadly wood beyond.

"You said this map would show us the quickest route to the Guardian." Viri paused briefly to inspect the moving line, tracing her finger along it all the way up to Nevarnost Tower. "But this still looks like it's going to take us days of walking. With the head start Braedan has, there's no way we'll—"

"I have a theory," Reeve interrupted before she could start

spiraling about how little time they had left. "I won't know for sure until we step into the Mistwood, though."

"What do you mean?"

Reeve didn't answer, just pushed open the rusted gates and gestured for her to precede him into the thick trees. There was no sign of the blackmist, but Viri knew it wouldn't be far away once they left the protection of the wards.

"You first," she said, eyeing her onyx ring warily and not wanting to admit just how nervous she was about having to rely on its ancient magic to keep her safe.

Sensing her misgivings, Reeve didn't argue. "Keep close," he said, leading the way forward. "Your talisman hasn't been used for years—the magic might have weakened in that time."

Viri's heart skipped a beat. "And if it has?"

"The three hunters in the legend only had one ring between them, so I assume as long as you stay in range of mine"—Reeve tapped his silver-runed band—"then you'll be fine."

"How far is its range?" Viri asked, following him through the gates and deeper into the forest.

Pointedly, Reeve said, "Let's not find out."

Viri shuddered and moved close enough for their arms to brush as they walked, unwilling to risk any distance between them. She indicated the map folded in her hand. "All right, we're in the Mistwood—what's your theory?"

Reeve's eyes were fixed on something up ahead. "We're not quite in it yet, but we will be in a moment."

Viri followed his gaze and inhaled sharply at the shadowy vapor appearing out of nowhere, saturating the forest like a dark cloud that floated between the trees and drifted lazily up through the canopy. Every survival instinct within her screamed at her to run back to the safety of the wards, but she fought the urge and stayed by Reeve's side, striding ever closer to the deadly blackmist.

When they were only feet away, Viri couldn't stop herself from grabbing his hand, clutching tight enough to bruise. "I swear, Reeve, if you're wrong about our talismans . . ." Anxiety clogged her throat, strangling the rest of her words.

He glanced sideways at her, clearly amused. "I thought we got past your trust issues when you threw yourself at me."

Indignation flooded Viri. "I didn't *throw* myself at—"

"I mean, I'm not surprised it happened," Reeve went on. "The first thing you did when you saw me in the Underlock last week was undress me with your eyes—"

Her face heated. "I did *not*—"

"—and you've obviously been thinking about me constantly since then—"

"I most *certainly* have not—"

"—so it was only a matter of time before you caved to your desires." He winked. "Not that I'm complaining. Feel free to do so again, anytime."

Viri couldn't *believe* him. "I—You—" She cut herself off when she suddenly became aware of her surroundings, realizing they'd passed into the mist without her noticing. It hovered all around them, and yet they remained safe, protected by an invisible shield, almost as if they were walking inside a bubble.

Slowly, Viri turned back to Reeve, only to find a satisfied smile tugging at his lips.

"You're welcome," he said simply.

Half of Viri wanted to yank the ring from his finger and shove him into the mist, while the other half wanted to hug him for distracting her from her fears long enough that they were no longer valid. She settled for doing neither and just repeated her earlier question. "Your theory about the map?"

Reeve chuckled at her clear attempt to ignore what had just happened, but he went along with it and answered, "Open it up again. If I'm right, the path will have changed drastically."

Viri hesitated, knowing she would need both hands to follow his instructions, but unsure whether the magical barrier would hold if she let him go, especially if it was his ring that they were solely relying on for protection.

Seeing her trepidation, Reeve's expression gentled into something Viri refused to identify, his voice soft as he said, "Do you really think I'd let anything happen to you? You're safe with me, Little Shadow. Always."

Viri's legs wobbled at the promise in his words, and then wobbled even more when he carefully but purposefully untangled their fingers. Her pulse skittered with alarm, but the mist remained out of reach, the protective shield provided by their talismans continuing to keep them both safe.

"Is this where I say 'I told you so'?" Reeve asked, his lips twitching as he flicked the ring on her finger.

She swatted his hand away. "Arrogance is unattractive."

A knowing smirk. "Apparently not to you."

Viri refused to rise to his bait this time, knowing it would only fuel his humor. Instead, she unfolded the map again, frowning when she saw the line through the Mistwood now led due west rather than angling north toward the tower.

She halted abruptly. "What does this mean?"

Reeve looked pleased as he inspected the path. "Ah, good. I was right."

"About *what*?"

"My theory." He tapped the line. "We know the map is meant to show us the most direct route to the Guardian, but that doesn't necessarily mean we have to walk the whole way there."

"What do you—"

"The story your parents told us," he interrupted. "I never understood how the husband could have hiked through the Mistwood if he was as weak as the legend claimed. Even with his wife and friend helping him, the journey would have been impossible for anyone siphoned within an inch of their life. I asked your mom about it once, wanting to know if anything had been left out of the tale, and she just smiled and said, 'Anything is possible with magic.'"

Pain stabbed at Viri's chest, since she'd heard her mom use those words more than once, always in a sneaky whisper, as if sharing a secret.

"I didn't dwell on it at the time," Reeve went on, "and just enjoyed the mystery of it. But after Brae and I found the map, and especially more recently, I considered what other possibilities there might be and came to one obvious conclusion."

"Which is?" Viri pressed.

Reeve tapped the line again, right at the very end. "There's a wayportal out here—or some equivalent of one that'll take us directly to the tower. *That's* how we're going to beat Braedan there. He's been stuck walking for days, while we'll only hike a fraction of that and portal straight over."

Viri squinted down at the map. "That's a lot of speculation."

"Maybe," Reeve admitted. "But the way I see it, we have two options: We do what Brae is doing and find our own way to the Guardian"—he indicated the northwest corner of the map and the miles of woodland between them and Nevarnost Tower—"or we follow the magical path and hope I'm right about there being a wayportal at the end."

"I don't like *either* of those options," Viri said, before sighing and making her decision. "If we try to find our own way, we'll still be days behind Braedan. We have to follow the map." She started forward again, her eyes tracking the moving line on the parchment as she mumbled, "Let's just pray this isn't a fool's errand—and that our talismans don't run out of juice before we're done."

"Talismans or not, the blackmist isn't the only thing to fear out here," Reeve said, peering into the thick trees. "I'd say it's fairly low on the list, actually."

Viri kicked a rock out of her path. "What do you mean?"

Reeve answered, "Did you ever hear that old nursery rhyme, 'Beware the Wood'?"

The words pulled a memory from the depths of Viri's subconscious, prompting a startled chuckle out of her. "Elders, that takes me back. I used to sing it so much that I drove my family crazy."

She could still recall it with ease, and quietly recited the two simple verses:

Beware the wood
Beware the mist
Beware the danger
In its midst.

Beware the beasts
They lie in wait
Beware the wood . . .
Or meet your fate.

"That's going to be stuck in my head all day now," she muttered when she was done, though it was her own fault for singing it.

"Just as long as it keeps you on your toes," Reeve said, still looking into the trees. "We're safe from the mist"—he touched his ring—"but this wood is ancient, as old as the island itself. There's no telling what might be lurking in the shadows."

Viri shivered, but said, "Nothing living can survive the blackmist."

"Nothing to our knowledge," Reeve corrected. "But that nursery rhyme had to come from somewhere, and if they mentioned 'beasts,' we'd do well to heed the warning. Stay alert, Little Shadow. That's all I'm saying."

23

Hours passed as they hiked through the dense forest, their talismans shielding them from the mist, rendering it little more than a dark haze—albeit a deadly, menacing haze that even the sunshine struggled to break through.

Soon enough, Viri almost forgot it was there, but that was because she was so distracted by the wonders of the Mistwood itself. She'd grown up hearing stories of its strangeness—how the trees moved from place to place, some sprouting up from nothing, others vanishing into thin air. She'd heard how the streams shifted, changing direction on a whim, with brooks becoming raging rivers or drying up into nothing. Even the ground itself couldn't be trusted, transforming underfoot, switching from solid dirt to slippery moss to knee-deep mud, sometimes all within the space of a few steps.

It was one thing for Viri to have heard the tales, but another entirely for her to witness it herself. She couldn't help marveling at the wild magic of the wood, not even caring that it left her skin constantly prickling from all the ellixen saturating the air.

Then again, it wasn't only ellixen that prickled her skin. At one point, a thornbush materialized around her and Reeve, covering them in cuts and scratches as they carefully picked their way out of its brambles. At another point, the soft earth transfigured into dagger-sharp scree that was impossible to traverse without falling, leaving Viri's hands and knees scraped so raw that she had to use some of Wynter's healing salve. Farther on, branches appeared out of nowhere, smacking into them both; vines curled around their ankles, tripping them onto hard rocks; stinging nettle attached itself to their flesh, burning relentlessly. The Mistwood was unforgiving, its magic as creative as it was cruel. And yet, even with the pain it elicited, Viri remained awed by its power—and by its beauty, the colors bright despite being shrouded by mist, the water crystal clear, the air fresh and almost sweet. It was like walking through a fairy tale, every step bringing a new visual enchantment.

Sometime around midafternoon, they reached a section of the forest that opened into a small clearing painted in wildflowers, with no mist in sight. Viri had begun to notice that it came and went in waves, sometimes so concentrated that it was difficult to see through, and other times the air was clear of it entirely. But even in those clearer patches, she never let down her guard, never moved too far from Reeve and the added protection of his ring, aware the mist could return at any moment.

"Let's take a break," Reeve said, gesturing to a fallen log at the side of the picturesque clearing. "A few minutes won't make a difference."

It *could*, Viri knew, thinking not just of Braedan but also of Jessalyn and the other missing kids. But she was tired, her feet were hurting, and every part of her ached after having tripped and fallen too many times to count from the unexpected forest changes, so she was grateful for a short respite. Part of her hoped a stream might appear so they could wash the mud and forest grunge off them, but it seemed as if the pretty clearing was content to remain as it was.

"I wish we'd thought to bring some food," Viri said, sitting on the log and groaning in relief.

"We did," Reeve said, dropping down beside her. He raised his arm, and from one blink to the next, there was a paper bag held between his fingers. He handed it over, and another blink later, there was a second bag that he kept for himself. "Jonas grabbed these when he got us breakfast. Eat up."

Viri gaped from the bags to him and back again. "What—How—*Where*—"

"It's called a magepocket," Reeve said, understanding despite her lack of eloquence. "Think of it as an intangible storage space. A place to keep things without having to physically carry them." He pulled a seeded roll from his bag and took a bite, as if he hadn't just blown her mind with his casual use of previously unheard-of magic.

Somewhat dazed, Viri unwrapped her own roll, finding it oozing with strawberry jam—an odd choice, but her rumbling stomach wasn't picky—and followed his lead, the two of them eating in silence and drinking from the canteens that came with their meals. The whole time, Viri fought to keep her mind calm, her worries about her brother and Jessalyn and the comets all pressing in on her, screaming for attention. But she shoved them down, knowing no good would come of her succumbing to her fears.

Once they had finished eating—and in Viri's case, licked the jam from her sticky fingers—Reeve made everything vanish back into the magepocket, before proceeding to pull more items out of it.

"I meant to give this to you earlier." He handed over a familiar dagger—the one Viri had left skewered in the female reaper last night. "Ardin returned to the alley to deal with the bodies after he got the kids home. He figured you'd want it back."

"I didn't think I'd ever see it again," Viri said in surprise as she slid the dagger into her boot, the other two already sheathed securely in her belt.

"He stopped by Jonas's apartment while you and I were sleeping," Reeve explained as he pulled more weapons from the magepocket: his black sword, which he strapped to his back, and a set of daggers that he fastened at his waist. "Jonas said Ardin wanted us to know that he, Sage, and Soren have picked up Jessalyn's trail, and he's hopeful they'll find her and the kids from her group quickly—which should then help lead them to the others."

Relief slammed into Viri at the possibility of Soren finding his sister so soon, and maybe even the rest of the children. Her voice trembled with everything she felt as she said, "That's great news."

"He also apparently had some choice words about Soren," Reeve added, humor threading his tone. "Jonas couldn't tell if Ardin hates him or is half in love with him already."

Viri's lips curled upward. "Sor has a certain charm about him. Apparently not even reapers are immune."

Reeve chuckled. "Poor Ardin."

"What's his story, anyway?" Viri asked, standing and brushing bark and dirt from her clothes. "Sage and Jonas, too." She might as well learn what she could about the reapers that she had somehow, for better or worse, found herself allied with. "How well do you know them? What made them decide to siphon only from each other rather than kids?"

"Wynter told you about that?"

"She did," Viri confirmed. "She also told me she likes all of you. Her judgment is clearly flawed, but if you're right about her having never Imparted, then that's the least of her worries."

Reeve chuckled again and rose from the log, following Viri—and her map—through the wildflowers and back into the mist-covered trees. "To answer properly, you'd need to know why they became reapers to begin with, and those aren't my secrets to share. What I *can* tell you is that they had certain regrets afterward, and those regrets were strong enough to lead them down a different path."

Viri eyed him as they splashed their way through a muddy brook that materialized in front of them. "Is that what made you stop siphoning? Regrets?"

"It's different for me," Reeve said, sidestepping her question. "Siphoning once wasn't enough to make me lust after ellixen the way they do. They'll never be able to stop needing it, their bodies too dependent on having a regular fix, even if they've disciplined themselves not to require it fresh from the source anymore."

"You mean, fresh from children."

"Mostly, yes," Reeve said, wading out of the water onto a bank of pebbles.

"Mostly?" Viri repeated.

"Reapers can siphon from adults—you know that."

Viri shoved away the image of her dead parents. "It's not a temptation, though, since adults don't have enough ellixen to be worth their trouble."

"*Most* adults," Reeve corrected, ducking beneath a leafy branch that appeared out of nowhere. "It's rare, but there are others like Wynter and me, people older than fourteen who chanced burnout and never Imparted. Most are shallows, not mages, but even shallows have more ellixen than those who have yielded to the obelisks. And for the few of us with mage levels of power, we have considerably more ellixen than everyone else, including children, so we're actually more appealing to steal from. A bigger meal, so to speak."

Viri felt queasy at the thought of anyone siphoning from Wynter.

"We're much harder to kill than kids," Reeve went on, as if that were meant to be a comfort. "It takes longer to siphon all our ellixen, and we usually have some control over our magic, at least enough to fight back. Still, you asked about fresh sources, and we technically count."

Viri shuddered, almost wishing she *hadn't* asked. She needed to think about something else, anything that would keep her from worrying about Wynter being targeted if her secret fell into the wrong hands, so she returned to their previous conversation. "You didn't answer my question before. Not properly."

"Which question?" Reeve asked as the ground shifted beneath them, turning into lush grass that grew higher than their heads.

Viri used her hands to push the stalks away. "The one about regrets."

"What about them?"

Annoyed by his obvious avoidance, Viri grabbed his arm and pulled him to a halt right there in the middle of the tall grass. "You said your friends all have regrets about the choices they made in the past. What about you? Do you regret what you did years ago?" Leaving no room for confusion, she clarified, "The girl you killed, the one you siphoned from—do you regret it?"

A storm of emotion rippled across Reeve's face as his eyes locked with hers. She hadn't realized until now just how important it was for her to hear him say the words: that he hated what he'd done and mourned his decision every day, that he wished he could go back in time and choose never to siphon from anyone, never to *kill* anyone. Her pulse thundered in her ears as she waited for any indication that he did have a heart buried beneath the monster he'd become, that there was some small chance of redemption for the boy she'd once cared so deeply for.

But then he answered, the words rasping out of somewhere deep inside him, laced with grief and yet painfully, brutally honest. "No. I don't regret siphoning from her."

Viri closed her eyes and turned away, wondering why she'd expected anything different. Why she'd *hoped* for anything different.

"Viri—" he whispered, reaching for her.

"Let's keep moving," she said roughly, resisting his touch, her voice full of disappointment.

He didn't try to offer an explanation or defend himself, as if he knew neither would do him any good. Instead, he just began walking through the grass again, seemingly oblivious to Viri's heart cracking in her chest.

Or more likely just not caring.

✦

They continued walking for another hour, two hours, three hours, with the forest ever-changing around them, but soon the lighting shifted as well, the afternoon sunshine dimming as the sky began to darken above the canopy. Viri's nerves thrummed at the thought of spending the night in the Mistwood, but she did her best to ignore them, checking the map repeatedly to confirm that the end of the magical trail was swiftly approaching. If all went to plan, Reeve's theory about the wayportal would prove true and they would be at the Guardian's tower by nightfall. And if not—

No, Viri rebuked herself, stifling her dread before it could take hold. There was no point worrying about a problem that didn't exist yet—or as her father used to say, *"A problem's not a problem until it's a problem."* Her energy was much better spent staying positive and hoping for the best rather than yielding to negativity and feeding her fears.

To keep from obsessing over what they would or wouldn't find at the end of the trail, Viri focused all her attention on where she put her feet, the forest becoming even more treacherous as the light faded, with hidden roots and rocks causing her to stumble with increasing regularity.

Tired, sore, and thirsty, she was just about to suggest to Reeve that they take a quick water break when the trees opened up in front of them, revealing another wildflower clearing, smaller than the last, with a trickling stream meandering through the middle. There was no mist in sight, the whole area bathed in sunset colors: oranges and pinks and purples that covered everything like a soft, cozy blanket. It looked so beautiful, so peaceful, that Viri could only stare in wonder.

But then she heard a sound, a whisper in her ear.

"Beware the wood."

Viri spun around, but there was no one beside her other than Reeve, whose brows rose in question.

"Beware the mist."

This time the sound was whispered into her other ear, and she spun that way, but still, there was no one.

"Beware the danger . . ."

"Did you hear that?" Viri demanded.

"In its midst."

"Hear what?" Reeve asked.

This time, the words came louder, as if they echoed from all around her.

"Beware the beasts."

"That!" Viri cried, her heart picking up speed. "The nursery rhyme—tell me you can hear it."

"They lie in wait."

Reeve tensed beside her. "I can't hear anything."

"Beware the wood . . ."

Goosebumps rose on her flesh as the final line whispered in her ears.

". . . Or meet your fate."

The ending of the song faded into silence, broken only by Viri's anxious breaths as she frantically scanned the clearing for any sign that they weren't alone, even though she knew that was impossible. They were deep in the heart of the Mistwood. No one could—

A gasp left her when something moved on the far side of the trees, a figure stepping out of the shadows. Reeve froze at her side, proving she wasn't hallucinating, his hands shifting to the hilts of his daggers.

But his weapons weren't necessary.

Because the figure—it wasn't some blackmist beast. It was a person.

A *familiar* person.

Every muscle in Viri's body locked in stunned disbelief at the sight of the young girl walking toward them, looking healthy and happy in a clean white cloak, her sandy curls as wild as ever, her brown eyes bright with mischief.

"Jessalyn," Viri breathed. "What—*How*—"

She couldn't finish her question, a strangled sound leaving her, part sob, part laugh, and she leapt forward, desperate to embrace Soren's sister, her relief too overwhelming to care how Jessy had escaped the reapers and found her way into the deadly forest. Those answers could come later; for now, Viri just needed to hold her and see for herself that she was truly safe.

But before Viri could make it more than one step, Reeve's arms wrapped around her from behind, hauling her backward.

"No, Viri, *stop*."

Something in his voice gave her pause—a combination of urgency and horror that she'd never heard from him before.

"Reeve, what—"

"That's not Jessalyn," he said sharply, still holding her tight, as if worried she would leap forward again.

"What do you mean? Of course it is!" Viri tried to push out of his grip, but his arms were like steel around her. "Let me g—"

She didn't finish her demand before Jessy's lips stretched into a wide, open-mouthed grin.

Viri jerked back into Reeve at the sight of razor-sharp teeth, three rows deep. She nearly gagged at the grotesque vision, and would have if Jessalyn hadn't still been transforming, her white cloak turning to black rags that covered her from head to toe, leaving only her hands visible—pale, too-long fingers with talon-like nails—and a sickly gray face belonging to a creature that was decidedly *not* Jessalyn. It was the eyes that were the worst, though, now vivid scarlet slits that glowed from within the shadowy hood, chilling Viri to the bone.

Reeve swore loudly and released her to draw his sword, snarling one word as the figure glided slowly toward them like a specter of death. *"Wraith."*

It shouldn't have been possible—wraiths had left the island long ago with the mages and all the other magical creatures—but Viri couldn't deny the evidence before her. She fumbled for her daggers, trying to recall everything she knew about them, her knowledge limited to what Wynter had shared while treating Reeve's grimblade poison: that wraiths attacked body, mind, and spirit. Viri could now add that they were shapeshifters, her heart simultaneously crushed and grateful that the real Jessalyn was nowhere near the beast they faced.

"Are you ready to meet your fate, Daughter of Death?"

The voice was the same as the one that had whispered the song in Viri's ears, but a quick glance at Reeve indicated he could hear it this time, too.

"Get ready," he warned, raising his blade.

Viri did the same with her daggers, knowing her fillium would be useless here. Any creature that could survive within the blackmist would have no ellixen left to drain. The wraith didn't even appear to have a physical body now that it had discarded Jessy's form, though Viri knew from the grimblade poison that it must be capable of bleeding, at least in theory.

Heart pounding, Viri grounded herself, part of her naively

hoping the wraith might have no intention of attacking. She knew nothing of its nature—if she and Reeve didn't strike first, it might very well leave them alone and go on its way.

Her hope dissolved, however, when it stopped gliding and suddenly flew at them, swiping its clawlike nails so fast that the air whistled. Viri ducked while Reeve jumped to the side and slashed forward with his sword, but his blade passed straight through the wraith's center, its rags rustling as if touched by a breeze.

A dark laugh echoed around them.

"You'll have to do better than that, Son of Shadows."

Reeve slashed again, and this time Viri leapt in to help him, hurling one of her daggers at the wraith's hooded head. The blade should have struck right between its scarlet eyes, but like Reeve's sword, it just sailed through the creature's intangible body.

Another dark laugh, and then the wraith stretched out its hand to point a taloned finger at Viri's chest. Her breath was punched straight out of her lungs, leaving her gasping violently, but no matter how hard she tried, she couldn't suck in any air, her throat closing as she choked on nothing. She knew it wasn't real, that it was some kind of mental wraith trick, but she had no defense against what she was feeling, and panic rose within her as she clawed at her neck.

She couldn't breathe—

She couldn't breathe—

A surge of ellixen from Reeve sent the wraith blasting backward across the clearing, its furious shriek echoing around them as it vanished through the distant trees. But Viri didn't care about the spine-tingling sound, because suddenly she could inhale again. She coughed and spluttered, her lungs screaming with relief that bordered on pain.

Reeve was beside her in an instant, looking as panicked as she'd felt mere moments ago. "Are you hurt? What did it do to you?"

"I'm all right," she wheezed out around her panted breaths. "Did you kill it?"

He shook his head. "Wraiths can't be killed. I just stunned it, but it'll be back any second." He held out his hand. "Can you run?"

Before Viri could answer, the wraith reappeared through the trees, hurtling toward them like a raging shadow, its arms outstretched and scarlet eyes promising vengeance.

"Go!" Viri shouted, taking Reeve's hand and sprinting into the wood. It was challenging to run while clinging to him, but she couldn't risk moving too far away from the extra protection of his talisman, the mist returning in force as soon as they left the clearing.

On and on they ran, the wind whipping at their faces as they raced between trees and around boulders, leapt through creeks and over fallen logs, all while the wraith gave chase, screeching at a pitch that felt like daggers piercing Viri's ears. At one point, the sound became so painful that blood trickled from her nose, prompting Reeve to throw his free hand back and send out another blast of ellixen. It gave them a momentary reprieve, but then the creature was soaring after them again, blending into the blackness of the mist and the swiftly approaching twilight. It felt as if it were everywhere and nowhere, around every corner and always at their heels.

"We—can't—run—forever," Viri panted as they bolted through the darkening forest, her lungs searing and muscles straining. It was a miracle neither of them had tripped on anything, almost as if the Mistwood sensed their plight and was trying to help.

"We just need to reach the wayportal," Reeve said, breathing nearly as hard, his grip on her hand close to bruising.

Viri hoped he was right, that there really *was* a wayportal waiting just up ahead. It was almost impossible for her to read the map while sprinting at breakneck speed, let alone in the dimming light, but it *looked* as if they were approaching the end of the magical line.

"We—should—be—nearly—" Viri stopped speaking when they burst through a thicket of leafy branches to find a small abandoned temple sitting in the middle of a pond covered in lily pads. The structure was ancient, made of pearlescent stone that shimmered with gold, appearing both welcoming and forbidding at the same time. There was no wayportal in sight, but Viri felt certain this was where the map had been leading them, and she bounded forward with Reeve, splashing through the pond and up the steps, only realizing when they reached the top that the wraith was no longer screeching—and no longer chasing them.

Viri tugged Reeve to a halt before he could keep running into the temple, both of them panting hard as they looked back to see the wraith hovering at the edge of the trees, its mouth open in the same horrific razor-toothed grin as earlier.

"Beware the wood. Beware the stone. Beware the beast. Who lost his throne," the wraith sang, the unfamiliar verse echoing all around them. *"Beware the lake. His sacred home. Beware the drop . . . Or die alone."* An ominous laugh. *"Farewell, Daughter of Death and Son of Shadows. Unlike you, I dare not tread where I am not welcome."*

With that, the wraith offered one last nightmarish grin and floated back into the forest, disappearing from sight.

"Um . . ." Viri said, her heart racing from the run, but now also from the skin-crawling sensation caused by the wraith's parting words.

"It's probably just mind games," Reeve said, though he looked as unnerved as she felt. He squeezed her hand in reassurance, his touch comforting her more than it should, prompting her to hastily untangle their fingers.

With a quick check of the map, Viri squinted through the growing dusk to confirm they were mere steps away from the end of the magical line. "It should be in here," she said, pocketing the parchment and moving deeper into the temple. "Let's look around for—"

A thunderous rumble interrupted her as the ground shifted around them, just like in the forest. Only, this time it wasn't changing into something new, but crumbling away into nothing, leaving a chasm of darkness—

Directly beneath their feet.

Viri didn't even have time to scream before they fell, the shadows swallowing them whole.

24

Down they plummeted, down, down, *down* through pitch-black nothingness, the force of the wind making Viri tumble and somersault through the air. Reeve was somewhere to her left, falling just as swiftly, but she only knew that because she could hear him bellowing her name into the darkness. She wanted to yell back, but her throat was closed again—not by the wraith's mental tricks this time but from the sheer terror of how fast and deep they were dropping beneath the earth.

And then, suddenly, the darkness lifted as they descended into a cavernous chamber, the expansive space lit by glowing blue moss covering the rocky walls and reflecting off the glassy surface of an immense underground lake.

Viri only had a split second to fill her lungs and brace for impact before she slammed into the water, her body barking in pain and then flooding with shock as the ice-cold temperature registered. She kicked upward, breaking through the surface with a gasp.

"Reeve!" she called, spinning frantically in place. *"REEVE!"*

A splashing sound came from her right as he appeared, coughing up lake water and yelling her name. *"VIRI!"*

"Here!"

He whirled toward her, then swam her way, the blue glow illuminating his worried features.

"Are you—"

"I'm all r-right," she answered quickly, her teeth chattering as she treaded water. "B-Bruised and c-c-cold, but alive. You?"

"Same," Reeve said. He pointed to a cluster of rocks resting like a small island a short distance away. "We need to get out of this water—I think I saw the shoreline as we fell, but I'll have to look around and get my bearings."

Viri immediately started swimming toward the rocks, her limbs tingling with pins and needles by the time she reached them, making it difficult to grip the slippery stone and pull herself up. With Reeve's help, she levered her body out of the water, shivering violently as she stood upon the island that was barely as wide as they were tall.

"Elders, you look like death," Reeve said, swiping water from his face—a useless endeavor, given his dripping hair—and eyeing her quaking form with concern.

"J-Just what every g-g-girl wants to hear," Viri chattered through frozen lips.

Before she could stop him, Reeve stepped forward and pressed his palm to her chest, right over her heart. She jerked backward, nearly sliding off the rocks, but his other arm snaked around her waist, holding her in place.

"Easy, I'm not trying anything." He winked. "No promises about later."

Viri was so cold that she couldn't even blush, though she did roll her eyes and try to pull away again.

Reeve didn't release her, just furrowed his brow in concentration. "This might feel strange."

That was all the warning Viri had before his hand heated and his magic flowed into her, spreading from her chest upward and outward, through her middle, along her arms, down her legs, his power thawing her from the inside out. A moan left her as every trace of ice vanished, leaving her no longer trembling but toasty warm.

"Better?" Reeve asked, tucking a tendril of wet hair behind her ear before letting her go entirely.

Viri swallowed against everything his tender, thoughtful actions made her feel and straightened her still-soaked cloak. "All that magic, and you can't even dry clothes? Some all-powerful mage you are."

A low chuckle. "You're welcome." He indicated the lake surrounding them. "And we still have another swim ahead of us. My magic doesn't come without a cost—I'll dry us both fully once we're out of here."

Shame hit Viri, making her feel like an ungrateful toad. "What kind of cost?"

Reeve's mouth curled upward, his eyes soft on hers. "The kind that was worth it."

This time, Viri *was* warm enough to blush, and she was thankful that the blue haze over everything would keep it from showing. She cleared her throat and asked, "Where's this shoreline you thought you saw?"

Reeve turned carefully on their rocky platform, squinting

around the luminous cavern, before finally pointing at what Viri could now see herself.

"There's a bank over there, and it looks like there's natural light coming from beyond it, so I'd say that's our way out." He gauged the distance. "It's a fair swim—do you think you can make it without turning into an icicle?"

His question was wry, but Viri answered seriously, her insides churning at the thought of getting back into the frigid lake. "As long as you're happy to heat me up again once we reach the other side, I'll be fine."

The moment the words left her lips, she knew she'd made a colossal mistake—as evidenced by the devilish grin that stretched across Reeve's face.

"I'll heat you up any time you want, Viridia Solace." His grin widened, his tone deepening with meaning—and promise. "No magic necessary."

Viri's cheeks warmed even more, but she refused to let him see her flustered. "Trust me, the only thing I want you for is your magic."

"Ahh, so you're finally admitting that you want me. We're making progress."

"That's not what I—" Viri snapped her mouth shut and glared at him.

"Careful." He touched his finger to her forehead. "They say if the wind changes, you'll be stuck like that forever."

Viri batted his hand away. "You're infuriating."

"If you mean infuriatingly good-looking, then yes, I am. I'm also infuriatingly charming, infuriatingly patient, infuriatingly loyal, infuriatingly—"

"—full of yourself," Viri said for him.

"I think the word you mean is 'confident,' and yes, I'm that, too. Admit it, it's one of your favorite things about me."

"I don't have any favorite things about you."

"We both know that's not true. Our little moment in the Summit showed us just how much you like my—"

Viri slammed her hand over his mouth, keeping him from finishing. His silver eyes shone ethereally in the blue light, his humor unmistakable. But then realization hit her and she released him to accuse, "You're trying to distract me."

He cocked his head to the side. "Why would I do that?"

"Because you know I don't want to get back in the cold water."

"Maybe *I* don't want to get back in the cold water. Only one of us has magic hands." He wiggled his eyebrows suggestively, and Viri snorted despite herself.

"Unless those magic hands can summon a raft or pull one from your magepocket, then we might as well get this over with." She turned on the narrow rock, preparing to dive back in. But she couldn't bring herself to take the plunge.

Seeing her hesitation, Reeve said, "Do you remember our last summer together before—" He broke off, winced, then cleared his expression to continue, "You were determined to beat me and Brae across the river mouth between Lake Mirtis and River Mort. You made us swim it at least a hundred times before you finally won."

A nostalgic smile touched Viri's lips. "And then I made you swim it another hundred more, just to prove I could keep beating you."

"Which you did, every time," Reeve said, pride clear in his

voice. "Let's see if you still have what it takes." He gestured toward the bank in the distance. "Race you?"

She acted as if she were thinking about it, when they both knew she was already going to be swimming as fast as she could to get out of the cold. "What do I get if I win?"

Reeve's devilish grin returned. "My magic hands making you hot."

Viri choked on a laugh. "And if you win?"

His eyes danced as he repeated, "My magic hands making you hot. It's win-win for me."

Viri bit her cheek to keep from laughing again. "You used to put a lot more thought into deciding prizes."

"Maybe I just know what I want now."

His meaning was impossible to miss, causing Viri's heart to skip a beat, but she didn't have time to dwell on his words or remind herself of everything he was—reaper, monster, killer—before he continued, "On three?"

She nodded, grateful to ignore what he'd just said and the contradictory feelings he elicited in her.

"One," he counted, bending forward and preparing to dive.

"Two," she said, copying his move and already dreading the cold she knew was coming.

"Thr—"

Reeve didn't finish before something large and black shot out of the water and slammed into him, propelling him forcefully back into the lake.

Viri shouted his name, having no idea what had just happened.

He reappeared with a splash, coughing and cursing. *"What the hell was—"*

His words cut off when he vanished beneath the surface again, as if something had dragged him under. Viri's pulse thundered in her ears as she peered frantically into the depths, but the blue glow barely penetrated the darkness.

"REEVE!" she yelled, unsheathing a dagger. *"REEVE!"*

A flare of light beneath the water, a tingle of ellixen, and Viri realized he was fighting whatever had pulled him down. The next second, he reappeared again, but he wasn't alone when he broke through the surface this time. There was something wrapped around him, an inky black tentacle that thrust him up out of the water, high into the air—

And then slammed him against the rocks with a sickening *crunch.*

Viri's stomach roiled at the sound, then roiled again at the sight of his shoulder bending at an unnatural angle and the blood dripping from his temple, his eyes dazed and unfocused from the hard blow to his head. That was all she saw before the tentacle lifted him again, and this time, the body it belonged to rose partially out of the water, revealing a monstrous black creature with glowing orange eyes and too many appendages to count.

"Beware the wood. Beware the stone. Beware the beast. Who lost his throne," the wraith's song whispered in her memory. *"Beware the lake. His sacred home. Beware the drop . . . Or die alone."*

Elders, this was what the wraith had warned them about—the drop from the stone temple into the lake. *This* was what had kept it from following them, the reason for its grotesque grin.

Dread rushed through Viri as she watched the lake monster haul Reeve beneath the water again, both his arms now trapped against his sides, stopping him from grabbing his weapons. But even if he'd been able to retrieve them, they would have been useless in his hands; he was barely even conscious after being slammed like a rag doll against the rocks. The only way he would survive this was if Viri fought for him—for *both* of them.

With Reeve's life on the line, Viri didn't think, she just acted, pulling a vial of zingzest from her cloak and downing the citrussy potion. Her nerves electrified as adrenaline shot through her system, and when the beast resurfaced moments later with Reeve's alarmingly limp form in its clutches, she didn't hesitate. Still holding one dagger in her right hand, she unsheathed her second—her last, after having thrown her third at the wraith—and leapt off the rock with a battle cry, barely noticing the frigid water thanks to Wynter's potent tonic.

Her aim was true and she landed halfway along one of the monster's slimy tentacles, instantly slashing into it with both her blades. The sinewy flesh peeled open beneath her, gushing oily black blood that stung as it splattered across her hands. But it was the beast's unholy shriek that really made her skin crawl.

It had been angry before.

Now it was *furious.*

Suddenly, Viri was hanging on for dear life as the tentacle twisted and bucked, flinging her into the air and plunging her beneath the water before doing both again—and again, and *again.* Another tentacle swatted at her, trying to loosen her grip, while a third sought to coil around her like the one that had ensnared Reeve, but she stabbed ferociously with her daggers, knowing that if it succeeded, neither she nor Reeve would be leaving the cavern alive.

"REEVE!" Viri screamed when he was tossed into the air again. His eyelids fluttered at her call, telling her he was still

alive, still fighting to stay conscious. Something about her cry roused him enough to send out a surge of ellixen—but instead of using it to free himself, he blasted away a tentacle that Viri hadn't seen coming toward her. The monster shrieked in pain, and then Reeve's mouth opened in a gasp as it squeezed him mercilessly, his eyes rolling to the back of his head as the beast dragged him under the water again—but this time, he didn't reappear.

"NO!" Viri cried, knowing she had to do something, *now*, or he would drown.

With a grunt of effort, she scrambled her way up the tentacle she was straddling, gripping with her thighs and fighting off the monster's other appendages with her blades, choking on water as it dunked her over and over again, trying to dislodge her. But she wouldn't let go—*couldn't* let go. Reeve still hadn't resurfaced, and if he was unconscious beneath the water . . .

Terror threatened to overwhelm Viri, but she shoved it down, slashing her way through anything that tried to stop her, black blood stinging her flesh until she finally reached the point where the tentacle attached to the creature's enormous body.

Her daggers were too small to hit anything vital—it would be like pricking a dragon with a pin—so she sheathed one and uncoiled her fillium, knowing she would have only one shot at this, and equally certain she was crazy for even thinking it possible. But now wasn't the time to doubt herself, so when another tentacle flew at her, instead of stabbing it away, she snagged it with her golden cord. As predicted, the appendage flung her straight upward, and she used the momentum to swing herself in the direction of the beast's head. It didn't have a chance to realize what she was doing before she thrust her dagger forward—

Right into one of its glowing orange eyes.

The monster's shriek was so loud, so *painful*, that Viri nearly blacked out—and she might have if she hadn't been thrown violently away, her fillium coming loose from the tentacle as she was hurled through the air and left to plummet down into the lake. The fall was jarring enough to knock the wind out of her, and she rose to the surface with a wheeze, panting hard and treading water as she braced for the next attack.

Only, it didn't come—the monster was retreating beneath the lake, its tentacles drawing inward to protect its remaining eye, like a dog running away to lick its wounds.

Viri could hardly believe it was over, her uncertainty so strong that she stayed on guard, even as the beast fled. But then, finally, the water rippled and Reeve appeared, his body released from the tentacle that had held him hostage.

Relief slammed into Viri at the sight of him, but it lasted only a second before she realized something was very wrong.

Because Reeve wasn't moving.

25

"*REEVE!*" Viri screamed, tearing through the water toward him.

Panic flooded every part of her as she swam faster than she ever had in her life, fearing she was too late, that he was already gone.

But then—

Reeve's eyes shot open, and water surged out of his mouth as he began coughing up half the lake, the sound causing a sob to leave Viri because it meant he was alive, he was *breathing*.

She reached him in time to help hold him above the surface as he continued purging fluid from his lungs. "Elders," she panted tremulously, "I thought you drowned."

Between splutters, he rasped out, "I feel like"—a hacking cough—"I did."

She kept supporting him, treading water for them both until his coughing began to ease. Only then did she ask, "How badly are you hurt?" His eyes were still dazed and unfocused in the blue light, but at least he was more alert now, even with the bloody smear at the side of his head. "Can you swim?"

His voice was hoarse and tinged with pain. "I think my shoulder is dislocated."

Viri swore, realizing for the first time that he was holding it close to his body rather than using it to stay afloat. "I'll help you," she said. "We need to get out of this water before that thing changes its mind and comes back."

Reeve nodded his agreement and then winced as the move jolted his head. But all he said was, his voice still rough, "My legs are fine, and I can still use one arm. Don't wait for me—I'll meet you on the bank."

Viri didn't entertain that with a response, just kept pace with him as they began the laborious swim toward the shore. Despite his injuries and the agony he no doubt felt, Reeve was able to move swiftly enough on his own, but she stayed close, watching for any sign that he needed her. Soon, though, she began to wonder if *she* might need help, since the zingzest was fading from her system with each stroke, along with the adrenaline of fighting the tentacled beast, leaving her no protection against the frigid temperature of the water.

By the time they reached the shallows and crawled out to collapse upon the pebbled shore, Viri had gone beyond pins and needles to complete numbness in her extremities. It was nearly impossible for her to draw herself into a sitting position, but she gritted her teeth and reminded herself that whatever she was feeling, Reeve had to be feeling worse. He'd been in—and under—the water for much longer, and his wounds weren't superficial. He might not be complaining, but there was no way he wasn't suffering.

"H-H-Here," she said, fumbling in her cloak until she clenched her unfeeling fingers around two vials, thrusting them at him. "T-T-Take th-these."

Reeve was shivering just as much as she was this time, and there was an alarming amount of blood dripping from his temple onto the pebbles, mixing with the water sluicing off them both. But even so, he ignored her, instead sitting up and reaching his uninjured arm toward her chest.

As much as Viri longed to be warm again, she hadn't forgotten Reeve saying there was a cost to his magic, and right now, he was in no state to pay it.

"N-N-No." She attempted to push him away, but her frozen limbs were like soggy noodles, barely able to follow her commands.

"If you think I'm g-going to sit here while you f-freeze, then you don't know me h-half as well as you believe," Reeve said, his teeth chattering nearly as fiercely as hers.

"B-But—"

He didn't let her finish her objection, his palm pressing gently against her heart, followed by delicious heat flowing into her. She could do little but whimper as feeling returned to her body, the burn a combination of pain and immeasurable relief.

Only when she was completely thawed did Reeve drop his arm, though he was still shivering violently enough that Viri leaned forward in concern and asked, "Can you heat yourself up the same way?"

"No, but my m-magic will help me recover f-faster than you." Seeing her question, he said, "Quicker h-healing, sharper reflexes, h-heightened senses. Not as m-much as freshly siphoned reapers, but better than n-nothing. It's what k-kept me alive b-beneath the water."

Viri had already seen how swiftly he could move when he chose to, and there had been times when he'd seemed to hear or see things before she could, but the healing was a welcome surprise—*especially* if his innate magic was what had saved him from drowning. Viri shuddered as she recalled the tentacle dragging his unconscious form beneath the water, certain she would have nightmares about it long into the future.

"Here, these will speed things along," she said, pushing the image from her mind and holding the vials out again—the last of the zingzest, and her only supply of morphenine. The former would revitalize him and warm him up, and the latter would help him tolerate what was coming next.

Reeve didn't argue this time, just swallowed both potions, color coming back into his flesh as soon as the energy booster hit his system, visible even in the blue glow of the cavern. But it was the morphenine that smoothed the pained tension from his brow, a moan of relief leaving him as the magic-enhanced painkiller took effect.

No longer shivering, he said, somewhat wryly, "Not that I'm ungrateful, but next time, maybe give me those *before* I have to swim across an icy lake with a concussion and a dislocated arm."

"The morphenine is only potent for a short amount of time," Viri said, "so if I'd done that, then it would have hurt a lot more when I did this." She grabbed his arm and yanked, *hard*, popping his shoulder back into place.

Reeve roared with pain, the sound tearing into Viri's heart, but then he clenched his jaw shut to stifle it, breathing fast and cradling his arm against his body.

"I think," he panted out, "you enjoyed that more than you should have."

Viri snorted and didn't deny it, though in truth, she felt queasy from what she'd just done. His agony still echoed in her ears, but the longer they'd waited to set his joint, the more pain it would have caused in the long run.

"Don't be such a baby," she mock-scolded, pulling Wynter's healing salve from her cloak and swiftly unbuttoning his wet shirt. She grimaced when she peeled the black material aside and saw the deep bruises across his muscled torso, a sign of just how tightly the tentacled beast had squeezed him. But she ignored those momentarily and shifted onto her knees to carefully rub the ointment into his upper arm, his flesh warming beneath her fingertips. Only after his shoulder was fully covered in the salve did she move downward, scooping more out and gently massaging it into the purpling marks on his stomach and along his sides, satisfied to note only a faint scratch left where the grimblade had stabbed him. Her fingers trickled back across his abdomen, his muscles contracting beneath her touch, feeling like steel beneath her hands—steel covered in silky-smooth skin.

Realizing he'd never replied to her comment, Viri glanced up and caught the look on his face, her fingers stilling and the breath leaving her. Heat scorched her cheeks, but she sternly said, "This is purely medical."

Reeve's eyes were sparkling like stars in the blue light. "If I'd known you were so eager to get your hands on me again—"

"Finish that sentence," Viri threatened, her cheeks still too warm, "and I'll throw you back in with the lake monster."

"I'm not the one who stripped my clothes off without a second thought," Reeve said, his humor impossible to miss. "If I didn't know any better—"

"You do," Viri ground out. "Now shut up and let me look at your head. You clearly have brain damage."

He chuckled, which she not only heard but *felt*, since her palms were still pressed to his bare abdomen. She hastily removed them, avoiding his too-amused gaze as she rose up on her knees and took his face in her hands, inspecting the bloody gash at his temple.

"How are you even conscious right now?" she murmured, brushing his dripping hair away from the grisly wound.

"You think I'd miss a moment of this?" His brows rose with disbelief. "I'd sooner throw *myself* back in with the lake monster."

Viri bit down on a smile and got to work, cleaning the cut as best as she could with her wet sleeve, then slathering salve over it. The magical ointment started working almost instantly, sealing the wound until it was little more than an angry red line.

"There, all better," she said, releasing his face and shifting away—only to be halted when Reeve's hand landed on her waist, keeping her close.

There was no humor in his expression now, his features solemn, even awed, as he said, "You saved my life."

Viri swallowed at the look in his eyes. "You would have done the same for me." Her gaze dropped to the scratch on his side where the grimblade had pierced him. "You *did* do the same for me." She glanced away and said, softly, "I never thanked you for that."

His finger touched beneath her chin, tipping her face back

toward his as he said, just as quietly, "You never need to thank me for that."

Viri swallowed again, holding his serious eyes as she whispered, "Then you never need to thank me, either."

He stilled, his gaze searching hers, and her heart began to quicken at the thought of what he might see. But as if he could read the fear that was suddenly overwhelming her, the intensity vanished from his features, replaced by quirking lips and amused eyes. "We're agreed, then," he said lightly, dropping his hands. "We'll both be ungrateful assholes."

A startled laugh left Viri, and she grabbed on to his offer of levity like a lifeline. "That's nothing new to you—the asshole part, I mean."

Reeve clutched at his chest. "Hey, I'm injured here. Show some compassion." He tapped his temple, which was now almost completely healed. "You didn't even kiss it better. Some bedside manner you have."

Viri grinned and shook her head. "Nice try. But you've had all the kisses you're getting from me."

He smirked. "That sounds like a challenge."

"Not a challenge—a promise."

A low laugh. "You shouldn't make promises you can't keep, Little Shadow."

Before she could respond—not that she knew *how*—Reeve stood up and rotated his shoulder, wonder touching his features as he said, "For someone with no proper training, Wynter sure knows her stuff."

"She's amazing," Viri agreed, grateful to move on from any and all talk of kissing. "There's a lot of trial and error, though. With heavy emphasis on the error."

"The best way to learn is by failing," Reeve said sagely.

"Say that *after* you've been the test dummy on some of her illegal magical experiments," Viri muttered.

"Speaking of experiments . . ." Reeve offered his hand to Viri and pulled her up beside him, the pebbles shifting under their weight. "I haven't tried this before, so bear with me."

Viri didn't have a chance to ask what he was talking about before she felt the tingle of ellixen, followed by an odd but not unpleasant sensation, like warm liquid dripping from the top of her head downward. When it passed, she was completely dry again, from her hair all the way to her toes. Moments later, Reeve was the same.

"That's better," he said, rebuttoning his shirt over his now barely bruised torso.

"You mentioned before that there's a cost to using magic," Viri prompted, marveling at her newly dry state. There wasn't a hint of dampness left, not even in her cloak pockets.

"Think of it like a muscle," Reeve said. "The more you use it, the stronger it becomes. But by the same rules, use too much and it gets tired—or worse."

"Burnout," Viri said, her stomach pitching.

Reeve nodded. "It happens when too much is used at once, whether that's from a concentrated burst of powerful magic or a slower release over a long period without resting."

"So in the case of kids who don't Impart . . . ?"

"It's the concentrated burst, but it's not by choice—it happens accidentally from an unstable buildup of ellixen." Before she could ask, he shared, "To avoid that, I had to learn how to control my magic—to train the muscle, so to speak. The same would have been true for Wynter."

"I still can't believe that," Viri murmured, though she knew deep down that it was true. Even so, she planned on having a *very* stern talk with her best friend after she returned to the city.

"Do you know what I can't believe?" Reeve asked, looking around the blue cavern, a frown creasing his brow.

"What?"

"The husband," he said.

Viri blinked. "Sorry?"

"The husband, the wife, and the friend from the story," he clarified. "I told you earlier that I doubted they hiked all the way to the tower, but there's no *way* they made it down here. Something isn't adding up."

Realizing he was right, Viri pulled the map from her cloak, relieved to see it had survived the lake and was now dry again thanks to Reeve's magic. But then she opened it, and any relief she'd felt vanished.

"No," she whispered, certain it had to be wrong.

Reeve peered over her shoulder, then tensed with disbelief. "That's not possible."

With a shaking finger, Viri traced the magical line—the one they'd been so close to reaching the end of . . . but now led to another place entirely, almost all the way back to the necropolis.

A stream of curses left Reeve's mouth, but Viri was staring at the map, thinking hard, words he'd said flitting across her memory:

"The map belongs to your family line, so the magic only works for someone with Solace blood."

And later:

"I never understood how the husband could have hiked through the Mistwood if he was as weak as the legend claimed."

Then finally:

"I asked your mom about it . . . and she just smiled and said, 'Anything is possible with magic.'"

A theory came to Viri, something that was surely a fool's hope, but she listened to her instincts as they guided her to unsheathe a dagger and prick the tip of her finger.

"The magic only works for someone with Solace blood."

Reeve was right that the husband never would have been able to make the journey . . . but what if he hadn't needed to? What if the wayportal wasn't located in any one place but moved around the Mistwood, just like how the trees shifted and the rivers turned and the ground formed and re-formed. *That* was why the map had changed—because the portal had *moved.*

And if it had moved once, then it could move again.

Especially if it was summoned.

"Anything is possible with magic."

If Viri's mother had spoken true, then maybe a Solace could do more than *read* the map—maybe a Solace could also *control* it.

Praying her instincts were right, Viri touched her bleeding finger to the line on the parchment, tracing it all the way back to where she and Reeve were standing, willing the map to recognize her, to *obey* her.

One second passed. Two seconds. Three—

And then a bright flash lit the cavern, and the shimmering wayportal appeared on the pebbled shore before them.

An incredulous laugh left Viri. "I can't believe that worked."

She turned to Reeve, finding him just as stunned as she was, but then he gave an amused shake of his head and drawled, "You couldn't have tried that *before* we were chased by a wraith, attacked by a lake monster, and had to hike for hours through a diabolical forest?"

Despite his sarcasm, she could see the pride clear in his eyes. But there was something else there, too. Something that made her stomach flip and her knees weaken.

Reaper, monster, killer—she said the words in her mind, desperate for anything to stifle what she could no longer deny was growing between them. The moment she'd seen his unconscious form go under the water, the terror she'd felt had exposed what she'd been refusing to acknowledge: that she cared for him, much more than she should. For all his teasing, for all her indignation and embarrassment, she wasn't fooling either of them. She wanted him, they both knew it. And yet—

Reaper.

Monster.

Killer.

That was what Reeve was, and regardless of anything else, she couldn't afford to forget it. He might not siphon anymore, but he also held no remorse for his past actions. He'd killed a girl, and by his own admission, he didn't regret her death. Viri couldn't ignore that—even if her heart was beginning to wish she could.

Summoning every scrap of self-respect she had, Viri stomped down her emotions and cleared her throat to answer, "Only one of us knows anything about magic, so excuse me if I didn't think to experiment with an ancient map and a wayportal that *moves*."

Reeve's lips twitched at her attitude, with him blissfully unaware of everything that had just passed through her mind—including her resolve to smother anything she felt toward him.

"At least we won't have to retrace our steps through the Mistwood after we're done with the Guardian," he said, looking thoughtfully at the wayportal. "No wonder the husband was able to get his magewish—not to mention his wife was able to return for hers, and then both of them a third time with their dying babe. It makes so much more sense now." He spoke the last part under his breath, his eyes oddly unfocused, but Viri was stuck on his mention of the Guardian, her insides swooping as she realized they were only steps away from discovering whether or not the legend she'd grown up hearing was true. If the Guardian of Elverdine Isle really did exist, if he was just on the other side of the portal . . .

Uncertainty barreled into her. "What's our plan here?"

Reeve shook off whatever musings had gripped him. "The same as it's always been: to beat Braedan to the Guardian and stop him from being granted a magewish."

"Right." Viri nodded mechanically. "We stop him from destroying the obelisks."

An unreadable look crossed Reeve's face before he wiped it clear. "We stop him from dooming the city, yes."

"What if we're too late?" Viri worried aloud.

"We'd know if we were."

"How? We've been out here for hours. What if he made it to the tower while we—"

"Viri," Reeve said firmly, placing his hands on her shoulders. "Take a breath. Everything is going to be all right."

Holding his eyes, she asked, her voice wobbling slightly, "How do you know that?"

He gave her a reassuring squeeze. "Because we're going to make sure of it."

His steely determination silenced Viri's fears. It was still daunting, the idea of traveling blindly through the portal and trusting it would deliver them to the Guardian, let alone having to convince him to refuse her brother should Braedan reach the tower on his own. But Reeve's confidence was the balm Viri needed to face what was ahead, along with his reminder that they would do whatever it took to succeed in their task—mostly because, if they didn't, everyone they knew would die.

"Come on, Little Shadow," Reeve said, watching with approval as she straightened her spine and indicated she was ready. "Let's go finish what we started."

With a fortifying inhale, Viri strode toward the wayportal with him, her heart fluttering nervously as she wondered what they would find on the other side. If she'd spared a moment to think about it, she might have assumed they would appear near a freestanding tower or fortress-like keep, or perhaps they'd arrive at the edge of the Mistwood overlooking an ancient castle. She might also have assumed they would need to go searching for the Guardian inside his expansive dwelling, and Elders knew how long that would take.

What she *wouldn't* have assumed was that the wayportal might open right inside Nevarnost Tower, directly in the center of a large, warmly lit circular chamber reminiscent of Wynter's laboratory, the walls covered in shelves full of books and potions and magical artifacts, the domed ceiling made of glass and revealing a moonlit sky full of stars.

Viri also wouldn't have assumed that a middle-aged man who could only be the Guardian would be standing mere feet away from the portal, his eyes a luminous blue, his dark hair flecked with gray, his tall frame clad in unusual purple robes, and his handsome face wearing a serene smile, almost as if he'd been expecting them.

But the one thing Viri *definitely* wouldn't have assumed—but really *should* have—was that the Guardian wouldn't be alone, her palm suddenly searing as her hunter's mark flared to life.

Because standing next to him—

Was the Reaper Priest.

THE JOURNAL OF
CELESTIAL MAGE KADMUS CASTRO

Fifty-Fourth Sun, Thirteenth Cycle, Twelfth Age

I did it.

I actually *did* it.

I used the power from the Aurora Comet and—

And—

I destroyed an obelisk.

Only one, not all four. I didn't know what I was doing, wasn't sure it would even *work*—and it nearly didn't. I'm strong for a mage, but the ellixen emitted by Aurora was unlike anything I've ever channeled during a celestial event. It was a struggle to maintain a connection, and I only managed to do so long enough to siphon a fraction of her power. Once I had it, instead of using it to bless my shallows, I speared its full force toward the southernmost obelisk.

At first, I feared nothing had happened.

But then I saw it: a small crack.

And then I felt it: the Hallow Stream. Roaring. *Raging.*

The crack destroyed the infusion on that one obelisk, but I couldn't hold Aurora's power long enough to bring down the other three. Even so, while most of the Stream's magic remained suppressed, a small amount was able to break free and surge outward.

It was angry. *Furious.*

And it came straight for me.

~~I have never~~

~~I can't begin to—~~

I don't have words for the amount of power that flooded me. How strong I felt. How *invincible* I was.

But then Tephryn and the fabricator mages repaired the crack, and the magic vanished, silenced once more.

I want it back. I *need* it back.

There's a hunger in me. An insatiable, relentless desperation to feel it again. No, to feel even *more*. But that can only happen if all four obelisks are destroyed—*permanently*. As long as an alchemist is on Elverdine Isle, as long as the fabricator mages are here, they will always be able to repair the wardstones, or build new ones.

But I think I know a way around that.

Because while the Stream's magic flooded me, it also whispered to me. Shouted. *Screamed*.

It wants to be free. *Demands* to be free.

And I can help make that happen, using Aurora's lover, Orion, the second of the Adastrum Devotis comets. His power matches hers, maybe even exceeds it. Either way, he will be strong enough to destroy all four obelisks.

The problem is, *I'm* not strong enough to channel Orion for the length of time needed to draw down the required power.

There is, however, a way that I could be.

Instead of a blessing rite, I could use a sacrificial ritual—a *forbidden* sacrificial ritual, in which the blood element involves not the drop of my own that I normally use, but instead blood from someone else.

And not just a drop.

The sacrifice requires *death*.

If I were to go through with it, the ritual would strengthen my ellixen to untold levels, which would enable me to maintain a connection with Orion for long enough to destroy the obelisks.

The idea is reprehensible. Sacrificial magic is forbidden for a reason: To use it is to leave a scar on your very soul.

And yet . . .

I can't stop thinking about how it would solve everything.

I shared my thoughts with Magistratus Garrin, fully expecting him to send me packing from the island. I didn't factor in just how hungry he and many of the other residents are for more magic, something they never knew was possible until I became their Priest. They've changed since I started performing my rituals here. They've *evolved*. Just as I have.

Garrin supports my plan, as do my devoted followers, though of course I didn't tell them everything. The details don't matter; they all suffer from the same ravenous yearning that ensnares me, with it driving us to do things we may not be proud of but accept as necessary. We will do whatever it takes, no matter the cost.

"For the greater good," Garrin said when I explained to him alone what the sacrifice requires, his eyes more wild and manic than when I first arrived. It was like looking in a mirror, the Stream's magic having left its mark on us both. On us *all*.

"We'll use someone with no family or personal connections and make it look like an accident," he added. "No one will ever learn the truth, and if they do, they'll still be thanking us when they're reaping the rewards."

Reaping.

That's exactly what we'll be doing.

Because once the Orion sacrifice is complete and the obelisks are destroyed, the Hallow Stream will be free—and we'll be reaping from it.

This is what it wants, I'm certain of it. It wants to be liberated, and the only way to ensure it stays that way is for me and my shallows to access its magic—to *siphon* its magic—which we'll then use to keep the fabricator mages from rebuilding the obelisks. The amount of ellixen we'll have at our fingertips will be more than enough to overpower them.

At least in theory.

I've never channeled anything other than a celestial body before. I tried to in my youth out of curiosity, as many do, but it's not possible on the mainland. I assume it has something to do with the wards around the two Hallow Streams, since they shield all ellixen flowing out into the natural world, so it makes sense that they also prevent it from being siphoned. It's why celestial magic is so unique, because we draw power from the cosmos, far beyond the reach of the Streams' wards.

Here on Elverdine, though . . . we're *also* beyond the reach of those wards. I never thought—or dared—to attempt it before the obelisks were built, but I'm confident that once the Hallow Stream's power is flowing once more, I'll be able to siphon from it and bestow it upon my shallows, just like I do with my celestial rituals. The magic will be a gift, a reward for freeing it, for protecting it. In return, my shallows and I will be strong enough to take on all the mages—and to show them who has the real power here.

Never again will the Stream's magic be suppressed. I'll make certain of it.

The mages will be incensed, but I care little about their tantrums. Tephryn, though . . .

She'll understand once I explain. She loves me. She'll forgive me. She'll accept why I had to do it. Why I had no choice.

And as for Zeranthe . . .

She's worried about me. Says there's something wrong with our bond, with *me*.

She's overreacting.

Our bond is fine, and I've never felt better.

But soon I will.

Soon I'll be *unstoppable*.

For the greater good, as Garrin said.

I will do this for him, for them, for my shallows.

And I will do this for me.

26

All the breath left Viri's lungs as she laid eyes on her brother for the first time in seven years.

No longer a fourteen-year-old boy, Braedan Solace was now a young man, albeit one who looked as if he'd battled his way through the entire Mistwood. His face was covered in dirt and scratches, his green cloak torn and muddied, his auburn hair mussed and windswept. But it was the black veins streaking up his arms and his familiar pale blue eyes—their father's eyes—that made Viri feel as if she'd been punched in the stomach.

Braedan, too, looked as if he'd seen a ghost as Viri and Reeve arrived in the center of the room, his eyes widening and his face draining of color. But he recovered quickly and spun toward the Guardian, words rushing out of him so fast that Viri didn't have a chance to think, let alone try to stop him as he declared, "Guardian, I wish for the death of—"

Reeve lunged forward and yelled over him, *"I wish for Braedan not to get a wish!"*

"NO!" Braedan roared, but he was too late.

With a wave of the Guardian's hand, ellixen flooded the room, strong enough to make the hairs on the back of Viri's neck stand on end.

"Your wishes are fulfilled," the mage said in a deep voice, looking oddly amused as he peered between them all.

Viri was so stunned by what had happened—or *not* happened—that she was frozen in place. In all their talks about the Guardian and the tower and the legend, she'd never once considered what it would mean if she and Reeve made it to Nevarnost. All along, she'd been worried about Braedan getting a magewish, and had forgotten that *anyone* who found the Guardian would get one.

But Reeve hadn't forgotten—and he'd just used his to save them all.

"What did you *do*?" Braedan rasped out to Reeve, looking horrified.

His words jolted Viri from her shock, reminding her that she'd spent the last seven years chasing him—the elusive Reaper Priest—and now she finally had a chance to capture him. She leapt forward, uncoiling her fillium as she raced across the circular room, readying herself for the fight of her life.

She expected a battle.

She *didn't* expect to make it barely three steps before another surge of ellixen forced her into a sudden stop, rooting her feet to the polished stone floor and immobilizing her body from the neck down. Betrayal flooded her as she slashed her eyes toward Reeve, but he wasn't even looking at her, his focus entirely on Braedan. The Guardian, however . . . he winked at Viri, the gesture revealing that *he* was the one who had turned her into a statue.

Before she could demand her release, Reeve marched forward to answer Braedan, the two of them squaring off face to face.

"What did *I* do?" Reeve repeated incredulously. "What the hell were you *thinking*?"

"Me?" Braedan's hands balled into fists. "You have *no idea* what you just—"

"It's *you* who has no idea what you nearly did!" Reeve fumed, throwing his arms out to the sides. "Elders, Brae, you can't kill the Reaper Lord!"

Viri jerked at the unfamiliar title—or jerked as much as she could, given her immobilized state.

"That's *exactly* what we need to do!" Braedan yelled back. "Never mind what that bastard has done to us both in the last seven years—if the Aurora sacrifice goes ahead, then it's not just a heap of kids who will die, but the obelisks will be destroyed and *everyone* will die!"

Viri jerked again, because *he* was the one who wanted to destroy the obelisks. It was *his* sacrifice.

"There's a contingency in place," Reeve said through gritted teeth. "If the Reaper Lord dies, there'll be a huge release of ellixen—years and *years* of stolen power. The magical surge alone will be enough to repel the mist from around Mount Mort, leaving the reapers free to escape Diaboros. *All* of them."

The words were nonsensical to Viri, but Braedan lurched backward as if slapped. "What?" he breathed, his temper fleeing.

Reeve loosed a shaky breath and ran his hands through his hair. "It's what I wanted to tell you before you took off without warning. We have to find another way to stop the sacrifice—something that *doesn't* involve killing the Reaper Lord. Otherwise the city will fall regardless." His face was grim. "We're stuck between a rock and a hard place, Brae, but if you'd gone through with this, if you'd used your wish to kill the Reaper Lord, then—"

"Everyone would have died anyway," Braedan whispered, looking like he was going to be sick. "If Diaboros falls . . ."

"Then Aravell falls," Reeve finished gravely. "The city won't stand a chance."

Silence fell in the wake of their heavy words, but Viri couldn't hold her tongue a moment longer. "Someone needs to explain what the hell is going on, *right now*." She slitted her gaze at the Guardian. "And you need to let. Me. *Go*."

His luminous eyes glowed with humor. "You could have freed yourself at any time, Daughter of Death," he said, using the same name the wraith had called her, causing goosebumps to prickle her flesh. But then he waved his hand, and she was released from his grip, leaving her free to lunge toward her brother. Only, she didn't move an inch, the conversation she'd just overheard keeping her in place—for now.

"Who's the Reaper Lord?" she demanded, looking between Reeve and Braedan. "What's Diaboros?" She turned her glare on Reeve. "You seem to have left a few things out in, oh, *everything* you shared with me."

Reeve's face was a mask of calm. "You wouldn't have believed me if I'd told you the truth."

"*What* truth?"

"That Braedan isn't evil," he said simply. "And he's not behind the Aurora sacrifice."

Fire burned in Viri's chest. "He's the *Reaper Priest*." She jabbed a finger toward her brother. "He killed our *parents*." From the corner of her eye, she saw Braedan flinch, but she kept her furious gaze on Reeve. "He's the *epitome* of evil. And in case you forgot, *you're* the one who told me he's using the sacrifice to destroy the obelisks."

Reeve shook his head. "I never said that. I only said we needed to stop him."

"From *doing the sacrifice* and *destroying the obelisks.*"

"No, from making his magewish."

"A magewish that would help him *destroy the obelisks.*" Viri's voice rose. "You *said* that."

"I didn't," Reeve said, still frustratingly calm in the face of her anger. "I told you the sacrifice is intended to destroy the obelisks, and that's true. I also told you we needed to stop Braedan, which was also true. But those were *two separate things.* You just assumed they were one and the same."

Viri couldn't believe what she was hearing. "You *let me* assume that," she snarled.

"I did," Reeve said shamelessly. "I needed your help to get here as fast as possible so we could prevent him from dooming us all. I never lied about that." He blew out a breath. "Be annoyed all you want, but everything I did was for all the reasons I said—to save the city."

"Then you need to *explain* that," Viri ground out, leaning forward with her hands on her hips. "No more misleading half-truths. If you want me to believe you, then you need to tell me everything you know."

Reeve sighed and rubbed a weary hand over his face. "I'm not sure you're going to believe me regardless of what I say. But here it is: You've been chasing the wrong person for seven years."

Viri saw red, a sound leaving her lips that was part hiss, part scoff, all rage. "Are you really going to stand there and tell me he's not the Reaper Priest? *Really?*"

"No, he is," Reeve said quickly, stepping closer as if to soothe her before thinking better of it and halting again. "But the title is a distraction, something used to keep you and every other hunter from learning about the Reaper *Lord*—the leader of all reapers who rules Diaboros, a reaper city hidden deep inside Mount Mort."

There was a ringing sound in Viri's ears after his declaration, a combination of shock and incredulity. "That's impossible," she said roughly, latching onto the first argument that came to mind. "Mount Mort is covered in blackmist."

"It's *surrounded* by blackmist," Reeve corrected. "But the inside is sealed like Mount Tembris and Mount Verta. There's an entire population of reapers living in there, with generation after generation of them growing up inside, all trapped in place by the mist."

Viri shook her head. Shook it again.

"They siphon from each other to survive," Reeve went on determinedly, "or from any kids they have—stopping before they kill them, so they can siphon again later—until those kids either succumb to burnout or become reapers themselves. They're all desperate to leave, starved for fresh sources of ellixen, but the mist is a death sentence to almost all who try to escape. Only a few ever make it out, always during rare pockets of time when the mist lifts just enough to offer a brief window of safety. It's a massive risk, but those who do manage to break free are the reason you and your hunter friends still have jobs."

Reapers are like rats—no matter how many we catch and throw in the Underlock, they just keep appearing.

Viri swallowed as her own words from a week ago replayed in her mind, hating how Reeve's admission explained why the hunters could never eradicate reapers entirely. But even so . . . "We would know if there was a city of reapers. That's not something that can be hidden."

"Where do you think we've been living for the last seven years?" Reeve asked, indicating himself and Braedan, the latter of whom was remaining wisely silent, as if aware that Viri was two seconds away from wrestling him through the wayportal and straight to the Underlock. "Where better to hide than in a city no one knows exists? *Especially* no hunters. There's a reason you never came close to finding us."

"But you said the mist keeps everyone trapped in—"

Reeve cut her off by raising his middle finger, making her temper flare to new heights, until she realized he was tapping his onyx ring—his blackmist talisman. His eyes then flitted to Braedan, with Viri following his gaze to see her brother was wearing one, too, the dark, silver-runed band gleaming against his black-veined skin.

Suddenly, Viri understood why they both needed them, and that it wasn't just to survive a trek through the Mistwood—it was so they could escape the blackmist-riddled mountain.

"I never told you how I ended up with one of these," Reeve said, twisting his ring. "Remember how I mentioned a teacher who helped me learn to control my magic and avoid burnout? Well, that teacher also possessed a vast collection of magical artifacts, including the original set of talisman rings left by the ancient mages. I was gifted one so I could come and go safely from the mountain, and as soon as I was able to, I stole the rest to give to Brae, Jonas, Sage, and Ardin so they could do the same."

Reluctantly, Viri could admit that his explanation made sense. But she still wasn't convinced about everything else he was telling her. He, however, wasn't close to being done.

"I know you must have a thousand questions," Reeve said,

"but for now, the main thing you need to know is that it's the Reaper Lord—*not* Braedan—who has been abducting the kids and plans to use the Aurora sacrifice to destroy the obelisks. We found out months ago"—he gestured to himself and Braedan again—"and together with Sage, Ardin, and Jonas, we've been doing everything we can to stop it. You already knew that part."

"You left out any mention of working with *him*." Viri's eyes speared back to Braedan, who remained so still that she wondered if the Guardian had frozen him with magic.

"As I said before, you wouldn't have believed me," Reeve returned, then continued before she could say she still didn't. "Throughout the ages, there hasn't always been a Reaper Lord like there's been a Reaper Priest, but when someone comes along with enough power, they're granted the title and given leadership over Diaboros." He paused. "The current Reaper Lord is unimaginably powerful, someone who can use siphoned ellixen to perform magic—a reaper who is *also* a mage. That's why Brae was desperate enough to come here and use his wish to—"

"Reapers can't be mages," Viri interrupted, before remembering who she was talking to and quickly adding, "Not by using siphoned ellixen." It was common knowledge that reapers couldn't access the magic they stole for anything outside their physical body. Heightened senses, speed, strength, healing, longer lifespan—that was the extent of their abilities. She'd hunted enough of them to know that for sure, as had every other hunter throughout history.

"The Reaper Lord isn't like other reapers," Reeve said, his dark tone making it clear how he felt about the supposed leader of all reapers.

"That would be my fault," the Guardian interjected smoothly.

"The current Reaper Lord learned how to control and use ellixen from me." He coughed and murmured, "Among other things."

All eyes turned to the purple-robed man. Even Braedan and Reeve looked surprised by his admission.

"A magewish," Viri breathed in realization. "You granted a wish to the Reaper Lord."

The Guardian's handsome face was impossible to read, though shadows crept behind his blue eyes. "Yes and no. But that's a story for another time, so"—he waved his hand and a roaring fireplace full of green flames appeared in the stone wall between two windows that overlooked the moonlit Mistwood, all materializing out of nothing—"please do continue. This is the most entertainment I've had in years." Another wave produced four golden velvet armchairs before the magical fire. "Shall we get comfortable? I can summon tea?"

Viri pressed her lips together to keep from telling him where he could shove his tea.

Reeve cleared his throat and got them back on track, none of them moving toward the chairs. "Brae came here intending to use his magewish to kill the Reaper Lord and stop the sacrifice, but what he didn't know was that, because of the Reaper Lord's innate power—and how much ellixen has been siphoned over the years to augment that power—in the event of the Reaper Lord's death, all that magic would explode out in an uncontrollable surge. That surge would be strong enough to pierce the blackmist surrounding Diaboros, allowing a city's worth of reapers to escape and swarm Aravell. *That's* why you and I had to intercept Brae—because while the Reaper Lord's death would save the kids and keep the obelisks intact, it would also leave Aravell overrun by reapers who are desperate for fresh sources of ellixen. Children and adults—they won't discriminate; they'll siphon from anyone with the smallest lick of magic, killing without prejudice."

His features were tight as he finished, "None of this is good, but at least now we still have until the comet arrives to stop the Reaper Lord in a way that won't risk freeing the reapers trapped in Diaboros. It's not ideal, but it's the lesser of two evils and our best chance at saving Aravell."

He trailed off into silence, leaving Viri to stare at him. Then stare at Braedan. Even stare at the Guardian. Everything she'd just learned swirled around her mind, until she came to the only conclusion that would keep her from vomiting all over the shiny stone floor.

"I don't believe you," she said hoarsely. Whether or not the Reaper Lord and Diaboros existed, she could look into that later. Sarielle, Meera, Darik . . . *someone* would have to know, and if it turned out to be true, she would act on it—with them. Reeve's performance was convincing, and much of what he'd said answered questions she'd had for a long time, but she couldn't simply accept his explanation without confirming it with those she trusted, and that would have to wait.

For now, there was something else she needed to do before she risked losing her chance forever, a mission that had consumed her for the last seven years: to bring vengeance upon the Reaper Priest.

For the first time since he'd killed their parents, Braedan stood mere feet away, and she knew it was a matter of seconds before he decided to fight or flee. She wouldn't allow either. In all the years she'd been hunting him, she'd always dreamed of catching him and throwing him in the Underlock, but she'd also never felt as if that would be enough. Death was out of the question—it was much too easy. She wanted him to *suffer*, to feel the same pain that she and his other victims felt, with it torturing him every day for the rest of his miserable life while he wasted away somewhere deep and dark until his final breath. She'd never known how to make that happen before—but now there was an opportunity before her that was too good to resist.

Before anyone could stop her, Viri turned to the Guardian and declared, "I want to make my magewish. I wish for—"

"I'm sorry, Viridia Solace," he interrupted, his knowledge of her name making her jolt in surprise, "but I can only allow one wish per person, and you've already used yours."

Viri's brow creased into a frown. "No, I haven't. It was Reeve who made the wish earlier."

"I'm not referring to tonight," the Guardian said, summoning a steaming mug out of thin air with a flick of his fingers. "You used your wish seven years ago."

Viri's frown deepened. "What are you talking about? I've never even met you before."

The Guardian sipped his tea, seeming amused. "We've met twice, actually," he said. "Though the first time, you were too young to remember. And the second . . ." He made a humming sound. "Well, you've forgotten because you *asked* to forget. That was your wish—and I granted it."

27

Shock slammed into Viri so hard that she stumbled back a step. Then another. She caught herself just before tripping over a crack in the stone, but still didn't take her eyes off the Guardian, not understanding what he was saying, yet knowing deep down that he was telling the truth.

She glanced at Reeve, at Braedan, and the looks on their faces—

They knew something. Something that their wide-eyed, pale expressions revealed they didn't want her to know.

"What did I want to forget?" Viri choked out. "And why?"

"I can show you if you want," the mage offered, sipping more of his tea, unaware of the roaring in her mind. "That was included in your wish—that if you ever desired to have your memories restored, I would return them to you." He smiled and leaned in as if sharing a secret. "That was my idea. You were too distraught at the time to care, but I added it, just in case this day came." He eased back again. "Say the word, and you'll remember what was forgotten."

"Of course I want to—"

"Viri, wait," Reeve said quickly, panic threading his voice. He closed the distance between them and took her clammy hands in his. "Think about this. If you asked to forget something, then it must have been for a good reason. Maybe you should trust that and just—" His throat bobbed. "Just let this go."

Viri stared into his eyes, seeing a turbulent storm in their silver depths, but if anything, that made her even more determined to find out what was going on. He was hiding something, and he had been since they'd reunited—she was sure of it. Whatever it was, it went beyond his claims about a Reaper Lord and a hidden city and Braedan's supposed innocence regarding the Aurora sacrifice. This secret, this thing he didn't want her to learn, to *remember*, was something else entirely.

Yanking her hands from his, Viri looked at the Guardian and said, firmly, "I want my memories back."

"No, Viri—" Braedan started, the first words he'd spoken directly to her, but she cut him off with an inhuman snarl.

"Don't talk to me," she spat. "Don't even *look* at me."

He recoiled as if she'd struck him, but then straightened his spine and opened his mouth to argue, halting only when Reeve placed a steadying hand on his cloaked shoulder and whispered something into his ear. The fight left Braedan and he nodded stiffly—to Reeve or to Viri, she wasn't sure—though his face was pinched with worry and his pale blue gaze dropped to the ground, as if he couldn't bear to watch whatever happened next.

"It's decided, then," the Guardian said, gesturing for Viri to follow him over to the green-flamed fireplace. "This may be disorienting—I suggest you take a seat."

Viri ignored the pleading look Reeve sent her, and ignored

Braedan entirely as she sat on one of the lush velvet armchairs beside the Guardian.

"As I said, this will likely feel strange," he warned again, his eyes glowing brighter in the light of the magical flames as he set aside his mug and took her hands in his. "It won't hurt physically, but the mind is a powerful thing, and it will do what it can to protect you—even from yourself. Try to relax. It'll make this easier."

That wouldn't be possible, since Viri was as tense as the stone surrounding them, wondering what might have been so terrible that she'd deliberately *chosen* to forget it. The Guardian had said she'd used her magewish seven years ago, but there was only one day back then that she would have wanted to forget, and yet, she vividly recalled every tragic moment of it. So whatever this was about, it couldn't have had anything to do with—

"Ready?" the Guardian asked, interrupting her thoughts.

Unable to help herself, Viri's eyes flitted to Reeve for reassurance, despite knowing she wouldn't receive it. He'd moved since she'd taken her seat and was now leaning against the wall beside one of the windows, his arms crossed as he stared out into the darkened forest, his expression oddly resigned. There was a smear of dried blood on his temple over where the wound had healed, his hair was a tousled inky mess, and his black clothes were as ragged as hers after their perilous journey, but even so, standing there bathed in moonlight, he'd never looked better, like a brooding hero straight out of one of Wynter's romance novels.

Reaper. Monster. Killer.

The reminder of what he was rose up from deep inside Viri, prompting a fierce ache within her, a potent mix of anger, despair . . . and grief. She tore her gaze away, telling herself she didn't need his comfort. Didn't *want* his comfort. He'd been lying to her—or at the very least, hiding things from her and letting her believe the wrong things. It was time for her to learn why, and she was certain those answers were trapped in whatever memory the magewish had stolen.

Tightening her grip on the Guardian, she confirmed, "Yes, I'm ready."

The last thing she saw before the room blurred was Reeve's chest rising and falling in a deep sigh, and Braedan slumping onto one of the spare armchairs to stare glumly at the fire—with Viri belatedly realizing she should have bound him with her fillium to keep him from escaping. But it seemed he was as resigned as Reeve about whatever was happening here, and intended to wait it out with them. Regardless, it was too late for her to secure him now, since ellixen slammed into her and her world turned upside down, leaving her no longer in the tower at all, but somewhere else entirely.

Somewhere painfully familiar.

Viri had been certain she remembered every horrible second of her Impartation ceremony, but there was no denying the formidable figure of the Southern Obelisk rising up before her, the obsidian stone tapering toward the cloudless blue sky. The area surrounding it was sparse, nothing compared to the farms on one side in the distance, and the forested necropolis on the other side. Instead, the obelisk sat innocently in the middle of a manicured grass circle bordered by a hedge of glowing angelroses. It was peaceful. Inviting. *Magical.* Exactly what kids needed to see when they came to sacrifice their ellixen—exactly what *Viri* had needed to see as a ten-year-old girl.

Because there she was, skipping beside Braedan through the

gap in the angelroses and coming to a wide-eyed halt as she stared up at the obelisk in awe.

It was strange for Viri to be watching her younger self, almost like she was viewing the scene as a spectator rather than experiencing it firsthand. She wondered if that was an effect of the magewish, but she didn't think on it for long, mostly because the breath left her when a much younger Reeve appeared through the angelrose hedge with Jorth and Amity Solace at his heels.

Viri's parents.

Tears filled her eyes at the clarity of the memory, her mom and dad so close that she could almost reach out and touch them. Her father had always been a handsome man, standing tall and proud, his hair a deep copper, his eyes the same as Braedan's pale blue. Amity, too, was strikingly beautiful, with rich auburn hair—like Viri's, just without the silver streaks—and uncommon lavender eyes, which Viri had also inherited. Both Jorth and Amity wore scarlet hunting cloaks over their black leathers, indicating they would be returning to work after the Impartation ceremony, but for now, they were wholly focused on their two children.

Viri thought she remembered everything about what happened next. In the memories she recalled, Braedan stepped up to the obelisk to reluctantly yield his magic, and then she did the same right after him, during which time she lost consciousness for the briefest of moments before awakening to find her parents dead and her brother standing over them with blackened veins. He and Reeve then took off before the Nox and hunters could arrive, leaving her alone and abandoned, her world having crumbled around her. But the scene playing out before her now . . .

there was something different about it. Almost like a haze had been lifted, her mind shifting and rearranging as if it were unlocking a door she hadn't even known existed.

Viri only had a split second to feel the brush of anxiety before her consciousness dissolved, her perspective changing until she was no longer looking upon the memory as a spectator, but *inside* it, returned to the thoughts and feelings of her ten-year-old self, the scene playing out as if it were a dream.

"It's so tall!" Viri said, turning from the obelisk to beam at Braedan and Reeve. "Do you think anyone has ever tried to climb it? Do you think we *can?"*

"I'm up for it." Reeve nudged her with his elbow before turning to his best friend. "What do you say, Brae? A friendly competition to see who can make it the farthest?"

Braedan grinned. "There'll be nothing friendly about it when you're both crying because I won and you lost."

Viri stuck her tongue out at her brother. He might be the oldest, but she and Reeve always managed to keep up with him on their adventures, and he knew it.

"Big words," Reeve said, his starry eyes twinkling in the way Viri loved. Then again, she loved his eyes when they were stormy, too. The only time she didn't *love them was when they were sad, but she hadn't seen him sad in a long time. "Maybe it'll be* you *who's crying after Viri and I kick your—"*

"There'll be no kicking of anything, and certainly no climbing the obelisk," Jorth interrupted in a stern voice, though he couldn't hide the humor in his expression.

"Daaa-ad,*" Viri whined, turning a pleading look on her father, then on her mother when it didn't work. "You're the ones who always tell us to challenge ourselves."*

"Challenge, yes," Amity said, her lavender eyes dancing. "But let's try to wait at least another year before you get yourselves arrested by the Nox."

Viri pouted, but then Reeve nudged her again and winked at her, silently telling her they'd sneak away later and have their competition. Braedan was staring at the ground as if to not give away their plans, but the dimple in his cheek showed he was on board to return after their ceremony ended. The three of them had plenty of experience getting up to mischief while Jorth and Amity were off hunting—today would be no different.

"Fine," Viri grumbled to keep her parents from becoming suspicious, before her attention returned to the obelisk. "How long is this going to take?"

Amity brushed Viri's hair behind her ear, smiling down at her daughter. But then she bit her lip as her gaze caught on the silver strands amid the red, concern flitting across her features. Uncertainty, even.

Viri had never seen her mom uncertain about anything in her life. "What's wrong?"

Amity shared a look with Jorth, who wrapped his arm around her, as if she—or both of them—needed the comfort.

Clearing her throat, Amity said, "Nothing's wrong, darling. It's just . . . you're so young. Maybe we should wait another few years for you to Impart."

"I'd like to wait another few years," Braedan said with a huff. "I'd like to not do this at all."

"You know you can't do that, son," Jorth said, though not unkindly.

"I know, I know." Braedan rolled his eyes. "The laws. The wards. The burnout. Blah blah. I get it—I just don't have to like it."

"I don't mind Imparting." Viri shrugged. "It has to happen sometime." She glanced questioningly at her mom and dad. "I heard you talking about me maybe burning out early—I thought this was what you wanted?"

Her parents looked startled to learn about her eavesdropping—almost nervous, really—but it wasn't like they'd said anything interesting. Most of it hadn't even made sense, like how she was "special," and how someone had warned them about a "cost" and told them never to let her Impart—which was ridiculous, because of course she had to Impart. Not just because of the laws, but because if she didn't, she would burn out. Her parents wouldn't have suggested she yield her magic four years early if they weren't worried about her. But Viri was happy enough to get rid of her ellixen today, since she knew Braedan was sad about it, and having her do it at the same time would make it easier on him.

"We think it's for the best, darling," Jorth confirmed, smiling at her, though it was tinged with unease. "We just want you to be as safe as possible."

Viri wasn't sure if he meant from burnout or from reapers, but either way, after today, neither would be a problem for her anymore. She wished Reeve was Imparting as well, but he'd stubbornly said this should be a family moment, claiming he didn't mind waiting for his own ceremony.

"Are we doing this or what?" Braedan asked, looking slightly green as he glanced at the obelisk again.

"Whenever you're ready," Amity said, laying her hand on his shoulder and sending him an encouraging look. "You remember what to do?"

Braedan nodded. "I just have to touch the stone and—and will *my ellixen into it, like an offering, and it'll automatically draw it out of me." His face was hesitant but also curious as he added, "Erlis Milton told me siphoning works the same way, just in reverse. That instead of willing the magic out of you, you will someone else's magic* into *you. Is that true?"*

Viri looked at her brother in surprise, as did Reeve, but both Amity and Jorth frowned.

"Young Erlis shouldn't be talking about things he doesn't understand," Jorth said tightly. "I'll be having a word with his father."

"Is he right, though?" Braedan asked, undeterred. "Is it really that easy to siphon magic?"

"There's nothing easy about killing someone for your own gain," Amity

said reprovingly. "The act itself might require little effort, but the scars it leaves behind are eternal. To deliberately steal ellixen—to steal life*—from another person changes who you are on a fundamental level. So no, it's not like yielding your magic to the obelisks. That's a gift, freely given, used to strengthen the wards and protect our community. Siphoning is selfish and hateful and brings nothing but death." With apparent effort, she smoothed her features. "But today's not for such unpleasant talk. It's a day of celebration. So let's do this, and then we'll all go out for a nice lunch at the Juniper Grill. Sound good?"*

Viri nodded eagerly, her stomach rumbling at the thought of visiting her favorite restaurant in the Entertainment Guild. Reeve nodded with her, as did Braedan, though his came slower, his mind still distracted by whatever Erlis had told him. Viri nearly kicked him so he would hurry up, but Braedan managed to shake himself out of his own reverie.

"All right, I'm ready," he said, still looking queasy at what he was about to do.

"You've got this, son," Jorth said, smiling proudly.

"We'll be right here, cheering you on," Amity added, wrapping him in a tight hug and kissing his cheek before stepping away again.

Braedan's throat bobbed, but then a sigh left him and he turned and strode stiffly across the grass, halting in front of the obelisk. He glanced back just once, his expression unsure, but Amity and Jorth sent him reassuring looks—while Viri and Reeve pulled faces, causing his lips to quirk upward and his tension to ease. With a visible exhale, he placed his hand against the obsidian stone and closed his eyes, concentrating hard.

Viri's palms turned sweaty as she watched her brother, but only a few seconds passed before his body relaxed and his eyes reopened, a relieved smile curling his mouth as he lowered his hand and walked back to them.

"That's it?" Viri exclaimed, squinting at him. "Are you sure you did it right?"

Jorth chuckled. "That's it, darling. It's not meant to be difficult. It's a gift, remember? Imagine it like the obelisks are grateful to receive your offering and take it as effortlessly as possible."

"Did it feel strange?" Viri pressed her brother. "Did it hurt?"

"Yes to the first, no to the second," Braedan said, rolling his shoulders and flexing his fingers, as if feeling for something that was no longer there. "No pain, just a kind of . . . warm tingle?"

Viri kept squinting at her brother, trying to see if he was lying. He'd always been protective of her—too protective, sometimes—so if it really had *hurt, then he would have already started arguing with their parents to let her wait another few years. His open expression said he was telling the truth, and Viri uttered a quiet* phew *sound, not realizing how worried she'd been.*

"My turn!" she cried. "Then we can eat!"

"I gave you half my vanilla bun on the walk over," Reeve said, shaking his head with amusement. "How can you still be hungry?"

"Because you only gave me half*."*

His lips twitched, but before Viri could see it turn into a full grin, she spun on her heel and began skipping toward the obelisk.

"Viri, dearest, wait."

Amity's anxious voice made Viri turn back to find both her mom and her dad looking oddly apprehensive, their cheeks pale, their eyes brimming with fear.

Viri peered around frantically, wondering if maybe their hunter's marks had begun to burn, indicating a reaper was nearby, but there was no one in sight except the five of them. No danger at all.

"What's the matter?" she asked.

Amity loosed a shaky breath and opened her arms. "You forgot to give us hugs."

Viri scrunched her nose. "Really, Mom? I'll be, like, twenty steps away."

"She gave me a hug and a kiss, too," Braedan reminded Viri. "Just let her do it, or we'll be here all day."

Blowing out a breath, Viri walked back and let her mom embrace her, then her dad, both of them squeezing fiercely, as if they didn't want to let her go.

"We love you, darling," Jorth said, his voice husky. "We'll be—We'll be right here watching, just like with Brae."

"Don't try to force anything with the obelisk," Amity warned, her fingers clenched in front of her, as if she were stopping herself from hugging her daughter again. "Just—Just let it take what it wants. Don't fight it. And definitely don't try to take anything from it."

Braedan frowned. "How would you even do that?" He seemed confused, but reassured Viri by saying, "It feels a bit like knocking over a bucket of water—by the time you realize your ellixen is gone, it's already done. There's nothing to fight, nothing to take back. Don't worry, you'll be fine." They shared a look only siblings could, mutually agreeing their parents were just being weird.

"No fighting the obelisk," Viri dutifully promised her mom and dad. "Got it."

With that, she turned and hurried away before they could change their minds about letting her Impart today, her thoughts on the garlic chicken and crispy potatoes that awaited her at the Juniper Grill when this was over. But when she came to a stop before the obsidian stone, her hunger was replaced by butterflies rioting in her stomach.

Viri had never been this close to an obelisk before. A heavy, insistent humming vibrated over her skin and into her bones, causing goosebumps to rise on her flesh and her blood to stir in her veins. It was like she could feel *the power within the stone, like the air was saturated with magic. There were times in her life when she'd felt a prickle of ellixen no one else seemed to notice, but she'd never experienced anything this strong before, like something deep inside her was calling out to the obelisk—or perhaps the obelisk was calling out to her.*

Braedan hadn't said anything about this. Nor had her parents.

Viri wasn't sure if she was more anxious or exhilarated by the strange sensations electrifying her nerves, but she was wholly mesmerized by the power she felt, and helpless to resist stretching her hand out toward the stone.

The moment she touched it, a gasp left her—

And her world exploded.

Fire—she was on fire. *Only, there were no flames, just a searing, agonizing burn spreading across her body as pure energy—pure* magic*— flowed from the obelisk into her. A suffocating, possessive feeling encompassed her, like the stone was searching for something while also claiming her as its own, a dark voice seeming to whisper, "Mine. Mine. Mine."*

The burning increased so much that Viri screamed, certain it was boiling her alive. She tried to yank her hand free, but whatever magic was coursing through her kept her trapped in place, connected to the very thing that felt as if it were killing her.

Another tortured scream left her, and through teary eyes she saw her mom and dad running forward while shouting at Braedan and Reeve to stay back. Terror gripped her at the sight, because while she didn't know what was happening, she could tell it was so very wrong, and she didn't want her parents anywhere near her. They were mere steps away when she threw her free hand out to warn them, but the most blistering surge of magic yet flooded into her from the obelisk, scorching like an inferno in her chest, before rushing down her outstretched arm—

And slamming into her parents.

Amity and Jorth barely had time for their eyes to widen in horror before the ellixen struck them, blasting them off their feet. Even Reeve and Braedan were blown backward by the shock wave, both landing in the angelrose hedge, looking dazed. But Viri's parents weren't looking dazed. They weren't looking anything at all.

Because they weren't moving from where they'd fallen.

The magic—

The obelisk's magic—

Viri's *magic—*

A strangled sob left her even as the burning continued to rise, but the flames were nothing compared to what she felt as she stared at her parents, their eyes open but unseeing, their bodies unnaturally still.

All the fire in the world couldn't melt the icy numbness sweeping through Viri as she realized the horrible truth.

Her parents were dead.

And she'd killed them.

⋆ ✦ ⋆

Viri wrenched herself out of the memory and leapt to her feet in front of the Guardian's crackling green fireplace, tears streaming down her cheeks as she rasped out to everyone and no one, "I killed them. *I killed them.*"

Braedan hadn't murdered their parents—*she* had. She couldn't look at him. Couldn't look at Reeve. Couldn't even look at the Guardian. Her mind was a mess, her grief so acute and shame so severe that it was impossible to string a rational thought together. The only thing she knew was confusion, having no idea what had gone so wrong with the obelisk, or why she'd been so certain of her brother's guilt. The answers were within her now, the door to the memory unlocked, but she couldn't bear returning to it yet, too overwhelmed by everything she was feeling.

The stone walls were closing in on her, her vision swirling as she tried to fill her lungs, but every ragged breath felt like daggers piercing her throat, her chest, her *heart.*

"Viri?" came Reeve's tentative voice, as if from far away.

She needed air.

She needed air.

"Viri, are you—"

The room spun around her, the urge to vomit rising with every second. She needed to escape. Needed to *breathe.*

So she did the only thing she could.

She ran.

28

Viri bolted from the circular room, sprinting past the way-portal and through a doorway hewn into the wall, then along unfamiliar stone corridors and down perilously steep staircases. She heard her name called with urgency, but she didn't stop, *couldn't stop*, desperate to put distance between her and what she'd just discovered, needing a moment to process, to think, to *understand*.

She didn't know where she was going, was only vaguely aware that she was in some kind of ancient castle, her surroundings passing in a blur of gilded portraits, regal statues, and elaborate tapestries. Silvers and golds rushed past her at eye level, while rich blue carpets lined her path, the colors blending hypnotically as she raced blindly down, down, down—

And then, finally, she burst through a set of double-arched doors out into the frigid night, the air thick with the scent of honeysuckle and jasmine. A quick, light-headed glance revealed she hadn't left the castle entirely, but was in a small garden courtyard bordered by stone pillars and surrounded by more ancient towers like the one she'd just fled. Glowmoths drifted lazily through the air, their radiant little wings fluttering from strange glimmering flowers to trees with bioluminescent leaves, and hovering around sparkling mushrooms in beds of glittering grass. The moon shone down upon a three-tiered fountain sitting in a pond at the center of the enchanted garden, the crystal clear water gleaming with iridescent fish.

The courtyard was impossibly beautiful and unfathomably magical, but Viri barely saw it as she stumbled toward the fountain, trying desperately to draw air into her lungs. She was choking and wheezing, just like when she'd been under the wraith's thrall, and equally incapable of unblocking her throat. The garden began to tilt around her, the kaleidoscopic lights making her nausea so intense that she slammed her eyes shut against the dizzying sight. Only, the moment she did, all she could see were her parents lying on the ground in front of the obelisk, staring out into nothing.

I killed them. I killed them. I killed them. I killed—

"VIRI!"

Hands landed on her shoulders, grounding her in place. Her eyes shot open to find Reeve's blazing silver gaze locked on hers.

"You need to breathe. *Now!*"

It wasn't a request—it was a command. But Viri couldn't obey it, the colorful garden spinning around her as her vision began to fade at the edges.

Reeve cursed when he realized she was beyond listening, and he quickly shifted one of his hands until it curled around her neck. His eyes kept holding hers as he sent his ellixen into her, like liquid sunshine filling her veins. The peace she felt was instant, a supernatural calm that made her feel languid and dreamy, her knees becoming so weak that Reeve had to circle his other arm around her waist to help support her weight.

"Breathe, Little Shadow," he murmured into her ear as she collapsed fully against him. "Just breathe."

This time, she could follow his command, her throat unclogging enough for her to inhale once, twice, three times, her burning lungs cooling as blissfully sweet air rushed into them, her heartbeat slowing, her vision settling.

Soon, she felt almost normal again, but that was when it happened.

A sob left her, then another, her body buckling with the force of her grief.

"I—I—I—" She was crying so hard that she couldn't say the words, couldn't share what the memory had shown her, what she'd *done.*

"I know," Reeve said quietly, holding her close, his fingers combing through her hair as she wept into his chest, saturating his shirt with tears. "I know."

"Wh-What happened?" she blubbered out. "Wh-Wh-Why did they—did they—"

Die. Why did they *die*? That was what she wanted to know, but the words continued to fail her.

Reeve tensed against her, though his voice remained soft, gentle, as he asked, "How much did you see?"

Viri finally managed to control her sobs enough to pull back slightly, though she couldn't bring herself to step away completely.

"Something h-happened with my magic when I t-tried to Impart," Viri answered tremulously, tears still leaking from her eyes, but at least she wasn't bawling as fiercely anymore. "It e-exploded out of me and—and—"

And killed her parents.

The shock of the discovery was beginning to wear off enough for Viri to understand that whatever had happened, it hadn't been her fault. Something had gone wrong, some unexpected reaction from the obelisk that had triggered a magical surge and resulted in tragedy. It had been an accident, nothing more, and yet, the weight of her guilt was crushing.

"There's more for you to remember," Reeve said, still stroking her hair. "But only—only if you want to know everything."

His hesitation made her look at his face, the moonlight revealing uncertainty in his expression. Fear, even. Seeing it, she almost decided not to finish the memory, but she knew that if she didn't, she would forever wonder what else she'd chosen to forget.

She owed it to her brother to find out why she'd believed he'd murdered their parents, just as she owed it to herself to find out what had really happened next.

"How do I w-watch the rest?" Viri asked, only stuttering slightly now as her tears began to dry.

Reeve seemed just as resigned as he'd been in the tower, though his unease was stronger this time, as if he knew exactly what she was about to see, and he dreaded it even more than what she'd already witnessed. The thought made Viri's stomach twist, but she gathered her courage and braced herself as best as she could.

"Just close your eyes," he answered, seeing her resolve, "and think of the last thing you remembered. Now that the magewish has been revoked, your mind should unlock the rest instinctively."

A shaky breath left Viri as she followed his instructions, not once thinking about leaving the comfort of his arms. He was solid and strong and safe when everything around her felt like it was crumbling—and something told her it was about to get so much worse. She didn't care that she needed him right now, didn't care that he was a reaper, a monster, a killer. Because he was also Reeve, and he was the only thing that stood a chance at keeping her together as she delved back into her past. *Their* past.

One second, she was staring up at him, seeing his conflicted, stormy gaze on hers, and the next, she was closing her eyes and tumbling back into her memory.

⋆ ✦ ⋆

Ice swept through Viri at the sight of her parents lying on the ground. Just seconds ago, they'd been running toward her, and now, they would never run again. They would never hug her, kiss her, hold her, love her. A thousand memories flashed across her mind, moments of laughter and tears and everything in between, none of which would ever be repeated.

Her parents were dead.

They were dead.

And it was all Viri's fault.

But—no, it wasn't. She hadn't done this. The obelisk *had.*

Fire broke through her numbness, the renewed magical burn so fierce that she cried out, tears still streaming down her cheeks as pain enveloped every part of her. She wanted to give in to it, to let it consume her so she could join her parents in peaceful oblivion, but even as the thought hit her, another one, a stronger one, told her that her mom and dad wouldn't want her to give up. She needed to fight. She needed to live.

"VIRI!" Reeve screamed her name, the sound barely penetrating her agony. "Brae—we have to do something! We have to help her! Brae! BRAE!"

Viri's pained gaze lifted to see Braedan standing over their parents, his face white with shock as he stared down at their lifeless forms.

But then Viri's attention moved to Reeve as he sprinted toward her, just like her mom and dad had done. She wanted to shriek at him to stay away, but the stubborn look on his face told her he wouldn't listen.

"You have to let go of the obelisk!" he yelled urgently, skidding to a halt right in front of her. He was so close—dangerously close. If there was another surge of power, if her magic exploded again—

"I c-c-can't," she gasped out around her pain, certain her skin had to be melting from her bones. "I'm s-scared, Reeve!"

"I'm right here, Viri," he said, his face pale with fear, but then it shifted with resolve as he reached toward her.

"No!" she cried, flinching backward into the obsidian stone.

"Do you trust me, Little Shadow?" Reeve asked, his hands still raised between them. "I think—I think I know how to help you, but you have to trust me."

"I—"

*Another scream left Viri, keeping her from answering. She trusted him more than anyone, but the pain—*the pain—

She couldn't speak beyond the agony tearing through her, her torment growing until, suddenly, her vision flooded with light, ellixen radiating out of her, turning her into a living sun.

Reeve cursed against the brightness and didn't wait for her response, taking her free hand in his and wrapping his other palm around her neck, skin to skin.

"What are you doing?" Braedan croaked out, finally shaking off his shock enough to lunge toward them.

Reeve closed his eyes in concentration. "There's too much magic inside her—it'll kill her if I don't stop it."

"You're—You're—" Braedan was at a loss for words.

"Yes." Reeve spoke through gritted teeth, fighting hard against the ellixen searing through Viri.

But then she realized, he wasn't fighting it at all.

He was absorbing it.

Stealing it.

Siphoning *it.*

A gasp left Viri as the burning eased a fraction and the veins in Reeve's arms began to change color, right before her eyes—something Viri shouldn't have been able to see, not without a hunter's mark. They didn't turn the inky black of reapers, though; instead, silver streaks shot along his tanned skin and disappeared beneath his dark sleeves. But that was all Viri saw before her inner flames raged to new, excruciating heights, as if the obelisk realized what Reeve was doing and was angry about it. If he siphoned her magic away, then the obsidian stone would lose its grip on her—it would have to let her go.

But by the same argument, if he siphoned her magic away, then—then—

Viri didn't have a chance to finish her thought, the inferno blazing so fiercely that it was all she felt, all she knew, *and her body simply couldn't handle the pain anymore.*

The last thing she saw before her eyes rolled to the back of her head was Braedan's terror and Reeve's determination, the two of them yelling her name, begging her to stay with them.

But she couldn't.

Because everything turned black.

✦

"You could have killed her! You did *kill her! What were you* thinking?"

"Calm down, Brae. Look—she's breathing. She's going to be fine."

Viri began to rouse, the familiar voices of her brother and Reeve blurring around her.

"She might be breathing now, *but she wasn't a minute ago!" Braedan sounded furious—and scared.*

"Now is all that matters," Reeve said in a firm tone. "And keep your voice down—she's going to be in enough shock as it is when she wakes up. She doesn't need to know what happened."

"What did *happen?" Braedan demanded. "How is she alive?"*

There were arms around Viri—arms that tightened protectively when Reeve answered, the closeness of his voice revealing he was the one holding her. But unconsciousness tugged her back before she could hear what he said, muffling his murmured words, her clarity returning only as he finished, "You know I would die before I let anything happen to her."

Braedan sighed shakily, his rage having fled at whatever Reeve had told him. "I can't believe you did that. But I'm—I'm so glad you did. The obelisk was about to rip her apart. And our—our parents—" A choked sound left him.

His grief managed to finally pull Viri awake, her own horror returning as she sat up in Reeve's lap and groggily looked around, seeing the once-perfect grass now charred and the angelrose hedge no longer glowing, but lifeless—just like her mom and dad, who lay mere feet away.

It wasn't a nightmare, then. It had been real.

But the pain was gone—the burning was gone. And she was no longer trapped against the obelisk, which stood innocently in the center of the scorched grass, as if it hadn't just shattered her life.

Tears started pouring from Viri's eyes, tears of shock, of fear, of anguish. Her parents were dead. The obelisk had tried to kill her. Reeve had broken the law and siphoned from her to save her life—and if what she'd heard was true, she'd died in the process, even if she was somehow alive again. It was too much—everything was too much—

Her shuddering sobs became so violent that Reeve drew her closer and Braedan's arms encircled them both, all three of them weeping as they held on to each other. Viri tried to tell them she was sorry, the words tumbling out in blubbering howls, but they kept shushing her, saying it wasn't her fault, that they didn't blame her, that they would get through this together. Their strength was the only thing that kept her from falling apart, the knowledge that, while she might have to face a future without her parents, at least Braedan and Reeve would be with her. They had each other, and they always would.

"Oh dear, it looks as if I missed all the excitement."

The silky, dark voice slid over Viri like oil, causing the hairs on her arms to stand on end. Braedan and Reeve pulled back, scrubbing their cheeks as they stared up at the cloaked figure who had appeared through the dead angel-rose hedge. Viri's tears continued to fall silently, though her sobs had quieted, if only because all her energy was gone, leaving her exhausted and numb. It was better than her grief, though she knew that would return soon enough.

"Who—Who are you?" Braedan asked, standing to his feet and holding his hand out to pull Viri up. He didn't let her go, his fingers gripping hers firmly as Reeve rose on her other side, moving near enough to brush shoulders.

"Can you h-help us?" Viri asked the newcomer, her voice hoarse from crying. "Our p-parents—The o-obelisk—"

A hiccup left her, but she swallowed it back.

The cloaked figure made a tsk*ing noise. His voice was deep and masculine, but his features were hidden by a hood that created unusual shadows covering his face. "It's tragic, to lose one's parents so young." He* tsk*ed again "But they knew better than to meddle with magic they didn't understand. What happened here was their own doing—in more ways than you can imagine."*

Every word felt like a punch to Viri's stomach, even as confusion flooded her.

"What do you mean?" she rasped, feeling Braedan's fingers tighten around hers, while Reeve vibrated with rising anger at her side. "What magic?"

"Nine and a half years ago, your parents made a choice." The figure

stepped closer, his physique hidden by his voluminous dark cloak and the shadows that seemed to follow his every move. Even his hands were concealed by black gloves, covering every trace of skin. "They did something they shouldn't have, took something that didn't belong to them, awoke magic that was best left undisturbed. Their actions had consequences, and today, they foolishly paid the price."

Reeve made a growling sound, but Braedan spoke before he could say whatever furious thing he was about to hurl at the man.

"How dare you!" Brae snarled, his eyes puffy from crying. "Our parents just died *and you're calling them fools?" He turned to Viri and Reeve. "Ignore this creep. We need to go and summon the Nox. We need to—" His voice broke. "We need to find out what to do next."*

Before they could move a single step, the man raised his hand to fiddle with his glove, the edge of his cloak sliding up along his forearm, revealing a sliver of pale skin.

But that wasn't all it revealed.

Viri gasped and lurched backward, tugging Braedan and Reeve with her. They resisted, having not seen what she had. She *shouldn't have been able to see it either, but maybe the magic of the obelisk had done something to her, changed something inside her. Whatever the reason, there was no denying the black veins she saw vanishing beneath the man's sleeve.*

"Y-You're a reaper," she stammered, fear making her voice tremble. A murderer stood before them, someone who had no qualms about killing children. Someone who enjoyed *it.*

"Not just any reaper, Viridia Solace," the man said, amusement threading his voice. "I'm the leader of all reapers—the Reaper Lord." His shadowed head swiveled to Braedan. "And you're not going anywhere."

Viri's body began quaking, and she felt the same terror emanating from her brother and Reeve. The feeling only grew when the Reaper Lord waved a hand and her skin prickled with ellixen before her feet suddenly became rooted to the scorched grass. She tried to move but was trapped in place, with Reeve and Braedan just as stuck as she was.

"You can do magic," Reeve breathed, staring at the Reaper Lord in shock.

"That was barely a party trick," he said dismissively, lowering his hands so that his sleeves concealed his veins once more. "I suggest you don't anger me enough to show you what I can really *do."*

A shiver traveled down Viri's spine.

The Reaper Lord's tone lightened, turning almost pleasant. "Now, I'm here to offer you a deal." He brushed invisible dust from his cloak. "I need something from you, and one way or another, you're going to give it to me. Only, I won't need it for another few years. I do, however, need to make sure I have it when that time comes."

Viri shared a puzzled look with her brother. Braedan's face was alarmingly white, his grip near bruising.

"We're not giving you anything," he said, trembling as much as Viri.

"I wasn't talking to you, Braedan Solace," the Reaper Lord said. That sense of amusement returned. "Though something tells me you'll be the one who ensures I get what I want."

Braedan squared his shoulders, looking more like their father than ever—something that caused a stabbing pain to ripple through Viri's chest. "I'll never help you."

"You have two choices," the Reaper Lord went on, as if Braedan hadn't spoken. He raised a gloved finger. "One. Viridia comes with me and, in a few years, after she's done what I need, she'll be free to leave—assuming there's anything left of her."

Viri swallowed back a whimper.

"Or two . . ." The Reaper Lord's attention returned to Braedan. "It's your sister who I want, but until I need her, I have no use for her. You, on the other hand, are old enough to be of value. So she can be my prisoner while

she waits . . . or you can take her place. A safeguard, so to speak. She can grow up and live her life, and you . . ." A dark chuckle. "You'll serve another purpose, while relaxing in the knowledge that she's protected and content as the years pass by."

"No," Viri said sharply, not letting her brother consider it. "You can't have either of us."

"Take me," Reeve offered.

"NO!" Viri and Braedan shouted in unison, both glaring at Reeve, with Viri digging her fingernails into his forearm to keep him from doing or saying anything else stupid.

"I don't want you." The Reaper Lord sniffed. "I don't even know who you are."

"I'm Reeve Ashton," Reeve said, standing taller. "And if you want my friends, you'll have to go through me."

The Reaper Lord stilled, his attention wholly focused on Reeve now, almost as if he'd been taken by surprise. But then he shook off whatever had gripped him and repeated, "I don't want you." He turned to Braedan. "I can take your sister, or I can take you. It's your choice."

Viri tried to move again, but she was still trapped in place. "You're crazy if you think either of us are going anywhere with you," she spat.

The Reaper Lord's head tilted to the side. "It seems you need some . . . motivation."

With a flick of his gloved finger, she flew backward, hitting the ground hard. But it wasn't the impact that ripped a scream from her—it was the pain that erupted beneath her skin, like she was being stung by a thousand firewasps all at once. It was a different kind of burning from what the obelisk had caused, but no less excruciating, causing her to writhe and shriek on the charred grass, the agony growing with every second that passed.

"STOP IT!" Braedan yelled.

"LEAVE HER ALONE!" Reeve bellowed.

Through teary eyes, she saw them straining against their invisible bonds, but they had no defense against the magic holding them in place.

"This is merely a taste of what she'll experience as my prisoner," the Reaper Lord said, another flick of his finger causing the pain to increase so much that Viri rolled over and retched. "Every day, I'll find some new way to torment her. But you, Braedan—if you come with me, I won't hurt you, not like this. You'll be revered among reapers, given a place of honor as their next Reaper Priest. You won't even want your freedom by the time I'm ready for your sister—you'll be begging to keep the power I give you."

"N-N-No," Viri moaned.

The Reaper Lord's voice became so soft that she barely heard him continue, "After everything that happened today, are you really going to let your sister keep paying for the mistake you made nine and a half years ago? There's only one ending for her, but if you do as I say, she'll be able to enjoy a normal life before that time comes. So make your choice, or I'll take her with me right now."

Viri retched again, the stinging turning to blades piercing her nerve endings. "D-D-Don't do it, B-Braed—"

She didn't even finish saying his name before he shouted, "I'll go with you! Just stop hurting her!"

A wave of the Reaper Lord's hand, and Viri's pain vanished, leaving her curled in a ball, trembling and weeping. She cried out when gentle fingers touched her, only to find Braedan and Reeve had been freed from their magical bonds and were crouching beside her.

"Y-You can't go with him," Viri pleaded with her brother, shaking violently. "I n-need you."

"And I need you to be safe." Braedan's face was still pale, but his eyes were resolute. "If this is the only way to ensure that, then so be it."

"We can f-fight him." Viri looked toward where her parents lay, trying to see their daggers or the magical fillium they shared when hunting, but there were no weapons in sight.

"You saw what he can do with his magic." Braedan shook his head. "I won't risk him hurting you like that again."

"I can t-t-take it."

"Don't you understand, Viri?" Braedan ran his hands through his auburn hair. "I can't *take it. I can't watch that again, not after what happened with the obelisk, not after you—" He broke off, his voice cracking. "Mom and Dad are dead. I can't lose you, too."*

Fresh tears streamed down Viri's cheeks as she realized her brother's mind was made up. She inhaled deeply, steadying her voice enough to argue, "But if you do this, you will *lose me. He said—He said it'll be years. Anything could happen in that time. What if I never see you again?"*

Braedan pulled her in for a kneeling hug, his arms tight around her as he whispered into her ear, "I swear, Viri, we'll be together again one day. I'm going to figure out what he wants from you, and I'm going to find a way to stop him. As soon as you're safe, I'm coming back to you." He drew away to look into her eyes, his own watery. "Do you trust me?"

Viri's lip wobbled. "Always, Brae."

"Then trust me to do what I must to protect you. I've already let you down once, and I promised myself I'd never do it again."

Her brow furrowed. "You've never let me down."

Braedan closed his eyes. "I wish that were true. If it were, today never would have—"

"As touching as this is," the Reaper Lord interrupted in a drawl, "I'd prefer to leave before any hunters or Nox arrive. Braedan, it's time to seal our deal in a way you can't return from."

Braedan helped Viri rise weakly to her feet, but then he handed her off to Reeve, who wrapped his arm around her in support.

"What do I need to do?" Braedan asked, his expression grim but determined.

The Reaper Lord waved lazily toward Amity and Jorth. "Siphon from them."

Braedan jerked backward. "What?"

"Ellixen lives on after death," the Reaper Lord said, "and while they won't have much of it, a taste of stolen magic is all you need to become a reaper. Prove your loyalty to me, become my Reaper Priest, and your sister will be safe for as long as I can give her."

Braedan looked as if he were going to be sick. "You want me to—to—"

"Siphon from your dead parents, yes," the Reaper Lord said heartlessly. "Do it now, or I'll rescind my offer."

Viri wanted to scream at her brother, to yell that it wasn't worth it, to say she *would go with the Reaper Lord, but she knew it would be no use. Braedan had made his choice—he was going to protect her, no matter what it cost him.*

Reeve's arm was the only thing that kept her upright as Braedan walked stiffly over to their parents and knelt between their bodies. His hand shook visibly as he reached for their dad, his throat bobbing as if he were swallowing back bile—just like Viri was—but he wrapped his fingers around Jorth's bare forearm and closed his eyes in concentration.

One second stretched into five, ten, twenty, before Braedan finally squinted up at the Reaper Lord and said, "Nothing's happening."

"You have to want *it," the shadowy man instructed, sounding impatient. "Others become reapers because they want the strength, the heightened senses, the* power. *Some just enjoy the euphoric high. But you? Think of what you want, why you're doing this, and then* use *that to reach out and steal their magic, claiming it as your own."*

Braedan glanced back at Viri, his eyes roaming over her face until they turned steely with resolve, then he slammed them shut again to concentrate once more. He looked like he had during his Impartation, only instead of willing his ellixen into the obelisk, he was willing their father's ellixen into himself.

This time, it worked.

Almost instantly, Braedan's veins began to blacken, the sight of them—and what they meant—so disturbing that Viri had to turn away. As she did, her gaze locked on Reeve's hands, finding no trace of the strange silver lines she'd seen when he'd siphoned from her. It didn't make sense—he was technically a reaper now, and she could apparently see reaper veins, and yet, there was no evidence marked into his flesh, as if he'd never taken her magic to begin with.

But Viri couldn't think about that now, because Braedan's tremulous voice called out, "Done," and her gaze returned to him just as he released his grip on Amity, having siphoned from her as well. He rose to his feet above their parents, his blackened veins spreading all the way up his arms, proof of what he'd done, what he'd become.

Braedan was a reaper now.

And he'd done it to protect Viri.

A sob left her, but she clamped her mouth shut over it, not wanting to make this any harder on her brother. She knew he was doing this for her, and while part of her hated him for it, she hated herself even more.

"Say your goodbyes," the Reaper Lord said. "It's time to go."

Viri shook her head as her brother walked woodenly toward her, refusing to believe this was it, that he was really going to leave her. Her tears were coming so fast now that it was hard to see as he stopped in front of her and pulled her in for a tight embrace.

"I love you, Viri," he whispered. "Promise me you'll do whatever it takes to live your life. That's what Mom and Dad would want—for you to be happy."

"They'd w-want us b-both to be happy," she wept against his chest.

"And we will be, one day," Braedan vowed, pulling back to meet her

blurring, tear-filled eyes. "Until then, make sure you live well enough for both of us." He kissed her forehead, then stepped away to haul Reeve into a bruising hug, rasping out, "Look after her for me. You're all she has now."

Reeve said something in reply, something Viri didn't hear, and then Braedan was releasing him and striding away, following the Reaper Lord through the lifeless angelrose hedge toward the wayportal. He didn't look back, not even once.

*The moment he was out of sight, Viri crumpled to the ground, sobbing so hard that she was sure her heart was tearing in two. Reeve sat and pulled her into his arms, telling her everything would be all right. But he was wrong—*nothing *was all right, and it never would be again. Her parents were dead. Braedan was a reaper. And she—she—*

She didn't know what she was, only that she was alone.

"You're not alone," Reeve said fiercely after she wailed her fears aloud. "I'm here, Little Shadow. I won't leave you. I'll never leave you."

His words only made her cry harder. Everything that had happened flashed through her mind, torturing her in a way that not even the obelisk had managed.

"I c-can't l-live like this," she howled, certain the strength of her loss was going to destroy her. Braedan had asked her to live, to be happy, but it wasn't possible. She knew that to the very depths of her being.

"Perhaps I can help with that," a soothing voice interrupted.

Viri jolted in Reeve's lap, fearing another monstrous reaper had come to add to her grief. But instead, a handsome man stood before her wearing a vibrant emerald cloak, his hood lowered to reveal a kind face with gray-flecked black hair and bright blue eyes.

"Wh-Who are you?" Viri asked.

"Who I am doesn't matter as much as what I can do for you," he said, crouching before them. "You wouldn't remember me, Viridia Solace, but we've met once before, and because of that, I now owe you something."

Viri wiped her face. "Wh-What?"

"A wish," the man said. "A magical wish, for anything you want."

Her swollen eyes widened. "A m-magewish?"

The man cocked his head to the side. "I'm surprised you know that term."

"Are you the Guardian?" Reeve breathed. "The Guardian of Elverdine Isle?"

The man looked amused. "I'm even more *surprised you know that term."*

Reeve's gaze flicked to Viri, as if, like her, he couldn't believe the legend they'd grown up hearing about was really before them. In an incredulous whisper, he said, "You're a mage."

"I am," the Guardian said solemnly. "And I'm breaking some very strict rules by being here right now." He swiveled back to Viri. "But as I said, I believe I can help you. You just have to make your wish."

Viri looked toward her parents and tremulously asked, "Can you—"

"I'm afraid there's nothing I can do for them," he said gently.

"But—in the story about the three hunters—" Viri hiccuped. "Their magewish brought the child back to life."

The Guardian's blue eyes turned guarded. "That was a different situation, and the wish had already been spoken before the babe passed, so the magic had no choice but to find a solution—the cost of which was far graver than anyone could have imagined." He shook his head. "Not all stories have happy endings, and despite what you may have been told, that one certainly didn't. I'm sorry, but I won't risk it happening again. I can't change your parents' fates." He paused. "But I can help in another way."

"How?" Reeve asked suspiciously.

The Guardian's gaze remained locked on Viri. "You said you can't live like this. Well, I can make you forget."

She sucked in a breath. "You can?"

"Not everything," he warned. "Your parents will still be gone, but I can

give you a purpose beyond your pain. I can make it so you don't remember what happened with the obelisk and the role you played in their deaths, and so you don't feel the loss of your brother on top of everything else. You'll recall that your parents died and that Braedan is gone, but your mind will create a reason that removes the guilt from your shoulders. It will still hurt, but it'll be bearable, enabling you to keep your promise to live—and eventually, to live happily."

"Are you saying I'll f-forget Braedan?"

"No. But you'll forget the sacrifice he made for you, and your longing to free him from the Reaper Lord's clutches. You'll likely forget about the Reaper Lord entirely in order to have peace of mind about the future without any threat hanging over you."

Viri was shaking her head before he even finished speaking. "I can't do that to Brae. I can't just—just forget, *and live my life like nothing happened."*

The Guardian held her gaze. "Isn't that the whole reason your brother accepted the Reaper Lord's deal? So you could do exactly that?"

Viri swallowed. "It doesn't matter. I can't— I can't—*"*

"Viri." Reeve's voice was gentle but insistent. She turned to find his silver eyes soft on hers. "This is what Brae would want. What your parents would want. You're going to drown in guilt otherwise. I think—I think you should do it."

"But—"

"No buts," Reeve said. "This is the only way you'll be able to keep your promise to Brae."

"But he's all alone," Viri whispered, another tear falling down her cheek. "If I forget what he did for me . . ." Her gaze lost focus as she turned it over in her mind, coming to a decision. She clutched Reeve's shirt and declared, "You need to go after him."

His eyes rounded. "No. I'm staying with you."

"I can't go through with this unless I know you're with him."

His arms tightened around her. "I told him I'd look after you."

"This is how you do that," Viri said hoarsely. "He needs you more than I do—I won't need you at all if I don't remember what happened." That was a lie, since she would always need Reeve, and the thought of being away from him made her want to start crying again and never stop. But then she imagined her brother on his own for the next however-many years, and she couldn't stomach that unless she knew Reeve was with him. Viri's wish would keep the worst of her grief at bay—her brother didn't have that luxury, so the least she could do was make sure he and Reeve had each other.

"I don't want to leave you," Reeve said quietly, his eyes dark with sorrow. "But if this is what it takes for you to use the magewish, then I'll do it. I'll go after Brae, I'll keep him safe. And one day, we'll all be together again."

Viri's chin wobbled as new tears pooled in her eyes, soaking into his shirt when he pulled her into a tight hug.

"I swear it, Little Shadow," Reeve whispered into her ear. "We'll see each other again." A shaky breath left him. "Now make your wish."

Viri didn't want to let him go, but the longer she waited, the harder it would be for him to follow Braedan and the Reaper Lord, so she pulled away and croaked out, "My heart will always remember you, Reeve Ashton. I might forget what happened today, but as long as I live, I'll never forget you."

She turned away from his sad silver gaze and announced to the Guardian, her voice trembling but firm, "I wish to forget."

He waved his hand, causing ellixen to prickle her skin. "Your wish is granted, Viridia Solace." A knowing smile curled his lips. "But when the time comes that you want to remember, you need only ask, and it will be done."

With that promise, Viri's eyes closed . . .

And she forgot.

29

Viri's memory faded like a dream, her mind rearranging to accommodate everything she'd just recalled and reconciling it with what happened next. The Nox arriving. Sarielle comforting the shell-shocked Viri before inviting her into her home. The High Council asking questions that Viri struggled to answer, unable to believe her parents were dead despite having seen Braedan standing over them with blackened veins; unable to believe Reeve had abandoned her when she'd needed him most, fleeing with her murderous brother and leaving her alone in her grief.

Only now, Viri knew none of that was real.

The garden rematerialized around her, the bioluminescent trees and flowers glittering at the edges of her vision, the fountain bubbling softly into the pond, the glowmoths fluttering through the air, and Reeve—

He was exactly where she'd last seen him: standing in front of her, his arms still circling her waist, holding her, supporting her, protecting her.

Just as he always had.

Reaper, monster, killer—none of those things were true. They never had been.

"The girl you killed," Viri had asked him mere hours ago, *"do you regret it?"*

"No," he'd answered. *"I don't regret siphoning from her."*

A tear dribbled down Viri's cheek. Then another. Soon her eyes were flooded with them, but she didn't utter a sound, crying silently as she held Reeve's understanding gaze.

He'd saved her life.

He'd never abandoned her.

And she'd—she'd—

She'd *forgotten.*

She'd believed he was a *monster.*

She'd *hated* him for it.

And he'd let her, saying nothing in his own defense, knowing she wouldn't trust anything he said.

Her tears continued falling like rivers down her face, until slowly, ever so slowly, Reeve leaned forward and kissed them away.

"It's not your fault," he whispered against her skin. "None of it is."

He was wrong—*all* of it was her fault, even the parts she didn't understand. *Especially* those parts.

He kept saying the words over and over, one hand rubbing her back and the other wiping her tears away until, finally, they began to ease. Her mind was a jumbled mess that seemed impossible to untangle, but there was one thing she needed to say, her words coming out rough with emotion.

"You didn't want to leave me."

"No," Reeve said, brushing her tear-damp hair behind her

ears. "But you asked me to. And you were right—Brae needed me, more than either of us realized."

"Does he—" Her voice broke. "Does he hate me?"

Reeve's arms tightened around her, his expression turning fierce in the moonlight. "Never, Viri. Everything he's done is because he loves you, and he'd do it again in an instant. We both would."

Another tear dribbled down her cheek, and Reeve caught it with his thumb.

Viri closed her eyes at the tenderness of his touch, unable to resist leaning forward to rest her head against his chest, his heart beating steadily beneath her ear as she wrapped herself fully around him. She had so many questions, and yet, all she could do was whisper, "I missed you."

"You have no idea," he returned hoarsely, pulling her even closer, until there was no space left between them. "Every day, every minute, every second of the last seven years, all I thought about was finding my way back to you. And now that you're here, standing in my arms, I'm terrified I'm going to wake up and realize this is all a dream."

Viri swallowed against the lump in her throat. She drew back slightly, but only far enough to look at his beautiful face. "If it is, then I'm dreaming, too. And I never want to wake up."

Reeve's eyes softened at her admission. But then a hint of familiar wryness touched his features. "Finally something we can agree on."

Despite the torrent of emotions she was feeling, Viri couldn't keep her mouth from quirking upward. "A miracle."

As if he could sense how desperate she was to not fall back into her despair just yet, Reeve's tone shifted into something lighter, something more conversational. "Speaking of miracles," he mused, "for a while there, I feared I might need one of those. But I think I'm going to be all right now that your memories are restored."

Viri's brow furrowed, not following. "What?"

"In fact," he went on, as if she hadn't spoken, "I'd go as far as to say it'll be almost too easy for me to prove you wrong."

Viri's confusion only grew. "About what?"

Reeve's lips curled up at the edges—the only warning she had for what he was about to say next. "When we were in the Summit, you swore there would never come a time when you'd ask me to kiss you again." Her breath hitched in surprise—and something else entirely—causing his smile to widen. "We both know you were struggling to keep your word when you hated me, but now . . ." His eyes sparkled knowingly in the moonlight. "Let's face it. You don't stand a chance against my vast array of charms."

Heat touched Viri's cheeks, but she grabbed on to the reprieve he was offering and squinted incredulously at him. "Vast array of charms?" Her squint deepened. "Who's been lying to you?"

A delighted laugh left him, his relief at having helped ease her pain clear to see—and soothing something deep within her. "That hurts, Little Shadow."

"The truth often does," she said. But then she added, "You deserved it. We were having a moment, and you ruined it." She would be forever thankful that he had, that he'd known her well enough to give her exactly what she'd needed, just like always. But even so . . .

Reeve arched a brow. "A moment?"

"We were sharing our *feelings*," Viri said. "Something that's clearly a foreign concept to you."

His brow arched higher. "I'm pretty sure my prediction that we'll be making out again in the near future is covered under the topic of 'feelings.'"

Viri rolled her eyes. "So presumptuous."

He smirked. "Am I wrong?"

She pressed her lips together and looked away.

Reeve chuckled, knowing he had her. But then he sobered again and trailed his fingers across her dried tear tracks, quietly asking, "Better?"

Viri swallowed and nodded. She wanted to stay in the light-hearted bubble he'd just given her forever, forgetting everything she'd remembered about her parents, her brother, and the Reaper Lord, forgetting the threat of the Aurora Comet hanging over their heads and how they still needed to figure out how to save Jessalyn and the other children—and the city. She wanted to stay in this magical garden with Reeve's silver eyes locked on hers . . .

Just as she wanted to utter those two words he already knew she was longing to say: *Kiss me.*

But she couldn't do it—not yet. Because as much as she wished she could ignore the questions nudging at her mind, they were becoming more insistent with every passing second. When she and Reeve finally kissed again, she wanted no distractions, and that wouldn't be possible unless she received some answers first.

Clearing her throat, she eased away slightly and made herself say, "I need to understand what happened that day. What went wrong with the obelisk? How am I alive if you siphoned from me? Why didn't your veins turn black? Why could I see reaper veins at all?" She ticked the questions off her fingers, finishing with, "And what does the Reaper Lord want with me?"

Reeve's gaze slid past her shoulder just as a warning seared across her palm. "I think someone else would like to explain."

Viri turned to find Braedan walking across the courtyard toward them, looking apprehensive enough that she half expected him to bolt back into the castle. But he continued striding forward, his torn green cloak billowing behind him until he halted beside the pond where she stood with Reeve.

For a long moment, no one spoke, the tension so thick that even the glowmoths kept their distance.

"I'll just . . . go for a wander," Reeve said, glancing between the two siblings. "It's not every day I get to explore an ancient magical castle." That was true, though he couldn't have been more obvious about giving them privacy. "Come find me when you're done, and we'll make a plan to stop the sacrifice."

Viri only had a second to note Braedan's nervous but grateful look before her focus was wholly diverted when Reeve leaned in and pressed a whisper-soft kiss to her temple. She sucked in a startled breath, and then shivered when he murmured into her ear, "I won't be far if you need me." His hand trailed down her side until his fingers twined with hers, squeezing once. "Whatever happens in the days ahead, that'll always be true. No matter how dark the shadows seem, you'll never be alone in them. I promise."

There was a strange weight to his words, and an even stranger expression on his face before he wiped it clear, his emotions passing too quickly for Viri to read them all, but she could have sworn she saw uncertainty, dread, and even a hint of despair. They were gone again in an instant, though, replaced by an encouraging look as he prodded her toward Braedan, then turned on his heel and left the glowing courtyard, vanishing between a pair of pillars back into the castle.

The silence was even more tense with Reeve gone, enough that Viri hugged her elbows, having no idea what to say. Braedan had sacrificed seven years of his life for her, and the whole time, she'd been hunting him, consumed by her desire for vengeance over something he'd never done. She wasn't sure whether to leap into his arms and sob her gratitude, or curl into an ashamed ball while begging for his forgiveness.

She settled on something in between, blurting out the words that had been bubbling within her ever since her memory had returned. Only, she wasn't alone in saying them, both she and Braedan speaking at once.

"I'm sorry."

Viri's mouth dropped open. "What are *you* sorry for?"

Braedan ran a hand through his messy hair. It was longer than he'd worn it as a teenager, and tangled enough that small twigs and leaves fell out as he combed it back, no doubt collected during his arduous trek through the Mistwood. "What am I *not* sorry for?"

Viri shook her head in disbelief. "I'm the one who used a magewish to forget something I've spent years blaming you for. You have *nothing* to be sorry about."

"I'm glad you used that wish," he said firmly, his dirt-smeared features showing he meant it. "When Reeve told me, the only thing I felt was relief."

"But—But we lost seven years." Viri's eyes burned almost as much as her palm. "And that whole time, I thought you—"

"I know what you thought," he said gently, his pale blue gaze soft on hers, making him look so much like their dad that her heart clenched painfully. "In many ways, it was better that you believed that than remembered what really happened. It gave you the chance to grow up and live your life without guilt, just as I wanted."

"But you didn't get to do the same," Viri said croakily, wrapping her arms tighter around herself. "You were hunted and scorned and vilified. And I can't even imagine what the Reaper Lord made you suffer through on top of that."

A shadow crossed Braedan's face. He turned away from her, staring down at the rainbow fish. "Actually, the Reaper Lord left me pretty much alone after the first few weeks." His tone darkened. "That was all it took for me to become his obedient little Reaper Priest."

Tension lined his body, his hands hanging stiffly at his sides, as if he wanted to ensure his torn sleeves covered his arms. But Viri had already seen his veins, and even if she hadn't, her mark was scorching incessantly in his presence.

She moved a tentative step closer. "I have . . . a lot of questions. About what happened that day. And about what you've been doing in the time since then." Her gaze traveled to his hidden arms. "Reeve said in the tower that the 'Reaper Priest' title is only a distraction, but . . ." She chewed her cheek, then forced herself to say the words, "We both know those aren't tattoos."

His body stiffened even more. But then he blew out a breath and faced her again, the moonlight showing his resigned features. "No, they're not." He gestured to a stone bench on the other side of the pond. "It's a long story. We might as well sit."

Viri followed him around the edge of the water and lowered herself at his side. It was the closest they'd been in seven years, and part of her longed to embrace him, but he was holding himself so rigidly that she feared one wrong move would send him running. Whatever he was about to say, he clearly needed space, so she sat on her hands and waited, ready to hear anything he was willing to share.

"I should start at the beginning, but . . ." He grimaced. "I need to work up to that."

Viri wanted to ask why, but she bit her tongue to keep from interrupting.

"Instead," he said in a detached voice, "I'll tell you what happened after I last saw you." He avoided her eyes, his attention returning to the rainbow fish. "The first few weeks were the worst. The Reaper Lord took me straight from the obelisk to the slums and tried to make me siphon again, saying I deserved to enjoy more than the small amount I took from—from Mom and Dad." He recovered quickly from his stumble. "I wasn't willing to kill an innocent kid, so I refused, and kept refusing, regardless of how angry it made him. In my mind, our deal only required that I go with him in your place. But he . . ." Braedan's jaw clenched. "He'd already mentioned making me the next Reaper Priest, but it didn't sink in what that meant until he used a blackmist talisman to drag me to Diaboros, and I was suddenly surrounded by a city of reapers. When I kept refusing to become one of them, I was thrown in a dungeon and left to rot."

It took all of Viri's willpower not to reach for him, but she stayed resolutely still as she envisioned the nightmare he was describing.

"Despite everything Mom and Dad told us about reapers," Braedan went on, still staring fixedly into the pond, "I'd somehow forgotten that it only takes a single taste of ellixen to create a hunger for it, so while I was locked away, I was *starving*. Not for food—that was delivered regularly, almost tauntingly. It was magic that I longed for, especially when the small amount I'd stolen started fading from my veins." He rubbed his arms, as if remembering the color returning to normal. "But no matter how desperate I was, when the Reaper Lord brought kids to me to siphon from, I wouldn't do it. And then he finally lost patience and started—started hurting me." A shaky exhale. "It was similar to what he did to you at the obelisk, magic unlike anything I knew existed. So many different ways of causing pain. But still, I didn't break. You were safe. Reeve was safe. Those two things gave me the strength I needed to keep resisting, despite the torment I felt.

"Then one day, a few weeks in, the Reaper Lord appeared for our daily torture session, and instead of dragging in some nameless kid for me to siphon, it was Reeve who was suddenly in my cell. He was filthy and covered in bruises just like me, having suffered the same magical abuse for weeks. I had no idea he'd been locked away the whole time—I didn't even know he'd followed me. I only learned later about the magewish and how you begged him to find me, which led to him getting captured by the Reaper Lord and kept alive for the sole purpose of being used against me."

Braedan still wouldn't look at Viri, but if he had, he would have seen the horror in her eyes. She couldn't imagine feeling the pain of the Reaper Lord's cruel magic every day for weeks, and yet, not only had her brother endured that, so had Reeve—all because of *her*.

"How was he used against you?" she rasped out.

Braedan tossed a pebble into the pond, its ripples reflecting the colors of the garden. "The Reaper Lord said that if I didn't siphon, then Reeve would die."

Viri stilled, her heart breaking at the position her brother had been put in, her horror growing as she realized what was coming next.

"I'm not going to say I didn't have a choice," Braedan said in a dead-sounding voice. "And I won't lie and say part of me wasn't relieved to have an excuse to siphon, since the hunger I felt was all-consuming. It wasn't the same for Reeve—even after he siphoned from you, he didn't lust for ellixen the way I did, the way all reapers do. He was never tempted, not once. But I . . ." His throat bobbed. "When the Reaper Lord dragged in another kid and told me to decide if Reeve lived or died, I didn't hesitate. I—I killed the boy. And while I hated myself for it, I also felt *good.* The ellixen made me strong. My pain vanished, my body healed. I could hear better, see farther, move faster. I felt invincible." His hands fisted in his lap. "So when the Reaper Lord returned again with the same threat—siphon or Reeve dies—I killed the next kid, too. And the next. And the next."

Viri had to swallow back bile, grateful Braedan couldn't see her face.

"The power, the *magic* . . . it's indescribable." His words ached with both longing and shame. "But even so, I soon realized that no matter how good it made me feel, I couldn't do it anymore. *Wouldn't* do it anymore. The guilt of it all . . . the blood on my hands . . ." A jagged breath left him. "And then there was the ellixen itself, which I could feel changing me, creating this—this *addiction.*" Another jagged breath. "I feared that if I didn't stop, then I'd *never* be able to stop. So I came up with a plan."

He straightened slightly, though his gaze remained on the pond. "With so much stolen magic in me, I was stronger than I'd ever been, so I decided to try and take the Reaper Lord by surprise. I wasn't naive enough to think I could overpower him, but I just needed to fight him off long enough to grab Reeve and run. I knew it was a risk, knew I'd be putting you in danger, but I had a plan for that, too: I'd get to you first and we'd go into hiding, somewhere the Reaper Lord could never find us. It wasn't the life I wanted for you, but at least you'd be safe, and Reeve and I would be free."

Braedan threw another pebble, this time hard enough to make the water splash loudly, scattering the fish. "What a fool I was."

"What happened?" Viri whispered.

"It was too easy—that's what happened," Braedan said bitterly. "I know now that the Reaper Lord *let* me shove him away, *let* Reeve and me run from the dungeon, *let* me think we were about to escape. Because in all my planning, I'd forgotten where we were—and what we were surrounded by."

Realization hit Viri, along with sorrow. "The blackmist."

A stiff nod from Braedan. "We didn't have our own talismans at that point, so we were trapped inside Mount Mort with nowhere to go. That's when things got worse."

Worse? Viri wondered in disbelief, unsure how that was even possible.

"The Reaper Lord was amused by our escape attempt, but it also made him lose what little patience he had left," Braedan said. "He warned me that if I didn't start behaving, then he would consider it as me reneging on our deal . . . which would mean he could do the same."

It took Viri a moment to understand. When she did, her heart clenched as a new wave of guilt tore through her.

"Me," she breathed. "He said he'd come for me."

Another stiff nod. "After what I'd experienced in just a few weeks, there was no way I was going to let you suffer the same way. And Reeve—his life was still at stake, too, both of your fates tied to my decision. So as much as I despised it—despised *myself*—I agreed to siphon again, and this time, I stuck with it. I blocked out the guilt, the pain, the shame, didn't let myself feel anything other than the power. It was the only way I could survive." A weighty pause. "Until it wasn't. Because soon enough, the ellixen changed me on such a fundamental level that I stopped caring at all. About anything. Or anyone."

Braedan curled in on himself, but his words came quicker now, as if he was eager to get the rest over with. "My compliance meant I was eventually released from my cell and given a lavish living space, but by then, I was so ellixen-high that I didn't realize the Reaper Lord had stopped threatening Reeve's life, stopped threatening to go after you, and I was siphoning simply because I wanted to. *Needed* to. I'd become a full-blown addict, having no idea that was what the Reaper Lord had intended all along, all so he could use me as a scapegoat for the hunters and Nox to focus on. He gave me the title of Reaper Priest and the menacing reputation that came with it—a ploy to distract hunters from learning of his existence—then kept me locked in a guarded apartment drugged out of my mind on ellixen. By that point, the only thing I cared about was my next fix. I just wanted to get high and stay high. Nothing else mattered."

He finally turned to Viri, his face haunted as he revealed, "I stayed that way for seven years."

Seven years.

The whole time he'd been gone.

Tears blurred Viri's eyes, even as she fought back more nausea.

"Reeve tried to pull me out of it, so many times," Braedan admitted, looking away again. "The Reaper Lord released him when he was no longer needed for my cooperation, but instead of a cushy apartment, he was cast out into Diaboros, like a fish among sharks. To this day, I'm amazed he was able to stay alive, something that only happened because he figured out how to use his magic to protect himself, and befriended some young reapers who cared more about atonement than siphoning from him. By the time he managed to find me again, I was too far gone to even recognize him. He did everything he could to snap me out of it, told me I needed to fight, reminded me that I'd promised to return to you, but I was beyond listening. The only thing I cared about was getting more ellixen."

Braedan rubbed a hand down his face, but then squared his shoulders. "That all changed a few months ago, when Reeve learned about the Reaper Lord's plans to destroy the obelisks. For seven years, he'd found a way to survive Diaboros and avoided doing anything that might risk the Reaper Lord breaking his deal to stay away from you, but the Aurora Comet changed everything. If the sacrifice went ahead and the blackmist flooded the city, then you—and everyone—would end up dying anyway. He realized it was time to act, so he and his friends broke me out of my apartment to wean me off my addiction, all so we could work together to try and stop what was happening."

"Sage, Jonas, and Ardin," Viri guessed.

Braedan nodded. "I hated them at first. I raged and screamed and fought them at every turn, my withdrawal symptoms so violent that they had to be with me constantly to make sure I didn't hurt myself. But they were patient, all of them having gone through it themselves, and I was eventually able to tolerate doing what they do—siphoning from reapers."

Viri nearly wilted with relief at learning her brother's blackened veins weren't from a recent kill, though her heart struggled to make peace with all the years before that—*especially* since those years were her fault. Everything he'd done, every child he'd siphoned from . . . he'd mentioned blood on his hands, but it wasn't on his.

It was on *hers*.

She wasn't sure how to reconcile that, wasn't even sure it was *possible*. Seven years of murdering innocents, all to keep her safe. The burden of those deaths weighed heavily on her soul—until she realized that burden *wasn't* hers to bear. The Reaper Lord had done this. He'd forced Braedan's hand, giving him no choice but to become a monster. Her brother had committed unspeakable acts, there was no denying it. But the blame lay squarely at the feet of his captor.

Fury simmered within Viri, but she stifled it—for now—because Braedan was still speaking.

"It's not the same as fresh ellixen," he said, "but siphoning from the others keeps my addiction manageable, and also keeps me in control enough to turn my remorse into something practical—a desire to make the Reaper Lord pay for everything he's done to me, and for everything he plans to do with the Aurora sacrifice."

Viri could relate to that desire, her fury rising anew.

"It's the whole reason I came here to Nevarnost," Braedan said, "because I realized it was the simplest solution for making sure he never hurts anyone again. Only—"

"You didn't know about the magical surge that would free the reapers from Diaboros," Viri said, "and that we need to find a way to stop him that doesn't end up with him dead."

Braedan released a frustrated breath. "Yeah. I should have known it wouldn't be so easy. But I was so fixated on the idea that if he died, then not only would the city be safe, you would be, too, and Reeve and I would be free to return to you." He swallowed and admitted, "I never found out exactly why he wants you. But I—I assume it has something to do with your magic. And that would be . . . very bad."

The sudden turn in conversation caught Viri by surprise. "What magic?"

A hesitant pause met her question, until her brother answered, "I said earlier that I needed to work up to starting at the beginning. The truth is, I'd rather not go there at all. But . . . there's something you need to know. Something Mom and Dad never told you. Something I think caused the obelisk to . . . do what it did that day."

Viri's throat turned dry. "What didn't they tell me?"

Braedan stood up so fast that she jumped, then began pacing between her and the pond, as if he were too nervous to sit still. But then he halted just as quickly and sat down again, though this time, he angled toward her, taking her hands in his.

"When we were young," he said in a shaky voice, "Mom and Dad had some friends who lived out on the surface. They had a nice house in a good neighborhood at the edge of Elders' Grove, but the best part was their yard, because it stretched right into the trees. You and I used to love visiting, because it meant we got to play in the grass and flowers."

"I don't remember that," Viri said, frowning. She also didn't know why he was telling her this.

"You wouldn't. You were only six or seven months old the last time we went. You'd just—You'd just started crawling." His fingers twitched around hers. "Mom and Dad usually sat outside to keep an eye on us, but that day, their friends wanted to show them something inside, and since you began howling when they tried to take you in with them, I said I was a big boy and could watch you until they returned. You were obsessed with the glowmoths fluttering around their angelrose bushes, so we all assumed you'd just stay there giggling at them, like you always did." Guilt bled into his voice. "But I got distracted when a glimmerfox bounded into the garden, and I chased it around, forgetting all about you. By the time Mom and Dad came back out . . . you were gone."

Viri started. "*Gone?* As in abducted?"

Braedan shook his head, though his pale face indicated that whatever he was about to say was worse. "You'd crawled away, following some glowmoths deeper into Elders' Grove. It was early afternoon, nowhere near a risky time of day, but . . . that close to Mount Mort, the wards aren't as strong, and the blackmist is unpredictable. When Mom and Dad found you, it was already too late."

A coldness came over Viri, her body tingling with dread. "Too late for what?"

Braedan's eyes were full of regret. "A small wave of blackmist had wafted in and back out again, right where you'd crawled. There was nothing anyone could do."

Numbness replaced the cold, though disbelief had Viri shaking her head. "No one can survive the blackmist. If that really happened, how am I still alive?"

Her brother just looked at her, waiting for her to put the pieces together.

She stared back at him, her heart racing, her thoughts spinning, only one possibility coming to her, but that—that—

"No," she breathed, tearing her hands from his and leaping to her feet, scrambling backward into a bed of glowing mushrooms. *"No."*

"It's true, Viri," Braedan said, standing slowly with his palms raised, as if to calm a wild animal.

He was wrong—it wasn't true. It *couldn't* be.

And yet . . .

"We've met twice, actually," the Guardian had said earlier that night. *"Though the first time, you were too young to remember."*

And the second time, she'd used her magewish to forget—a magewish she'd received when she'd met him as a babe.

A *dying* babe.

. . . And then a *dead* babe.

Viri pressed her trembling fingers to her lips as the full weight of her realization hit her. Her eyes were too wide, her breathing too shallow, her heartbeat too fast as she whispered, her words barely audible, "I'm the child in the legend."

30

It wasn't some ancient ancestor who had been touched by the blackmist—it was *Viri.* Her parents were the husband and wife in the story. They'd used their friend's magewish to have the Guardian bring her back from death, which meant—

"The obelisk," Viri gasped. "That's why it reacted the way it did. Because—Because—"

"Because your magic is different," Braedan confirmed quietly. "The blackmist stole all your natural ellixen, so the Guardian had to fill you with more, binding you to the raw magic of the isle—something powerful, but also volatile." His face turned sad. "When you tried to Impart, instead of the obelisk absorbing your ellixen, it did the opposite, turning your magic against you and flooding you with its own, pulled directly from the wards, which sent you straight toward a self-combusting burnout. Everything was amplified, your connection to the obelisk opening an unstoppable river of ellixen flowing into you, but also *out* of you. That's what—" He broke off, but Viri didn't need him to finish.

"That's what killed Mom and Dad," she choked out.

"It wasn't your fault," Braedan said quickly, hearing the pain in her voice. He stepped closer. "No one knew the obelisk would respond that way. It's a miracle it didn't kill you, too."

"Because Reeve saved me," Viri said in wonder. But then she realized, "I still died, though, didn't I? That was the only way he could break the connection between me and the obelisk—by siphoning all my magic."

Braedan shifted on his feet, looking uncomfortable. "Don't be mad at him."

"Mad?" Viri repeated incredulously. "He saved my *life*. I just don't understand *how*."

"I don't fully, either," Braedan said, though he didn't meet her eyes. "Every guess I have comes back to the strangeness of your magic, with the normal rules of siphoning not applying to you." She opened her mouth to ask what he meant, but he distracted her by flicking the end of her braid and sharing, "Before the magewish—the first one, when you were a babe—you didn't have any silver streaks. The little hair you had was like Mom's, like mine, but it changed after what the Guardian did. And when Reeve siphoned from you—"

"His veins turned silver, not black," Viri whispered. "And even those faded much faster than they should have." As if the magic had refused to be claimed by another and had fled his body near-instantly.

"Again, I think it has something to do with the uniqueness of your ellixen—which is also why I assume he never felt the same hunger for it that all reapers do. Your magic is too different."

"Was," Viri said. "Past tense. My magic is gone—I Imparted it, but even if that didn't go as planned, Reeve took the rest from me."

"And yet, you're standing here, which means you must have

some ellixen in you," Braedan pointed out. "You also just admitted that you saw Reeve's veins change color, and that's something only hunters, reapers, and mages can see."

Viri jolted. She'd already known about hunters and reapers, but—

"Mages can see reaper veins?"

Braedan nodded. "Or anyone with comparable levels of ellixen, which is what I think you must have." Before she could object, he went on, "I've had a lot of time to consider this, and everything circles back to you being connected to the magic of the isle, since my guess is, you're still able to tap into that power, consciously or unconsciously. That's what flows in you now, keeping you alive, while also keeping you from burning out."

Viri stared at him. "I think I would know if I could 'tap into' a magic source like that."

Braedan tilted his head to the side, rousting a glowmoth from his hair. "When we were kids, you always felt ellixen more strongly than others. You hid it well, but I could tell. Has that changed?"

"No," she admitted reluctantly. "I'm still sensitive to it." Even more so than when she was younger.

Braedan looked troubled. "I was afraid you'd say that." He scrubbed a hand over his face, then explained, "I told you before that I think the Reaper Lord wants you for your magic. It's the only thing that makes sense. And if I'm right about all this, if you really are able to access the raw magic of the isle . . ." He visibly shuddered. "Elders know what he might want to use that for. Use *you* for."

A chill snaked down Viri's spine. She wished Wynter were here, not just for comfort, but because her friend—who was supposedly a *mage* and could therefore *see reapers*—would dive straight into researching Viri's hypothetical magic. If they knew why the Reaper Lord wanted it, then they could figure out how to keep him from using her.

. . . Assuming she was even alive beyond the next two days. His intentions for her wouldn't matter if he succeeded in destroying the obelisks, since her chances of surviving after that would diminish by the second.

"Who *is* the Reaper Lord?" Viri asked, still struggling to believe she possessed some mysterious power that appealed to him. She wasn't like Reeve—she couldn't perform magic with a wave of her hand. All she had was a heightened sensitivity to ellixen, with the closest she'd come to using it being when she'd located the warded chest in the Summit storage room. It was hardly an awe-inspiring skill.

"No idea." Braedan shook his head. "In seven years, I've never met anyone who has seen beyond the shadows hiding his features. He could be a wraith, for all I know."

Viri shivered as she recalled the one she and Reeve had encountered in the forest, her memories of the Reaper Lord making her confident that he, at least, was flesh and blood.

"I hate this," Braedan croaked out suddenly, covering his face with his hands. "I hate that I did this to you. I hate that you're in danger because of me. I hate that Mom and Dad died because of me. That you died *twice* because of me. I hate that Reeve suffered—"

"Brae—*stop*." Viri's heart clenched as she pulled his hands away to reveal his guilt-ravaged expression. "What are you talking about? None of those things are your fault."

"You're wrong—*everything* is my fault," he cried, tears lining his eyes. "You crawled into the blackmist because of *me.* I promised I'd watch you, and I *didn't.* Everything that's happened since then was because I failed you. The magewish, your magic, the obelisk reacting, Mom and Dad dying, the Reaper Lord wanting you—*everything.*"

Tears welled in Viri's own eyes at the devastation she saw in her brother's features, making her realize this was something that had haunted him for seven years. Longer, even.

"Brae, listen to me." She tightened her grip, forcing him to meet her eyes. "You were *four years old.* There's no one in the world who would blame you for not noticing me crawl away."

"But I—"

"No." Viri's voice was unyielding. "You told me I'm not responsible for what happened to Mom and Dad, so hear me when I say the same is true for you. You were barely old enough to *read*, let alone babysit. You need to stop carrying guilt that doesn't belong to you. If anything—" She inhaled deeply, then made herself continue, "If anything, the fault lies with Mom and Dad. Not just for leaving you to watch me, but for knowing what they did about me and still wanting me to Impart early. Even the Reaper Lord said they knew better than to meddle with magic they didn't understand, and he was right. We both know he was."

Braedan looked down, refusing to accept her words.

"Please, Brae," Viri whispered. "You once told me Mom and Dad would want me to be happy—don't you think they'd want the same for you? You've suffered enough in the last seven years. It's time to let this go." She squeezed his hands and begged, "If you can't do it for you, then do it for me."

A ragged breath left him. Then another. Finally, he looked up again, his voice rough as he said, "I'll try."

"That's all I ask." She offered him a small, encouraging smile. "And I'll be here to remind you whenever you need it, because I'm not forgetting anything this time, and you're not leaving me again."

His eyes were still sad, but they were lighter than before, like a weight had been lifted, bringing a sense of healing, of hope. That light deepened when his lips tipped upward the slightest fraction and he said, "I know you meant for that to be reassuring, but it sounded more like a threat."

Viri's smile grew. "Then maybe you should take it as one." With a pointed look, she said, "No more self-sacrificial rubbish. I'm not ten years old anymore. Whatever comes next, we face it together. Agreed?"

He hesitated, but at the tightening of her fingers, he gave in. "Agreed."

"Good," she said. "Now, can I finally hug you without either of us bursting into tears?"

His eyes lightened even more, a familiar spark of mischief touching them, something that made her heart give a pang of grief for how much she'd missed it, how much time they'd lost. But they were back together now, and that was what she would focus on.

"You can hug me," he said, "but I can't promise about the tears. We both know how dramatic you can be."

Viri scrunched her nose but didn't deny it, just threw her arms around him for the first time in seven long, painful years. Sure enough, tears leaked from her eyes, but she sniffed them back and held him tighter, only letting go when he made a wheezing joke about needing to breathe. That more than anything told her he was going to be all right. They both were.

"On the topic of hugs . . ." Braedan said after she stepped

back again, his voice turning unexpectedly teasing, which only strengthened Viri's relief. "You and Reeve seemed pretty cozy earlier. Anything you want to share?"

Her relief vanished instantly, replaced by a blushing scowl. "Definitely not."

"Are you sure? Because it looked like—"

"It looked like 'mind your own business,'" Viri stated firmly.

Braedan chuckled and raised his hands in surrender. "Fine. But next time, get a room. I do *not* need to see my best friend and my sister—"

"Don't even think about finishing that thought," Viri warned, her blush deepening.

Braedan grinned broadly enough to show his dimple, something she'd never imagined she'd see again. But then he sighed, his playfulness fading as he said, "We should go find him and come up with a plan. We might not be able to kill the Reaper Lord, but we sure as hell need to stop him."

Viri wholeheartedly agreed, but the castle was huge, and it could take a while to hunt Reeve down—time she could use to get the last of her questions answered. "You get him, then meet me up in the Guardian's tower."

Braedan understood immediately. "Do you want us to delay—"

"No," Viri said. "We've lost enough time already. Find him, then head straight there."

Braedan nodded, his humor reappearing as he said, "Don't get turned into a frog. I doubt even Reeve would kiss you then."

Viri blanched. "Is that possible?"

Braedan scratched his jaw. "I mean, I guess it depends on how much he likes y—"

"No, the *frog*," Viri gritted out.

Her brother laughed and threw his arm over her shoulders, guiding her across the glowing courtyard to the tower she'd sprinted out of what felt like years ago. What he didn't do was answer, but she shook off her unease as they parted ways, Brae heading in the direction Reeve had gone, while Viri retraced her steps through the double-arched doors all the way back up to Nevarnost Tower.

Part of her wanted to stop and admire the blue, silver, and gold castle furnishings this time, but she told herself she could come back again when everyone she loved wasn't in danger. Another part of her—a very large part—wanted to duck into one of the many cozy-looking sitting rooms and take a minute to process everything she'd learned that night. Her head and her heart felt ravaged, and she desperately longed for a moment of peace to try and come to terms with her emotions. But with the comet nearly upon them, it had to take priority over all else. So she barricaded her feelings behind her mental wall and strode purposefully along the gilded hallways, climbing up the steep, spiraling staircases until she reached the Guardian's circular stone room.

For some reason, she wasn't at all surprised to find him in the same armchair before the green-flamed fireplace, a smile touching his lips as he caught sight of her.

"Welcome back, Viridia," he said. "I've been waiting for you."

31

Nerves bubbled within Viri as she walked past the way-portal toward the Guardian, barely glancing at the rare books and magical artifacts lining the walls, or the glass windows and ceiling that showed a starry sky that seemed to be oddly lightening. She frowned at that, before telling herself it must be a trick of the moonlight, then directed her full attention toward the purple-robed mage as she sat in the golden chair next to his.

She launched straight in.

"I know I'm the child you brought back to life."

He showed no surprise at her statement. "I assume you have questions?"

Viri licked her lips, not having expected it to be that easy. "What can you tell me about the magic in me?" She couldn't bring herself to say the words *my magic*. "The story goes that you bound the chil—*me* to the magic of the isle, but what does that mean?"

The Guardian crossed one leg over the other, his robes shifting with the move. "That isn't entirely accurate," he said. "I didn't bind you to the magic of the isle itself—that would have been too dangerous. Not to mention impossible. The Hallow Stream has been inaccessible since before the ancient mages left these shores."

"Hallow Stream?" Viri repeated, having never heard that term before.

"One of three sources of pure magic that fuel our world with ellixen," the Guardian explained. "Or it was, long ago, but now only a trickle flows from it, most of which lingers in untamed places like the Mistwood."

The wild magic of the forest—Viri had experienced it herself. If that was only a *trickle* of the Hallow Stream's power, then she didn't want to imagine it at full strength. She wondered why it wasn't accessible anymore, and nearly asked, before realizing it was irrelevant if she had no connection to it.

"So I'm *not* bound to this Stream?" she clarified, just to make sure.

"Elders, no," the Guardian said with an incredulous laugh. "No one could survive that. But I *did* bind you to something else, something arguably as powerful, in a different way."

His luminous blue gaze held hers, waiting to see if she would figure it out.

Her own eyes widened as she breathed, "The obelisks." The wards they produced were powered by generations' worth of ellixen; there was nothing else that could compare.

He inclined his head in confirmation. "To save your life, the magewish created a connection between you and the obelisks, allowing their concentrated ward magic to flow into you—which had the added benefit of purging any remaining blackmist from your body, not just returning you to life, but enabling you to remain alive."

Ward magic. No wonder Viri was so perceptive to them, her lifelong sensitivity making so much more sense.

"Unfortunately, that kind of deep, ancient magic has a sentience about it," the Guardian went on. "It's unpredictable, even volatile. As far as the obelisks were concerned, you took something from them. Something that didn't belong to you. And they weren't happy about it."

Viri shuddered as she remembered pressing her hand to the obsidian stone and hearing the dark voice whispering, *"Mine. Mine. Mine."*

"I told your parents there would be a steep cost to bringing you back." Sorrow touched the Guardian's features. "I even warned them to keep you away from the obelisks, to never let you Impart. But they became anxious as the years passed, fearing the unfamiliar magic brewing in you and what it might mean for your future. They ignored my warnings, hoping that if you gave your ellixen back to the obelisks, then the danger would no longer exist." His sorrow deepened. "They knew the risks, yet they did it anyway. And the moment you touched the obelisk, they tragically paid the price."

Viri had to take a moment to breathe deeply and swallow back fresh tears, her voice coming out croaky and full of accusation. "You said you warned them, but why didn't you just *stop* them? You're an all-powerful mage—you froze me with a wave of your hand earlier, so why didn't you do the same to them that day? Why appear after they were dead, not before it ever happened?"

She knew she wasn't being fair, but her grief felt raw, like a reopened wound.

The Guardian wasn't angered by her outburst. If anything, he seemed even more compassionate. "I wish I could have. But as I told your younger self, I broke some very strict rules by coming to you, and I was only able to do so by using your magewish as a loophole. The Guardian of Elverdine Isle isn't supposed to leave Nevarnost Tower, nor is he or she supposed to interfere in the lives of the isle's inhabitants, aside from those who make their way here and earn a wish." His solemn eyes held hers. "There must be a balance in all things, Viridia. When the balance is disturbed, the consequences are dire, not just for me, but for all who live on this isle. I risked coming to you that day only because—" He stopped suddenly and looked into the fire, as if reconsidering what he'd been about to say.

"Because what?"

The Guardian sighed loudly and turned back to her, his handsome face tinged with shame. "Because I felt partially responsible for what happened to you. Not just the deaths of your parents as a direct result of their wish, but also . . ." He sighed again. "Also how you lost your brother to the Reaper Lord. *That's* why I appeared, so I could grant you the means to alleviate your pain and guilt, if only for a while."

"Why would you feel responsible about the Reaper Lord?" Viri asked. But then she remembered something he'd said earlier that night—something that had meant little to her at the time, since she'd barely believed in the Reaper Lord's existence, but now . . .

"You taught him how to use ellixen," she whispered in horror. "The power he has is because of a magewish, because of *you*."

The Guardian's eyes flickered a few times while she spoke, but he didn't deny her allegations, just rubbed a weary hand over his forehead. "It's more than that. I'm the reason the Reaper Lord *became* the Reaper Lord." Viri jolted, but he wasn't done. "My guilt goes beyond what happened to you, though the rules I must abide as Guardian of this isle mean I'm unable to correct my past mistakes. I stated before that I can't interfere, and unfortunately, that includes anything involving the Reaper Lord." He inhaled deeply. "You, however, I was able to help, since you'd come to my tower as a babe and had therefore earned your magewish. Like I said—it was a loophole, and a perilous one at that, since I also told you I'm not supposed to leave Nevarnost. But magic granted us both some leniency that day, and while I did suffer for my actions, the isle, thankfully, did not."

The shadow that passed over his face was enough for Viri to keep from prying into how he'd suffered. Instead, she asked, "You said you can't interfere when it comes to the Reaper Lord—does that include telling me who he is and why he wants my magic?"

The green flames sizzled and popped while the Guardian considered her question, but when he spoke, it was in a tone full of regret. "I'm afraid so. And before you ask, I can't tell you anything about the star-crossed comets or the Aurora sacrifice, either."

Viri slumped in her seat. "Is there anything you *can* tell me? We know we can't kill him without risking the magical surge, but is it even *possible* to stop someone with the kind of power he has?"

The Guardian's steady gaze held hers. "I'm of the opinion that nothing is ever truly impossible. Don't lose heart, Viridia Solace. All is not yet lost."

His words were encouraging, but not exactly helpful. Still, they gave Viri the smallest ray of hope.

"There's one more thing you should know," he added, his face serious. "You're already aware that the Reaper Lord intends to destroy the obelisks, but with everything I've explained tonight, that now means something more specific to you."

Realization slammed into her. "If I'm bound to the obelisks, then—then—"

He nodded gravely. "If they fall, you'll no longer have their magic keeping you alive."

A sudden, impending sense of doom had Viri rubbing her arms, but she shoved her fear away, having already known she wouldn't survive long if the obelisks were destroyed. The only difference now was that her death would be instant, rather than drawn out underground with the rest of the city.

"Can you share anything else?" she begged. "Even a hint about where the sacrifice is taking place?"

The Guardian looked as if he were warring with himself, like there was some unknown force keeping him from speaking. "I'm sorry, I can't help you. But I can say this: You already have everything you need to succeed. Trust yourself. Trust your friends. Trust your magic."

Viri blew out a resigned breath at the finality in his voice. She glanced toward the door, anxious for Braedan and Reeve to appear so they could head back to the city, meet up with their friends, and discuss next steps. With any luck, Wynter and Jonas would have learned more about the comet by now, and Soren, Sage, and Ardin would have found Jessalyn and the other missing kids. And if not . . . well, they still had two full days until Aurora arrived. A lot could change in that time. Elders, Viri's entire *world* had shifted within the last few hours, so anything could happen between now and the sacrifice.

She was just about to ask the Guardian more about his

interactions with her parents—partly to make small talk while she waited for Braedan and Reeve, but also because she still couldn't believe the bedtime story she'd grown up hearing was true—but her stomach got in first, rumbling loudly and reminding her that she hadn't eaten since before the wraith and the lake monster. She looked sheepishly at the mage, who chuckled and waved his hand, a tingle of ellixen producing a platter of fruit and pastries, along with a crystal chalice full of sparkling elderberry juice.

Viri moaned her thanks and began to scarf down the food, which only made the Guardian's chuckle deepen.

"I don't often have visitors for breakfast. Or any meal, for that matter."

"Breakfast?" Viri repeated around a mouthful of honey cake, washing it down with a hearty swig of the sweet juice. Its bubbles tickled her nose, making her sneeze, before she was able to say, "Don't you mean dinner?" She glanced pointedly toward the windows but then did a double take, startled by how much lighter the sky was, almost as if dawn were touching the horizon. "Are your windows enchanted?"

The Guardian cocked his head to the side. "No. Why do you ask?"

The food Viri had just binged sat uneasily in her stomach. "Why is the sky getting lighter?"

The Guardian seemed unsure whether or not to laugh. "That's what happens when the sun rises."

Viri's unease grew. "But . . . the sun only just set before we arrived here. It shouldn't be anywhere close to rising."

Understanding hit the Guardian's face—as did alarm. "Just to be clear," he said slowly, "what day do you believe it is?"

"It's Friday night." Her last twenty-four hours might have felt as if they'd lasted three thousand years, but she wasn't so confused as to have lost track of them. A pang of sadness hit her as she realized she would normally be at family night right now; last week's game of Mage Quest seemed like forever ago. She thought of Jessalyn and her bright yellow pajamas, praying the young girl had been found and was back home, safe and sound.

"Viridia, I'm sorry to tell you this, but you're wrong," the Guardian said, banishing her plate and chalice with a flick of his fingers. "Time passes differently in the Mistwood, sometimes faster, sometimes slower, depending on the path you take." He held her shocked gaze and declared, "It's Sunday morning."

Viri's ears rang, certain she must have misheard, but knowing from the look on his face that she hadn't.

"What?" She leapt to her feet, the food she'd just eaten roiling within her as she realized the Aurora sacrifice was happening *today.* They didn't have two days left. They didn't even have a full day left. They had until *tonight.*

Panic flooded her as she all but shouted, *"Where the hell are Reeve and Brae?"*

The Guardian raised his hands helplessly, having no answer.

Viri spun around once, twice, so overwhelmed that she couldn't think straight. "Can you use your magic to locate them?" Desperation crept into her tone. "Or to call them back here somehow?"

A shake of his head. "The castle has many rooms spread across multiple levels in each of the different towers, all full of distracting magical wonders. The grounds are even more expansive and equally enchanted. There's no telling how far they might have wandered."

Viri wanted to scream her frustration, something that only grew when he asked, "Are the two of them together?"

She had no idea. If Nevarnost was as vast as the Guardian claimed, then Braedan might not have even *found* Reeve yet, let alone told him they were ready to leave.

"I'm not—I don't—" Viri was at a loss. She raised shaky hands to her mouth and said, "The comet is coming in *hours*. We need to leave. We need to plan. We need to—"

"How about this," the Guardian interrupted in a soothing voice, rising beside her and placing a calming hand on her shoulder. "You go on ahead of your companions, and I'll track them down and send them after you."

"But—I—" She looked at the door, praying Braedan and Reeve would materialize, but there was no sign of them, making her realize the Guardian was right. She couldn't risk waiting however long it might take for them to appear, not when they were now at the point when every *second* counted.

Unwilling to waste any more time deliberating, Viri gestured to the wayportal in the center of the room and asked, "Does that connect to the city portals?"

"No. Only the roaming Mistwood one."

Viri cursed, though she was unsurprised, given how secretive Nevarnost was. But at least the magical map would allow her to skip another journey through the forest. She quickly pulled it from her cloak and pricked her finger with her dagger, using her blood to send the Mistwood portal to the very edge of the forest, right by the necropolis. Reeve had his own blackmist talisman, as did Braedan, so she would just have to pray that her ring held enough magic to protect her until she reached the boundary of the Southern Obelisk's wards.

"Here." She handed the map to the Guardian. "Reeve knows how it works, and Brae has Solace blood. Once you find them, please tell them to hunt down Sage, Ardin, and Soren for news, then meet me in Wynter's lab. Make sure they know how little time we have left."

"I will," the Guardian promised somberly. He squeezed her shoulder once before releasing her. "Best of luck to you, Viridia Solace. If anyone can stop the Reaper Lord, it's you."

Viri wished she had his confidence, but all she felt was knee-weakening dread. "Thank you," she choked out. "I hope I'll see you again." Mostly because that would mean she was still *alive*.

"I hope so, too," the Guardian said quietly, lifting a hand in farewell.

That was the last she saw of him before she turned and leapt through the wayportal, coming out the other side to find the forest bathed in the first light of dawn, with no blackmist in sight.

Relieved not to have to test her ring, she hurried from the Mistwood into the safety of the ward-protected necropolis, keeping her pace swift as she passed through the rusted iron gates and carved a path between the twisting trees and tombs. The burial ground was as silent as death, the ancient white graves glowing like specters against the shadowy light of the early morning, their gleam inadvertently protecting her from tripping over any of the smaller headstones or down the crumbling stairs into the underground crypts. She didn't have time to sprain an ankle, the urgency she felt to hurry, hurry, *hurry* driving her forward across the leaf-strewn ground, the only sounds being the crunching of her boots and her anxious, panting breaths.

Viri's thoughts whirled as she rushed past mausoleums and vaults, the earth beginning to rise as she approached the spiraling white cathedral sitting on its grassy knoll at the heart of the necropolis. Plans and possibilities flashed rapidly across her mind, part of her wondering if all fifty of the missing children might have been found during the time she'd lost, with the rest of her instinctively knowing that hadn't happened. The Reaper Lord had proved himself too clever not to have contingencies in place. And as much as Viri respected Meera and Darik as leaders, they had no idea who was really behind the sacrifice, or the kind of power the Reaper Lord had at his disposal—both his control of magic *and* the mountain full of reapers under his command. She had to warn them about what the Nox and hunters were really facing. Sarielle, too, needed to know, so she and her council could prepare the city in case the sacrifice ended up going ahead.

Bile rose in Viri's throat at the thought, but she kept hurrying through the necropolis, the spooky cathedral coming nearer, her skin tingling at the sight while her mind remained focused on forming a plan. The city needed all the warning it could get, so she would wake Sarielle first and urge her to rouse the council, then she would seek out Meera and share everything she knew. As for Darik . . . well, Viri would let Meera update the Nox captain, since his general dislike of her meant he probably had a million reasons to throw her in the Underlock by now—and not just for breaking Reeve out in the first place.

Elders, that felt like centuries ago.

Viri began to feel steadier as her plan solidified, deciding that after Sarielle and Meera, she would head straight to Wynter's lab to find out what she and Jonas had discovered. By then, Reeve and Braedan should have arrived with news from Sage, Ardin, and Soren, and then . . . then . . .

Then they would figure out what to do next.

Another tingle traveled over Viri at the enormity of the task before them, but she refused to entertain the worst-case what-ifs while there was still time. There were fifty children who needed to be saved before tonight—Jessalyn likely among them—and an entire city that needed to survive beyond that. She couldn't give up. *Wouldn't* give up.

Determined, Viri increased her pace as she approached the rusted iron gates leading up to the cathedral, intending to speed through the last of the necropolis and take the wayportal directly to Sarielle. But just as she reached the warped, corroded fence, another tingle ran over her flesh, this time prickling enough for her to realize it had nothing to do with her emotions—it was *magic* she could feel.

But it was also more than that.

Because as she staggered to a halt in front of the iron entryway, she became aware of something else.

Her palm was burning.

Years of training had Viri crouching into a defensive stance and uncoiling her fillium, looking left and right for the reaper who had triggered her mark. But there was no one in sight, her hand warm but not searing enough to indicate she was in imminent danger, nor that anyone nearby was being siphoned.

She bit her lip, debating what to do. Logic told her to ignore her hunter duty and continue onward, since stopping the sacrifice took priority over all else. But something inside her was resisting, her intuition whispering, *"Wait. Look. Listen."* She heeded that inner voice, sparing a moment to close her eyes and concentrate on her palm.

Her eyes shot open again as she realized what her mark was tugging her toward.

The cathedral.

And it wasn't just her mark—as soon as she stepped up to the iron gates, the prickle of ellixen grew stronger, too.

But it wasn't either of those things that made Viri tense all over.

It was the faint sound of crying.

She'd heard something similar when she and Reeve had walked through the necropolis on their way to the Guardian, but she'd convinced herself it had been nothing more than creaking tree branches and the whistling wind.

There was no wind now, the early-morning air still and silent.

Viri's breathing shallowed as something deep within her urged her through the rusted gates and up a short, winding path ending at a set of weathered stone steps. The crying had vanished, making her wonder if she'd imagined it, if she was wasting time and should stick to her plan to head straight to the wayportal. But her palm was burning hotter now, and her skin was prickling incessantly from magic, both convincing her to ascend the crumbling staircase and press her hand to the rotted white doors.

The entrance should have been sealed.

It wasn't.

The doors opened at her touch, not because she'd pushed them—but because someone had *pulled* them.

Before she knew what was happening, a black-veined hand was clutching the front of her scarlet cloak and hauling her through the entryway. She raised her fillium to bring the reaper down, but the moment she crossed the threshold into the ancient building, she suddenly found the cause of the ellixen prickling her skin.

The cathedral was warded, and now that she was inside, the crying she'd heard faintly from outside was crystal clear.

Only, it wasn't just one person crying. It was many.

And they weren't just crying—they were also screaming.

Young, terrified screams.

The missing children.

They were *here*.

But Viri couldn't do a single thing to help them, couldn't even *see* them beyond the lights flashing across her vision as the strength of the ellixen ward slammed into her, blinding her with pain, forcing her to stumble and curl in on herself as her nerve endings shrieked in agony—something that only deepened when the hilt of the reaper's dagger smashed into her temple.

Her pain vanished in an instant.

Because she dropped to the ground, unconscious.

THE JOURNAL OF CELESTIAL MAGE KADMUS CASTRO

Eighth Sun, Fourteenth Cycle, Twelfth Age

~~They're coming for me. The mages. Tephryn~~.

~~I can't—I don't—~~

~~Zeranthe~~

~~She's—She's—~~

~~What have I done? WHAT HAVE I DONE~~?

Orion came tonight—and death came with him.

Just not the death I had planned.

At first, everything went exactly as it was supposed to. My followers and I were gathered inside the White Tomb awaiting the comet's arrival, our sacrifice laid out on the altar stone, ready for what was about to unfold. Magistratus Garrin didn't even need to stage an "accident," because a volunteer came forward—a devoted shallow who believed in our cause so deeply that she was willing to pay the ultimate price. It eased my conscience, knowing she'd agreed to it, and that I wouldn't be committing cold-blooded murder.

As it turned out, I was wrong about that. Though it wasn't her who I killed.

I never had the chance.

Because just as Orion appeared at the edge of the night sky, just as I started chanting and began to reach for the comet's power, just as I was about to drive my ritual bone dagger downward and complete the sacrifice—I remembered something.

In my desperation, in my <u>hubris</u>, I'd forgotten that Orion requires one more element than Aurora for the channeling to work.

Ellixen abyssus.

Before I could find a way to salvage the ritual, disaster struck. Because out of nowhere—

Magic slammed into me.

It wasn't Orion's magic.

It wasn't the magic of the Hallow Stream, breaking free on its own.

No, it was my beloved Tephryn.

And she wasn't alone. Every mage on the isle had come for us, having somehow learned of our plans to destroy the obelisks.

Quickly, so very quickly, everything went wrong.

Or maybe it went right.

. . . But then it went very, *very* wrong.

~~I can't~~

~~I don't~~

~~Zeranthe~~

I'm not sure what happened. How it happened. How it was even *possible*. But instead of siphoning Orion, I siphoned something else.

Some*one* else.

One moment, I was standing at the altar, trying frantically to recall everything I knew about *ellixen abyssus*, and the next, the mages were swarming the White Tomb. They drove me and my shallows outside, then started slapping nullicuffs on anyone who displayed the slightest hint of ellixen, silencing what little power they had. Seeing that, witnessing my devoted followers being repressed with barely any effort, that's when I lost it.

I'm not sure if it was my devastation about Orion.

If it was the Hallow Stream's influence over me.

If it was simply *me*.

But when one of the mages who had mocked and derided me for months came forward to bind me, something inside me changed. Shifted. And suddenly, I was *hungry*—not for food, but for *power*.

His power.

I could *feel* the ellixen running through him. And I wanted it. *Needed* it.

So I took it.

It was instinctive, what I did. For years, I've siphoned from celestial bodies. It's become second nature to me, reaching for them and channeling their power, then releasing it outward so my shallows can absorb it.

This time, that's not what I did.

Because when the mage tried to bind me, I grabbed his wrists, skin to skin—and I *fed*. There's no other word for it. I siphoned the ellixen right out of him, reaped every last drop. My veins turned black, something that's never happened during my rituals, but I've never stolen power from a living being before. I didn't know I *could* steal from a living being. It's not possible on the mainland—the wards around the Hallow Streams there prevent it—but here on Elverdine . . .

I couldn't stop—didn't *try* to stop. His ellixen . . . I was *starved* for it. It was better than anything I've ever siphoned, like the finest, purest delicacy.

I needed more.

So when he fell at my feet, drained of magic—drained of *life*—I couldn't resist the hunger driving me to siphon again. To *reap* again.

In that moment, I became something new, something powerful, something unstoppable—a *reaper*. And when I began yelling instructions to my shallows, telling them what to do, *how* to do it, I was no longer their Mage Priest, but their Reaper Priest.

The first ever Reaper Priest.

No—the first Reaper *Lord*.

A powerful title, for a powerful leader.

And lead I did. My shallows followed me, as they always have, drawing magic into themselves. *Reaping* magic.

Once the oppressed, now the oppressors.

The mages didn't know what was happening, not even when they began falling to the overwhelming number of shallows, their power stolen, their lives extinguished.

But the dragons—the bonded dragons—they knew.

Zeranthe knew.

She came for me, screaming into my mind as she flew down from the mountain. It took mere minutes, but when she landed among the moonlit tombs, it was already too late.

I was too far gone in my lust for more magic.

My shallows—my *reapers*—were too far gone.

And Zeranthe . . . the strength of her ellixen . . . the sheer *amount* of power inside her, emanating like the light from a thousand suns—

I no longer had any control over myself. All I knew was *need*.

By the time I realized what was happening—that I was siphoning from my beloved dragon, that my reapers were doing the same, that we were *killing* her—

The other dragons arrived then, having come to save their mages. They forced me and my reapers to scatter.

But Zeranthe—

The dragons had to carry her away, her ellixen all but gone, her vibrant blue scales turned a deathly white.

She didn't fight back.

Why didn't she fight back?

Our connection is gone. I can't feel her anymore.

~~I think I~~

~~I think we~~

~~I don't know if she~~

The mages are coming for me. They believe I've lost my mind, that the Hallow Stream's magic has corrupted me.

Maybe it has.

Maybe it happened when I cracked the first obelisk, when the Stream's power flooded me, when its rage filled me.

Maybe the Stream is the reason for my hunger, my desperation, my *addiction*.

Maybe it drove my actions tonight.

Or maybe that was just *me*.

The mages will have figured out what happened by now, what I did, what my reapers did, and they'll have rallied. I don't know what they're planning or how they intend to stop us, but Tephryn is smart, and she—they—

I won't go down without a fight.

I won't let them take this from me, from my reapers, from <u>us</u>.

The hunger—it's relentless.

I need <u>more</u>.

They're coming for me. Coming for my reapers. Tephryn is—

<u>They're here.</u>

32

"Viri."

"Viri, please—you have to wake up."

"P-Please, Viri!"

Viri groaned as her eyelids fluttered open, her head throbbing so ferociously that she nearly blacked right out again—and would have, if not for someone shaking her, begging her to rise.

Not just someone. Viri knew that voice.

She sat up with a gasp, seeing nothing and fearing that the knock to her head had left her blind. But she squinted through her pain until she could focus past the darkness of the musty room she was in, the dimmest of everbeacons revealing damp walls covered in mold and a cluster of white stone coffins lined up beside each other, all cracked and crumbling.

Viri's stomach clenched as she took in the crammed space, the moistness of the air telling her she was in an underground crypt, the lingering tingle of the wards indicating she was somewhere beneath the cathedral. But she spared only a second to get her bearings and note the staircase leading up to the only exit—

a wooden door that was undoubtedly locked—before her attention was fully diverted by the person who had woken her.

Because it was Jessalyn.

"Thank the Elders you're not dead," the young girl whimpered, wrapping her arms around Viri's neck. She was trembling violently, her grip so fierce it was bruising.

"Jessy," Viri breathed, hugging her just as tightly. "Are you all right? Are you hurt?"

Jessalyn shook her head against Viri's shoulder before easing back enough to show her puffy, tear-stained face. Her brown eyes were wide with fear, her sandy hair tangled, her clothes filthy, but aside from her messy appearance, she didn't seem to have suffered any physical harm in the days since she'd been abducted.

"They don't hurt us," Jessalyn confirmed shakily. "The reapers—we only see them when they bring food and water. They haven't even tried to siphon from us."

Viri noticed then that there were other children in the room, peeking out nervously from behind the stone coffins and hiding in the shadowy corners, all in similar states of neglect.

"Have you come to save us?" Jessy asked tremulously. "Are we going home?"

"Yes," Viri said firmly, unwilling to let on how dire their situation was. Her mind was spinning, largely from her head trauma, but also because she realized with a sinking feeling that no one had the slightest idea where she was. Reeve and Braedan would know something was wrong when she didn't show up at Wynter's lab, but they wouldn't have the first clue how to find her. She needed to think, to come up with a plan, but, Elders, her head was *hurting*.

Gritting her teeth against the thundering pain, Viri reached into her cloak and pulled out the last of the healing salve, slathering it against her swollen temple and moaning with relief as it began to work almost instantly. She did a quick inventory of what remained from Wynter's supply, noting that the zingzest and morphenine had been used up during their lake encounter, and she'd lost the impedidust somewhere along the way—likely while fighting the tentacled beast—but she still had the scarlet powder that could nullify the heightened abilities of any reapers it touched, and she made sure it was secured within easy reach.

Patting her sides, Viri cursed as she realized her last two daggers had been confiscated. But at least she still had her fillium and the scarlet powder, both of which she decided she would use against whoever appeared next in the crypt, giving the kids a chance to make a run for it while she fought back any pursuers.

It wasn't her strongest plan, but it was better than nothing, and she felt her confidence grow.

. . . Until she glanced at her forearm and saw that her fillium wasn't actually there.

Her blood turned cold as she remembered she'd been holding it when she'd lost consciousness, which meant—

"Looking for this?"

Viri startled, her palm searing as she scrambled to her feet and whirled toward the staircase. The door had opened without her hearing it, and standing there, bathed in shadows, was an eerily familiar form.

The Reaper Lord.

"Hello, Viridia Solace," he said in his deep voice, his bulky cloak covering him from head to toe, just like last time. The only difference was, he now held her fillium in his gloved hands.

Viri froze at the sight. It should have been impossible. He

was a *reaper.* The golden cord was most debilitating when touching skin directly, but it still worked over clothes, and unless the Reaper Lord had the same rare immunity as Viri and Reeve, then there was no way he should have been able to hold it without feeling its effects.

"I wish you could see the look on your face right now." Dark amusement threaded his tone as he waved the weapon tauntingly. "If you're wondering how I can touch this, it's because it used to belong to me, and unlike people, magic is loyal. But it was stolen long ago, along with something even more precious. I swore I'd get revenge one day, so when I say I'm going to enjoy this, I mean that more than you can know."

A prickle of ellixen was the only warning Viri had before her fillium rose magically into the air in front of the Reaper Lord, hovered like a thrashing, golden snake—

And exploded into dust.

"No!" Viri cried, watching in horror as the glittery specks floated gracefully to the filthy ground.

Her fillium—her *parents'* fillium—

"So satisfying," the Reaper Lord crooned. "You have no idea how long I've wanted to do that."

Viri stared at the gold dust in disbelief, her eyes burning at the sense of loss, of *grief.* Her weapon had saved her life countless times since she'd become a hunter, had saved her parents for many years before her. For it to now be destroyed . . . for the Reaper Lord to have had enough power to make a magical artifact *shatter* . . .

Trembles began to rack Viri's frame, a heady combination of fury and fear. She motioned to the pale-faced Jessalyn to back away, and the young girl scurried over to a group of children cowering behind one of the white coffins. Only when Jessy was safely out of the Reaper Lord's firing line did Viri turn to face him head-on, her voice hard as she promised, "You'll pay for that—along with everything else you've done."

A lethal laugh. "Pay? I just did you a favor. Someone had to show you that you're deluding yourself if you still believe you stand a chance at stopping me." He cocked his hooded head to the side, the shadows moving with him. "Though I suppose I should also thank you." His humor returned. "You've been so painfully predictable, you made my task almost too easy."

Viri glared at him, denying him the satisfaction of asking what he meant.

He told her anyway.

"Did you really think I wasn't aware of your brother's escape from his cozy little prison? That I didn't know about his plans to find the Guardian and how he intended to use his magewish? That I didn't make sure Reeve oh-so-conveniently learned about the danger that would come with my death?" A mocking chuckle. "Poor Reeve. He played right into my hands by seeking you out, and you did exactly what I expected in freeing him from the Underlock. The two of you saved my life—just as I knew you would. So as I said, I should thank you."

Viri hated everything he was saying. Hated *him*. "We only saved you because we had to," she snarled, loathing how easily she and Reeve had been manipulated. "That doesn't mean we're not going to stop you."

"What you still haven't realized is that you shouldn't *want* to stop me. I'm doing all this *for* you, Viridia. If you haven't figured that out yet . . ." The Reaper Lord shook his head as if disappointed, though all Viri could think was that he was insane if he believed that. "Shame. But it matters little, because contempt alone won't help you, and no one else is going to, either—not in the next eight hours before Aurora arrives."

The blood drained from Viri's face. It had been barely dawn when she'd left the Guardian's tower. If the comet was only eight hours away, then she'd been unconscious for much longer than she'd thought.

"But I also know better than to underestimate you," he went on, "which, unfortunately for you, means I can't risk any problems between now and nightfall. After all, we both know how adept you are at getting yourself out of tight spots."

Viri scowled. "You don't know anything about me." Though in this case, what he'd said was true, and she was going to make damn sure he found out *exactly* how adept she was.

Another dark laugh. "You think I haven't been watching you closely for the last seven years? Before that, even?"

A shiver traveled down Viri's spine at the thought of him spying on her. But then she processed something else he'd said.

"If I'm such a risk, why am I here? Why keep me alive?" She'd been at the mercy of whatever reaper had knocked her out, and instead of being harmed, they'd dragged her down into the dank crypt and left her there. At any other time, she'd be thanking her lucky stars. But now . . . something more was going on here.

"Because if things don't go as intended tonight," the Reaper Lord answered, "then I'm going to need you after all."

"What does that—"

"I'm done answering your questions," he said impatiently.

"I'll see you soon, Viridia Solace. Best you rest up before all the excitement."

Rest was the last thing Viri would be doing. She had eight hours left and planned to use every one of them to get out of the cathedral, save the children, and stop the Reaper Lord from hurting anyone ever again.

But then she discovered his words weren't a suggestion.

They were a warning.

Because a wave of his hand sent a surge of ellixen her way, and for the second time that morning, she fell to the ground, out like a light.

33

When Viri startled awake again, she was no longer in the underground crypt, but instead in a vast, vaulted hall, the air so cold that her breath clouded in front of her face.

Everything came back to her in a rush, adrenaline flooding her as she realized she was tied to a cracked marble pillar, one of many lining the arched inner walls of the cathedral's immense central chamber. Moss and mold covered most surfaces, as if nature had claimed the space as its own, with vines curling around the pillars and twisting along the fractured ground like serpents waiting to strike. Everywhere she looked, there was something broken or decayed: crumbled statues, splintered pews, shattered glass, a field of debris scattered around stained white coffins, all leading up to an elevated dais, the only place that looked untouched by time. Behind it was an enormous figure of an ancient firebird—a symbol of death and rebirth—with its wings outstretched and tail feathers fanning like flames. It was as beautiful as it was terrifying, its beady eyes seeming to glow as it stared down at a raised stone slab sitting atop the dais.

Viri inhaled sharply at the sight of the slab, but it wasn't only from realizing what it was intended for. It was also because she could *see* it—and everything else in the vast hall—due to the moonlight flowing through the smashed glass ceiling.

Bright, brilliant moonlight.

No, Viri whispered to herself, knowing that if night had fallen—

Then she was out of time.

A whimper on her left had her turning so fast that her neck cricked, the pain dull compared to the dread she felt at finding Jessalyn tied to the next pillar along. Beyond her, more children were bound, all the way around the cathedral. Like Jessy, they were beginning to rouse from whatever magic had left them there unconscious, their fearful cries and wails echoing throughout the moonlit space.

Viri wondered if they knew what purpose the Reaper Lord intended them to serve tonight, but a searing burn kept her from asking, her mark warning that a reaper was coming—or reapers, as she soon discovered, with them streaming through an archway and marching along the debris-strewn nave toward the dais.

One . . . five . . . fifteen . . . thirty . . . She lost count as their cloaked forms continued appearing, their bare hands showing blackened veins that vanished beneath their sleeves, some even having so much stolen ellixen that the dark lines traveled up their necks and over their jaws toward their hardened eyes. None of them spared a glanced at Viri and the children, their focus solely on reaching the steps leading to the stone slab and spreading out before it, like a wall of witnesses in front of an altar.

There, they waited.

Viri's heart was pounding in her ears, the rapid beats sounding like a clock ticking down far too quickly. She tugged against her bonds, but a sharp sting of ellixen revealed it wasn't rope that tied her to the pillar, it was *magic.* Rope she could saw her way through, but she didn't have the first clue how to break out of bindings she couldn't even *see.*

A sobbing sound had her turning to Jessalyn again, finding the young girl with tears streaming down her cheeks.

"It's going to be all right, Jessy," Viri said in a hushed voice. "I won't let anything happen to you."

She had no way to promise that, and they both knew it.

"If—If I don't make it—" Jessalyn started.

"You *will.*"

"—tell Soren I love him." Jessy hiccuped. "Tell him I w-want him to be happy."

He would never be happy without his sister. He would never forgive himself if she didn't survive. He would never forgive *Viri* if she didn't do everything she could to save her.

"You tell him yourself," Viri said firmly, "as soon as we get out of here."

A dark, amused voice interrupted before Jessalyn could respond.

"I don't know whether it's admirable or pathetic that you still believe that's possible."

Ice and fire filled Viri simultaneously as the Reaper Lord appeared, striding casually between the pillars until he stood before where she sat against the cracked marble. She hated having to look up at him, but her magical bindings didn't allow any wiggle room, let alone enough to stand.

"The comet will be appearing any minute, and you *still* think you can stop me?" He chuckled. "I knew you were stubborn, but this is ridiculous."

Viri strained against the magic holding her, pain lancing along her wrists as if blades were slicing into her flesh, but she didn't care, just continued struggling.

"Don't bother," the Reaper Lord said, watching her pitiful attempt. "There's nothing you can do now anyway."

His hooded head turned toward the dais, where his reapers waited obediently. He made a satisfied sound, then snapped his gloved fingers, causing Viri to flinch as ellixen overwhelmed her senses. Magic swept through the room in a fiery wind, lighting candles scattered amid the debris all the way up to where they bordered the stone slab, and behind it—

Jessalyn gasped and Viri's eyes widened as the firebird seemed to come alive, flames leaping along its feathers, blazing from the crown of its head to its outstretched wings and down through its fanned tail. It was even more beautiful and terrifying now, like an inferno made flesh.

"That's better." The Reaper Lord hummed his pleasure. "I intended to make tonight's ceremony more of a visual spectacle, but your friends have proved themselves to be surprising little pests and have managed to figure out where we are, so this will have to do."

Viri sucked in a breath, hope blossoming within her.

"Don't look too excited," the Reaper Lord said with a menacing laugh. "The Magistratus was notified of this location by her daughter, of all people—"

Viri sucked in another breath, since if Wynter had told Sarielle, then she would have also told Meera and Darik. Reeve and Braedan would know, too, plus the rest of their friends. That meant there was still a chance—

"—but I've strengthened the wards enough that they'll never

make it through the doors," the Reaper Lord finished smugly. "An entire army could be amassing outside, and none of them can lift a finger to help you."

Viri's hope vanished like smoke, leaving her slumping against the pillar.

The Reaper Lord laughed darkly again. "I'm sorry to disappoint you, Viridia. If it helps, imagine Sarielle Starling's surprise to learn her precious daughter has been studying forbidden magic beneath her nose for years." He *tsk*ed. "Loyalty is so hard to come by these days."

"Wynter has more loyalty in her little toe than you do in your whole body," Viri spat. "And Sarielle loves her, so she'll understand." *Eventually,* she added with a mental wince, wondering what, exactly, Wynter had been forced to reveal to her mother in order to share what she'd learned about the comets. Viri hoped her friend was all right—just as she hoped to survive long enough to find out for herself, even if that was looking less likely with every passing second.

"Love is a lie that only fools believe in," the Reaper Lord said in a disgusted tone. "How the Magistratus feels about her daughter is irrelevant—unless, of course, she can be used in some way. Power matters. Love doesn't."

"Said by someone who has clearly never been loved."

"Or perhaps said by someone who has been betrayed by love, in all its wretched forms," he countered sharply, before waving a dismissive hand. "I'm not discussing this with you. The time has come to say your goodbyes."

Another snap of his fingers beckoned a burly reaper who reached for Jessalyn, her magical bonds dissolving as she was yanked to her feet.

"No!" Viri cried, struggling anew. *"No!"*

"I have to start somewhere." The Reaper Lord gave a heartless shrug. "Would you prefer another child take her place?"

Yes, Viri thought, revolted by her own thoughts.

"Viri!" Jessalyn cried, sobbing harder now as the reaper dragged her away, hauling her resisting form toward the dais with little effort. *"Viri, help me!"*

"JESSY!" Viri screamed, fighting with all her might but unable to move even an inch.

"Such passion," the Reaper Lord murmured, watching Viri's battle. "Maybe love does exist." He sniffed. "Pity."

And then he turned and strode after Jessalyn, his cloak billowing behind him as he stepped over the vines and around crumbling coffins, following a glass-strewn, candlelit path to where his obedient reapers waited. They bowed as he approached, then shuffled aside, making room for him to ascend the short staircase up to the dais. There, Jessy was lifted onto the stone slab, with her thrashing wildly until the Reaper Lord waved a hand to flatten her against the surface, binding her arms and legs in place by magic, his burly helper quickly falling back beside the other acolytes.

Viri was going to be sick. She was peripherally aware of the children sobbing around her, the sounds and smells of their fear only adding to her nausea. But her gaze remained locked on Jessalyn writhing against the stone slab, the moonlight streaming down onto her visibly quaking form while the flaming wings of the firebird stretched out behind her.

"Not long now," the Reaper Lord announced, his voice echoing throughout the hall. His head was tilted back as he peered up through the shattered ceiling, shadows rippling around him, like always, but they now danced with firelight, making him look like a demon straight from the pits of hell.

Viri fought and fought and *fought* against the ellixen holding her to the pillar, panting hard as she tried desperately to free herself, her wrists screeching in pain. But no matter what she did, the magic holding her was too strong.

Helplessness overtook her as the Reaper Lord continued to stare up at the night's sky, as Jessalyn continued to strain against the bonds pressing her down, as the children continued weeping and screaming. It couldn't end like this, and yet, there was nothing Viri could do, her years of training having never prepared her to fight someone as powerful as the Reaper Lord. Anger rose within her at the unfairness of it all—at her parents dying when she was a child and never telling her the truth about her own past, at her brother sacrificing seven years of his life just to protect her, at Reeve being forced to abandon her, at her forgotten memories that had stolen so much time from them all, and lastly, at the all-powerful Guardian who had refused to help stop the Reaper Lord, offering nothing more than trite words that—

Viri stilled suddenly as she remembered exactly what the Guardian had told her.

"You already have everything you need to succeed. Trust yourself. Trust your friends. Trust your magic."

Viri trusted her friends, but they were stuck outside, beyond the cathedral's impenetrable wards. She also trusted herself, though right now, she was trapped by the Reaper Lord's power, unable to move. Her magic, however . . . that she *didn't* trust. She didn't even *understand* it. But if what the Guardian had said was true—perhaps even veiled advice—then maybe it was time she stopped physically fighting and tried something different, something . . . *magical.*

Her mind scrambled to consider everything she knew about the magewish bond that tied her life to the obelisks, how their pure, potent ward magic flowed within her, heightening her sensitivity to ellixen. She'd learned in the Summit that she could focus that sensitivity to locate warded objects, but . . . what if she could do more than that? What if she could *create* wards, just like the obelisks did?

And more importantly . . .

What if she could *break* them?

Viri's palms began to sweat as an idea came to her. The cathedral's wards were all that prevented anyone from coming to their aid, so if those wards were destroyed . . .

It was a long shot, and something she needed to test first, unsure what might happen if she attempted such magic—or *any* magic—without knowing what she was doing. She could make the wards worse, unintentionally strengthening them or even making them permanent. She needed to experiment with something smaller, so she closed her eyes and cast her mind back to Reeve's instructions in the storage room, imagining herself like a mage blossom unfurling petal by petal, reaching for her heightened sensitivity, her *magic*, ready to release it.

Nothing happened.

Anxiety rose within Viri, but she forced herself to breathe through it, knowing her desperation was only working against her. She summoned the memory of Reeve's lulling, hypnotic voice as he'd guided her, willing her thoughts to settle, her heartbeat to slow.

And then she tried again, reaching deep inside herself once

more, coaxing her magic to flow out, to break past the embankment of her mental river.

This time, it worked.

A gasp left Viri as the power inside her erupted outward and slammed against the wards of the cathedral, the sting of their ellixen so strong that she had to stifle a groan. She hastily reeled her river back in, wrestling it under as much control as she could, using nothing but the memory of Reeve's calming voice and her own intuition to guide it toward a different point of focus.

Her awareness homed in on her own wrists, making her realize that the bonds holding her to the pillar must be a kind of ward—or perhaps the strange magic within her didn't discriminate between wards and general ellixen. Either way, she concentrated hard on the tingle binding her in place, brushing her peculiar, unknown magic up against it, like a hand stroking a pet, and mentally whispered, *"Let go, let go, let go."*

She had no idea what she was doing, was certain it wouldn't work—

But then, suddenly, she was free.

Shock stole Viri's breath, but she shoved her incredulity aside, knowing she could marvel over what she'd done later. For now, all she wanted was to leap up and sprint for the dais, but she made herself remain in place, aware she would get barely two steps before the Reaper Lord waved his hand and flung her away, or worse, forced her back into unconsciousness until the sacrifice was over. His hooded head had already swiveled in her direction, like he'd sensed a change in the magic binding her—or *not* binding her—and it took all her willpower to stay immobile under his perusal.

A chillingly long moment passed before he looked away again, his head tilting upward once more, causing a shaky exhale to leave Viri. But then his shoulders straightened as something caught his attention, and she followed his gaze up through the shattered ceiling, ice flooding her as she saw a bright purple streak traveling ever so slowly among the stars high overhead.

Aurora had arrived.

Panic rippled through Viri, with it only growing when the Reaper Lord withdrew a white bone dagger from his cloak and held it between his open palms, then began to chant in a foreign language, likely that of the ancient mages.

It was now or never, Viri realized, staring at the dagger in horror and knowing exactly what would happen as soon as the Reaper Lord's chanting ended.

Her inexperience made her technique raw and clumsy, her intuition still all she had to guide her, but Viri speared the river of her magic outward again, this time letting it slam against the cathedral wards—and stay there. They were so much stronger than the small amount of ellixen that had bound her wrists, like a mountain compared to a pebble, and she strained against them, raising her whisper to a mental shout: *"SHATTER! SHATTER! SHATTER!"*

Her head began to throb as she pushed with everything she had, ramming her magic against the wards over and over again, each time screaming louder, *"SHATTER!"*

And then, finally, they did, causing a harsh ripping sound to tear through her mind and make her partially black out, her magic no longer contained by any wards and instead streaming beyond the cathedral and into the necropolis. In her half-lucid state, she was somehow able to sense what it sensed, aware of the scores of people waiting outside in the moonlight, Nox and hunters alike, none of whom realized the wards had come down. She had to find a way to tell them they could now enter the cathedral, but *how*—

Her magic suddenly jerked in another direction, flowing toward someone hiding with a smaller group in the shadows of a tomb—someone her magic was being pulled toward, like a moth to a flame. *"Mine, mine, mine,"* it whispered, but unlike when Viri had been attacked by the obelisk during her Impartation attempt, this voice wasn't dark and menacing—it was soft, affectionate, loving.

And it was talking about Reeve.

His magic—there must be something in it that called to her own, like power attracting power. She didn't understand enough about ellixen to guess beyond that, just continued trusting her instincts and brushed her magic against his like she'd done with the wrist bonds, saying, *"Reeve, if you can hear me, the wards are down. Please hur—"*

Her magic was wrenched backward as full lucidity returned to her, leaving her nauseatingly dizzy as her power was contained once more. Her ears rang, not from being hurtled back into her own consciousness, but from Jessalyn's screams—

Because the Reaper Lord had raised his dagger high above her, his chanting beginning to slow, the blade pointed directly at her heart.

Viri didn't know if Reeve had heard her, didn't care that she was light-headed and weak after destroying the wards, because she wasn't waiting another second to save Jessalyn. Even knowing the Reaper Lord could swat her away, she scrambled to her feet and sprinted forward, hurdling over crumbled statues and broken pews, swerving around white coffins and fallen pillars, leaping past twisted vines and flickering candles. The Reaper Lord didn't seem to notice her mad dash, not even with the racket of glass crunching under her boots, as if he were stuck in a trance while chanting in the moonlight. His reaper underlings saw her coming, though, and a group of them lunged forward to intercept her.

At any other time, Viri might have been flattered that they thought ten of them were needed to bring her down, but right now, she had no defense against even *one* of them. She had no fillium or weapons to counter their heightened strength and speed, her only option being the scarlet powder that could nullify their inhuman abilities. She wished she could wait to hit more of them at once—including the Reaper Lord—but she didn't have a choice if she wanted to survive beyond the next few seconds.

Thumbing the vial from her cloak as she ran, she waited until the reapers were mere steps away before screeching to a halt and hurling it at their feet, the glass smashing and the powder rising like a red cloud. Viri was careful to stay out of its explosive radius, not wanting to risk nullifying the newly discovered magic within her, and she watched in awe as the reapers stumbled clumsily upon losing access to their stolen ellixen.

Unsure how long the effects would last, Viri leapt forward again, grateful for all the hours Meera had spent training her in unarmed combat as she aimed her fist at the nearest reaper, who crumpled to the ground with a satisfying thud.

The rest didn't succumb as easily, with them quickly adjusting to their dulled senses and coming at her together, blades drawn. Stinging cuts tore her skin open, blood smearing across her flesh and seeping into her clothes, but she was nimble enough on her feet to avoid any major wounds, ducking and dodging their attacks while kicking and striking in return. Nine against one were challenging odds—even without their enhanced strength and speed—but they couldn't all assault her at once without harming each other, and she used that to her benefit. She brought one woman down with an elbow to her temple, brought another down with a kick to her nose, shattering the bone. She managed to steal a dagger from a man and stab him with it, using the same blade to fell two more, leaving just four of the original ten remaining.

Four—plus the dozens still standing between her and the dais, none of whom had been touched by Wynter's nullifying powder.

But Viri refused to think about that, focusing only on the battle at hand, and struck forward with the blade once more—or she would have, if it hadn't flown from her fingers.

By magic.

Viri whirled toward the Reaper Lord, who was no longer chanting, but looking straight at her. Goosebumps prickled her flesh, from fear but also from the wave of ellixen she felt rushing in her direction—a wave she was certain would send her crashing to the ground, unconscious. If that happened, Jessalyn would die. Viri was sure of it.

Dread enveloped her, but so did determination, both making her react instinctively by throwing her hand out to meet the power surging her way, bracing herself to push back against it. Wards by definition were barriers, and she had ward magic within her, which meant—

The Reaper Lord's ellixen slammed against her invisible shield, the force of it so strong that Viri stumbled a step, but that was all it did. She was still standing, still conscious.

As stunned as she was that it had worked, she didn't let on, only stared right back at him, reveling in his shock.

And his fury.

But then he snapped his gloved fingers and the rest of his reapers sprang forward, a veritable army lunging Viri's way.

Only, it wasn't just his army that was rushing toward her, because with a loud *boom*, the doors to the cathedral burst open, unleashing a river of black-uniformed Nox and red-cloaked hunters into the vaulted hall.

Viri's heart leapt with hope, and she swore she heard the Reaper Lord cry out an enraged, *"No!"* before she became fully preoccupied by the reapers, who were now swarming all around her. She quickly brought down the four remaining ones whose strength had been nullified, then spun just in time to meet the attack of an ellixen-heightened man, the speed of his movements alarming, the power behind his slashing sword enough to carve her in two.

He didn't get a chance, because Reeve was suddenly there, his black blade slaying the reaper in three effortless moves.

Viri was so relieved to see him that she could have jumped into his arms and kissed him—and might have, if they hadn't been surrounded by death. Instead, she ducked when a knife soared past her head, then demanded, somewhat irrationally, "What the hell took you so long?"

"Walnut was hungry," he answered, tossing her two daggers and executing an impressive sideways kick that sent an approaching reaper flying backward. "We had to stop for snacks."

Snacks? Viri's brain almost exploded, but then she saw the teasing glint in his silver eyes and rolled her own, stabbing forward with her blades when a male reaper lunged for her. As soon as he fell, a woman took his place, followed by two more who pushed Viri closer to where Reeve was battling three reapers at once, his black sword reflecting both moonlight and fire.

Beyond him, Viri spotted Braedan fighting beside Sage and Ardin, the three of them moving in sync, a perfect, deadly team. But it was the two people battling a few feet away from the trio that stole Viri's breath, because Wynter and Jonas were also here, not using swords and daggers but instead tossing vials left and right, an assortment of liquids and powders, some of which Viri had seen before and others she most definitely had not. The impedidust was familiar, immobilizing any reapers it touched and allowing the Nox and hunters to swoop in and take them out with ease, but there were other things that left Viri cringing, like the orange potion that ignited on contact, burning a reaper to ash, and the brown sludge that made another's skin melt away like dripping wax, his screams audible even over the sounds of clashing steel echoing throughout the cathedral.

But it was a different scream that captured Viri's attention, one younger and much more familiar—a warning scream that caused her to spin toward the Reaper Lord just in time to see him wave his hand outward, not to attack her personally, but to make the hall come *alive.*

There was nothing she could do to ward against his ellixen as the cathedral itself became a weapon. Vines coiled around the legs of the Nox, sending them crashing to their knees. Pillars cracked and crumbled, dropping lethal chunks onto the heads of anyone standing too near. The ground fractured into deadly fissures, with hunters vanishing into blackness. Coffins opened for victims to stumble into, then closed again, trapping them inside. And perhaps worst of all, the candles erupted, creating a firestorm that burned without fuel, like a wall of flames bearing down on them all.

"Reeve!" Viri shouted in alarm, but he was already throwing his magic to douse the fire, only for it to rise again almost instantly.

She was about to ask if there was anything her own magic could do to help, but another scream from Jessalyn had her whipping back toward the young girl—

Just in time to see the Reaper Lord's bone dagger plunge downward.

"JESSY! *NO!*" Soren bellowed from somewhere to Viri's right, the terror in his voice feeding her own.

Her heart stopped as the blade seemed to move in slow motion, both Soren and Jessalyn's screams piercing her eardrums, but then her pulse sped twice as fast as resolve burned through her. Before she could second-guess herself, she flung out her arm and released her magic, visualizing an invisible shield forming around Jessalyn, just like the one she'd created to protect herself from the Reaper Lord's ellixen attack. She had no idea if it would work against a solid object, but she pushed everything she had into it, begging, *pleading* with her magic to do the impossible.

The bone dagger continued downward, now just inches from Jessalyn's chest. Viri was aware of the reapers still surrounding her, of Reeve fighting them off while trying to combat the raging flames, of Braedan and Sage lunging forward to assist, of Wynter tossing her scarlet powder at yet more attackers heading their way. But while all that was happening, Viri's concentration remained on pushing her magic outward, praying, praying, *praying* for it to work.

The Reaper Lord's dagger was a hair's breadth away from striking Jessalyn's heart—

And then it met Viri's barrier and shattered like glass, falling in harmless white shards to the ground.

"NO!" the Reaper Lord roared over the chaos. He flung out a furious hand, and Viri was too busy keeping Jessalyn protected to stop his magic from slamming into the people closest to the dais—Nox, hunters, and reapers combined—all of whom flew violently through the air and smacked hard against the arched walls and pillars before crumpling to the ground.

None of them rose again.

Viri's blood turned cold at how many people had just died with a single blast of the Reaper Lord's magic, the power he commanded unfathomable. She reinforced the barrier around Jessalyn, fearing he would shift his rage onto her, but as Viri watched, he seemed to peer across the cathedral, taking in the battle with a calculating air.

She realized what he was going to do an instant before he did it, and she leapt forward to stop him, dodging between fighting opponents and avoiding the snaring vines and crumbling stone, tripping once and cutting her palms on broken glass before scrambling back up to continue her sprint toward the dais.

But when she finally made it there, it was too late.

The Reaper Lord was already gone.

THE JOURNAL OF

~~CELESTIAL MAGE KADMUS CASTRO~~

TEPHRYN ALEMEDES

Eleventh Sun, Fourteenth Cycle, Twelfth Age

I stole Kadmus's journal.

I needed to read the truth for myself, in his own words.

He really did it.

He turned himself into a monster.

A reaper.

And he's not the only one. They're spreading like wildfire all across Elverdine Isle, the temptation of magic too strong for so many of the shallows, who have longed for power their whole lives.

But more than that, now that they've had a taste for siphoning, they can't stop. Their addiction is only growing, with them stealing ellixen from mages, from creatures, from other shallows.

They're even stealing it from children.

Killing children.

It's—It's—

"Evil" is too tame a word.

We're doing what we can to capture as many as possible, imprisoning them in the Underlock—a warded prison the fabricator mages have constructed deep beneath the mountain. The reapers are too strong to contain anywhere else. They're also fast, and heal much quicker than they should, making them unnaturally difficult to kill. I thank the Elders that they seem unable to use the magic they siphon in any practical way—once a shallow, always a shallow, at least when it comes to stolen ellixen. Kadmus is the sole exception, most likely because he was a mage before he became a reaper, and he continues to have his own stores of power.

Mage. Reaper. Mage Priest. Reaper Priest. Reaper Lord . . . I don't know what Kadmus is now. What he's become.

My heart has never hurt this much. But despite my sorrow—or perhaps because of it—I knew I had to help stop him. His strength, his speed, his power . . . it was nearly impossible for us to seize him, and even then, unlike the other reapers, the Underlock's warded cells weren't strong enough to hold him. But we also couldn't risk executing him, not with so much stolen ellixen inside him and the deadly magical surge it would cause if released. What he siphoned from Zeranthe alone . . .

If I hadn't seen it with my own eyes, watched her glorious scales fade as her life drained away, then I never would have believed it.

Kadmus loved me, I know he did.

But his bond with his beloved dragon—there's nothing more sacred.

So we did what we had to do.

I did what I had to do.

Kadmus couldn't be contained, and he couldn't be killed, so we did the next best thing.

We [redacted]

His strength was such that it took the combined powers of three healer mages, two enchanter mages, and my own alchemical elixirs to restrain him as he fought us magically and physically right until the end. But finally, he succumbed.

He's not dead—but he also won't be able to harm anyone again. Ever. We'll ensure it by returning him to the mainland, entombing him somewhere deep and forgotten, hidden from anyone who might seek to aid him. It's a peace many believe he doesn't deserve, but I'm relieved. Despite what he did, what he chose, he was once good. I want to remember him that way, not as the monster he became.

With Kadmus no longer a threat, our attention must turn to the danger all around us—and on the horizon. Because try as we might, we haven't been able to hunt down all the reapers, and their numbers are growing daily as more shallows succumb to the temptation of siphoning. Here on Elverdine, this is a worry, but it's an isolated one. If, however, any of the reapers were to make it to the mainland . . .

The consequences would be catastrophic.

Kadmus was wrong when he theorized that the wards around the two other Hallow Streams are what prevent mages and shallows from siphoning from the natural world. It's not the wards—it's runes etched by the Elders themselves, powerful mental enchantments that make anyone who attempts to steal ellixen believe it's impossible. It's a safeguard to protect all living creatures, one I've never understood the need for until now.

If Elverdine's reapers make it to the mainland, the runes preventing siphoning will be ineffective, because they already know it's possible to steal magic—and how. Not only would they have a near-endless supply of ellixen-rich beings to siphon from, but they could also teach the shallows there to push through the mental enchantments of the runes. The sheer numbers of shallows who might be tempted to steal power, especially if it meant they could take it from the mages who have governed them throughout the ages . . .

The reapers cannot be allowed to leave Elverdine Isle. Because if they do, they'll siphon, and keep siphoning, until there's nothing and no one left.

Only death.

We can't allow that to happen.

We won't allow that to happen.

The lives of every human and creature in this world are depending on us.

We must find a way to protect them—before it's too late.

34

The battle died down swiftly after the Reaper Lord fled like a coward from the cathedral, his magic dissolving with his hasty exit, allowing the Nox and hunters to overcome the remaining reapers without having to worry about tumbling into coffins and fissures or being crushed by falling stone.

Viri left her colleagues to finish off the stragglers, focusing instead on guiding the shell-shocked Jessalyn over to where the other children were huddled near a broken pillar in the corner of the hall, their bonds having vanished at some stage during the commotion, enabling them to seek shelter from the worst of the fighting. Miraculously, none were harmed beyond a few minor scrapes, though all were clearly traumatized by what they'd experienced.

They weren't alone in that—Viri herself would need time to recover from what she'd witnessed that night, the sights, the sounds, the smells. The blood, the screams . . . the death.

So much death.

Viri shuddered as the battle replayed in her mind, every moment burned into her brain—including the all-too-vivid memory of the Reaper Lord's bone dagger striking toward Jessalyn's heart.

She shuddered again and held the young girl close, only releasing her when Soren appeared and drew his sister into his arms, both siblings weeping with relief at being reunited.

Tears burned Viri's eyes as she watched them, but then she turned away to give them privacy. The other kids were already being seen to, so she cast her gaze around the mess of the cathedral, searching the moonlit wreckage for Reeve, Braedan, and Wynter, even Sage, Jonas, and Ardin, needing to reassure herself that they were all safe. It was difficult to see much of anything through the blurs of black and red as the last of the reapers snapped and snarled at the Nox and hunters, but she managed to catch brief glimpses of all six of them—just enough to let her know they were alive and ease the tension from her shoulders.

But a quick glance upward brought the tension straight back again as she watched the purple glow of the Aurora Comet continue to travel slowly across the starry sky. Her stomach churned with a renewed burst of dread, with it only fading when she reminded herself that the threat had passed. The children were safe, as were the obelisks. The Reaper Lord had lost his chance to complete the sacrifice. He'd failed—and he'd run.

Part of her was upset about him fleeing, since he'd been *right there*, and while she might not have known how to counter his terrifying range of power, she could have attempted to capture him somehow, especially with Reeve's magic backing her up, and an army of hunters and Nox ready to drag him to the Underlock. But another part of her couldn't help remembering how a single wave of his hand had killed dozens at once, and a shiver swept through her as she realized someone like him probably *couldn't* be captured. It was frustrating that he remained free, but at least she and her friends would live to fight another day—and hopefully, the next time they encountered the Reaper Lord, they would have the means to bring him down, forever.

"Viri!" Braedan cried, dragging her gaze from the comet to where he appeared before her, climbing over crumbled stone and withered vines to pull her in for a hug. "Elders, when we left Nevarnost and couldn't find you—" He cut himself off, his arms tightening around her, making it clear how worried he'd been.

"I'm sorry," she murmured into his torn green cloak, unsure if she was apologizing for scaring him or for leaving the castle without him. Either way, she embraced him just as fiercely, then drew away to glance around for Reeve and the others again. All she saw was a cathedral full of reapers, Nox, and hunters—the latter of whom made her belatedly shove Braedan behind the broken pillar and whisper, "Can you be here right now?"

A smile quirked his lips. "No one knows who I am, so as long as you don't start calling me 'Reaper Priest'"—he lowered his voice for the two words—"then I'll be fine."

Viri winced at the title, but shook off everything it made her feel, and said, "Still, you *are* a reaper." She eyed the black veins on his blood-smeared hands. "And we're in the middle of a hall filled with people who would lock you away without a second thought."

"Little sis has a point," Sage said, striding confidently into sight, then ducking behind the pillar with them. Her beige leathers were covered in almost as much muck as the night of the thunderstorm skirmish, her purple hair splattered with a sickening amount of red. To Braedan, she added, "The confusion of the battle kept us hidden—there were too many reapers for hunters to see and sense anyone individually—but we're pushing our luck now as they thin out. Ardin and Jonas are waiting outside. We need to go before we draw attention." She swiveled to give Viri a surprisingly respectful nod. "Nice job tonight, hunter. Maybe you're not as useless as I thought."

Viri snorted at the backhanded compliment. "A pleasure, as always, Sage." She still wasn't sure how she felt about Reeve's—and Braedan's—reaper friends, but they *had* helped save everyone, so she settled on being grateful they'd survived. She would figure out the rest later.

A quick flash of a grin was all Sage offered in reply before she tugged at Braedan's sleeve to draw him away. But he resisted.

"Aren't you coming with us?" he asked Viri.

"I'll join you later," she promised, her nerves igniting as she peered through a missing chunk of the pillar and spotted Meera heading their way. Both Braedan and Sage wore cloaks that hid most of their veined arms, and there were still too many other reapers around for hunters to sense them specifically, but even so . . . It would be nearly impossible to convince Meera that they were *good* reapers, not without having time to explain, so Viri hurriedly said, "Meet you at Wynter's lab?"

"Don't take too long," Braedan warned, "or I'll come find you, risks be damned."

Outwardly, Viri huffed her annoyance, but inwardly, she was filled with warmth at having her big brother back, something she'd never imagined would be possible—or that she'd even *want*. There was a lot they needed to work through—not the least of which was him being a reaper, and she a hunter—but they had time now, and knowing that brought a sense of peace to her for the first time in seven years.

"Reeve's still around here somewhere, using his magic to help the wounded," Sage told Viri. Her hazel eyes narrowed in threat. "Don't let him get arrested. *Again.*"

"The first time was his own choice," Viri pointed out. "If he's stupid enough to let it happen again, then that's on him."

They both knew she didn't mean it, her gaze already doing another scan of the vast cathedral. Unlike earlier, she couldn't see Reeve anymore, and she felt a niggle of concern, before reminding herself that he'd managed to stay clear of hunters and Nox for years. Some might recognize him now, those who had laid eyes on him during his imprisonment, but he could use his magic to defend himself, if needed. He also wasn't at risk of being sensed by a hunter's mark, unlike the rest of his friends. Braedan and Sage, however . . .

"You need to go," Viri urged as Meera neared, and this time, the two reapers heeded wisdom, vanishing into the crowd of Nox and hunters who were slapping nullicuffs on any struggling survivors.

Viri didn't breathe easy until she saw her brother and Sage slip out into the night. She then turned her attention to her mentor just as Meera climbed over some debris and moved around the crumbling pillar to halt in front of her. Much like Viri, she was covered in cuts and bruises, her clothes torn and her magical amulet slightly askew around her scarred neck, but there was triumph in her eyes—and pride, too.

"Looks like your half-baked plan ended up fully cooked," Meera said, reminding Viri of her parting words in the Summit.

With a wry smile, Viri said, "Turns out it just needed a little seasoning before it was ready." *Or a lot of seasoning,* she admitted to herself, as shocked as anyone by the success of the night. Her smile spread as she realized, "Darik is going to hate that he won't have an excuse to lock me up anymore." She *had* saved the kids and the city, after all. Surely that was enough to earn her some grace with the difficult Nox captain. "Where is he, anyway? I assumed you'd want to question me together?"

Her mentor's brow furrowed. *"I haven't seen—"*

"I'm here," Darik announced as he strode into view, straightening his uniform. Unlike Viri and Meera, he looked as if he hadn't lifted a finger in the fight, his attire as immaculate as always, from his boots to his gloves, even his polished buttons and buckles. There wasn't so much as a strand of his salt-and-pepper hair out of place, making Viri aware of just how bloody and bedraggled she was in comparison.

"It seems you have quite the story to tell us, Solace," Darik noted, glancing toward the gathered children, where Soren and Jessy were still huddled on the ground in front of the group. "There's obviously much to discuss." He paused, then declared, "We'll debrief first thing tomorrow."

Viri started. "Tomorrow?" she repeated, unsure what she'd expected but definitely not that. Darik hadn't said one word about her freeing Reeve from the Underlock—or how he himself had been attacked in the process—let alone how they'd broken into the Summit afterward and then vanished for days without a trace.

"Go home, Viri," Meera said gently, though her jade eyes seemed amused by Viri's stunned reaction. *"Get some rest. We'll see to the kids and take care of things from here."*

"But—" Viri stopped herself, unsure why she was arguing when the very word "rest" had her suddenly swaying with exhaustion, her adrenaline swiftly dissolving now that the danger had passed.

"Don't worry—we have plenty of questions for you," Meera added, a dry note in her mental voice now, *"but we also want to keep our jobs, and Sarielle has been anxious enough that we might very well lose them if we don't let you have the rest of the night off."* She jerked her chin toward the space in front of the dais, where Wynter was in the middle of what looked like a strained conversation with her mother, the firebird blazing steadily behind them despite the rest of the flames having been extinguished.

Viri was torn between wanting to huddle on the ground with Soren and Jessalyn, wanting to help Meera and Darik return the children to their families, wanting to go find Reeve, and wanting to be there for her best friend. The latter won out, so she ducked down to say goodbye to Soren, whispering that everyone was meeting at Wyn's lab later but they'd understand if he wasn't willing to leave his sister. He replied with a ragged "Thank you"—something she knew wasn't in response to the information she'd shared, the depth of feeling in those two heartfelt words making her blink back tears.

With a quick kiss to his cheek, then Jessy's, Viri stood again and started in Wynter's direction, only to pause when Darik's deep voice stopped her.

"Tomorrow morning, Solace," the Nox captain reminded her—unnecessarily. "Come prepared for an interrogation. A *long* one."

Viri barely managed to resist rolling her eyes—or sighing. She chose to ignore his stern face in favor of the pride Meera still wore, infusing false brightness into her tone as she replied, "Sounds fun. Can't wait."

Before Darik could say anything else—or change his mind and demand answers immediately—she turned and strode away, wobbling slightly as fatigue slammed into her with every step. But her night wasn't over yet, so she willed strength into her aching body and stifled the yawn that tried to break free as she headed toward the dais.

"Viri!" Wynter cried upon seeing her approach, running to meet her halfway and throwing her arms around her. "Thank the Elders you're all right!"

"You were amazing tonight, Wyn," Viri said as they drew apart. "I saw you and Jonas using your alchemy—"

A strangled sound left Wynter, and Viri broke off hastily, remembering the Reaper Lord saying that Sarielle had learned about her daughter experimenting with forbidden magic.

"How much trouble are you in?" she asked quietly.

"Never mind that," Wynter said, though the waver in her voice suggested things were going to be uncomfortable when they all returned to their apartment. "Jonas and I learned something about the comets that you need to know. Not about Aurora—about Orion."

Viri tensed at the reminder of the second comet. "You know when it's arriving?"

"No, not yet. But we're pretty sure we have some time."

Relaxing again, Viri said, "Then anything else can wait until I've slept for about fifty hours. Give or take."

"But you need to hear this," Wynter said urgently. "It's about the *ellixen abyssus* requirement. I had the translation wrong—"

"Viri, darling, I've been so worried," Sarielle interrupted, arriving at their sides and drawing her into a trembling embrace. "I think I lost ten years off my life tonight alone."

"You and me both," Viri said, returning her guardian's hug, feeling safe for the first time in days. She pulled back to ask, "You weren't here during the fighting, were you?"

"Me? Elders, no. My hunter days are long behind me." Sarielle shook her head firmly, her blue eyes shuttering slightly as they flicked toward her daughter. "I know my place, and it's not in a battle against reapers."

Wynter looked down at the ground, her cheeks flushing.

Sarielle didn't reprimand her further—for now—only offered her hands to both of them. "Come. We can't do any more here tonight. I need to get my girls home."

"I'll follow in a minute," Viri said, glancing around for Reeve again, unwilling to leave without seeing for herself that he'd made it through the fight unscathed—and that he wasn't on his way back to the Underlock. "There's someone I need to talk to first."

Sarielle looked like she was going to object, and Wynter looked like she was bursting to share what she and Jonas had learned about Orion, but Viri turned and walked away, deciding both could wait. Her energy was fading quickly, and she needed to use what little remained to make sure Reeve left the cathedral without getting caught.

Only . . . she couldn't find him anywhere, not even after walking the entire length of the vast hall. She scanned the room again, noting plenty of familiar faces among her hunter colleagues and the Nox Custodia, some supervising the nullified reapers, some searching the debris for survivors, and some dragging bodies away—the last group making Viri's stomach clench at just how many had fallen, Nox, hunters, and reapers alike.

Still, there was no Reeve. But an odd, affectionate tug inside her had her heading out the front doors, the sensation similar to what she'd felt when her magic had been drawn to him earlier that evening. She followed it instinctively, stepping out into the cool, moonlit night and passing beyond the rusted iron gates, finally finding him leaning against a tree growing between a cluster of white graves, his midnight hair a perfectly tousled mess, his silver gaze watching her approach.

"What took you so long?" he asked, his eyes dancing as he repeated her own words from earlier.

She hid a smile. "I stopped for snacks."

His lips twitched. "Very important."

"So I hear."

He pushed off the tree, his face turning serious. "You scared the hell out of me today. When you didn't meet us, when I realized the Reaper Lord must have taken you—"

Viri stopped him by moving forward and wrapping her arms around him. "I'm all right," she whispered. "You found me."

"I'll always find you," he said hoarsely, pulling her closer. *"Always."*

Her heart stuttered at his vow, then stuttered again when he pressed his lips to her temple, but he didn't take it further, instead stepping back and eyeing her from head to toe.

"May I?" he asked, raising a hand.

She wasn't sure what he meant but nodded anyway, only understanding when he placed his palm against her chest and his magic flowed into her, her aches and pains vanishing along with all her wounds.

Sending him a grateful look, she stretched her arm into a moonbeam, seeing nothing but smooth, healed flesh. "Neat trick."

"It is, though it inconveniently only works on others." Reeve indicated the shallow cuts that flecked his skin. "But speaking of neat tricks . . ." His tone shifted. "That was some seriously impressive magic you did earlier. Both the cathedral wards and protecting Jessalyn."

Viri released a shaky breath. "I got lucky. I had no idea what I was doing."

"Lucky or not, you saved her—and everyone else."

"It was a group effort. If you and the others hadn't been waiting outside, tonight would have had a very different outcome."

"You can thank our friends for that," Reeve said. "Jonas and Wynter found some obscure reference to where an ancient Aurora sacrifice had taken place"—he gestured to the cathedral behind them—"and Soren, Sage, and Ardin figured out that there were wards silencing what was happening inside. Only, by the time we all arrived, those wards had been strengthened to prevent anyone from entering." His eyes locked with hers. "I heard your voice in my head when they came down, like you were whispering right into my ear. How did you do that?"

Viri shuffled her feet, reluctant to admit that her magic seemed to be *attracted* to him, of all things. He would never let her live that down. "You're the mage. You tell me."

He studied her as if sensing she wasn't being entirely truthful, but thankfully, he let it go. "However it happened, you were incredible tonight."

The sudden tenderness in his expression made her breath catch. "You weren't half bad yourself."

"Not half bad?" His mouth curled upward. "That's high praise, coming from you. Next you'll be saying—"

Whatever he thought she'd be saying, she never found out,

because something over her shoulder caught his attention, and his eyes widened in alarm—and fear.

"No—*wait*—" he cried, throwing out an arm.

But it was too late, because a surge of ellixen slammed into Viri, and then—

Darkness.

THE JOURNAL OF

~~CELESTIAL MAGE KADMUS CASTRO~~

TEPHRYN ALEMEDES

Thirty-Third Sun, Fourteenth Cycle, Twelfth Age

As I write this, the mages are preparing to leave Elverdine Isle. The native dragons have already fled to the mainland, along with the magical creatures who called this place home. There are simply too many reapers now, and the risk they pose to all living beings is too high.

But as dire as things are, there's a light in the darkness: the shallows who have resisted temptation, led by my dear friend Anissa Solace, daughter of Magistratus Garrin. She's devastated that her father and so many others have followed Kadmus down such a dark path, but even in her anguish, Anissa continues to fight, protecting her people from the reapers we've failed to capture.

I've told her she needs to leave Elverdine with the mages, that there's nothing but death for her here. She won't go, nor will any of the other shallows. They've all lost loved ones to these monsters—friends, family—and they refuse to lose their homes, too.

As much as I understand, I wish they would listen to reason.

Because what we plan to do—what I plan to do—

They know exactly what will happen if they remain here.

They're staying anyway.

"It's our island," Anissa told me, her lavender eyes dulled by grief and exhaustion, but there remained a spark of life in them, of determination. "They can't have it."

"But you'll—" I tried, for the thousandth time.

"These reapers are our people, Tephie." She placed her hand on my shoulder, comforting me, when it should have been the other way around. "They're our responsibility. We'll hunt them until there are none left."

"That could take—"

"Even if it takes generations," she interrupted firmly. "We won't give up. We won't give in." Her lips lifted into a sad smile. "You know me better than that."

I did, and for that reason, I helped her as much as I could, gifting her a hollowed stylus infused with everlasting, magical ink. On their own, the shallows can't recognize reapers, not until it's too late. I'm unsure why that is, why only mages can see the black veins crawling along their skin. But now Anissa and those she believes capable can use the stylus to brand themselves with the ink, the power of which will amplify their senses, allowing them to see the reaper marks and know when the monsters are near.

I'm confident she'll use my gift wisely. She's already started training a group of what she calls "hunters," and while none have the abilities of a full mage, I've witnessed them battling reapers with my own eyes, and they're not unskilled. They'll only improve with time, something I tell myself whenever my concern for them threatens to overwhelm me.

Along with the stylus, other magical artifacts are being left behind by my fellow mages: weapons and talismans and all sorts of helpful items. We've also ensured the permanence of any ellixen-fueled creations, like the wayportals, elevators, wards, and more. To avoid the risk of reapers siphoning from these—or worse, from the obelisks that, thank the Elders, continue to suppress the mighty, vengeful power of the Hallow Stream—the enchanter mages have laid runes all around Elverdine to safeguard inorganic objects. There's no magic that can protect living beings in the same way—not without killing them—but at least these runes will limit what the reapers can siphon from.

Anissa and the other residents are grateful for everything we're leaving them, but I feel it's the least we can do, not just because it was one of us who doomed them all, but also for another reason:

None of them will remember the truth of what happened here.

The plan we've devised requires full cooperation throughout the coming ages. Full trust. And such a thing is too perilous to depend upon. Not when the future of the world is at stake.

Because it <u>is</u> at stake.

The more the reaper numbers grow, the greater the chance that one will leave the isle and venture to the mainland. The moment that happens, all will be lost.

So we have to make sure the reapers can never leave.

<u>I</u> have to make sure.

As the only alchemist here, I alone am capable of the magic this task requires.

It took me weeks, but I finally figured it out. I know how to keep the reapers confined to Elverdine. How to keep everyone on the mainland safe.

I have created death.

A mist—that's what I've developed. A dark, deadly mist that will surround the isle and act just like a reaper, sucking the ellixen straight out of any living being it touches.

It's complicated magic. The only way I can make it work indefinitely is to bind it to the most powerful source on the island. Normally, that would be the Hallow Stream, but since its magic is suppressed, it's the obelisks themselves that I require. Even then, I need . . . more.

Because the mist—the blackmist—must be fueled.

And for that to happen, it needs a continual supply of fresh ellixen.

If the Hallow Stream were free, then the flow of magic would enable this. But we can't risk releasing the Stream's power, not with how volatile, how *furious* it is. The effect a mere fraction of it had on Kadmus alone . . . how it corrupted him, made him hunger for more, led to him becoming a monster, a reaper . . .

No, the Stream must remain suppressed, for the sake of everyone on the isle. But that means we need another source of fuel for the blackmist.

It was Anissa who came up with the idea. Anissa who suggested the ultimate sacrifice for her people. But also, the ultimate protection.

"Our children," she declared. "Once they reach fourteen, their ellixen is at its strongest, unless they're one of the rare few who has the capacity to become a mage. So at that age—or close to it—they'll yield all but a drop to the obelisks, keeping just enough to survive but not enough to tempt the reapers. They'll be safe, and the obelisks will have the power needed to feed the mist. It's the perfect solution."

"What about before they're fourteen?" I argued. "If we do this, children under that age will still be targeted."

"My hunters and I will protect them."

I wished I had her confidence. "Why would anyone give up what little ellixen they have?"

"Because we'll lie," Anissa answered without hesitation. "We'll tell them the obelisks are warding us from the blackmist, and that their magic is needed to keep those wards strong—which is true, if you ignore the fact that the obelisks are also fueling the mist." She waved a hand, as if that last part hardly mattered. "We'll also tell them that if they don't yield their ellixen, they'll burn out. That alone is all the incentive they'll need."

I shook my head. "Only those who develop enough power to become mages are at risk of burning out. Everyone knows that."

"Then it's a good thing we still have some mentalist mages here," she returned, "since we're going to need them to modify our memories." Seeing my shock, she leaned forward and added, with emphasis, "We need to forget, Tephie. We need to believe the lies. It's the only way we can protect them all—my people and yours."

And so the full scope of our plan was formed.

At Anissa's urging, the mentalist mages have begun preparations to cast widespread memory enchantments over all who live on the isle, shallows and reapers alike. When the last of the mages leave, they'll take with them any items that might expose the deception—books, notes, journals—as well as teachings on how to use magic or avoid burnout. Anything that might make the shallows resistant to giving their ellixen to the obelisks.

Then the mages will depart on their dragons, gone forever.

All but one of them.

Because someone needs to stay and release the mist around the isle, rounding up as many reapers as possible in the process and trapping them inside the northernmost mountain. The shallows won't remember that the monsters are in there, or the sheer numbers of them—a parting gift from the mentalist mages to help limit their nightmares—but, Elders willing, the mist will keep the bulk of the reapers contained throughout the coming ages. If nothing else, their initial confinement will give the hunters a fighting chance against those who manage to remain free.

Beyond that, there's one more reason why someone must stay behind: to watch over the Aravellians from afar, ensuring the obelisks protect them from the very mist that they themselves are fueling. We owe them that much.

I owe them that much.

So I'll be staying. I'll retreat to the far edge of the island, to a place I've been using for my experiments, a castle I've called

Nevarnost. There I'll remain in seclusion, watching—always watching—as the Guardian of Elverdine Isle, making sure the residents keep believing the lies and using their children to power the obelisks.

Because if they ever stop sacrificing their ellixen . . .

If the blackmist falls and the reapers leave their mountain . . .

If they find their way to the mainland . . .

May the Elders have mercy on our souls.

35

Viri woke up on a bed.

She was so comfortable that she just lay there, basking in the feeling of soft blankets beneath her and a fluffy pillow under her head. It took her a long moment to realize that something wasn't right, an insistent warmth in her palm making her memories return in a rush, prompting her to sit up so fast that her head spun. She pushed through it to leap to her feet, whirling around and searching for the threat, finding herself in what appeared to be a large bedroom. An everbeacon chandelier showed dark walls and closed scarlet curtains concealing what she assumed were windows, with similar scarlet drapes tied elegantly to the four corner posts of the lush bed she'd just scrambled away from.

Once, twice, three times she scanned the room, but there was no sign of anyone else in it with her, let alone a reason why her mark might be warm. She focused on the sensation, but instead of it pulling her in one direction, it seemed to be pulling her in *every* direction, something she'd never experienced before.

Dread pooled within her as she moved on shaky legs toward

the windows, drawing back the curtains to find a view that, a week ago, she would have said was impossible.

Because she was looking out at two mountains bathed in moonlight: the jagged-topped Mount Tembris . . . and the round-peaked Mount Verta.

"No," Viri whispered, stumbling backward as she realized where that left her.

Inside the deadly, blackmist-covered Mount Mort.

Home of Diaboros, the city of reapers.

That was why her mark was warm—because even if there were no killers in the room with her, she was *surrounded* by them.

"No," she whispered again, her body tightening with fear—a feeling that only grew when her mark gave a searing warning before a familiar dark voice spoke from the now-open door.

"Oh, it's not so bad." The Reaper Lord's shadowy form stepped into the room. "If nothing else, the décor is pleasing."

Panic slashed through Viri, and she immediately reached inward for her magic, certain she would need to protect herself from whatever revenge he had planned. "Where's Reeve? If you've hurt him, I'll—" She broke off as she realized that, try as she might, she couldn't feel anything within her, the river of power still and silent.

The Reaper Lord chuckled as if he sensed her struggle. "Reeve is unharmed. It was only you I wanted. Though I had to take precautions." He tapped his gloved wrist pointedly.

Relief tore through Viri upon hearing about Reeve, but that turned quickly to unease as she glanced down at her hand, finding a shimmering red cuff circling her flesh. It was clearly magical, and yet, she felt nothing. Not even a tingle of ellixen.

"You revealed some clever new skills earlier tonight," the

Reaper Lord said, his tone mild, but there was a hint of rage behind the words. "Forgive me if I want to ensure you can't do anything like that again."

Viri tugged at the cuff, but it wouldn't budge. "What is this?"

"My own version of a nullicuff, something not even your magic can destroy," he answered. "Consider yourself cut off from your power until the time comes for me to remove it."

Viri swallowed, surprised by how anxious she was to have lost access to something she'd only recently discovered. "And when will that be?"

"When the Orion Comet arrives, of course."

She jolted. "What?"

The Reaper Lord smoothed a hand down the front of his dark cloak. "You really should have listened to me, Viridia. I told you earlier—if tonight didn't go as planned, then I was going to need you. If you hadn't intervened, you wouldn't be here. But you did, and now it's not fifty children who will be sacrificed. Just you."

The room spun around her, her voice croaking as she repeated, *"What?"*

"Didn't your little friends tell you? Orion requires a different kind of sacrifice than Aurora—it needs *ellixen abyssus*." A meaningful pause. "Also known as 'ward magic.'"

Viri felt as if she'd been kicked in the stomach. *This* was what Wynter had tried to share earlier. It wasn't "void magic" the comet needed—it was the magic *inside Viri.*

Her lungs began to constrict, but she forced herself to take steadying breaths, knowing a clear mind was the only weapon she had left. "What makes you think I have what you're looking for?"

"Don't play coy," the Reaper Lord said flatly. "We both know about your connection to the obelisks."

Viri jerked backward, a denial rising swiftly to her lips before she realized it was pointless. She'd already known that the Reaper Lord wanted access to her magic; her brother had warned as much in the garden at Nevarnost, even if he'd been unsure why. The reason—the Orion sacrifice—was an unwelcome surprise, but Viri would worry about the comet later. Right now, her most burning question was how the Reaper Lord had learned about her ward magic to begin with. The Guardian knew, having been the one to grant the magewish, and her parents, too, who had carried the secret to their graves. But the Reaper Lord . . .

"How—" Viri began to ask, only to be interrupted.

"I told you before. I've been watching you your whole life."

"But *why*?" she demanded. "How did you even know *to* watch me?"

"Have you really not figured it out yet?" the Reaper Lord returned, his disbelief clear despite his face still hidden by shadows. "Truly?"

"Figured *what* out?" Viri cried, welcoming the frustration, since it offered a reprieve from her terror. But both emotions fled at what the Reaper Lord said next.

In a taunting, singsong voice, he recited, "Once upon a time there were three young hunters: a husband"—he held up one finger—"his wife"—he added a second finger—"and their best friend." This time, he didn't add a third finger, but instead—

He pointed at himself.

Viri's eyes rounded in shock. "You're—You're—"

"The best friend of your dead parents? Yes. I was, once. Until they stole my magewish to save your life—a magewish I needed to save someone *I* cared about." His tone darkened. "When I returned to the Guardian, begging for another wish, there was nothing he could do, but he was sympathetic enough to teach me some magic. Only, when I dared to want more, he took it all away from me. So I became this." He waved a hand at himself. "And now I have all the power I could ever want."

Viri gaped at him, struggling to process everything he'd just shared but still managing to rasp out, "You don't, though, or you wouldn't need me."

"I don't *need* you," the Reaper Lord scoffed. "But I do want what only you can give me—the means to destroy the obelisks."

"That'll never happen," Viri said, still reeling from what she'd just learned. Her hands fisted by her sides. "I won't sentence Aravell to death."

"Death?" An incredulous laugh. "I don't want to *destroy* the city—I want to *liberate* it. And you, Viri darling, are going to help me, whether you want to or not."

His response echoed jarringly in Viri's ears, not because of his liberation claim, which she didn't believe at all, but because of two words he'd used, spoken with familiarity—and mocking affection.

Viri darling.

"Who are you?" she breathed, staring into his shadowy hood.

"Finally, a question I want to answer," the Reaper Lord said, sounding pleased. He reached for his left glove and pulled it off, revealing a black-veined hand. But before Viri's eyes, the inky streaks faded from his skin—and as they did, the searing in her hunter's mark eased as well, as if there weren't a reaper standing in the room with her.

"How?" she whispered, not understanding.

"Another good question," the Reaper Lord said, but this time, his voice was different, no longer deep and masculine. Instead, it lightened, the pitch becoming higher. Feminine.

And familiar.

Viri staggered back a step.

Then another.

She stopped only when she crashed into the bed frame, clutching the post for dear life as the Reaper Lord raised his—*her*—hands to lower her hood, the shadows vanishing entirely.

Viri stared in disbelief.

In *horror*.

"Surprise, darling," Sarielle said with a dark smile, a wave of her hand making her black veins return and Viri's mark start searing once more. "Glamour magic truly is a wonder, especially when I have to spend my days around you pesky hunters."

Viri shook her head. "No." She shook it again. *"No."*

Sarielle *tsk*ed. "Are you really so shocked? I promised your brother I would leave you alone until I needed you—but I didn't promise I wouldn't keep an eye on you. Why do you think I took you in seven years ago? It certainly wasn't because I cared about you."

Tears burned Viri's eyes, denial scorching through her, leaving a trail of agony. "No," she said again, not wanting to believe it. *Unable* to believe it.

"I must admit," Sarielle went on, "even I was impressed by my ability to act the part so well, and for so long. I had you convinced I was a loving, softhearted mother figure." Another chuckle, this one taunting. "The night I told you about Aurora was some of my best work. The trembling, the weeping . . . Oh, how I struggled not to laugh as you did exactly what I wanted and went straight to free Reeve, neither of you realizing you were my pawns all along."

Viri continued to shake her head mutely, beyond words. Beyond *anything.*

"Don't take any of this personally," Sarielle said, as if she hadn't just thrust a dagger into Viri's chest. "Your parents claimed to love me, and they stabbed me in the back. I'm merely returning the favor." She shrugged coldly, no sign of the devoted guardian who had taken Viri in and cared for her—*pretended* to care for her—for years.

"And besides," Sarielle went on, "at least I'm not leaving you to rot in a dark cell while we wait for Orion to arrive." She indicated the lush bedroom. "You'll have all the comfort you need until that day comes, and then, well . . ." She laughed, the sound making a shiver travel down Viri's spine while bile crawled up her throat. "After that, comfort won't matter, will it?"

With a slash of a smile, Sarielle reached into her cloak and withdrew a leather-bound book, tossing it at Viri's feet. "Here. Something to keep you entertained while you await your fate."

Numbly, Viri looked down at the cover, seeing ancient runes with a translation that read: *The Journal of Celestial Mage Kadmus Castro.*

Sarielle didn't offer an explanation for the journal, only turned and headed for the door. She was just about to walk through it when Viri finally found her voice, hoarse and croaking as it was.

"My friends will find me. Reeve and Braedan will come for me. They'll stop you. *We'll* stop you."

Sarielle turned back, her smile widening. "You think I haven't already dealt with them? Your brother is locked up again, safe and sound. Your friends, too. Even Wynter—yes, my own daughter. She's too dangerous to leave running around, especially now that I know about her useful little alchemy secret."

Viri's stomach plummeted. But Sarielle wasn't done.

"And as for Reeve?" A low, wicked laugh. "He's free, but he won't be coming for you."

A tendril of hope rose within Viri. "He will. He'll find me." He'd promised he would, always.

"He doesn't need to find you—he knows exactly where you are," Sarielle said smugly. "But he won't do a thing about it, because I've ordered him not to. And after all, blood is thicker than water."

Everything inside Viri stilled. "What did you just say?"

Sarielle smirked. "Oh dear, did he forget to tell you?" She stepped through the doorway, turning back to offer three final words that shattered Viri's world:

"He's my son."

Then Sarielle slammed the door behind her, the lock bolting into place, leaving Viri alone in the middle of a reaper city, her mark burning, her mind roaring . . .

And her heart breaking.

THE JOURNAL OF

~~CELESTIAL MAGE KADMUS CASTRO~~

TEPHRYN ALEMEDES

Thirty-Ninth Sun, Fourteenth Cycle, Twelfth Age

It's done.

The blackmist has been released.

The reapers are trapped inside Mount Mort.

The residents—good and bad—have all forgotten.

I've relocated to Nevarnost Tower, where I'll remain until the time comes for me to breathe my last. When that day approaches, I'll send word to the mainland, and another mage will adopt my role as Guardian of the Isle, ensuring the obelisk wards hold and the blackmist stays in place—forever.

This is my fate, my penance for what I and my kind have created.

The reapers.

The mist.

Death itself.

Not so long ago, this island was a haven, isolated from the rest of the world because of its volatile magic. Now, we must isolate it again, for a different, darker reason, damning all who reside here to a life of exile.

They can never learn the truth:

That Elverdine Isle is no longer a haven.

It's a prison.

Acknowledgments

Shadow Reaper is my fourteenth published novel (yikes!), so you'd think by now this part would come easier. Seriously, who's left to thank?! But as the old adage goes, it takes a village, and that's *definitely* true for this book (more like a city!), so bear with me while I pour out my heart for a few paragraphs of gushing gratitude. (Don't worry, I've only been allocated two pages—let's face it, I've been known to get a bit rambly—so this'll be short and sweet!)

First up, to my agent, Jen Azantian—this book is dedicated to you for good reason. It really wouldn't exist without you holding my hand through some horrible, no good, very bad times. It's not an exaggeration to say I'm thankful for you every day.

To my incredible editors—Katherine, Awo, Rebecca, Mary—I'm in awe of how different this finished book is from the first draft. If not for your incredibly insightful notes, we wouldn't have Kadmus and Tephryn (and Zeranthe!!) or the journals at all! I'm forever grateful for the days and weeks and months you lovingly put into this book, and how you helped make it shine brighter than any everbeacon in (fictional) existence.

To my teams at Knopf (USA), Penguin (UK), and PRH (AUS)—there are so many of you on the front lines and behind the scenes working magic on this series. From sales to marketing to publicity to design and everything in between, please know I see you, I adore you, and I'm thankful beyond description for all that you do. Alas, there are too many of you for me to mention by name in my two-page allocation (sorry! Rambly, remember? *Hides face*), but I do want to give a quick shout-out to Casey Moses for the cover of my dreams and to Francesca Baerald for a map that makes me gasp with delight every time I see it.

To everyone at ALA and Mushens Entertainment, and also to my film agent Mary Pender and the team at WME, thank you for all your hard work in sharing my books around the globe—I'm so excited for all that's ahead! (And speaking of around the globe, thank you to all my foreign publishers, who have embraced this series with such passion. I can't wait to meet you all in person one day!)

To the early readers of *Shadow Reaper* who read it in various states of, well, *mess*, truly, thank you. Alison, Krystal, Paige, Bridey, Sarah—you're all the actual *best*. Thanks also for being sounding boards for all the artwork and numerous other things, especially when my decision fatigue made so much of that feel impossible to navigate on my own.

Also big thanks to Rebecca Yarros for reading the draftiest draft to ever draft and still being kind enough to offer such a glowing endorsement quote. Don't worry about accidentally leaking the title over your socials—I'm sure no one saw it. (Lollll!)

As always, I want to thank God for being by my side through the good times and the bad (especially the bad), and of course to Mum, Dad, Steve, Reesh, Noah, and Caleb—I love you guys.

Thanks for being the best family I could ever ask for. I genuinely don't know what I'd do without you. Ditto to my friends, near and far—you know who you are. <3

Lastly, to my readers . . .

I really don't have the words. Just . . . *thank you.* I've said it before and I'll say it forever: You're the reason I get to keep creating new characters and worlds and stories. Thank you for reading my books, for sharing about them over social media and (lovingly? heh) forcing your friends and family to read them as well. Never doubt the power you have to make a difference in this world—the light inside you is something we all need. Trust me on that.

Also . . . please don't hate me for the cliff-hanger. Yeah, I know, it's nasty. I wish I could say I didn't mean to do that to you, but . . .

I'd be lying.

Insert author grin here

About the Author

LYNETTE NONI is an Australian author who studied journalism, academic writing, and human behavior at university before venturing into the world of fiction. She is the #1 bestselling and award-winning author of the Prison Healer series, the Medoran Chronicles, the Whisper duology, and *Wandering Wild*. Her books have sold more than one million copies in over twenty countries. When not writing, you can find her living on the beautiful Sunshine Coast, baking, reading, watching Disney movies, and—always—dreaming of more adventures.